BROKEN
THRALL
BOOK TWO

K. A. RILEY

MAP OF KRAVAN

THE SEVEN RULES OF THE REALM OF KRAVAN

1. From their birth inside the Tower, humans with unnatural powers, otherwise known as "Tethered," are the property of Pureblood Nobles. If deemed worthy at the age of nineteen, they are offered a Placement with the Noble families of Kravan.

2. No Household other than Kravan's Royal Family shall own more than two Tethered at once.

3. To be a Tethered is to be allowed no physical intimacy whatsoever. There are no exceptions.

4. No Tethered shall marry or produce offspring with another Tethered or a Pureblood. If impregnation occurs, the child will then be born and raised in the Tower.

5. Any Tethered who represents a threat to the Nobility may be killed without trial.

6. *A Noble may choose to kill a Tethered without fear of punishment.*

7. No Tethered shall be made privy to rules Five or Six.

*To those who feel too deeply and
curse themselves for it.*

"Only people who are capable of loving strongly can also suffer great sorrow, but this same necessity of loving serves to counteract their grief and heals them."

— LEO TOLSTOY

PROLOGUE

SOMEWHERE CLOSE—A mere hundred or so feet from where I sit —Thorne is shackled to a cold stone wall in a cell similar to mine.

He's so near that I can almost *taste* him, and my craving for him is so powerful that I could weep with the pain of it. I would kill right now to have his arms around me. To hear his voice in my ear, telling me that together we will rise up against those who did this to us.

I would kill to feel his lips on my skin.

But Lady Verdan and her prick of a son, Prince Tallin, will never let that happen. And though Thorne is powerful enough to take on a small army, I know perfectly well that he won't fight back or attempt escape.

Not if it means risking my life.

He would endure physical and mental agony for years, just to keep me safe.

And I would do the same for him.

He and I are one. We are bound together by fate, by love, by a force far greater than any I've ever known.

It's why Kravan's powerful Nobles try so hard to keep Tethered from loving one another. They try to convince us not to feel, because they know what will happen if we find our true mate.

The power that stirs inside us when we fall in love is terrifying to them.

I suppose I can't blame them for being afraid.

They should be.

One day, we will bring them all to their knees.

CHAPTER
ONE

"Maude," I murmur. "What day is it?"

~*Tuesday,* she replies. *It's late morning on May the seventh, to be precise.*

The Artificial Intelligence unit implanted inside my left forearm is my mentor, my advisor, my teacher...and a general pain in my ass.

Still, for the last several days, I've been more grateful for her existence than I can possibly express.

The cell's inky black depths are damp and cold, but right now, I feel nothing. I've long since forced numbness upon myself, and I refuse to succumb to the cruelty of my surroundings.

More importantly, I refuse to let the assholes beat me.

I'm in this place because I betrayed the Nobility. Because I infiltrated the Prince's Ball and learned secrets no one of my station—no lowly Tethered—should ever know.

I'm here because I stuck my nose in where I shouldn't have.

But I don't regret my actions for a second. It was those actions that led me to the truth and forged my bond with Thorne. That one, wild night revealed to me the extent of my powers and taught me that my purpose is greater than that of a mere servant to some Noble sadist.

I'm a Gilded Elite, the title given to a Tethered with multiple powers. I have the ability to heal myself and others. Only recently did I discover that I also have the power to identify other Tethered with nothing more than a touch or a look into their eyes.

I am what's known as a Hunter, considered by some the most dangerous of our kind.

Hunters see the truth even when it has long been hidden. We have the power to expose hypocrites—which means exposing those who are in control.

What I've already learned could bring the realm's powerful to their knees. The secrets I've uncovered could stir up a second Rebellion.

If the Tethered of Kravan rose up, we could eradicate the laws that imprison our kind in the Tower from birth until the age of nineteen. For such freedom, I would gladly suffer a thousand days in this cold cell...as long as I knew Thorne would survive, too.

I press my head back against the cool stone wall and wonder silently whether I smell like death. If I do, I've grown accustomed to it—which is both comforting and absolutely horrifying.

~*You smell more like a teenaged boy's dirty sweat socks after they've been stewing in a lagoon,* Maude croaks out. *If I'm being honest.*

I suppose I should be grateful that my mocking A.I. unit hasn't lost her edge during our time in the darkness. But as always, I find myself wishing she were a physical entity so I could punch her.

"You're seriously saying you can *smell* me?" I stammer.

~*Of course I can, Shara. I am equipped to tap into all your senses.*

"But I can't even smell myself anymore. It's like I'm immune to it or something."

~*You may be, but I'm not, and I'm telling you, you smell foul.*

"Thank you so much."

~*You're welcome.*

As I let out a long, low moan of frustration, I hear a quiet scratching, followed by the scurrying of tiny feet against stone.

I slip my fingers over my left wrist, and a dim green light illuminates the space around us just enough for me to see the tiny form of a mouse scampering over to stand on his hind legs before me.

"Mercutio!" I whisper. "Where have you been? I've been worried sick about you!"

~*You do realize he won't reply, don't you?* Maude asks.

Sure enough, he stares at me blankly before scrambling over and leaping up my shin until he reaches my knee. He rises onto his hind legs again to reveal a small switch in his belly—one I have never noticed until now.

"I don't want to shut you off," I tell him. "If that's what you're asking of me."

~*You won't,* Maude tells me. *I suspect that's a Play button.*

"Play? Play what?"

Instead of waiting for a response, I reach out and, taking the mouse gently in my hand, press the button. The rational part of me knows I won't actually hurt Mercutio—he's made of chips, wires and fake fur, after all—but some corner of my mind can't help but think of him as a living creature.

The last thing I want is to risk breaking the one link I have to Thorne.

"Shara." When I hear the familiar, deep voice vibrate

through the air, my body tightens in the best possible way. Small explosions of hope overtake every inch of me, and my breath catches as though an exhalation would banish the sound.

"Thorne?" I breathe, glancing around in the darkness for any other sign of him.

The voice continues, and only now do I realize how exhausted and strained he sounds. "I need you to know I'm all right, and that I don't care how long they keep me in here. I can still feel you, you know—despite the fact that these damned walls are thick as all hell. I think of you constantly...and I *want* you constantly."

"I want you, too," I mouth, despite the disappointing realization that I'm only listening to a recording of his voice, and that he hasn't magically appeared a few feet away.

"Listen to me," Thorne continues. "You need to do whatever that rat-fuck of a prince tells you, do you hear me? Whatever it takes to get yourself free of this hell-hole and expose the truth about him, about Lady Verdan, all of it. Leave me here, if you must. Gather every bit of evidence you can, and then find your way to the rebels who are still hiding out in the Capitol. Along with you, they're the key to changing the world. But whatever you do, beautiful Shara, look after yourself. You're everything to me. You're everything to Kravan. You alone have the power to heal this realm."

With a click, the recorded message ends.

I could weep with how badly I want more.

"He doesn't know," I say when the message has finished playing. "Tallin hasn't told him about the plan to have me go to the palace and pose as his fiancée."

~No, Maude says. *It looks like they intend to leave your Thorne quite literally in the dark.*

"Fuck that," I snarl. "I won't leave him in shackles. He's spent enough of his life in a prison."

6

I play the message a few more times before Maude warns me Mercutio's battery might die.

~*There's no sunlight down here to charge him,* she cautions. *He needs to get up to the main floor before too long.*

"May I record a message?" I ask Mercutio. "For you to give Thorne? Do you have enough power?"

The mouse offers me a small nod, and then rises up once again onto his hind legs.

I take that as a sign to speak. "Thorne...I can't stand being in here, so close to you but so impossibly far away." I hesitate for a moment, then add, "I need to see you. Somehow, we're going to be together, and soon. I promise you that. There's something I have to do...for the good of everyone. The prince has given me a task, and it's the only way for us to get out of this place. I hope you can forgive me, and I hope you understand that I have no choice. I'm going to do everything I can to get you out of your cell. I promise, I won't leave you behind."

When I'm finished, I tell Mercutio to find his way back to Thorne. "Once he's listened, go recharge yourself. Find me here before I leave for the palace. And thank you, little friend."

The mouse lets out one squeak, then scurries back to the tiny hole he squeezed through to enter my cell.

"There was a time I thought I despised Thorne," I say softly, snickering. "I was sure he was just a destructive, cruel man like so many others. I told myself from day one that he was cold and deceitful—and arrogant as hell."

~*The line between love and hate is finer than a silken thread,* Maude replies. *Or so they tell me.*

"They who?"

~*The whole world and all its history. Every love story that has ever gone wrong, and every one that's gone right. But something tells me your story has only just begun, Shara. How it unfolds will ulti-*

7

mately be up to you. Use your strength and your mind, and set your own destiny in place before someone does it for you.

Maude's right.

I need to figure out how to convince the prince to let Thorne out of his cell. I need him close to me—even if we can't be together.

In Lady Verdan's home we were forced apart at every turn. Only once, for a few short, perfect hours, did we have the freedom to love one another.

Our punishment for that sin was this dungeon.

I only fear our future punishments will be far worse.

CHAPTER
TWO

FOR DAYS, I've wondered whether Devorah and Pippa, Lady Verdan's step-daughters, care that Thorne and I have vanished from their home.

I've also asked myself whether the Verdans' cook, Mrs. Milton, has any idea why Thorne and I are no longer serving our former Proprietor.

Then again, I don't suppose any of them has lost sleep over our absence. Apart from the fact that Devorah enjoyed flirting shamelessly with Thorne, I can't imagine there's any part of her that misses either of us. She's probably delighted that I'm gone.

Still, I can't help but wonder if they have any inkling that we're being kept prisoner in their basement.

For the last several days, someone has been bringing us our meals—someone who's not part of the Verdan household. I've only managed the occasional glimpse at them when an opening appears at the base of my cell's door to push food through on a small, metal tray.

All I know is the person is a tall, faceless servant. A woman, I think—though I'm not entirely sure, given that I only ever catch brief glances of her silhouetted form.

But right now, the footsteps I hear approaching my cell don't belong to any woman. They have the distinct weight of a man's tread, which can only mean one thing.

I steel myself, prepared for the worst.

When the door flies open and light floods the space around me, blinding as a sea of licking flames, I cover my eyes with my arm, wincing at the sudden onslaught.

"Hello, my sexy little captive," Prince Tallin says, his voice velvet smooth. I might almost think he sounded charming, if not for the fact that I despise him with every fiber of my being.

As always, I want to tell him to fuck off, or to shove a royal scepter up his ass, or any equivalently hostile greeting.

I just *barely* manage to bite my tongue.

Slowly, I lower my arm and peer up at him, trying my best to hide the disgust that permeates my every cell.

"I take it you've been having a wonderful time?" he says.

"I'm pretty sure it would be more wonderful if I were outside this rancid place."

"Ah. Does this mean you're ready to accompany me to the palace?"

"I've been ready for days," I grunt. "*You* were the one who —" I stop myself before I say something that risks setting him off. "I mean, you wanted to teach me a lesson. You've succeeded."

"You're telling me you've learned your place, then?"

Reminding myself of Thorne's words, I nod. "Yes. I'll do whatever you want. Only..."

The very hint of a condition makes Tallin tense, his mouth contorting instantly into a grimace.

"Look," I say, "I'll do what you asked of me. I'll seek out and identify Tethered within the Nobility's ranks—whatever you want. But I have one request."

The dark-haired prince moves closer—*too* close. He

crouches down and slides a hand onto my neck, pulling the collar of my filthy pajamas aside to stroke the skin beneath.

"Oh? And what request might that be?" He breathes the words onto my flesh as he caresses me, and the sensation is the most brutal form of torture I've ever endured.

I want to scream. I need to do something—*anything*—to make him stop. Not only do I abhor the feel of his fingers on my flesh, but the images that infiltrate my mind when he comes into contact with me are ghastly.

I feel the chill of death with the merest touch of his fingertips. In my mind, I hear the screams of pain and horrors suffered by his victims. Tallin's touch is foul and nightmarish, and with it comes a stark vision of the cruelty he's wrought with his unseen, unidentifiable powers.

I recoil, my breath clenched like a fist inside my chest.

As if pleased by my discomfort, Tallin lets out a sound like a purr, then whispers, "What is it that you would like to ask of me, Shara dear?"

Against my will, I pull my eyes to his. "I want you to free Thorne from his cell and grant him a position in the Royal Guard. I need to know he's safe if I'm to do as you ask—I need him close to me, or I won't be able to focus enough to be useful to you."

At that, Tallin yanks back his hand, raising it in the air as if he intends to strike me.

I know what you're capable of, I think. *Do your worst, or grant my request. Those are your options.*

My chin high, I stare him in the eye, waiting for the bite of pain that's sure to come.

But it never does.

He lets his hand drop. "You want me to invite that traitor into the palace," he mutters. "To endanger my people. My servants. My father, the *king*."

"He won't endanger anyone," I reply, and this time, I do something that makes bile rise into my throat. I slip a hand onto the prince's firm chest, eyeing him up and down as if I'm strongly considering consuming him. "Trust me, your Highness. Thorne wouldn't risk your wrath, because he knows you would hurt me if he did anything foolish." I pull myself a little closer when I add, "And if you bring him into your service, I promise I'll make it worth your while."

A half-smile twists Tallin's lips. "How, exactly, do you intend to do that?"

~Appease him. Flatter him. Convince him you're as twisted as he is.

The words are Maude's and mine at once.

Swallowing down my nausea, I ease closer still and whisper into his ear. "I'll play my part like a seasoned actor. I will convince every member of the Nobility that you and I are madly in love. Before you know it, Kravan's high society will become convinced that I suck your cock every morning, every night, and every single hour in between. When you and I are together in their presence, I will look at you with so much desire you won't know what hit you. They'll never doubt that I am at your mercy —heart, body, mind, and soul."

"Ah—but you won't *actually* suck my cock," he says mournfully. "Will you, little thing? There's the tragedy of it."

I'd sooner chew glass.

I draw back, sickened, but force a smile onto my lips. "We'll see, won't we?"

At that, something like hope crosses his features. It's almost an innocent look—but I know better. There's not an innocent bone in this man's body, and I'm pretty sure there never has been.

I suppose he reads the look in my eye, because he grabs hold of my arm, squeezing hard enough to draw a wince, and pulls himself close once again. "I can take you by force any time I choose. You know that, don't you?"

"You're hurting me," I snarl between gritted teeth.

"You say that like you think I should care."

Rage barrels through me, and though I try to fight back the emotion, it conquers me with ease.

With tears in my eyes, I hiss, "Without my help, you're fucked. You know it as well as I do. At any moment, one of the Tethered hiding among the Nobility could take you and your father down. Maybe one of them has the power to turn your Guards against you. You can't know what their gifts are— whether one of them might be able to murder your entire army, or destroy your beloved palace with one violent blast of flame and fury. I can help you. I can see straight into their souls and identify their powers. But I will only do this if you swear to me that you'll free Thorne from this hell-hole."

The truth is, I'm not sure that I *can* identify their powers. For all the times I've tried to figure him out, Tallin's are still a mystery to me. All I know is that he's seen death and suffering at close range...and that he's one of the cruelest people I've ever had the misfortune of meeting.

Grimacing, he drops my arm and says, "Fine, then. I'll speak to my father and see what I can do. In the meantime, I will send my servant later to bring you to the palace. You will have your own quarters there, since I know you will refuse to sleep in my bed. But you may change your mind soon enough."

I sincerely doubt that, you walking scrotum.

"And Thorne?" I ask.

"*If* my father approves his release, Thorne will be brought to the palace to serve at the lowest level of the Royal Guard. He will run errands and do tasks only of *my* choosing. He will have very little freedom to roam—and will not be allowed to see you in private—ever. But he will be free of this dungeon—which, I suppose, will have to be reward enough for you." His eyes flare when he adds, "Just be aware that if I ever find Thorne in your bed—if I discover that you two have sought to make a fool of me in front of my staff and my Guards—I will kill you both, and I will relish every moment of it."

My mind turns again to the tumultuous night when Thorne and I made love. The night when I learned at last what it was to connect with another person, body and mind—and I finally came to understand why I had craved Thorne so painfully since the first moment I'd laid eyes on him.

I would kill to be with him again. I would risk everything, even my life.

The one thing I'm not willing to risk is *his* life...which means I will have to exercise self-control in quantities I'm not sure I possess.

"You won't find him in my bed, your Highness," I say at last. "You have my word. I only want him safe."

"Good," Tallin says. "You haven't seen the full extent of my wrath, Shara, but I *will* unleash it if you defy me. Trust me on that."

I have seen your wrath, I thought. *At least, I've seen the consequences of it. I know perfectly well what you're capable of, you sick bastard.*

CHAPTER
THREE

HOURS AFTER TALLIN leaves me to languish in the dark once again, I find myself wondering whether he might have lied about sending a servant to bring me back to the palace.

Still, when Mercutio skitters in for another visit, I snatch him up and tuck him into the pocket of my pajamas, hoping he can find a way to charge his battery once we get to the palace.

~He simply needs a sunny spot, Maude informs me. *Thorne designed his small body to absorb solar power, even without the help of a charger. The process is slow, but it will work.*

"You're sure?" I reply, wishing I could ask Thorne about him myself.

~~I'm certain of it. Thorne is clever. It's no mere fluke that he gave you Mercutio as a gift. That little mouse is resourceful, and remember—he's programmed to protect you, which means protecting himself as well.

I can only hope she's right.

After Mercutio goes dormant in my pocket, it feels like several more hours pass before I finally hear footsteps on the stone floor.

The cell door creaks open a few seconds later, revealing a silhouette starkly outlined in the doorway.

It's a woman, tall and slender, dressed in what looks like a Guard's uniform—though in the relative darkness, I can't see her eyes to decipher whether she's a Harmless or a Crimson Elite.

I have no doubt this is the same woman who's been bringing my meals—and who has likely been bringing Thorne his as well.

"Come with me," she says, her voice ice cold.

It's probably naive of me, but I had hoped for a little warmth from a fellow Tethered. Then again, I suppose she sees me as a threat.

~*You've been imprisoned by your Proprietor*, Maude says. *Which means in her eyes, there's likely a reason for it. Maybe she assumes you're violent, unhinged, or something far worse.*

Without a word, I follow the young woman into the corridor, then stop, turning to look toward Thorne's cell door. Part of me is tempted to dart over and try to pry it open, but the Guard, reading my body language, turns to me and says, "Don't even think about it."

I twist around to face her under the glow of the corridor's less than adequate torchlight.

I can see now that the crest of her uniform is purple. She's a Violet, a Tethered who is perceived as non-threatening to the Nobility.

My friend Nev, who grew up with me in the Tower, is also a Violet. Her power is that of a Porter—someone who can move from place to place with nothing more than a thought.

A Violet's power may have the potential to be dangerous, but most of them are judged honorable and trustworthy by those in charge—which means the young woman before me has probably shown unwavering loyalty to Tallin and his father the king.

That's bad news for me.

I stare briefly into her eyes, watching as her irises swirl with a multitude of colors.

I can see now that she's what's known as a *Netic*—a Tethered who can manipulate objects with their mind. I've heard of them, though I have never met one.

"Are you a member of the prince's personal Guard?" I ask.

She nods, her expression sullen, almost hostile. "I am."

I suppose I shouldn't be surprised; Tallin is a sleazy asshole, after all, and she's...well, beautiful. Her hair is jet-black, her cheekbones sharp enough to cut glass. Her lips are dark pink and full, and when the swirling colors fade away, I see that her eyes are light turquoise.

Rarely have I seen a woman so striking. I have absolutely zero doubt Tallin requested her for his Guard, and I have one guess as to why.

"What's it like, working for a man who..." I begin to ask, but forbid myself to finish the thought. "I mean, what's it like, working for Prince Tallin?"

"He's a good and kind Proprietor. I'm fortunate to work for him."

The sentiment is so absurd that without thinking, I snicker. "You can't possibly mean that."

~Watch yourself, Shara, Maude hisses into my mind. *Don't alienate her. Clearly, she's not your friend.*

A look of pure rage crosses the young woman's face. Faster than I can register, she thrusts a hand out sideways. A flaming torch comes loose from its place on the wall and flies toward me.

Maude, sensing the projectile before I do, forces me

instantly to the floor. The torch goes flying over my head only to slam into the opposite wall.

"Never question my loyalty again," the Guard snarls. "I don't care who or what you are to Tallin. I *will* fucking kill you."

"Fine," I reply, rising to my feet and brushing myself off. It doesn't escape my notice that she refers to him as *Tallin* and not a more formal title. "I'll accept that exactly one Tethered in Kravan actually likes the prince. So, will you at least tell me your name?"

"Valira."

"Pretty name."

She responds with a sneer before turning to guide me back along the corridor toward the stairwell at the far end.

"If your friend Thorne is to be released into Royal Guard duty," she tells me, sensing that I'm dragging my feet as I trudge along behind her, "it won't be until tomorrow morning. Prince Tallin is speaking to his father tonight to seek his approval."

"He's really asking the king?" I reply, stunned.

"He told you he would. The prince is a man of his word, whatever low opinion *you* may have of him."

She seems so confident, as if she made me the promise herself.

"I'm a little surprised that you know about my request, to be honest," I tell her. "Does the prince tell you everything?"

As she walks, Valira glances over her shoulder at me. "He tells me what I need to know. The prince trusts me. I know everything that's happened between you. I also know what you pulled at the ball."

The accusation in her tone is unmistakable, and I wonder if Tallin fed her a host of lies, or if she knows the actual truth about me. Does she know I'm a Hunter? That Thorne and I are both Gilded Elites?

Not that it matters. If she's as loyal to Tallin as she claims, my guess is that she despises me—particularly if she knows her beloved prince has tried his best to persuade me to have sex with him.

Then again, he probably didn't tell her *that* part.

The biggest question in my mind is whether or not Valira knows what Tallin really is. Can she possibly be aware that he's a Tethered—not to mention the illegitimate son of the king and Lady Verdan?

Tempted though I am, I can't bring myself to ask. If I do, I risk giving my entire game away—as well as risking Thorne's and my futures.

If Tallin's secret were exposed to the wrong people, my purpose in the palace would come crashing to an end—as, no doubt, would my life.

"I'm sorry if I've offended you," I say in a measured tone as I accompany her to the stairs. "I'm simply trying to figure out if you really are loyal to the prince. I need to know whether you're on our side. Prince Tallin's and mine, I mean."

"*Your* side?" she scoffs. "You really want me to believe you're an ally to the prince?"

"Of course I'm an ally," I lie poorly. "I'm as devoted to him as you are. He and I have an agreement in place. He freed me. I owe him my allegiance."

"I don't believe you mean any of that for a second."

Irritated, I scowl. "You seem pretty determined to think the worst of me, Valira. May I ask why?"

When she reaches the top of the stairs, she turns and glares down at me. I stop in my tracks, hesitant to move any closer. "Maybe I simply don't like you. Maybe I don't want you inside the palace, where you pose a danger to the Royals and to others —myself included."

"You don't know me—which means you can't possibly

know whether or not I pose a danger to anyone. But if you did, you'd know I've never hurt a soul. I have no powers of aggression. I'm just a Healer. A Harmless."

Well, it's *partly* true, at least.

"*Harmless,*" she parrots, her voice like a hammer slamming viciously into a nail. "I know more about you than you think."

We continue in silence into the foyer. To my surprise, the Verdan house is quiet enough that you could hear a pin drop.

"Where's the family?" I ask. "Lady Verdan and her...daughters?" I'm hesitant to say *step-daughters,* as I have no idea how much Valira knows about their private affairs. "Why aren't they home?"

She rounds on me, arm stretched skyward as if she's intending to bring the chandelier high above crashing down on both of us. "You ask far too many questions," she snarls. "I won't answer them. I'm not your fucking friend. I'm not your ally. You may be valuable—powerful, even—but, if not for the fact that I promised Prince Tallin I'd bring you to him, I would lock you back up in that godforsaken cell and leave you there to wither away. Do you understand me?"

Instinct tells me to come back with a smart-ass retort, but some quiet survival mechanism in my mind is warning me to keep my mouth shut. She's right—I'm powerful, but not in any way that would help me to vanquish her in a fight. Even with Maude on my side, I'm pretty sure I couldn't move fast enough to duck out of the way of every projectile Valira could fling at me.

My lips seal into a tight line, and I gesture to her to head out the front door.

I follow her to a vehicle waiting outside—an elegant silver Flyer, ready to take us to the palace.

Smart, I think.

It's a quick walk to those grounds, but I suspect the prince doesn't want the servants witnessing my arrival. After all, I'm about to take on the guise of a Noble—not just that, but his fiancée, and it would be difficult to explain why I'm wandering over from the Verdan grounds.

When we're both inside and the Flyer's doors have sealed, Valira takes hold of the vehicle's controls. But instead of flying us over the wall directly to the Royal Grounds, she takes us out over the Verdan property's gates and down the main road, past the entrance to the laneway leading to the palace.

After a minute, I realize we're actually heading directly toward the island's coast.

"Where, exactly, are we going?" I ask, knowing the very utterance of a question probably raises Valira's hackles.

"You can't be seen entering the palace through ground level," she says, confirming my theory. "Not dressed the way you are, in those foul pajamas. There are too many inquisitive sets of eyes around and too many gossiping servants and Guards. I'm taking you in another way—a secret one."

At that, I seal my mouth again.

Reaching into my pocket, I stroke a finger over Mercutio's small head in hopes that he'll understand what I want.

He juts his head out and watches through the window, taking note of every tree, every shrub, every gate we pass. If there's a secret route into the palace, it could be incredibly useful for getting back out.

That is, if I survive long enough to come up with an escape plan.

FOUR

"Your quarters are in the palace's eastern wing," Valira informs me. "You will be allowed to wander the grounds as you wish, but if you stray beyond the walls, you will be followed and killed, so don't even think about it. I'll be your contact should you need anything, but if you make demands of me like you're an actual Noble, I promise you, I'll break your face."

"I'm not exactly a demanding person," I reply, watching as we turn onto a narrow, tree-lined drive. "I only left the Tower a short while ago. I'm nothing more than a servant—it's the only life I've ever known."

"That may be true, but the prince seems to think you're something special. For some insane reason, he wants you close at hand."

Her voice sounds like it's on the verge of breaking, as if the words are wounding her soul.

Is she...jealous of me?

He's not a good man, I want to tell her. *He's cruel. He's cold. He will use you then kill you, if it suits his needs.*

~Don't say it, Maude cautions silently. *If she loves him, she won't want to hear it—even if she knows it to be the truth.*

Instead, I say, "Valira, I don't intend to spend much time with the prince. I just want you to know that. I'm only in the palace to play a role. I'll be attending a few social functions with him, that's all. It's not like we'll be sleeping together."

"Why do you think I care?" she growls. "You can fuck anyone you want to. It's irrelevant to me."

Okay, *now* I'm just confused.

"I figured you might be worried that I was planning to use him, or hurt him, or something."

"Hurt him?" At that, she laughs for the first time. "There's no way you could possibly hurt him more than he's—"

She stops talking, as if she was just teetering on the verge of saying too much.

"I didn't mean that I'd attack him physically," I reply. "I mean—in case you're worried I'll try and seduce him, or something. It sounds like you and he are close. I just want you to know that I am not, in any way, shape or form, attracted to the prince."

"I hope you mean that." Valira tightens like my words have rendered her wretchedly uncomfortable. "Don't seduce him, Shara," she says softly, her voice almost pleading. "Please."

The last word comes as little more than a whisper.

"I won't," I reply. "I promise."

I glance at her reflection in the rearview mirror, then back in the direction the vehicle is heading. We're coming to the end of the long laneway, and before us lies a dark forest. Tucked among the trees is what looks like a small, tidy wooden shed.

Valira says nothing more as she lands the Flyer. After the doors open automatically, she slips out of her seat and I climb out of mine. She leads me over to the shed, as if I'm supposed to know what the hell we're doing here.

When she keys in a code and pulls the door open, all I can see is darkness in the shed's depths.

I vow to fight her to the death if she decides to lock me inside. I have no interest whatsoever in stepping inside what looks far too much like the cell where I just spent several awful days.

As if to appease me, Valira pulls a flashlight from her waistband and holds it up, illuminating the small space before us. To my temporary relief, I can see now that it's no cell. It seems it's just a simple garden shed, with tools hanging along the walls and what looks like a wooden floor, a rectangular woven mat at its center.

"It's all right," she says, her voice taking on a surprisingly soothing edge. "Just follow me, and you'll be fine."

She reaches down and pulls the mat away, revealing a small silver ring embedded in the floor. She crouches and yanks it upward, and with it comes a hatch, which opens easily to reveal a staircase leading into some velvety-black depth beyond.

"This entrance leads down to a series of tunnels," Valira tells me. "And one of those will take us directly into the palace. We'll get you settled and clothed before the other servants and Guards see you."

We? I think, but I say nothing.

~She probably has an accomplice on the inside, Maude says. *Someone who can help if you turn unruly.*

Now, why would I do that? I reply internally.

~Because you're stubborn as a mule, and you frequently do inadvisable things. Also, you're impulsive, foolish, and—

Enough. Thanks, Maude.

I nod, ready to accompany Valira in silence, my body tense.

The last time I was in the palace was a horror from beginning to end. I watched one of my oldest friends draw his last breath—and almost watched Thorne die.

Not to mention that the prince of Kravan came perilously close to violating me.

I can only hope this time will be slightly less traumatic.

When we descend a set of rickety stairs, I'm relieved to find a series of lights flaring to life in sequence as we begin our advance through the tunnel. Occasionally to our left and right, other dark corridors branch off, leading into the distance. I do my best to keep track of our route, memorizing every small variation in the wall, every curve in the tunnel.

Maude, are you mapping this?

~Every inch of it.

"Has any Tethered ever attempted to escape the palace through these tunnels?" I ask out loud. It may prove a foolish question, but I'm curious to see Valira's reaction.

She glares sideways at me. "Yes. A fool, not long ago," she replies. "A Harmless maidservant who claimed someone inside the palace was abusing her. She was quickly discovered thanks to her wrist implant, and dragged back. It didn't end well for her, so I don't recommend that you think too hard about doing the same."

I shudder with speculation about what happened to the poor young woman.

It doesn't take a genius to guess which man in the palace was probably abusing her. For all I know, she may have been one of the victims I saw in my mind's eye when I touched Tallin and witnessed the aftermath of his powers.

"Valira," I say quietly. "Has the prince ever hurt you?"

It's the wrong question to ask.

Valira spins around and comes at me so fast that I don't have time to muster fear. She shoves me backwards, pinning me to the frigid stone wall, her eyes flaring with rage.

"What goes on between the prince and me is none of your damned business, do you hear me?" she hisses. "I am not your fucking confidante. You need to get that through your head right now. You may think because I'm a Tethered—because I know what it is to be locked inside the Tower for years on end —that we're the same, you and I. But we're not, and we never will be."

Her fingers curl around my neck, thin but powerful, and I stare into her swirling eyes, perplexed and curious about her at once. She's violent. She's short-tempered and highly emotional.

But something—some deep instinct inside me—tells me she won't hurt me. She's not as cruel as she pretends to be.

In fact, if I had to guess, I'd say she was fragile as a porcelain vase.

I just wonder if Tallin knows his attack dog has no fangs.

CHAPTER
FIVE

TWENTY OR SO MINUTES PASS BEFORE WE finally come to a set of stone stairs that lead up to a hatch embedded in the ceiling above the tunnel.

But instead of climbing up and pushing it open, Valira lets out a long, low whistle. The hatch flies open above us to reveal what appears to be a small white room with rounded walls, as if it's inside one of the palace's turrets.

A tall young man—a member of the Royal Guard, judging by his uniform—holds the hatch while we scramble up and out.

When we've stepped into the room and he's closed and locked the hatch, I assess the Guard. He's handsome, with messy reddish hair and a mischievous grin. His eyes are caramel-colored and intelligent, and when his gaze lands on Valira, a distinct air of admiration overtakes his features.

"I'm...taking the prince's special guest to her suite," Valira tells him as if she's talking about a dog she's holding on a leash. Her tone, while a little stiff, is warmer than it has been. "Of course, I know you won't say anything to anyone about her, Archyr."

Whoever this Archyr is, he must be trusted by the prince if he's in on this little scheme of ours.

If Tallin trusts him, he's probably an asshole.

~Perhaps, Maude says. *Or maybe he's decent enough that the prince knows he won't do anything dishonorable.*

"I'm no gossip, Val," the young man says. "You know I'm the last person who would ever tell anyone about Tallin's new pet. I'm just happy to know she's here and that you made it back safely."

"You're a gossip and a half, and you know it," Valira retorts, and with those words comes the first time I've seen a genuine smile on her lips. "I'm surprised half the Royal Guard aren't here waiting for us, to be honest."

"I'd never tell anyone," he protests with a mock-pout. He steps toward her, and for a second I feel as though I'm intruding on a moment of intimacy. His voice goes low when he says, "I'd never put you at risk. You know that. The prince's secrets—and yours—will always be safe with me."

Valira reaches out and squeezes his hand. There's some profound emotion passing between them, though I can't quite work out whether they're close friends or something more.

"I know," Valira says. "I trust you with my life."

The exchange could almost seem sweet—if not for the fact that we're clearly on opposite sides.

I study Archyr for a moment, wondering how long he's been serving the Royals. The crest on his chest tells me he's a Crimson Elite. In his eyes, I see brute strength, despite his relatively slim build.

I don't remember seeing him at the Crimson Championship, and I find myself wondering if he knew Ilias.

But I have no desire to ask him—particularly given that Ilias was my friend and this guy clearly isn't.

28

Still, something about him feels far more open than Valira. He's easier to read, his face riddled with expression.

"So," he says, turning my way to eye me up and down. "You're Tallin's fake lady love. I can see why he chose you. Nothing like a dirt-covered urchin to please a prince."

A hit of self-consciousness assaults me. I look atrocious, I know.

I've never been so eager for a shower in my entire life.

"That's not why the charming prince chose me," I retort. "Though I will say—if my foulness repulses him, so much the better."

"Well, unfortunately for you, it looks like you'll clean up nicely," Archyr says. "Still, I've got to say, it's a little hard to grasp why the prince would bring a Tethered into the palace under the guise of a Noble—unless, of course, you're horny for him. If that's the case, I can't say I blame you. Even the most beautiful of women has trouble resisting him." With that, he glances briefly at Valira before turning back to me.

I want to tell him and Valira I'm here to help our kind. I'm here because I want the Nobility's secrets revealed. I want Tallin exposed for the fraud he is.

But I can't say any of that out loud. As far as Valira and Archyr know, I'm simply the prince's mysterious property, here to be used until Tallin grows weary of me.

"With all due respect—which isn't much," Archyr says, "it seems to me only a traitor would sneak in here posing as one of *them*. Why would any Tethered hide behind an assumed identity, rather than serve the Nobility like the rest of us? What are you trying to prove?"

"I have my reasons for being here," I say. "You can assume whatever you want about my relationship with the prince. The fact is, he and I have a mutual understanding. I'm here because I want the realm to become a better place—whatever it takes."

"Mutual understanding? Really, now?" He takes a threatening step toward me as if testing the waters, and says, "So, you are admitting you're here to fuck Tallin, then?"

With that, I glance over at Valira to see her reaction. She glares at me with loathing in her eyes.

"She's not going to fuck him," she mutters. "She's already promised me she won't seduce him."

"Ah," Archyr replies, and there's something approaching disgust in his tone when he adds, "I suppose if she *did* seduce him, it would be a little awkward for you, wouldn't it, Val?"

She looks pained—almost ashamed, and I can only guess at the underlying meaning behind Archyr's words.

Is Valira *actually* in love with Tallin? Is that really why she's so loyal to him?

"The prince can do as he pleases," she says. "But this wretched Harmless isn't for him. He's using her for some end—and I'm sure he'll dispose of her when he's done, just as he does with everyone else."

I can't help but chuckle. I've been called many adjectives in my life—weak, pathetic, useless. But *wretched* is a new one.

"Let's just hope he's never done with you, then, Val. For both our sakes. But maybe having her here will mean some relief for you. The prince demands far too much of your attention."

I still don't understand the nature of their friendship—but it feels laced with a pain that neither of them can quell. The tension between the two of them has grown palpable.

"Arch—enough," Valira says under her breath. "Please."

"I'm just saying, let the Harmless have the prince, if she wants him," he replies, an intensity in his eyes I can't quite read. "It would be best for everyone."

"You don't know Tallin like I do." Valira's voice quivers slightly as she speaks. "You don't know what he needs. You can't just throw a woman at him and hope he'll change, Arch. You know it's more complicated than that."

"But I *do* hope—every day—that he'll change. I hope—"

"Stop."

She presses a hand to his chest. I can't see her eyes, but I see his, and I can almost feel the wordless message being conveyed between them.

There's fear in the air, as well as pain—though where that pain comes from, I'm not sure.

"I'd really like to take a bath," I finally say in an attempt to defuse the situation. "Could we get on with this, or are you two planning to stand here all night, speculating as to why I'm unworthy of the almighty Prince of Kravan?"

"Take her up the eastern staircase," Archyr says, waving a dismissive hand toward the door. "Cast her into her luxurious quarters to languish in wealth and opulence, the poor, sad creature."

Valira huffs a sigh of defeat, then turns to lead me through a door to our right.

"I'll see you around, Wretch," Archyr says to me, and I raise my hand, holding my middle finger aloft as I follow Valira out of the small room.

Behind me, Archyr lets out a laugh, and I smile against my will.

He may be an ass, but something about him reminds me of my friend Ilias...which means I have to admit he's a *likable* ass.

As it turns out, Archyr wasn't exaggerating when he said I'd be "languishing in wealth and opulence."

The wing Valira brings me to is clearly intended for guests far higher up in Kravan's social chain than I could ever be. If the prince's and the king's quarters are in a more opulent part of the palace, I can't entirely imagine it.

The first hallway we come to is at least twenty feet wide. Its floor is solid, gleaming marble, and lining both walls is a vast collection of what appear to be priceless busts and statues. No doubt they were stolen long ago from distant realms and placed here to make the wealthy look even wealthier.

When we've made our way down a series of hallways and Valira has finally opened the door to my quarters, I expect to see a bedroom. But instead, what greets me is an enormous, extravagant living area. Two comfortable looking yet elegant couches are positioned in an L-shape next to a fireplace large enough to stand in. Its surround is gray stone so clean that it looks like no fire has ever been set in its depths.

The room's floor, like that of the hallway, is marble, but here and there, expensive-looking carpets are scattered around the large space, ornate patterns woven into their colorful surfaces.

Stunned, I move through the suite toward a wide doorway that leads into a bedroom. The bed is enormous—far too large for one person—and all I can picture is lying at its center, Thorne climbing in and slipping over me, the braided muscles of his arms tensing as anticipation eats away at us both.

What must it be like, I wonder, to live with that kind of freedom? To be able to spend each night with the person you love, without fear of discovery?

It's a freedom few Tethered ever know.

I can almost taste Thorne as my mind veers to delicious fantasies and the question of how I can possibly find my way into his arms soon—because at this point, desperation has begun to eat away at me.

I don't want the luxury of these quarters—not if I can't share it with him. All I want is to feel him here—close to me. I want the right to love.

Thrusting the thought aside, I venture into the bathroom. It alone is larger than my entire quarters in the Verdan house. Every inch of it is white, from the towels to the tiles on the wall to the floor—except for the faucets and towel racks, which are burnished gold.

I'm not a fan of gold—but then, I've never had much exposure to it.

I suppose it's an acquired taste.

"Where do *you* sleep?" I ask Valira, more out of an awkward need to make conversation than anything else as she shadows me around the suite.

"In the servants' quarters, a level down," she tells me. "Though each of the palace's wings has its own servants, and its own quarters."

"And Archyr?" My tone is cautious.

"He sleeps in the western wing," she says, a chill in her voice.

"Will I be seeing you often?"

"That's up to the prince. A household servant will come in each morning to draw the curtains, tend to the bedding and to your other needs. I have little doubt the prince will check in on you frequently, as well. Needless to say, it's not my job to wait on you."

She speaks the last sentence with clear annoyance.

"I want you to know I'm not here to betray our kind," I tell her quietly, looking her in the eye. "Whatever you and that...*friend*...of yours may think. I'm not here because I asked for this. I'm here because the prince gave me no choice. I'll admit that it's preferable to the Verdan dungeon—but it's far from ideal."

"Whatever," she snaps, clearly not interested in anything I have to say. "Anyhow, you should be accustomed to a cell by now. All Tethered are, aren't they? We huddle between walls like caged dogs and learn to crave a prison."

"I don't like prisons," I tell her. "I can't imagine you loved being inside the Tower, either."

Valira hesitates for a moment, then begins to speak. "Of course I didn—"

She winces, grabbing at her left arm as though she's suffering a sudden onset of pain. An abstract design on her forearm glows a violet so bright that it's visible through her uniform.

Her pain is one I know all too well—one that Maude inflicted on me during every fight class I was ever part of.

No doubt Valira's A.I. unit is reprimanding her for what she was about to say. Those who were raised inside the Tower are not allowed to refer to it as a prison—ever. I can only get away with it because my Maude has been reprogrammed to work with me, rather than against me.

Though I still don't know who it is that reconfigured her behavioral patterns to grant me more freedom.

Whoever it was, I'm grateful.

"Of course, you're only joking," I say, hoping to calm Valira's Maude and persuade it not to report her defiance of Kravan's rules. "It's clear you're loyal to the Royal Family—any fool can see that."

The purple glow disappears from under her sleeve, and she shoots me a brief, almost grateful look before turning away. "You'll find clothing in the wardrobe," she says coolly. "It should fit you, but if there's a problem, the tailor will make any alterations you may need."

"I'm sure it'll be fine."

As she turns to leave, I say, "Valira..."

"Yes?" she replies sharply, turning back to me.

"Are you in love with the prince?"

Her brows knit, and for a moment, she looks like she might hurl something at me again.

But instead, she says, "What if I am?"

"Then I pity you. It's clear that Archyr has feelings for you, and quite frankly, he seems like a much better choice than Tallin."

"I can't be with a Tethered Guard. Or anyone, for that matter. You know the rules."

"Yes. I do. But I love a Tethered. I love Thorne—and he knows it."

"How the fuck do you get away with saying things like that?" she half-whispers, staring at my left forearm, clearly confused as to why my Maude unit isn't screaming internally at me. "What have they done to you?"

"No one has done anything to me," I tell her. "My Maude and I just have an understanding, that's all."

She falls silent for a few seconds, then peers down at her forearm, which is glowing brightly again. She speaks slowly, methodically. *"If I serve faithfully, I will be rewarded with long life. If I break Kravan's laws, I will pay the ultimate price. The choice is mine...and I vow to choose well.* I love and respect the prince. I love the king. I love Kravan. There. Are you happy now?"

I stare into her eyes, convinced she was speaking more to her Maude unit than to me. "No, I'm not happy, because I think you're full of shit."

I can see the chokehold the Royal Family has on her. Valira is trapped, body and mind, in this place, her loyalty tested at every turn. One false step would no doubt land her a punishment harsher than anything I've ever imagined.

I wish I could disable her Maude unit as Thorne could do. I wish I could tell her there's hope—that I'm here to help her and all of us to find a way out of this place and to turn the Nobility on its head.

But instead, all I can do is watch her shoulders slump, her body betraying defeat as though she's taking a silent, internal punishment for her very thoughts.

"I know what you're thinking," she says. "But believe it or not, Shara, I serve the Royal Family by choice. I'm here because I want to be—for the sake of others, as well as myself. I'm here because this place is my home. I don't care whether you understand that or not. Your opinion means nothing to me."

"I know," I tell her. "But I think Archyr's opinion *is* important to you—and I don't think he likes you being so devoted to the prince."

"Archyr knows exactly why I stay close to the prince," she replies. "He knows his highness needs me."

I'm about to say something else when Valira spins around and heads for the door.

"Be mindful in the palace," she tells me over her shoulder. "The surveillance systems aren't the most reliable as the king prefers humans to machines. But there are Guards everywhere. Keep to yourself, and play your role at all times. If you're caught defying the Royals, it won't go well for you—I promise you that."

"The Verdans had surveillance, too," I reply, feeling in my pocket for Mercutio, who is stirring slightly. No doubt his battery is low, and I remind myself to lay him on the windowsill when I'm alone. "I'm used to being watched."

"Perhaps," Valira replies, pivoting to narrow her striking, light eyes at me. "But the Verdans didn't have the Royal Guard at their disposal—and they didn't have Prince Tallin."

With that, she leaves me alone, slamming the door behind her.

CHAPTER
SIX

AFTER THE GREATEST shower of my life, I change into a pair of dark gray trousers and a white cotton blouse—clothing that is probably perfectly normal for a Noble's daily wear but more luxurious than almost anything I've ever worn.

My entire life has been spent in the Tower's uniforms and the ones Lady Verdan provided. The only exceptions were the red gown I wore on the night of the Prince's Ball, and the once-white pajamas I had on during my time in the Verdans' dungeon—pajamas that are now crumpled into a ball at the bottom of the trash can in the bathroom.

I never care to see—or smell—them again.

As good as it feels to be clean, all I can think about is Thorne, languishing in that filthy, cold cell while I enjoy the luxury of my surroundings.

Only, I'm not enjoying them.

It's all I can do not to scheme and plot a way back to the Verdan residence in hopes of freeing Thorne from his cell and running off with him.

Then again, where would we go? We're on an island, and not a very large one. It's not like we can swim to the Capitol.

I make a mental note to research how to swim...not that it will help.

"I just hope you're all right," I say softly. "I need you safe and strong, for all our sakes."

Mercutio is resting on the living room's windowsill, set to soak up tomorrow morning's sun. If Maude is right, he will be rejuvenated by it—at least a little. By this time tomorrow, I'm hoping he'll be back to his old, energetic self.

"Maude," I say quietly. "Do you have any way to connect to Thorne and find out if he's okay?"

~*Perhaps you should ask yourself that question, Shara.*

I'm about to ask her what she means when I realize she's right. Thorne and I are connected by more than mere mutual attraction. We're *bound* to one another.

On the night of the ball, Thorne explained the truth behind why our kind are called Tethered. He told me that when we find the person we're meant to be with, our powers grow—that the connection between us is so intense that it literally makes us stronger, both physically and mentally. It's why the Nobility has worked so hard for so long to keep our kind from falling in love.

In the Tower, we were punished if we so much as accidentally brushed up against one another. The Warden always claimed the greatest sin we could commit—greater, even, than killing—was to kiss. Because kissing led to bonding...and bonding led to untold power.

When Tethered are assigned to their "Proprietors," the title given to the Nobles who take ownership of us, we're meant to keep to ourselves. We're not allowed to touch one another or anyone else—not allowed to love, to care, to speak intimately with anyone.

Those who lack powers have tried for generations to breed emotion out of us as if it's a disease.

When I was first placed in the same house as Thorne, I didn't think there would be any risk of our breaking the rules. After all, I was certain he hated me, and some part of me was convinced I despised him, too.

Just like Maude said, there is the finest of lines between hatred and love, and one of them can very quickly turn on the other.

I love Thorne. I love his protective nature, his strength, his generosity. I love his sense of humor, though I'll admit he's occasionally used it to drive me to the verge of fury.

When he and I made love the night of the Prince's Ball, I saw—perhaps for the first time—who he truly is. I saw his goodness, his gentleness...his feral protectiveness.

I felt his heart and mind from within, as well as every other part of him, as if they were my own. I absorbed his strength, his power coursing through my body, rendering me invulnerable, if only for a little while.

I knew then, without a shadow of a doubt, that he loved me —and that he would lay down his life, if it meant making Kravan a better place for me and for our kind.

Heeding Maude's advice, I search my mind for any sign of him. I don't exactly have high hopes, given that in the dungeon, I tried for days to do the same and failed.

But now, calling his name silently and desperately, I feel the faintest voice echoing its way back to me. It's almost instant, a breathless whisper slipping along the edges of my mind.

I'm here, Shara. I'm alive, and happy that you're safe. For now, that's all that matters.

I inhale a quiet gasp.

I don't know whether I imagined the words to make myself feel better or if he actually sent them my way.

I assure myself it's the latter—that he's okay.

But just as I'm allowing the thought to settle into my mind, a wrenching pain bites at my abdomen, as though I've been stabbed with the sharpest blade.

I double over, crying out.

"Thorne?" I whimper. "Thorne!"

The agony I'm feeling right now...it's *his* pain. His torment. I don't know what's causing it, but knowing he's feeling the same vicious assault is enough to make me sob.

"I have to go to him, Maude," I say, my voice quivering as tears streak down my cheeks. "I have to see him. He's in so much pain..."

~*You will see him soon. I'm sure of it. But if you try to escape this palace tonight, you will be killed, and I can't let that happen, Shara.*

Maude may be an artificial intelligence unit, but she's remarkably caring—to the point where I'm convinced I hear tears in her voice.

~*Let it pass,* she says. *The prince is deliberately pushing him to the brink in hopes of breaking his spirit. If you ask me, his highness greatly underestimates Thorne's strength...and yours.*

She's right.

Even now, I can feel the pain lessening and Thorne's mind fighting back, forcing our mutual enemy into a retreat he's not even aware of.

I've just managed to inhale a slow breath when a knock sounds at the door to my quarters.

"Who is it?" I call out, afraid that if I move, I'll double over again.

"Valira," comes the reply from the hallway.

Wiping the tears from my cheeks, I push myself to my feet and tread over to open it, leaning against the doorframe for support. I can feel the glistening perspiration on my face as I stare out at her.

"What the hell happened to you?" she asks, looking half concerned, half irritated by my state.

"I—nothing," I tell her, almost grateful that the discomfort I was feeling a minute ago is rapidly being replaced with annoyance of my own. "What do you want?"

"The king sent me to get you. He wants to speak to you in his study."

My first reaction is one of horror.

Speaking face to face with the man I've only ever seen at the Crimson Championship—a man whose lover is Lady Verdan, my harpy of a former Proprietor—is not something I ever wish to do, let alone right now.

But, given that he's the one who holds Thorne's fate in his hands, I suppose I don't have much of a choice.

"Fine," I tell Valira. "Do I need to dress up?"

She looks me up and down and, with a dour expression, says, "What you're wearing is fine, I suppose. Come with me."

Reluctantly, I follow her out of the room, closing the door behind me. She guides me along a number of seemingly endless hallways, down several ornate staircases lined with priceless art, and down more lengthy passages. We pass a number of Guards, some of whom eye me curiously.

Most, however, ignore me, oblivious to the fact that I'm a Tethered like them.

Each time I spot someone in the uniform of the Royal Guard, my heart jumps a little in my chest. The first time I saw the crest of the Guard, it was on Ilias's chest.

He wore that same crest the night he was killed in this very palace.

The night I watched him die.

I can only hope that one day soon Thorne gets to wear that same, terrible uniform—and that one day after that when we've gathered enough evidence to bring down the Royals, we can both flee this awful place.

~*Be pleasant to the king,* Maude cautions when she senses

my ire. *My records indicate that he has a soft spot for young women. You'd do well to end up in his good graces.*

"Gross," I mutter. "But hardly surprising, knowing the nature of his disgusting son."

~I would suggest you not say things like that out loud, Shara.

"Oops," I whisper in a snide tone.

"Here we are at the king's private library," Valira says before knocking softly on a red wooden door to our right.

"Come," a deep voice replies.

Valira pushes the door open, gesturing for me to enter.

When I've slipped inside, she shuts the door behind me. I tremble to find myself sealed into a private sanctum with the king, who's seated in one of two leather armchairs by the large fireplace.

"You asked to see me?" I'm unsure whether to bow my head or scowl at him.

"Yes, Lady Ingram," he says jovially. "Shara, rather—though I probably shouldn't call you that too often. Come, sit with me. Let's have a chat."

I step over and seat myself stiffly in the other chair, forcing a smile onto my lips.

The king is a handsome man, like his son. His eyes are bright and joyful, his countenance more pleasant than I had expected of the man who oversees the Crimson Championship. I hate to admit it, even to myself, but I can see why Lady Verdan cares about him. There's a warmth in the man—something drawing me in against my will.

"I want to thank you for the service you have agreed to render us," King Tomas says. "I know you've only just arrived, but I appreciate that what you're about to do won't be easy. Snitching on your own and all, I mean."

Snitching on my own.

He's not wrong. That's exactly what I agreed to do.

When I accepted Tallin's proposition, I pictured myself bringing down the Nobility and the traitors within—but the king is right. I'm expected to turn against my own, to report them to Tallin—and I have no idea what will become of them if I do.

Maybe Archyr and Valira are right to look at me with disdain. Maybe I *am* a traitor to our kind.

"I...it's not easy, of course...your Grace," I say, awkward in my attempt at faux-reverence. "But I will do whatever is necessary to keep myself and Thorne safe—and to help you to seek out those who are disloyal to you, of course."

~Liar, Maude whispers to my mind, and I swear I can hear a smile in her voice.

Shut up.

"Ah, yes," the king says. "There is the matter of Thorne. You care for him, I assume? He is a handsome young man, after all."

I swallow, fighting to keep my hands from balling into fists. "His looks are far from the first reason I care for him...your Grace."

With a laugh, the king adds, "Of course you don't love him just for his pretty face or sculpted body. Just as I didn't fall in love with Lady Verdan for her beauty—though she *was* beautiful when we met—as you can imagine. I'm sure your Thorne has many wonderful qualities. Unfortunately, one of them is an uncanny ability to take down his enemies, as he did the night of the ball. I'm sure you would agree that inviting him to join the Royal Guard would be more than a little foolish on my part."

"Thorne would never turn against you," I protest. "He only wants to—" I'm about to say *protect me,* but that would hardly solidify my case. "He's loyal to you, and always has been."

"Was he loyal to me when he brought you to my palace in hopes of exposing my son as a Tethered?" he asks.

For the first time, anger has begun to seep into his tone.

"He just wanted to know the truth," I reply. "He and I are sorry for what we did. We never meant to hurt you."

The king lets out a slow breath, then issues me what I can only describe as a genuinely kind smile.

"I believe that, Shara. I really do," he says, and behind his words, something nefarious lingers—though I'm not sure I want to know exactly what. "But if I am to take the risk of bringing Thorne into the palace, I need you to prove your loyalty to me."

Fear trembles its way along my skin, penetrating into my veins and to the very marrow of my bones.

Does this mean...is he going to try the same thing his son did?

"What can I do to prove myself, your Grace?" I ask, my voice trembling slightly.

"My son will be inviting you to a dinner party which is to occur tomorrow evening. It will be your first social event together as a so-called couple. I have it on good authority that there may be a traitor in attendance—a Tethered, posing as a Noble. I need you to identify that person, if in fact the rumor is true. Prove to me that you are willing to fight on the right side of the Quiet War, and I promise—things will go well for you."

The Quiet War. Yes, I've heard whispers of the silent conflict between members of the Nobility.

"I'll do as you and the prince wish and attend the dinner." I reply uneasily. "But what happens if I don't find a Tethered among the guests?"

"If you come to me, look me in the eye, and tell me you didn't find a Tethered in attendance, I will have no choice but to believe you," the king says. "Trust goes both ways, after all. It's entirely possible that my informant has it wrong. Of course, I would feel better if I knew with certainty you were willing to turn one of your kind in."

I stare at the king, confused. If there really is an informant who's told him about a traitor, why does he need me? Why hasn't he already brought them in?

Maybe *that's* the test—maybe he's seeing if I would throw a Noble under the proverbial bus just to appease him and to save my own skin.

Not that it matters. I need to get Thorne free of the Verdan prison. Even now, the pain in my abdomen has returned, and is coming in silent, agonizing waves. I don't know what's happening to Thorne—whether he's being starved or tortured —but I need to get him out of that vile dungeon as soon as possible.

"I'll do as you ask," I blurt out, desperate. "In the meantime, could I ask something of you, your Grace?"

King Tomas's eyebrow arches, and he looks amused. I suspect he's unaccustomed to anyone asking favors of him.

"You may ask whatever you like of me," he chuckles. "Whether or not I'll oblige is the only question."

I let out a quiet laugh. "I would feel much better if I knew Thorne was free of the dungeon. I know I can't ask to see him or speak to him. But if I'm supposed to go to a dinner party and focus my power on the guests, it would help to know Thorne had been freed from his shackles. The thought of it is distracting me, and I'm worried it will keep me from doing my job successfully."

The king contemplates this for a moment, then says, "Of course, dear girl. I will send Valira immediately—and Thorne will be looked after. As I said, trust goes both ways, and I would like for you to trust me. You and I have the potential to be great allies, Hunter—and I am not here to cause you pain or suffering. I am not the sadist my son is—but then, I realize it will take time to convince you of that."

I look into the king's eyes, trying to figure out what he's

playing at. He just called Tallin a sadist. What sort of man says something like that about his own son?

Then again, he's right.

It occurs to me then that the king might simply be an honest man.

He's a Normal, which means he lacks the glint of devious mischief that lingers behind the eyes of so many Tethered. He's not guarded like Lady Verdan or Tallin, or even me. He is as free as any person I've ever met—which means he's probably also the most *straightforward* person I've ever met.

I hardly dare think it, but King Tomas seems almost...good.

Perhaps Tallin inherited his malice purely from his mother. His sadism, his cruelty. All of it. Maybe there's a reason Lady Verdan fell in love with Tomas when they were both teenagers —maybe she saw the good in him that she lacked, and wanted to latch onto it in hopes of absorbing it.

"Thank you, your Grace," I finally say. "It means the world to me that you're helping Thorne. I just...I want you to know that I wish to do what's best for Kravan."

"I know you do," he says in a gentle, soothing voice. "Now, go. Rest. I'll have Thorne brought to the palace immediately. Understand that he will not be allowed to visit you or stay in your quarters, however. You have a role to play and appearances to keep up. While you're under my roof, you are Lady Ingram, and you are devoted to my son. Understood?"

"Of course," I say, working hard to conceal my excitement. "Absolutely. Thank you."

The king nods a final time and gestures to me that I may leave. With a quick bow of my head, I rise to my feet and head for the door.

"Send Valira in, would you?" the king asks as I reach for the doorknob. "She has an errand to run for me."

"Yes, your Grace."

When I find Valira waiting in the corridor, I tell her the king wishes to see her. She doesn't look surprised in the least as I watch her slip into the chamber and close the door behind her.

In a hopeful daze, I wend my way back through the labyrinthine corridors until I find my quarters. Once inside, I dash toward the bedroom and throw myself down on the enormous bed, my head spinning.

Tomorrow, I will attend the dinner with Tallin. I'll study the guests, hunting for traitors.

The question that keeps twisting its way through my head is whether or not I am about to become the very thing I despise. By this time tomorrow evening, I may well have turned into a power-hungry monster who preys on the innocent—all because I value my own life and well-being over theirs.

AFTER A FEW MINUTES, a quick series of knocks slams against the suite's door.

I force myself up from the bed and hurry into the next room to open it, hoping for news from Valira that she's about to head to the Verdan residence.

Surprise overtakes my features when I open the door to see Tallin, a wicked smile on his lips.

"I've come to officially welcome you to the Royal Palace, Lady Ingram," he says with a mockingly reverent bow of his head. With a snicker, he wheels a silver cart through the doorway and into the suite.

I back away, apprehensive of his proximity.

The cart is laden with a number of plates elegantly concealed under shiny silver domes.

"Thank you," I say, a hint of a chill in my voice. "I appreciate the food—I *think*. But I assume you don't make a habit of delivering meals to guests. Couldn't a servant have come instead?"

"Of course they could have," he says, striding back to shut the door and seal us in. "But I wanted an excuse to talk to you. You know, to see how you're settling in." He slips uncomfortably close to me when he adds, "I'd like to make plans for our blissful future together."

I have no future with you.

The words are so sharp in my mind that I may as well have uttered them out loud.

~Don't even think about it, Maude warns.

So instead of speaking, I allow my internal tirade to continue.

In fact, your Highness, it's my sincerest hope that you will have no future whatsoever. Once Thorne is here in the palace and we find our way to each other, we'll come up with a plan to escape this place and expose you for the fraud that you are.

~Don't forget, Maude reminds me, *angering the prince may result in a punishment inflicted on Thorne, or even on both of you. Smile, nod, and be pleasant. Best to keep the bastard happy for now.*

Ugh, I reply silently.

But she's right. Thorne has been tortured long enough, and I'm not willing to risk another minute of it.

"Have a seat, your Highness," I say with a forced grin, gesturing toward the couches. "Have you eaten dinner, yourself?"

Tallin flicks a hand toward the cart and says, "Yes, I have. This is all for you. I thought I'd spoil you a little tonight while we discuss our strategy."

I step over and lift the gleaming silver domes off the food, staring in awe at what looks like an assortment of steak, potatoes, asparagus, fresh bread, cake, and all sorts of other delicacies.

The only "steak" I've ever eaten in the Tower was so thoroughly cooked that it felt like I was chewing leather. But the cut of meat taunting me from a few feet away makes my mouth water. From the scent greeting my nose, I can already guess how delectable it will be.

"Dig in," Tallin commands. "Valira told me you're famished —and I'm sure she's right."

"How would she know that?" My tone is more defensive than I intend. "I mean, I didn't say anything to her about being hungry. At least, I don't think I did."

Tallin chuckles. "You haven't figured out her powers, then?"

"I didn't need to figure them out. Even if I weren't a Hunter, I would know perfectly well that she's a Netic. She showed me by hurling a torch at my head."

"Ah, yes. But Valira's powers go far deeper than that."

"Oh. You mean she can hurl multiple torches at once? Good to know."

Tallin snickers. "Let's just say she's the greatest drug known to humankind—if she cares about you enough to offer her services."

The way he utters the words, I'm convinced he's actually fond of her—something I didn't know Tallin was even capable of.

"Well," I say, taking a bite of buttered bread, "I somehow doubt that she would offer them to me."

Tallin snickers. "No, I don't suppose she would. She doesn't like you much. Hell, from the sound of it, she doesn't like you at *all*." He leans forward when he adds in a loud whisper, "It may surprise you to learn, but I suspect she thinks your intentions here in the palace are less than noble."

"She's not wrong," I confess, serving myself a loaded plate before seating myself on the other couch, slicing into the steak, and popping a piece into my mouth. I can't help but moan with pleasure at its tenderness. "If I'm really here to hunt down the Tethered who are hiding among the Nobility, I'm not exactly proving my loyalty to our kind, am I? It makes me look like a snake, at best."

"I beg to differ. What you're doing is for the good of the

entire realm—Tethered included. You're restoring order and helping to turn the tide of the Quiet War. My father and I have many detractors, and it would be best if the traitors were silently taken down."

"Taken down?" I repeat. "What does that entail, exactly?"

I can guess, but I want to hear the words from his lips.

"Oh, let's see," he says. "Loss of a little of their power. They'll probably receive an ultimatum of some sort from my father. He will want to persuade them to work with him—tell them he knows their secret and see what they can offer one another. He needs allies, after all, and the world is a better place if we all work together, don't you think?"

I narrow my eyes, though the truth is that I want to roll them. Tallin, of all people, speaking of "working together" sounds patently absurd.

It's hard to resist pointing out that if Kravan's king really wanted to restore order, Tallin and his cruel mother would be the first two Tethered who should be "taken down."

"Speaking of which, what did my father want with you?" Tallin asks. "I hear you and he had a little tête à tête."

I pause for a moment, then swallow another piece of steak.

I don't suppose there's any point in lying, so I come clean. "He wants me to attend a dinner party with you tomorrow. He says he needs me to prove my loyalty before he's willing to give Thorne any privileges."

"Ah," Tallin replies, watching me intently. "There is indeed a dinner, and yes, I want you to accompany me. I'll need you to wear something nice. Something...enticing. After the spectacle you made of yourself at the ball, you're going to need to work a little to redeem yourself in the eyes of the Nobility. There are some people out there who thought you were a little...hysterical...that evening."

My cheeks flush with horror at the memory of that night—

sprinting out of the palace after I'd called out Ilias's name and betrayed my connection to him. I nearly gave away who and what I was—nearly got myself killed in the process.

"Don't worry," Tallin says, seemingly reading my thoughts. "Most of the Nobles thought you were simply a sensitive young lady, horrified to see a handsome young man getting butchered. That sort of reaction happens from time to time—you're hardly unique. Still, from here on out, I suggest you hold your head up high and try your best to convince them that you have a strong constitution. We have some trying times ahead of us, you and I, and neither of us can afford to let on that we're anything other than blissfully happy."

It's a tall order, given that I was raised never to lie or act a part. In the Tower, playing a role was considered a grave sin. We weren't even allowed to mimic the actors we'd watched in films.

I can't imagine convincing a room full of strangers that I'm excited to be with Tallin, of all people.

"Where is the dinner tomorrow going to take place?" I ask, trying my best to shake off the thought of what I must do.

"At the home of someone you may know," Tallin replies. "The Prefect of Kravan."

CHAPTER
EIGHT

My knife squeals against the plate as Tallin's words penetrate my mind.

"The...*Prefect*?" I choke, fixing my baffled eyes on his. "I can't possibly go to his home."

Instant irritation etches itself into Tallin's brow. "Why the hell not?"

"Because it would be suicide. Like you said, I know him. I met him in the Tower—everyone in my cohort did. We spoke when he came to examine my..." I'm about to say *"cell,"* but my years of conditioning—and Maude's myriad reprimands—have taught me better. "My Whiteroom," I finally say. "The Prefect and I spoke to each other there. He'll recognize me."

"Don't worry. With your makeup and hair done, and with a new dress, I can't imagine he'll think you're the same innocent girl he met in the Tower. Hell, at the ball, I thought you were the sexiest woman I'd ever laid eyes on, and when I saw you in that dungeon of my dear mother's—well, let's just say you had turned into a sad, mousy little thing. You're perfectly capable of transforming as a chameleon does, Shara. All you need to do is exhibit the confidence of a Noble, and those around you will be none the wiser."

"And how am I supposed to do that?"

With a shrug, he says, "Easy. Just act like an asshole."

I wonder if Nobles always refer to one another in such glowing terms.

"It's not that simple," I protest. "I can act as objectionable as you'd like, but there's still a high risk that the Prefect will realize he knows my face, not to mention my voice. I was wearing a mask when you met me at the ball, remember. I was disguised."

"A mask hides less than you think. Besides, it's all about presentation. If you wear something low-cut to dinner—something that shows off those breasts of yours, that waist, those hips..." He says all of this while moving his eyes over my body like a set of groping fingers. "Let's just say the Prefect will never think to look you in the eye. The man would fuck a peanut butter sandwich if it had a nice set of tits. He's a foul little man, if I ever met one."

I can't imagine Tallin and I are even speaking of the same person. When I encountered the Prefect, he seemed polite, professional, and not at all lecherous. A little cold, perhaps, and clearly prejudiced against Tethered—but that was hardly surprising. Every Normal in Kravan is taught to think of our kind as less than human.

~If anyone can recognize a fellow creep, it's the prince, Maude mutters into my mind. *He knows the Prefect better than most people do. Take his word for it, and use it to your advantage, if you must. And don't worry—I'll help make you look unrecognizable.*

"Fine," I tell Tallin, just barely satisfied by Maude's assurances. "I'll see what I can do. But consider yourself warned—this is a big risk we're taking, especially for our first public outing."

"It's a risk we have to take. This dinner—it's important." Something in his expression reminds me of what his father, the king, told me. He's convinced there will be a Tethered at the dinner—and if I fail to identify him—or her—I suspect Thorne's and my future will be forfeit.

"Anyhow," Tallin adds, "even if the Prefect were to grow suspicious of you, he'd be a damned fool if he spoke a word about it. He owes his status and his life to my father. Trust me —he wouldn't dream of questioning my choice of betrothed."

"Betrothed," I repeat, barely masking the disgust in my voice.

Ever since we first spoke of our planned charade, I've pushed away the thought that he and I are supposed to present ourselves to the world as a newly engaged couple. I did agree to role-play a Noble, but the notion that I am pretending to be bound to Tallin for life—even if it's a mere act—is enough to gnarl my insides in the most unpleasant way.

"Have you forgotten?" he asks, reaching into a pocket and pulling out a small, black velvet box. "Because I haven't." He cracks the box open to reveal a platinum ring that features an obscenely large, teardrop-shaped diamond.

I've known since I was a little girl that such rings are worn by Normals and Nobles before they marry. I had always dreamed of seeing one in person—never of wearing one, of course. I knew perfectly well that it was forbidden for someone like me.

Knowing this one will find its way onto my finger as a symbol of my fake bond with Tallin is as horrifying as the idea of being shackled to him. It feels as if the prince is laying claim to me, chaining my hand to his against my will.

~*Do as he asks*, Maude warns, sensing my desire to tell Tallin where to shove his gaudy ring. *You can take the thing off when the time comes—or slice your finger off, if you'd rather. For now, though, don't give him any reason to punish you.*

I thrust my hand toward him, trying my best to offer up a sly smile rather than a wince.

Tallin removes the ring unceremoniously from the box, grabs my left hand, and violently slides it onto my finger. His nails dig hard into my skin as if to remind me who holds all the power in this twisted agreement of ours.

I stare down at the ring, its brilliant, gleaming stone reflecting every color in the world at once, and wonder how much it must be worth.

"Do you like it?" Tallin asks, his tone more irritable than tender.

"I'm not sure," I tell him, then swallow when I realize the foolish honesty of my reply. I lift my eyes to his and quickly stammer, "I mean, it's beautiful. It's just—I didn't expect it. I think I'm in shock. I've never seen anything like this, let alone worn it."

"If we're to be taken seriously, the Nobles of Kravan need to believe we're inseparable," he says. "They must think we're in love...and that you and I are fucking like wild animals each night. Easier to convey that illusion with a ring on your finger."

It's nearly impossible to hide the grimace that tries to yank my lips downward, and Tallin laughs. "You really do think I'm a monster, don't you?" he says. "The idea of being with me—even in jest—is horrific to you."

"I didn't say that," I tell him.

"You didn't need to. It's written all over your pretty face. I must warn you, your acting chops are going to need to improve before the dinner party if you want to last in this place."

"I'll do what I can," I say, dropping my hand to my side. "There's only one problem. The marks on my left arm give me away. At the ball, I wore long gloves. If you want the ring to be seen, I can't do that."

"So you'll wear long sleeves," Tallin says with a shrug.

"You told me you want me to wear a revealing dress to the Prefect's."

A grunt of annoyance erupts from the prince's throat. "Well, you're just going to have to figure it out, aren't you?"

~Ask him for silver cuffs, Maude says. Tell him they must be made of platinum.

Why?"

~I have my reasons.

I do as she suggests, and to my surprise, Tallin nods his assent. "Fine. I'll have the jeweler send something up."

"Oh—I should tell you, I have other news," the prince adds. "About your friend, Thorne."

I freeze, half expecting him to tell me he's changed his mind —or the king has—and decided to leave Thorne to starve to death in his cell.

"What is it?" My attempt to sound nonchalant only results in a slight break in my voice.

"He's free of the Verdan dungeon. He is currently in the Verdan home, in the process of getting cleaned up and outfitted for his stay in the palace. He will serve on the Royal Guard, as you requested. Rather, *demanded*. Whether he stays will be up to you and your good behavior."

I pull my chin up and meet his gaze but can't bring myself to ask him the question that's gnawing at my mind.

"You're wondering if he'll be in the palace tonight," Tallin says. "The answer is yes. He'll be sleeping under the same roof as you."

My heart begins to race so insistently that Maude expresses concern by buzzing gently inside my wrist.

I'm fine, I tell her silently.

I clear my throat. "Will Thorne be staying in the same servants' wing as Valira?"

"Yes," Tallin says. "But I warn you—if you make your way down there, you will be seen, and your actions will be reported. It will not end well for either of you. We have dozens of servants working for us—Normals and Tethered alike. The rumor will spread that you and your boy toy betrayed me, and you can imagine what I will be forced to do to each of you. Don't risk it, or you'll suffer for it, and our deal will come crashing to an end."

"What, exactly, would you do to us?" I don't particularly want to know the answer, but I'm morbidly curious to see how much of his sadism he's willing to divulge.

Tallin's lips curl up at the corners. "I would make sure your Thorne didn't get through the night without twenty or so shattered bones—and I'd have you brought to my quarters for your own...*special* punishment."

At that, my heart sinks to new depths. Some part of me had hoped I could secretly find my way to Thorne—to sneak into his quarters and be with him, if only for a few minutes here and there.

But as much as I hate to admit it, Tallin is right. It would be foolish to allow the palace's servants to think the prince's fiancée is cheating on him with a Guard. Still, it physically hurts to think Thorne will once again be so close and yet remain so cruelly far from me.

At least he'll be safe...for now.

"When can I see him?" I ask. "To make sure you haven't hurt him?"

Shit.

Only after I speak those words do I realize how much accusation lies behind them.

To my relief, Tallin cocks his head slightly, eyeing me with amusement. "Really, Shara? You don't trust me by now? Here we are in your suite, with the door closed and locked, and I haven't so much as dragged you into the next room and pinned you to your bed. Surely you have a *little* faith in me by now."

"Of course I do," I lie. "I simply mean I'd like to see him for myself. It wasn't easy for me, being imprisoned in Lady Verdan's dungeon. And Thorne had it even worse than I did, bound the way he was. I just want to know he's not injured, or sick, or anything else."

The prince lets out an exasperated sigh, as if the very thought that I could genuinely care even a little about Thorne is a massive inconvenience for him. "Then you'll be delighted to know you'll see him tomorrow evening."

CHAPTER
NINE

My heart beats violently against my chest. I can barely bring myself to look into Tallin's eyes in hopes of determining whether or not he's teasing me.

"Tomorrow?" My voice quivers. "Really? But your father said—"

"My father and I have come to an agreement. We both feel you will be more amenable to helping us if your mind is at ease. And so, Thorne will be on duty at the Prefect's house, as will Valira. I always have a few bodyguards with me, and I thought it might be wise to bring your special friend as an act of good faith."

"Valira?" I ask. "Really? I thought she was more a personal assistant than a bodyguard."

"Valira may not have the brute strength of many Crimsons, but she has gifts that are of great use to me. She's also proven her loyalty more than once, and for that, I have endless faith in her." He looks almost wistful when he adds, "God knows, she's already given her soul for me more than once. There is no Guard more worthy."

With a smile, he adds, "Did you know that she's a Violet?"

I nod. "I did—but I assumed Violets weren't generally chosen as members of the Royal Guard."

"Well," Tallin snickers, "she should technically be considered a Crimson. But I asked that her status be revoked. I never want her to fight in the Crimson Championship. I can't afford to lose her. That woman would die for me—and I recognize what that's worth. I am...very fond of her."

I'm not entirely convinced he's right—not sure Valira really *would* die for him. She's still an utter mystery to me. Then again, I've heard of people falling in love with their captors, and maybe it's as simple as that. Maybe she loves Tallin in spite of herself.

"I should probably tell you that Thorne knows the Prefect," I caution, changing the subject as I cut another piece of steak, which is rapidly growing cold. "But I assume you're aware of that."

"The Prefect has already been informed that Thorne has been chosen to serve among the Royal Guard. My mother sent him word. Apparently, he was delighted to hear it. It seems he thinks Thorne is quite a remarkable young man. Perhaps it will be up to me to let the Prefect know your lover is actually a traitorous piece of shit."

"Please don't," I half whisper.

Tallin laughs. "Fine. I can always have my mother do it."

The steak I just consumed threatens to come back up.

"Don't worry," Tallin says with a roll of his eyes when he sees my expression. "That was a joke. My mother won't be attending this dinner. But I should warn you, it's very likely you'll be seeing Lady Verdan quite soon. I suggest you remain on your best behavior around her. Shockingly, my mother isn't too fond of you."

I hate Lady Verdan almost as much as I hate Tallin, and it's so absurdly fitting that they're mother and son. I'm not sure which of them is the worse person, but they're both doing an exceptional job of competing for the title.

Tallin glances around the room, then claps his hands together. "Well, I have a few matters to attend to in the servants' quarters. I'm going to leave you before I'm overcome with the desire to consume you like you're devouring that meal."

Had those words come from Thorne, they would have aroused and excited me. I would have dropped my plate, leapt over, and straddled him instantly.

But from Tallin, they feel like a mental assault, and I have to swallow hard to keep the bile from rising up in my throat.

The prince seems to read my expression, because he lets out a mocking laugh, then says, "Oh, get over yourself, *Lady Ingram.* Stop being such a fucking prude." He leaps to his feet and strides over to the suite's door before adding, "Pick out a suitable dress for the Prefect's dinner—one as low cut as possible—and be ready at six p.m. sharp."

I nod before taking another bite of steak. "And don't forget," he says, "I'll be watching you—as will Valira. Fair warning: she's not nearly so kind as I am."

"*Kind* is not a word I'd use to describe you, Assho—" I mutter the moment the door is closed, but Maude sends a shock of pain up my arm to remind me not to be a fool.

~Focus, Shara. Keep your mind on your goal. Don't be clouded by hatred.

She's right. I need to prepare mentally for the Prefect's dinner, which means ridding myself of distractions.

Mercutio is perched on his hind legs when I slip over to the window, his small, shining eyes locked on mine.

"You should rest here until you're fully charged," I tell him. "But tomorrow, I need you to find Thorne and make sure he's really here, in the palace."

If it turns out the prince is lying to me, I will murder him.

I STAY true to my word and don't venture into the servants' quarters that night, despite the fact that I'm sorely tempted. More than once, I reach my mind out, searching for Thorne, hoping to feel him close.

But try as I might, I never quite manage to connect to him.

Around ten p.m., Mercutio scurries under the door into my room and climbs the bedclothes until he's perched on my knee.

"I didn't even know you'd left," I tell him. "What is it? Do you have news?

He rises onto his tiny hind legs and presses his paws to my left forearm, scratching gently. The markings under my skin light up green, and as if she's translating, Maude says, *~He wishes to tell you he's located Thorne. He's still in the Verdan home, getting cleaned up and prepared to join the Royal Guard. Mercutio raced back here rather than risk being seen.*

"Is Thorne all right?" I ask. "Is he hurt? Did he manage to record another message?"

Mercutio simply stares at me as if he hasn't understood the questions.

"Never mind," I sigh. "They're probably delaying bringing him here because they want to conceal his physical state. Tallin wouldn't want the other Guards seeing a new recruit looking like he's been abused."

I just wonder how long we can manage to resist seeking one another out when he finally arrives, knowing there's only one level separating us.

~One level, a malevolent prince, and his entire arsenal of Crimson Elites, Maude reminds me. *It would not go well for you to surrender to your cravings.*

"Oh, come on. Where's your sense of adventure, Maude?"

~*My sense of self-preservation ate it.*

When Mercutio has tucked himself away again to charge on his windowsill perch and Maude has gone into sleep mode for the night, I lie back in bed, my fingers trailing along my neck as I try to recall the sensation of Thorne's lips on my skin.

"Tomorrow," I whisper into the darkness. "I'll see you tomorrow evening. Whether I'll be able to touch you is another question entirely."

CHAPTER
TEN

THE NEXT MORNING passes at a glacial, torturous pace.

Dressed in an elegant off-white pantsuit with my hair perfectly styled, I explore the palace and its grounds, pretending to be interested in the landscape.

The truth is, all I can think about is the prospect of running into Thorne. I know it's unlikely, given that he's probably being monitored closely by the prince and his underlings.

But a girl can hope.

Seeing him, touching him again, kissing him as he wraps his powerful, protective arms around me, are all I want in the world right now. As important as our mission is, and as much as I want to turn Kravan's society on its head, I want Thorne even more.

"What sort of surveillance is in place out here, Maude?" I say softly as I meander down a winding path toward a small pond dotted with lily pads and a couple of perfect swans.

~I haven't detected much, other than the Guards constantly on the watch. Surprisingly enough, I've found no presence of cameras or recording devices in your quarters. There are cameras in various hallways in the palace, but they don't appear to be functioning *consistently. I suppose having so many members of the Royal Guard in service here means there's not much need of video surveillance.*

I smile to myself, curious to know whether the systems were fried the night of the Prince's Ball when I made my escape —with Maude's help, of course. "Let me know if you discover anything I should be aware of—or if they're monitoring my link to you."

~Once you have the platinum bands on your wrist, it will cease to matter.

"What do you mean?"

~I intend to manipulate the metal in your bracelets to block any potential signals. No one will be able to read our communications or your emotions—which, in your case, usually means unfettered rage.

"I guess it's wise to hide my wrath," I chuckle. "Clever Maude."

~Would you like to know how it works?

"Not really. I'll chalk it up to magic and leave it at that, if it's all right with you. I just need to know we're safe to speak to one another."

~We are safe...so far.

I wander the grounds for an hour or so, my hopes of spotting Thorne fading. Occasionally, I notice a member or two of the Royal Guard coming my way, but they're always strangers who eye me with a sort of hostile curiosity, as if they know I'm the prince's lover and despise me for it.

I don't blame you, I think. *I would hate me, too. It would take an absolute psychopath to fall for that asshole.*

Silently, I apologize to Valira for the mental insult I just inflicted on her.

I steer clear of the Guards, worried that if I engage in conversation with any of them, I'll end up confessing that I'm one of their kind and then beg them to understand that I'm only here for the greater good.

Something tells me they wouldn't care, even if I divulged the truth. Valira knows I'm a Tethered, after all, and she still abhors me.

As I'm headed back toward a side door that leads into the palace's eastern wing, I spot Archyr stepping outside and scanning the grounds warily.

"Ah. Lady Ingram," he says with a sly grin, striding toward me. "How are you settling in?"

The greeting feels friendly enough, though I'll admit I find it difficult to trust his motives.

"Just fine, thank you," I reply in the most obnoxiously high-class manner I can muster. It's my attempt to practice for the evening's outing, and I must fail miserably, because Archyr snort-laughs.

I'm about to walk by him into the palace when he mutters, "Look, I don't know why you've really come to this place—but I need you to promise me something."

I freeze and look him in the eye, more surprised than irritated. Glancing around, I whisper, "I'm not sure Guards are allowed to ask Noble guests for promises."

"You *wish* you were a Noble," he says with a smirk. "Well, whoever you are—whatever your reason for being here—you're not cruel. That, I can tell."

"Can you? Because your friend Valira seems to think I'm the devil incarnate."

"Valira is suspicious of many people. She has her reasons for it."

"The only person she should be suspicious of is—" I begin, but Maude buzzes a familiar warning into my arm.

~Don't speak ill of the prince. Trust no one.

"Tallin," Archyr says, completing the thought for me. He lets out a sigh before adding, "Look—I'm not so keen on Little Lord Hornypants myself, but there's a lot about the prince you don't know. He loves Valira, for one thing. Like, *genuinely* loves her. I could torture myself all day and night thinking about it—but there's no way I can lay claim to her when a prince is so demanding of her company."

There's pain in his eyes when he tells me this, despite his attempts to hide it.

"But why would she spend *any* time with him? He—" I begin, not knowing what to say. *He's an asshole? He's a monster? She deserves better, even if she's cold as ice?*

I know, I know," Archyr says, raising his hands. "Look—it's complicated. His relationship with her and hers with me. You probably see us as three very messed-up people. But for some reason, I want you to know Valira is good and kind. She happens to be the most generous person I know."

I glance around to make sure no one is close, then hiss, "Why are you telling me this?"

"Because if you spend time with the prince, you may feel resentful about their...*habits*. His and hers. I know I do sometimes."

"Habits?"

Archyr stares at me as if to ask, *Are you really this naive?*

"They fuck," he says. "In secret. I don't think the king knows about it, and most of the other Guards are either oblivious or tight-lipped. But yeah—they have sex regularly."

I'm somehow surprised and not at all surprised, all at once.

"Does Valira...want it?" I ask.

Archyr sucks in his cheeks, then says, "There's no right answer to that question. Besides, you'd have to ask her. Let's just say it helps keep the prince from blowing a gasket. She's saving us all from the worst side of Tallin."

I study him, trying to work out whether he knows Tallin is a Tethered, like us. Can he possibly know? Does Valira?

"What about you?" I'm not quite sure how to ask the question, but something in his voice, in his eyes, tells me he's more deeply involved with Valira than he's letting on. "Are you...I mean, do you care for her?"

"Does it matter?" He snickers, then focuses his gaze on the distance. "If you want an answer, then yes. But I have a feeling you know what it is to care about someone you can't have."

I nod. "I have some idea."

With a dismissive shrug, he says, "Just...do me a favor and go easy on her. I know she can seem hard as nails, but trust me when I tell you she is made of glass, and Tallin renders her more fragile every day. One misstep could shatter her."

So, I think. *I was right about her.*

She's made of porcelain, not iron.

"I'll do my best to be kind to her," I say, skeptical though I am. "I promise. But if she doesn't want to shatter, maybe she should stay away from the prince."

"If only it were that simple...Lady Ingram."

As I watch Archyr walk away, I realize why it is that he reminded me so much of my friend Ilias when we first met. He's kind, caring, and loyal.

Ilias's loyalty got him killed.

I can only hope Archyr's fate will be kinder to him.

CHAPTER
ELEVEN

By the time I've returned to my suite and paced its entire length a hundred or more times, I've begun to doubt Tallin's word.

I can't feel Thorne's presence. There's no evidence that he was ever brought to the palace. Archyr said nothing about it, and surely he would know if Valira had escorted him here.

I'm starting to wonder if I'm an idiot for putting my faith in the biggest prick I've ever met.

I know Thorne. If he were in the palace, he would do everything in his power to find out where my quarters are and come to me...*unless something was preventing him.*

"If that asshole of a prince is lying to me," I say under my breath. "If he's done something to Thorne...I swear I'll..."

~You'll what? Maude asks flatly. *You can't threaten the prince. You may be impressive in your way, Shara, but you're a Healer and a Hunter. You're still no fighter, and you have no power to take him on.*

I want to snap a retort at her, but she's right. The truth is, Tallin can do anything he wants to me—he could make my life as miserable as humanly possible, and I wouldn't be able to do a thing about it. All I have is a single, minuscule shred of faith that he's kept his promise and that Thorne has indeed been freed from his shackles.

"Do you really think Thorne is here?" I ask Maude. "Is there any way I can know?"

~You're tethered to him, don't forget. You should be able to reach for him, just as you would extend your arm to take hold of the book on that coffee table.

I glance over to lay my eyes on the table, which is positioned a few feet from the fireplace. A single, untitled tome lies at its center. I tread over, reach down, and take it in my hands to feel its leather cover, soft and smooth.

~Reach for Thorne, Shara, Maude commands. *Set aside your hatred of Tallin...and find the one who matters most.*

Doubt fills me at first. The truth is, even in Lady Verdan's dungeon, I could feel his presence only a little. It was as if the walls between us were blocking our connection. Like our bonds had been temporarily severed.

I let out a long breath and seat myself on the couch. Closing my eyes and raising my face, I call Thorne's name silently.

At first, nothing comes back to me but a feeling of sheer, echoing isolation, as if he's simply...gone.

But after a few seconds, I feel—or hear—something.

"Shara."

The voice is quiet and distant, as if someone is whispering my name a mile away and it's coming to me on a gust of wind.

But there is no doubt in my mind that it's him. He's nearby.

"Thorne," I whisper. "Are you in the palace—will I really see you tonight?"

There's a pause, and then that same, distant voice says, "Yes. But you need to know...I can't—"

I wait for him to finish, but nothing more comes.

I call to him again, seeking any confirmation that it really was his voice that I heard just now.

"Thorne?" I say out loud, and then I half shout, "Thorne!"
But all I hear is silence.

WHEN AFTERNOON COMES and it's time to settle on a dress from my wardrobe, reapply my makeup and style my hair for the dinner party, it's the thought of Thorne that inspires me.

I've been putting off the dress selection since last night. Knowing Tallin wants me to show off my body is nauseating and infuriating, all at once. I'd rather show up with one sack over my head and another one over my entire torso.

But, given that's not an option, I surrender and begin to rifle through my wardrobe.

If I want to look enticing, it's for Thorne's eyes only.

I select a flattering dress of green silk with a long, flowing skirt. Its bodice fits me like a glove, showing off my curves in a way that I hope will distract from my face, just in case Tallin is wrong and there's a risk the Prefect will recognize me. I grab a small clutch, slipping Mercutio inside, along with a tube of lipstick and a package of tissues.

By the time I'm ready to head to the dinner party, I have to admit Tallin had a point. I look entirely different from the girl I was in the Tower, her hair perpetually pulled back, not a drop of makeup on her face.

Now, with my features altered, my brows filled in, and my hair falling loose about my shoulders in waves, I actually resemble a Noble. My face is virtually unrecognizable, even to me, and I can't decide whether that's a good thing or a terrible one.

"Is there anything else I should change about my appearance, Maude?"

~I believe the prince will bring the wrist pieces. They'll help to

cover the markings on your left arm. Other than that, the Prefect might recognize your voice. But there's not much you can do about that.

"You can't change it for me?"

~No—at least, not to any degree. It's up to you to disguise it. My advice is just to act slightly intoxicated. Flirt and fawn over the prince. Laugh a great deal. Trust me, the Prefect will have no idea he's speaking to a former resident of the Tower. It will never cross his mind.

She has a point. The Tethered candidates the Prefect met in the Tower weren't exactly a barrel of laughs. We were frightened for our futures and irritatingly self-conscious.

"I'm not sure I know how to fawn and flirt," I tell Maude.

~It's easy. Simply pretend the prince is Thorne. Or pretend you're Kaleen, from your Tower days.

I wince. Kaleen used to flirt endlessly with our fight trainer, Ore, presumably in the hopes of gaining his favor. She was shameless, not to mention annoying as hell. Still, I spent enough hours observing her with a grimace on my lips to know exactly what Maude means.

Dressed in a dark navy suit with a gray shirt, the prince arrives at my suite at six p.m. He eyes me up and down with approval, his gaze dwelling far too long on my cleavage.

"If I didn't rely on you for your gifts," he says with a low whistle, "I would absolutely tear that dress off you right here and now, regardless of how repugnant you might find me."

With a sneer, I ask, "Is that threat of assault supposed to be a compliment?"

Tallin shrugs. "Take it however you like. I'm telling you I would very much like to fuck you. Luckily for you, we have other plans."

I'm about to counter with a remark about how much I would like for my kneecap to collide with his testicles when I remember Maude's advice to gush over him tonight. There may be no Prefect present, but I probably shouldn't risk pissing Tallin off just now.

"For the record, I don't find you repugnant," I say, forcing my voice to come out a little smoother, a little higher than usual. "You're a very...handsome man."

The last two words force bile into my esophagus.

Tallin smiles, pleased with my compliance. "A compliment? From Shara? The world must be on the verge of ending."

I mirror his expression, lowering my chin. "I'm just practicing for later," I tell him.

"Sure you are," he says, offering me his arm. "Come—it's time to make our way to dinner."

Together, we head down to the main entrance and the palace's curved front drive, where a Flyer awaits us—a sleek, silver work of art with darkened windows.

A driver stands beside the vehicle, his head bowed, hands clasped behind his back.

It's not until we're close that he raises his chin and a set of cold hazel eyes lock on my own.

A gasp escapes my lips.

Tallin had claimed Thorne would be on Guard duty tonight at the Prefect's, but he'd said nothing about the fact that he would be our actual *driver*.

For a second, I wonder if this is an act of generosity on Tallin's part—but then, I remind myself the bastard doesn't have a benevolent bone in his body. It could be the king's idea, I suppose—showing me a little kindness in hopes of encouraging my cooperation.

"Thorne," I breathe, almost against my will.

Why do his eyes look so vacant, so distant? Why can't I feel his mind as I should be able to?

He's looking straight through me as if I'm not even here.

In an instant, I feel the prince's hand on my back, fingertips digging in through the thin fabric of my dress.

"Do *not* acknowledge him," Tallin snarls under his breath. "It's me you're supposed to want—remember? You're not even meant to know this lowly Guard. He's only here to prove to you that he is unhurt. Now, get in."

As if stirring from a stupor, Thorne narrows his eyes at the prince but says nothing. Instead, he simply offers up one nod as if to acknowledge that he, too, heard Tallin's command.

"I...thought you said Valira was coming," I say, my voice strained. "Where is she?"

"She's traveling separately," Tallin replies. "She can be a little possessive. A little jealous, too. I don't want to inspire a cat fight in the Flyer, given that you and I will be snuggled together in the back seat."

I shoot him a look, wondering what he means by that. Is he seriously worried Valira will think I have my sights set on him —or is he actually intending to try something?

If that's the case, why isn't Thorne reacting?

I watch as he moves around to the driver's side door and opens it, ignoring both Tallin and me.

When we're inside the vehicle, I peer into the rearview mirror as Thorne slides into the pilot's seat and prepares for takeoff. The prince slips close to me, pushing my hair away from my neck and stroking a finger over my bare shoulder.

It doesn't take a genius to figure out the prince is manipulating us both, torturing us with proximity while forbidding us from touching. But knowing what he's doing doesn't make it any less infuriating.

"Highness, maybe you should keep your hands to yourself until we're at the Prefect's," I say, fighting the strain in my voice.

"I would," Tallin replies, "but you're just so...enticing."

Thorne's eyes shift to the reflection in the mirror. Gone is the dazed, vacant look, and I can almost taste the rage roiling inside him when he spies Tallin's hand possessively claiming my skin.

"Thorne," I say again when the doors are sealed and the engine thrums to life. "Are you okay?"

A second later, Tallin's fingers are around my throat, squeezing. "Tsk. I told you—do not acknowledge him."

Thorne twists around in his seat, his eyes flaring bright, the veins in his neck throbbing.

"Don't you fucking touch her," he hisses, his voice rough as sand. "Or I'll kill you."

The moment the words pass his lips, his features contort with pain, and a cry escapes his throat.

"Thorne!" I rasp, reaching for him, but Tallin tightens his grip on my neck, forcing me back against the seat.

"He's fine," the prince whispers into my ear. "Your dog is simply being disciplined. He knows the rules."

"What do you mean?" I croak under the pressure of his fingers as they threaten to crush my windpipe.

Tallin releases me and reaches into his pocket to pull out what looks like a small, flat, silver disc with a white sphere turning slowly at its center. "You may think I monitor all members of the Royal Guard closely—that I watch them and tap into their Maude units for information," he says. "But the truth is, I have no interest in omniscience. I am fully aware that those who wish to serve me are loyal. But sometimes, when one of the Guards displays a rebellious streak, I connect their internal wiring to this small creation." He holds up the device, and I see that the white sphere is glowing slightly. "If your Thorne develops the urge to, say, *injure* me, he receives a shock painful enough to bring an elephant to its knees."

His face glistening with perspiration, Thorne shoots me a

look in the mirror. *How long has this been going on? How many times has Tallin inflicted this very torture in the Verdan dungeon?*

Something tells me he's been issuing these cruel punishments for days now—and that it's why I've been unable to connect fully with Thorne.

"That seems like a bad idea when he's piloting us, doesn't it?" I ask, trying desperately to keep my voice light in hopes of defusing the situation.

"Which is precisely why your friend needs to learn to control his emotions," Tallin laughs. "He might wish me harm, but I don't suppose he'd want *you* suffering the residual effects of a fiery crash. Isn't that right...Guard?"

Thorne shifts in his seat, his stare now fixed on the prince's reflection.

"Uh-uh," Tallin says. "Eyes ahead, dog. Don't worry—I won't hurt your precious Shara. Not unless one of you breaks the rules. I don't care for a second that you two have fucked like rabbits. I don't care if you're desperate for each other and convinced you'll somehow find your way back into one another's arms. You need to understand that you're both *mine*—and I could make things very unpleasant for you both, if you insist on defying me."

"Please," I plead. "All I ask is that you let me speak to him—or at least, let him speak. I just need to know he's all right."

The prince chuckles. "He's fine. Aren't you, Thorne?"

The Flyer is silent for a few seconds, then Thorne clears his throat and growls, "I'm fine."

But I know him—and thanks to Maude, I understand now how to seek out his mind, at least a little. I can feel his anger now as if it were my own, churning like a sea unsettled by a brutal storm. He's just barely holding it in—barely maintaining control.

He wants Tallin dead, and I don't blame him for a second.

"There, you see?" Tallin says, leaning in close and pressing his lips gently to my neck.

I yank myself away, glowering at him. "Our agreement was no touching. Stop it."

The prince clicks his tongue and says, "Our agreement, if you recall, was no touching except when we're putting on a show for others. And that's what we're doing right now for our friend here, isn't it? Thorne needs to understand the rules. He needs to know I'm in charge."

"There's no need for a show," I snarl. "Save it for your Prefect and your precious fucking Nobles."

Tallin laughs, then lets his hand drop to my thigh, which he squeezes through the dress's too-thin layers of silk.

To say I want to slap him is an understatement. I'd like to grab hold of his hand and dig my nails in until he cries out in agony. I'd like to stab him in the heart with a shard of glass. There are many, *many* things I'd like to do—and not one of them involves him living to see the main course at tonight's dinner.

I can only hope Thorne can't see Tallin's groping hand in the mirror as he eases it slowly upwards.

Pleading silently, I stare ahead, hoping Thorne is somehow able to read my mind when I think, *Ignore him. We'll find a way to be together again. Somehow or other, this will all be over soon.*

As I pull my eyes to the window, I remind myself what Archyr said. Tallin and Valira are lovers.

If it's true, how can the bastard behave this way? How can any man be so callous and cruel—let alone so unfaithful to the woman he allegedly cares for so deeply?

Then again, Tallin is no man.

He's a goddamned monster.

CHAPTER
TWELVE

THE PREFECT'S house is situated on a small island called The Reach. According to Maude, it's one of Kravan's most elite residential areas, home to only a few of the realm's high-ranking officials.

Each property is surrounded by high stone walls—just like every single Noble home I've seen on Kravan's various islands.

As we glide low over the grounds in preparation for landing, I spot a pack of what appear to be large, menacing dogs creeping over a vast lawn.

"Sentinel hounds," the prince says when he sees me staring down at the beasts that stalk the territory like aggressive shadows. "They're mechanical, but far more dangerous than real dogs, which can too easily be manipulated with offers of food or affection."

I see Thorne tensing in his seat as he banks the Flyer around to bring us in for our landing.

"What do the hounds do if they find someone sneaking onto the property?" I ask, my voice sounding like that of a naive child.

"If you enter the grounds uninvited, they rip your face off, or worse," Tallin explains with relish. "They've been known to tear even the most powerful Tethered to shreds on occasion."

I shudder, recalling the time when a couple of Tethered broke into the Verdan house in search of a certain journal, clearly hunting for the truth about Lady Verdan.

To this day, I have no idea who they worked for—nor do I particularly want to know.

"I'd love to have some hounds on the Royal Grounds," Tallin adds, "and roaming the Capitol's streets to take down those damned rebels. But my father refuses—something about a fear of angering the peasants. He's worried the mechanical dogs would accidentally kill some Noble or other, and the war that's been raging for years between all the powerful families would escalate quickly. Then again, Father despises all things electronic and mechanical. He much prefers old fashioned forms of surveillance. Human eyes and ears. It's why he never bothers to have the palace's cameras updated."

~The king is wise not to include sentinel hounds among his arsenal of Guards, Maude whispers to my mind. *Knowing Tallin, he would probably have the beasts programmed to kill for sport.*

"The Quiet War," I say, briefly eyeing the reflection of Thorne's eyes in the rear-view mirror, "is it really as intense as I've heard?"

"More intense, even," Tallin tells me, leaning in close as if we're the best of friends. "You might be shocked to discover that many Nobles spend their days trying to figure out how to unseat my father."

"Why would they, though?" I ask, genuinely perplexed. "He's the king. It's not like they would be given the throne of Kravan in his place, is it?"

Tallin sits back, staring at me. Shaking his head, he says,

"There are many old tales of kings being overthrown and others taking their place. It's only a matter of support from other powerful Nobles. And trust me when I say there are worse men —and women—than my father out there."

Part of me wonders why any Noble would want to change the system. After all, they benefit from it on every possible level, while the Tethered continue to be born in captivity. Every single wealthy person who lives on Kravan's outer islands possesses property and wealth, and by all accounts, leads a pleasant life.

I tell myself I must be missing something—though I can't imagine what. There has to be more to this "Quiet War" than a couple of disgruntled Nobles.

Despite the rage I know he's still feeling, Thorne manages to bring us in for a gentle landing on a pad next to the large manor house.

It takes everything in me not to leap out the door when he slips out of the pilot's seat onto the tarmac.

"Oh," Tallin says, grabbing hold of my wrist to stop me doing anything impulsive. "I almost forgot to give you these."

He presses a button in the back of the driver's seat, and a small compartment opens between us. Inside, I spot two long metal cuffs.

"Put them on, and be sure your markings are concealed," Tallin says.

I slip the cuffs over each forearm, my fear of discovery lessening. The cuffs are elegant and stylish, and it's unlikely that any Noble will think to question why I'm choosing to wear them.

"Careful, now," the prince whispers, sensing my desire to pull away from him as we climb out of the vehicle. "There are eyes watching us both. Remember—you have only one job tonight, and my father will be hearing about it if you fail us."

Recalling the king's insistence that a Tethered will be among the guests tonight, I reluctantly push my arm through Tallin's and move with him toward the house's entrance, with Thorne stalking along behind us. My desire to turn and look at him is so great that it takes Maude issuing me a silent, desperate warning to keep me from caving.

"She looks incredible from behind, doesn't she?" Tallin calls over his shoulder. He slips a hand down my back, pausing when he's just about to reach my ass.

My hands coil into fists, my desire to punch the prince increasing to dangerous levels.

~He's being a dick for the sake of getting a rise out of you, Maude warns. *Don't let him control your emotions. If you do, he'll exploit your weakness. Stay. Focused.*

Thorne must be thinking the same thing, but he manages to stay silent as the enormous house's front door opens and the Prefect moves into its frame, a friendly-looking blonde woman by his side. Both smile in greeting as we approach.

"Your Highness," the Prefect says, his tone and body language filled with a reverence that makes me want to gag. "It's so good of you to come."

Tallin grins. "I was pleased to receive your invitation," he says. "Prefect, I'd like you to meet Lady Ingram, my betrothed."

The Prefect shoots me only a cursory glance and a vague smile before shifting his eyes back to the prince. "My congratulations," he says, his manner submissive, and I understand for the first time why Tallin wasn't concerned about him recognizing me.

He couldn't care less that I'm here. All he cares about is pleasing Tallin.

He's a simple kiss-ass.

Lucky me, I guess.

The Prefect's wife, on the other hand, looks me up and

down appraisingly, then finally nods her approval. "So nice to meet you, Lady Ingram," she says. "I can see why the prince chose you over every other lady in Kravan."

"I...thank you," I reply.

"This is Lady Weston," Tallin says, gesturing to her. "The Prefect's lovely significant other."

"Ah—*there's* a familiar face," the Prefect says suddenly, and I freeze in place until I realize that Thorne has slipped up next to me. "Thorne," the Prefect adds, "so good to see you again. I heard you're moving up in the world to Royal Guard—not that it surprises me in the least. You always were highly capable. And devoted to the Nobility."

Tallin lets out a snicker at my side, then covers it up with a cough.

"Thank you, yes," Thorne replies. It seems he's been temporarily released from Tallin's torture, and the sound of his smooth, deep voice sends a shockwave through me that doesn't stop until it reaches my core. The craving is brutal, relentless—almost a cruelty.

What I wouldn't give to be alone with him right now. I need to touch him, to taste him. I need to feel him inside me again...

"Come, Lady Ingram," Lady Weston says, taking me gently by the arm as if she senses my discomfort. "Let's get you a drink and let these fellows catch up. Several guests are already milling around the drawing room. Mostly men, I'm afraid. Such a bore."

I gratefully detach myself from Tallin and accompany her down a long hallway of tiled floor, multiple crystal chandeliers, and expensive-looking art, until we reach a kitchen large enough to cook for an entire army.

"White wine? Red?" my host asks, slipping toward a cupboard and pulling out two glasses.

"White," I reply. "Please, Lady Weston." Not that I'm any

expert, but white wine seems more refreshing than red, which always reminds me unsettlingly of blood.

"Please," she laughs, "call me Susan."

"Susan," I repeat with an awkward smile.

As she pours us each a glass, I notice Thorne standing in the doorway, watching me intently.

"Would your servant like anything?" Susan asks me. "Is he hungry?"

"My...servant?"

"Yes, your Guard. As I understand it, even Tethered need to consume food and drink now and then."

I turn to see a look of amusement flash over Thorne's features. "Oh! I...yes. Of course they do."

Good lord. Is this what it feels like to be a member of the Nobility? Being told that I own people? Calling them mine, as if each Tethered is nothing more than a pair of shoes?

"Thorne," I say, turning to him with a hint of authority in my voice. "Would you like something to eat?"

"Yes. I would," he replies, his eyes narrowing as they move down my body. There's a quiet hunger in his voice when he adds, "There's something I would like very much to eat. But I'm not allowed to have it...*your Ladyship.*"

My cheeks flush with the insinuation in his tone, and I can only hope Susan doesn't pick up on it.

All I want to do is grab him and leave this place—or, at the very least, find a quiet room where we can spend a few hours alone together, now that Tallin isn't here to torture us both.

"I...why ever not?" Susan asks. "We have plenty of food to go around. Not to mention wine."

"Thank you," Thorne says, offering her a charming, if reserved, smile. "But I need to fly Lady Ingram and the prince back to the palace later. So, no alcohol for me. It's very kind of you to offer, though."

"Goodness," Susan says, flushing bright red. "You're a charmer, aren't you?"

For a second, I'm terrified that she's going to put her hands on him as I've seen Lady Verdan do more than once.

I'm not sure I could restrain myself if she did.

"I was raised well by those who trained me in the Tower," Thorne says. "And I always aim to please."

At that, he lowers his chin and shoots me a veiled look. "I'll leave you ladies now. Let me know if there's anything you need...Lady Ingram."

My chest throbs with desire and pain as he turns and heads toward the drawing room where the other guests have assembled.

More than ever, I hate this need to put on an act and pretend for even a second that I don't desire him—that I don't crave him with every fiber of my being.

But we both know perfectly well that the alternative to pretending is death. So, if I can only have these few, brief moments of agonizing torture with him now and then, at least it's better than being separated again for days on end.

"*So,* you and the prince," Susan says, leaning back against the counter, her wine glass already half empty. "Tell me, how did you two meet?"

My eyes are still locked on the doorway, but I take a quick gulp of wine, shift my gaze to hers, and say, "We, um, met at the Royal Ball."

She looks baffled. "Really? That was only a few days ago. You're already engaged?" With a laugh, she adds, "Love at first sight, was it?"

She's eyeing my left hand, and all of a sudden, I remember the engagement ring Tallin insisted on giving me. I set my glass down and finger it nervously, self-conscious under her judgmental gaze. "Something like that," I tell her. "I'm still sort of in shock, to tell you the truth."

She moves closer when she replies, "I know the feeling. Engagement rings are hard to get used to, aren't they? Took me years to stop feeling strange about my own. It feels so much like a sign that someone has taken possession of us." She holds up her hand to reveal a ring with three diamonds set against a gold band.

Relief fills me to realize she's offering up more sympathy than judgment.

"I suppose it probably seems to everyone else like Tallin and I sprinted into this engagement." My eyes lock on the diamond. *If only it had come from Thorne. If only I were free to be with him—if only* **all** *Tethered were free.*

"Tell me everything," Susan says. "I want to know how you felt when you two first met. The prince was the most eligible bachelor in all of Kravan, and here you've snatched him away from all the other young ladies."

I don't want to tell her anything. Don't want her to know he was vile and disgusting—that he filled me with fear.

But I have to maintain my composure...so I tell her about my first encounter with Thorne, instead.

"I knew the second I saw him that there was something between us," I say softly, savoring the words as they come. "Something more than just attraction, I mean. It was deeper. To be honest, I wasn't sure I liked him at first—but I think I knew I *loved* him. I just didn't want to admit it to myself."

It's all true. The first moment I spotted Thorne in the training room inside the Tower, I endured a wave of emotion unlike any I had ever experienced—something so deep it infiltrated every cell in my body.

Thorne had, quite literally, taken my breath away during those first moments. After that, he'd pissed me off a thousand times and excited me a thousand more. And through it all, I knew, deep down, that he and I were bound by something far stronger than mere physical attraction.

"Well, he *is* extremely handsome," Susan says. "As I said, every lady in Kravan thinks so."

"Yes," I reply, smiling as I think of Thorne's face, his eyes. His body. "He is. We're meant for one another. There's no doubt in my mind."

As I speak, I look into Susan's eyes, wondering if she could possibly suspect I'm bending the truth to suit my narrative.

It seems she's oblivious, because she clasps her hands together and says, "That's such a wonderful feeling, isn't it? Ah, young love. You're very lucky, and so is his Highness."

"His Highness," I repeat softly as if trying to remind myself I'm supposed to be gushing over Tallin, and no one else.

"Excuse me, Lady Weston," a woman's voice says, startling me out of my thoughts. I turn to the doorway where Thorne stood a moment ago, only to see a Tethered in a Domestic's uniform with a telltale green crest on the left side of her chest.

She looks like she's forty or so years old, her dark brown hair pulled back into a tidy bun.

"Yes, Evangeline?" Susan's tone is suddenly ice cold. "What the hell do you want?"

As if she's torn a mask off her face, I suddenly see my host's true colors. The way she speaks to me—to Thorne—it's only because we're associated with the prince.

"I...I'm wondering if you need anything," the woman called Evangeline says, her hands twisting nervously together.

"We have caterers today," Susan says. "As you know perfectly well. Why would I need you?"

"Yes, Ma'am," the servant replies. "Of course. I only thought—"

"You weren't thinking at *all*, clearly."

87

"Quite right, my Lady." The Tethered begins to turn away, but stops when her eyes land on me.

On her face is a look of shock, as if she's seen me somewhere before.

Her mouth drops open for a moment, and she looks like she's on the verge of speaking.

"Is there something else, Evangeline?" Susan says impatiently.

"I'm sorry. I thought...it's just...your guest..." She looks me squarely in the eye and says, "It's nothing."

"If it's nothing, you should go about your business elsewhere in the house and stop disturbing us before I have you terminated."

The way she utters the last word is chilling, and I find myself glaring at Susan, enraged.

I know by now that Nobles think nothing of killing Tethered or having them killed. But the ease with which Lady Weston speaks of it is vile.

Evangeline sounds distraught when she replies, "Of course. My apologies for intruding."

Without another word, she turns and leaves.

"Honestly," Susan says, moving closer to me and speaking conspiratorially. "These Tethered are such utter flakes, don't you think? Not a brain cell between the lot of them. Except for your Guard, of course—that Thorne. Then again, it's not exactly his *brain* I noticed, if you catch my meaning."

She says the words like she expects me to rejoice in the fact that she objectifies Thorne like he's a toy for her to play with rather than an actual human.

My body tenses as rage seeps through my veins, but I force myself to smile and say, "When I was growing up, our family's Tethered were always quite intelligent—and reliable."

"Well, you're fortunate, then. I've had to get rid of more of them than I'd care to admit. It's an unpleasant business, I'll tell you. Such a pain."

"Get rid of?" I can barely keep my voice contained when I add, "By that, you mean..."

Drawing her finger across her throat, Susan lets out a laugh. "Oh, I don't do it myself, of course. Termination is the Prefect's business. He knows Kravan's laws better than anyone —which means he knows Tethered are as disposable as any other trash. He hires Crimson Elite specialists to come tend to the business themselves. As you can imagine, it gets quite messy at times."

Just when I thought I couldn't feel hatred deeper than what I feel for Lady Verdan and Tallin, Lady Weston is pushing me to the limit.

"Strange that you should feel the need to dispose of your Tethered," I say through a clenched jaw, "given that the Prefect is in charge of their Placements. I would have expected his judgment to be better than that."

Still oblivious, Susan laughs. "Oh, it's not his fault. The poor thing tries so hard. I must admit that I'm the one who's fussy. I can't stand a Tethered who thinks they know better than I do— it irritates me beyond words." She sighs, then adds, "It's a misery. I'll probably have to get rid of Evangeline, if only for that reason. She has a habit of sticking her nose in where it doesn't belong, as you just saw."

"What will happen to her? If you get rid of her, I mean."

Susan shrugs. "She'll be killed, of course. It won't exactly be difficult—she's a Green, after all, with no special powers to speak of. No Noble wants a rejected Green, so she would be useless to society—worth no more than a sack of compost."

A wave of scalding heat rises to my cheeks. I force down a large gulp of wine to hide my rage, then rise to my feet and excuse myself. "I'm going to look for the prince," I say, heading toward the kitchen door. "Thank you for the drink, Lady Weston."

Susan reaches a hand out to stop me, but when I shoot her a look of warning, she says nothing.

You're wise to keep your mouth shut, Lady Weston. Because if you keep me here for another minute, I swear to God, I will kill you with my bare hands.

CHAPTER
THIRTEEN

IN THE HALLWAY, I spot the Domestic called Evangeline standing some distance away, talking to Valira, who's dressed in her Guard uniform, as usual. Their heads are close together and they're speaking in whispers as if they know one another.

Confused, I freeze when I see them.

As Valira glances sideways at me, I notice a hint of silver under her sleeves.

Is she wearing wrist pieces to enhance her powers? I wonder.

~It's more likely they're intended to block signals from her A.I. unit, Maude informs me. *Perhaps Valira is tired of being monitored constantly.*

As I watch, Valira mutters a few final words under her breath, then with a nod and a quick look in my direction, Evangeline scurries rapidly away.

Striding over, I grab Valira, pull her into a room off the hallway—a small office with one narrow window—and shut the door behind us.

"What are you doing?" she spits. "If the Prefect sees us together in here..."

"He'll think I'm hurling harsh words at a member of the

Royal Guard," I hiss under my breath. "Which is exactly what Nobles in my position do on a regular basis. So tell me, why were you speaking to that woman?"

For a second, Valira looks as if she's at a loss for words. But she quickly rallies and raises her chin defiantly. "I wanted to ask her to make sure the prince has everything he needs."

"Sure. But why her? Lady Weston said there are caterers here today."

Valira glances at the door as if she's about to make a run for it. "You really do need to stop asking so many questions," she says. "Just let me do my job."

"Your job," I snicker. "Ah, yes. A Violet with some bizarre, unhealthy loyalty to the prince of Kravan. A Violet who watches over him at dinner parties, in spite of the fact that there are far more qualified Guards back at the palace."

"I'm perfectly capable of defending Prince Tallin, if I should need to."

"Are you saying that's why you're here? Is that why you were talking to that Domestic? Is there some threat against the prince?"

"There's always a threat in the air," she replies. "But I'm here because Tallin—the prince, I mean—asked me to be here. That's all."

I cross my arms and glare at her. "Valira," I say, my voice hard-edged. "What the hell is the deal between you and Tallin? Have you sold your soul or something?"

She fixes me with a cold stare and says, "I don't believe for a second that you're really this fucking naive."

I laugh. "Fine, then—you're his lover. Is that what you want me to say out loud? Is it such common knowledge that you tell everyone?"

It's not really a question.

Even if Archyr hadn't *told* me they were lovers, I know

perfectly well that Tallin sees her as far more than a mere Guard.

It also explains why she hates me so much.

The only question that remains is whether or not she's his lover willingly.

"Yes," she says. "It's not exactly a secret. Tallin and I are lovers."

A realization punches me in the throat then, and I reply, "Oh God—are you two tethered like..."

I'm about to say *like Thorne and I are*, but I don't want to offer up that information. If Tallin knew Thorne and I were fully bound together, he would probably do whatever he could to tear us apart.

"No," Valira snaps. "I am not Tallin's tethered mate. It's... more complicated than that."

"But?"

"Prince Tallin needs me." She seals her lips tightly, then adds, "Look, I do what I have to do. I perform my duty, which keeps everyone in the palace safe—including you and your precious Thorne. Nothing else matters."

I have no idea what the hell she means by that.

I want to ask, *Are you telling me your blowjobs are some sort of magical shield against Tallin's cruelty?*

But I have no desire to be slapped.

"Does your duty involve that Domestic, Evangeline?" I ask. "I don't believe for a second that you and she were only discussing the prince's wishes. Why was she staring at me like that?"

This time, Valira snickers, steps to the door, grabs its knob, and says, "I told you—you ask too many fucking questions, and it's going to get you killed. I have no intention of being a casualty of your too-curious mind. Some of us don't have the privilege of dressing up and posing as Nobles, and being in this room with you right now means I'm risking my life. No offense, Lady Ingram, but you're not worth it."

With that, she leaves, closing the door behind her.

"Maude," I whisper. "Is there a chance the prince will know what she and I just talked about?"

~There's a chance, Maude replies. *Or, rather, there would be— if not for her wrist braces, which may be blocking his access. Just to be on the safe side, though, I scrambled her Maude's signal.*

"Bless you for being a meddlesome bitch, I guess?"

~Meddlesome bitch is high praise coming from you, Shara dear.

Once I've cursed Maude out sufficiently, I take in several deep breaths then slip out into the hallway and make my way back toward the front of the large house.

I've only gone a few feet when the sound of low voices draws my eyes to an open door ahead and to my right.

I slip over and peek in only to see a small, elegant office containing a desk and a chair. Leaning against the desk, Tallin is holding Valira by the shoulders. His back is to me, and I can just barely see Valira's face, which is twisted and pained. The prince is speaking to her in what almost sounds like a soothing tone—if Tallin is capable of such a thing.

"A few hours," he says softly. "That's all. Then I'll do unspeakable things to you in my bed."

"Yes, your Highness," her strained voice replies.

"*Highness,*" he scoffs. "Why do you call me that when we're alone?"

He leans forward and kisses her gently on the neck. Pulling her head to the side, she lets out a moan as his hands work their way up her waist, slipping up her body to cup her breasts through her uniform. She throws her head back, letting him do as he wishes.

I can't see her face anymore, but from the low purrs she's emitting, she seems to be enjoying herself.

Maybe this moment answers every nagging question I have about Valira. Maybe she really *does* care for Tallin. After all, there are probably plenty of people in this world who are attracted to powerful Nobles like him.

If she loves him, then Valira must despise me simply for existing—for this play-acting of mine. She must hate knowing his hands will be on me tonight, even if it's just part of the act.

"I want you so fucking badly," I hear the prince say, and I find myself wondering where the Prefect and his guests are, and how this is happening right under their noses.

My question is answered when I hear male voices bellowing at one another somewhere farther down the hall. I turn and half-jog toward the open drawing room, where the Prefect is seated with several well-dressed men, each of whom looks like he's in his forties or fifties.

"Ah, Lady Ingram," the Prefect says, gesturing me into the room. "Come in, will you?"

The other men leap to their feet, their eyes moving down my body as each of them smiles a vile sort of approval. I step into the room and lay my small silk clutch on a side table. "May I introduce Lord Davies, Lord Southdown, and Lord Twain," the Prefect says. "You may have met them at the Prince's Ball."

"I'm afraid I didn't have the pleasure," I say with a smile, extending my hand for the first of the men to shake.

He pulls it to him and, after a brush of his lips, says, "You may not remember me, but I *certainly* remember you. One doesn't forget a spectacle like that. The entire palace was shut down when you ran off, you know. His Highness was eager to find you, but from what I hear, you provided him with quite a hunt."

"Oh?" Lord Davies grunts. "It seems I haven't heard the juiciest rumors about that night. What happened, exactly?"

"My little love wasn't a fan of the Crimson Championship," Tallin's voice says from behind me.

I spin around to see him standing in the doorway, throwing me a quick look of warning as if to say, "I've got this. Don't you dare say a word."

"The way your Guards sprang into action, I thought a new Rebellion had begun!" Lord Davies replies with a hearty laugh. "I'm glad to know it was simply that you were desperate to locate this lovely creature and ensnare her. I can't say I blame you for it."

"Her reaction was perfectly understandable," Lord Twain replies. "Many of the ladies are squeamish about bloodshed. I'm just glad his Highness found you again, Lady Ingram. It looks like a happy ending was had by all."

I force out a ringing laugh as the prince takes me by the waist and plants a kiss on my cheek. It seems Tallin has returned from his little tryst with Valira.

"What a charmer you are, your Highness," Lord Southdown says.

"Yes," I reply, taking Tallin by the hand. "He is, isn't he?"

"He must be. It seems the prince has acquired the most attractive woman in all of Kravan."

Movement by the door draws my eye, and I look over to see Thorne and Valira making their way into the room, each looking equally enraged. They position themselves against the far wall, hands behind their backs, and stand protectively close to the prince.

"Attractive doesn't begin to describe Lady Ingram," the prince replies, pulling me closer still and kissing me again. This time, his lips brush my cheek far too close to my mouth for comfort.

I look sideways at Thorne, whose eyes are fixed coldly ahead as if he's in denial about the scenario playing out in front of him. Even from a few feet away, I can feel the tension in his body as our mutual enemy lays claim to me in front of the small group of guests.

"She really is the sexiest thing, isn't she?" Tallin asks, a hand slipping down my back as his gaze settles on my chest. "Just lovely."

If Thorne doesn't kill you, I think, *Valira will. Stop being an asshole.*

"Are you all ready for dinner?" Lady Weston's voice calls from the doorway.

"Famished," Tallin says when the others have made their way out of the room, his hand slipping down still farther to cup my backside as he steers me toward the door.

When we've taken a few steps down the hall, I stop and say, "My clutch! I left it back in the drawing room."

To my relief, Valira has joined us and is now standing next to Tallin. Maybe she'll be enough to distract him.

"Go get it, then," Tallin replies with a huff. "Meet me at the table."

I run back to find that Thorne is still pressed to the wall, his eyes sealed shut.

Slipping over to him, I whisper his name.

"I thought I could do this," he breathes without looking at me. "I thought I could take on this charade, for the good of our kind. But if I have to watch that fucker put his hands on you one more time, I swear I'll..."

He opens his eyes and fixes them on my own.

"You'll what?" I whisper, reaching for my clutch as I eye the door to make sure no one is watching us.

"I will kill him for touching you. I swear it."

I'm about to issue him a warning when I hear a voice in the hallway. I gather up my clutch then move past Thorne, who grabs my hand and for a delicious, breathless moment, holds me in place.

"I need to taste you again," he murmurs.

I swallow, my eyes landing on his own. "I—"

Before I can finish my thought, Thorne drops my hand and nods toward the door. I turn just in time to see Susan appearing outside the room.

"Ah, Lady Ingram," she says from the doorway, where she's now staring inquisitively at Thorne—no doubt because my hostility earlier has made her apprehensive about looking into my eyes. "Come, come—we wouldn't want your dinner to get cold, now, would we?"

CHAPTER
FOURTEEN

WHEN I REACH the dining room, I discover that several more people have joined the party.

There are now eleven of us in total. Eight men and three women—though why there's such an imbalance in numbers, I can't begin to guess.

When I seat myself with Tallin to my right, I take in the guests, reminding myself I have a job to do. Lords Southdown, Twain, and Davies are scattered about the table. The Prefect and his wife sit at the ends, watching over the rest of us like proud parents—at least, how I imagine proud parents would look.

Seated across the table from me is a man who introduces himself as Lord Malloy. He strikes me instantly as jovial, friendly, and unassuming—unlike some of the other guests. By all appearances, he's approaching middle age, his brown hair graying at the temples.

A near-silent gasp escapes my chest when my eyes land on his, only to see his irises twist with numerous colors before settling once again on brown. It seems I've found the Tethered the king was searching for.

He looks as if he's about to ask me something when the man to his right engages him in conversation, thankfully drawing his attention away.

"What is it?" Tallin whispers, leaning in close to me. "Did you see something?"

I don't want to answer him.

When I agreed to play this role—to expose Tethered hiding among the Nobility—I expected to uncover traitors to our kind, monsters like Tallin and his spiteful banshee of a mother.

There's nothing about Lord Malloy that tells me he's cruel, or even moderately mischievous. If anything, he appears to be a perfectly decent, quiet man who enjoys the company of others.

But if I refuse to report him to the king, the consequences will be dire for Thorne and me. Tonight is a test of my loyalty, and *if I fail...*

No. I don't want to think about it.

For a moment, I contemplate lying and telling Tallin it's one of the others who is the Tethered. Lord Twain or Lord Southdown, who both seem almost as lecherous as Tallin himself.

"Say it," Tallin hisses, his face buried in my neck to conceal his rage. "Tell me what you've seen."

"Lord Malloy," I breathe miserably, pulling myself close and twisting around so no one will be able to read my lips. "He's a Velor—which means he has the ability to move incredibly fast."

"I know what a fucking Velor is," Tallin snaps, pulling his glass up to his mouth. "Are you certain?"

I nod. "I knew one in the Tower—I know the power very well. It can be used aggressively—but..."

Tallin isn't going to like what I'm about to say.

"But what?"

"Lord Malloy is harmless. I don't see any evidence that he's violent. Only that he likes to speed around his grounds when no one is looking. That's all he uses his power for."

"That may be all you see, but it doesn't mean he's harmless," the prince laughs softly. Those around us are speaking loudly now, their voices crescendoing alongside their wine consumption. "A Velor could do some serious damage—he could steal valuable items without anyone seeing him, and wreak general havoc on Kravan."

"It's not like he's *invisible*," I whisper. "He's just...fast. There's nothing wrong with—"

"Highness!" Lord Twain roars, interrupting us. "May we ask you to stop canoodling with your beloved long enough to regale us with tales from the palace?"

"Of course," Tallin says, shifting away from me to spew out stories about his great accomplishments, which seem mostly to involve punishing Tethered servants for minor infractions.

My eyes glaze over as he launches into a seemingly endless series of anecdotes, and I find myself glancing toward Thorne more than once to see if I can catch his eye.

"He's a handsome one, isn't he?" a woman's voice asks.

I had barely noticed the guest seated to my left, but I turn now and glance at her, then down at my plate, wishing I could disappear.

"I...who?" I reply, my cheeks flushing.

"It's all right to find the help attractive, you know," the woman whispers with a quiet laugh. "We all do. So many of their kind are beautiful. I've heard that a few have gifts that make them extraordinary lovers. What a power *that* would be."

"Indeed," I say. "I wouldn't know. The only man I have eyes for is the prince."

What a nauseating lie.

"Of course," she replies with a wink. "But if the prince were to propose a threesome with your gorgeous Guard, well...Let's just say I'd be tempted, if I were you."

"Somehow, I don't think the prince would ever propose such a thing," I sigh, and she laughs again.

"Pity," she says. "By the way, I haven't introduced myself. Lady Graystone is my name."

"Lady Ingram," I reply.

"Oh, I know. The whole of Kravan is talking about you." She pulls herself closer to me when she adds, "But don't worry—I'm no gossip."

With that, she introduces her son, Ellion, who is seated on her other side.

A pale man of twenty or so, he nods briefly when I acknowledge him, his eyes downcast. I find myself wondering why he's here and whether his mother dragged him out against his will.

It's only after I've said hello to Ellion that I notice Lady Graystone's left hand is a prosthetic. Though it moves naturally, it appears to be made of some sort of light golden metal—a mechanical hand, which must have cost a fortune.

When she notices me staring, she smiles and says, "I was in a crash quite a few years ago, when I was about Ellion's age. My family's Flyer went berserk, and we went down hard. That's how I lost it."

"I'm so sorry," I tell her. "I didn't mean to stare. It's just—it's quite beautiful."

She glances down at it, her smile never wavering. "This is about the tenth prosthetic I've had," she tells me, "and definitely my favorite. It was crafted for me by an engineer who specializes in artificial intelligence. It's directly linked to my mind, which means it feels like a part of my own body. Sometimes, I'm convinced my hand has a mind of its own."

She says the last words with a wink, and, as I look her in the eye, I inhale a quiet, sharp breath. For the first time, I see that her irises, like Lord Malloy's, are swimming with an array of colors.

Did I fail to notice before? Or was she somehow hiding her true identity?

Is it even possible for a Tethered to hide from a Hunter?

I pull my gaze to her son Ellion, who has begun watching me cautiously. His eyes, too, betray the nature of a Tethered—though their fluidity is less intense than that of his mother's irises.

Shooting a look at Thorne, I see him shake his head ever so slightly as if warning me against something.

~If he's cautioning you, Shara, Maude says, *he has a point. The king asked for the name of one Tethered. Not three. No need to sell every bit of your soul.*

As the dinner drags on, I choose to avoid conversing too much with the Graystones for fear that Tallin will ask my opinion of them and force me to lie.

While I eat, I find my eyes veering back and forth between Thorne and Tallin, who pokes me at regular intervals to ensure that I'm fawning over him sufficiently.

"Remember your promise," he growls softly, and I have no choice but to giggle and act like an absolute fool on more than a few occasions. I did promise, after all, to convince every Noble in existence that my life revolved around my unrelenting desire to give him endless, mind-bending blowjobs.

I watch Lord Malloy on occasion, chastising myself silently for what I've done. I have no doubt there plenty of Tethered among the Nobility who, like Tallin, are power-hungry and cruel. But I can't help thinking Lord Malloy deserves to be left alone.

He chats jovially with the guests to his left and right, and when I manage to listen in on their conversations, I realize he's probably the most humane person in the entire room.

"What's going to happen to him?" I whisper to Tallin.

"Oh, nothing," the prince says with a wave of his hand. "I'm sure my father will simply keep an eye on him. Your job is to point us toward possible treachery, that's all. If you're right and Lord Malloy is harmless, there's nothing to worry about."

When I breathe a sigh of relief, Tallin chuckles. "You were genuinely worried, weren't you?"

"Of course I was. I don't want someone getting hurt because of me."

The prince gawks at me like I have three heads. "You're telling me you care for this man you've never even met before tonight?"

"I care that I might be responsible for his downfall," I whisper. "I want to be able to look myself in the eye tomorrow morning."

"You went nineteen years in the Tower without a mirror, right?" he asks. "Trust me—you'll find life much simpler if you continue to avoid the curse of your own gaze. God knows, I'm an expert at it."

I don't know what he means by that, and I refuse to ask.

FIFTEEN

AFTER DINNER, the guests move to the Prefect's vast library for more drinks, throwing themselves down onto an assortment of leather couches and armchairs.

The room smells of wood polish and leather, and at first, I revel in the space, marveling at the beautiful patchwork of book spines covering every wall.

But very quickly, the conversation and infighting among most of the half-drunk Nobles becomes infuriating—not to mention that it seriously tests my ability to keep up the pretense that I'm one of them.

I've only ever seen hints of what's known as the "Quiet War" between Noble families. There were the two men who broke into the Verdan residence one night as I slept. Not to mention the ridiculously high walls surrounding every property. Whispers of threats to the Royals.

But watching a bunch of entitled, wealthy assholes stare one another down as if assessing each other for physical weakness, I'm beginning to understand the nature of this so-called "war."

Despite the smiles on the guests' lips, the room teems with loathing.

Everything the Nobles say seems intended to diminish their fellow guests in front of the prince. *Most* of them, that is.

Lord Malloy and the Graystones remain largely silent as they watch the other guests rage at one another.

"I've heard your Tethered have been spreading rumors about me," Lord Twain barks at Lord Southdown, waving a snifter of brandy in the air. "You'd best see to it that it stops or I'll have it stopped for you."

At one point, I hear Lord Davies tell another guest, "Rumor has it your wife was seen at the shops touching your Guard inappropriately. You ought to strap that one to your bed until she learns to behave herself."

Through it all, Thorne and Valira stand guard by the door. The Prefect's servants and caterers stream in and out of the room, bringing us copious amounts of alcohol—which is beginning to seem like a terrible idea.

Over time, the drinks loosen the Nobles' tongues still further, and most of them spend a good part of the evening discussing the uselessness of their respective servants while simultaneously boasting about their Tethered's powers.

I have no desire to make conversation with any of them, so I wander the room, gliding past Thorne to peruse the library's plentiful bookshelves, eyeing tome after tome with interest.

Intrigued, I pause when I come to a section made up of a large series of historical texts. To my disappointment, they seem to focus only on the time since the Rebellion.

"Interesting stuff, isn't it?" Lord Twain asks, his words slurred as he sidles over to me. "You're keen on history, I take it?"

"Oh, no," I tell him. "I mean, not really. And if I were, it would be the ancient stuff—you know, the times before..."

I stop myself, unsure whether Nobles are allowed to speak of pre-Rebellion times. In the Tower, it was forbidden—but then, we were the furthest thing from Nobility.

"Ah. The true, secret Histories," the Noble chuckles. "There's only one place in Kravan where those texts remain, and I'm afraid even one as important as the prince isn't allowed to see them."

"Too true," Tallin half-shouts from across the room. I turn to see his eyes narrowed in our direction. "Not even my father the king is supposed to know the true history of Kravan."

"Oh?" I ask, smiling at Lord Twain. "Where are these secret texts kept?"

He smirks mischievously at me, and for a moment, I'm certain he's seeing two of me in his drunken state. In a conspiratorial tone, he half-whispers, "In a secure vault—a top secret one in the possession of a certain Nobleman and his wife. They say the Nobleman is the keeper of the texts—though apparently, even *he* is not allowed to see them. As I understand it, it's nearly impossible to access them."

"Why aren't they kept inside the palace?"

"There's only one house in Kravan with a vault secure enough to keep the most powerful Tethered from breaking in. Besides, if they were kept in the palace and the realm knew, the Royal Guard would have a full-time job, keeping intruders from trying to find them."

"Ah," I say. "As for the secret Nobleman who keeps the texts —does *he* know what's in them?"

"They say he does not," Lord Twain replies, moving in closer, his tone and body language flirtatious in a vile, paternalistic way. "But if he did, I'm not sure even a lovely young thing such as yourself could persuade him to tell you the truth of it all. If he divulged the truth..."

He pulls a fist into the air as if he's miming hanging himself.

"Oh," I laugh, pulling back and shooting a look at Tallin. "I would never ask for that sort of information. I'm just curious, I suppose." I shrug. "You know, about how we all ended up living outside the Capitol, hiding behind our high, stone walls. I'm curious to know how the Tower came to be. All of it."

"If you want to know about that sort of thing, look no further than the Tethered scum," Lord Southdown half-shouts from the nearest couch, clearly inebriated. "Violent animals, all of them. It's no secret that they attacked the Capitol, and our ancestors were forced to flee. It's as simple as that. It's a wonder we managed to contain the monsters. You don't need historical texts to tell you Tethered are garbage. If you ask me, they should all remain in the Tower until they die of old age, or kill each other off."

"In windowless cells, you mean," Lady Graystone says, her voice smooth as silk. "With no knowledge of the outside world, no view of sky or land. You're happy to deprive the Tethered of love, of life, of ambition. You think that's the best way to deal with the so-called 'monsters'?"

I see her son reach for her arm and issue a squeeze of warning, and she seals her mouth.

"Had we not deprived them after we defeated them," Lord Southdown says, "their kind would be running Kravan—which means they would kill all of us and each other. You know it as well as I do."

"Perhaps she knows nothing of the sort," Lord Davies says. "Every Tethered I've ever known has been respectful and kind. My two Tethered servants are excellent people."

"Clearly, you haven't known many of their kind," Lord Twain retorts to a chorus of agreement from the other guests. "They're brutal creatures. Mercurial. They're ambitious, despite the rules against it. We've had to put many of them down— that is, when they weren't busy killing each other."

"If they really are as terrible as you say," Lord Davies replies, "then why not let us read the true Histories? Why hide the texts? If indeed the Tethered caused the Rebellion, shouldn't we be informed of how and why they did it so we can prevent it from happening again?"

Even from across the room, I feel Lord Twain's ire rising at his fellow guest's impertinence and irritating curiosity.

"We don't need to know why or how it occurred," the Prefect thunders. "When one sector of society is made up of animals, there is no need to understand anything other than that they must be put down when they act up. It's quite simple, really."

Now that our host has shut the conversation down, Tallin fixes his eyes on me. "If you're so curious about Kravan's history, my darling, you can ask my father about it. I'm sure he'll tell you anything you'd like to know. Trust me—there is no point in learning what some secret vault contains. We all know the texts are filled with vile lies."

I want to ask what, exactly, those lies are supposed to be, but Maude issues me a stern warning.

~If you throw out any more questions, they'll begin to doubt you're really a Noble. Most of these wealthy assholes are familiar with the rumors about the forbidden texts.

Do you know where they are, Maude?

~No, I do not, though I suspect there are some in this room who have an inkling. Secrets never last long among those with influence.

I nod slightly, my eyes veering to Thorne, who's watching me quietly, an intensity in his expression that tells me he's thinking exactly what I'm thinking.

We need to get our hands on those texts, and soon.

AFTER THE CONVERSATION has mercifully changed course and the Nobles are once again engaged in badmouthing their Tethered servants, I excuse myself to head to the bathroom, slipping out the door.

I manage to throw Thorne a reassuring glance, all too aware of Valira's appraising stare as I pass her.

When I return a few minutes later, though, Valira is nowhere to be seen. It takes me a moment to realize Tallin, too, has disappeared.

My voice takes on a fake formality as the curious Nobles in the room turn my way. "Guard," I say. "Where is the prince?"

"I believe he stepped out for a breath of fresh air," Thorne tells me. "Valira has gone to watch over him."

"Ah. Maybe I should go find him. Would you join me, please?"

As he shifts from his post with a curt nod, I notice Lady Graystone watching us, an approving smile on her lips.

Thorne follows silently as I turn and head down the hallway.

When we're some distance from the library, I whisper, "I need to be alone with you—*properly* alone. I can't stand being so close to you and not being able to..." I stop before I say something that makes my skin flush bright red.

"I feel the same way, my Lady," Thorne replies, and I look sideways to see him grinning slightly. It seems any residual pain from Tallin's earlier punishment is long gone. "By the way, I trust the evening has been a success for you?"

"If you can call it that," I reply out of the corner of my mouth. "I'm not exactly happy about turning in one of our own."

"I know. I can feel the conflict in you."

He reaches out and slips his fingers over the back of my hand, so gently that I wonder if I'm imagining it. I close my eyes against the sensation, memorizing it. Every nerve in my body comes alive —every vein throbs with the violent drumming of my heart.

The first time I met Thorne, he touched me like this, his fingers grazing the back of my neck in my cohort's cafeteria inside the Tower. Never had I felt a sensation like it—and to this day, I have never forgotten the surge of longing that over-took me in that instant.

Then again, the longing has never ceased—and right now, it's destroying me.

"Tell me," I whisper, forcing my mind away from the ache of desire at my core, "why did you shake your head when I looked at Lady Graystone and her son?"

Thorne stops in his tracks, glances back toward the library, and says, "When I first laid eyes on them, I saw something—a vivid snapshot of the future. I don't really know how to explain it, but I think those two are going to be important."

My brows rise, my eyes widening with confusion. "I thought you could only see a few seconds into the future. When you first told me about your powers, you said..."

"Our bond has changed me." He smiles and reaches a hand out to stroke my cheek, then thinks better of it and tucks it to his side. "My mind has opened up to visions of the future that are detailed and powerful."

"What exactly did you see?"

"Something that made me think the Graystones need to be protected at all costs." Thorne hesitates for only a moment before he adds, "I'm convinced they're the key to turning the tide, Shara. I just don't know how or why yet."

"I hope you're right," I tell him. "Lady Graystone is a Conjurer, as far as I can tell—she summons items with her mind. I can't see Ellion's gift yet—but he and his mother are so secretive, I wonder if he's somehow found a way to hide it, even from me."

"Maybe that's part of his gift," Thorne says. "A defense mechanism to mask what he really is."

"Maybe," I concur. "I just hope we're right to protect them." I glance around before asking, "Why won't you tell me what you saw in your vision?"

Thorne's jaw tenses. "Because it was a future you and I both hope for—but I can't say more than that for fear that it won't come to pass. If my vision affects your choices..."

"It may alter my behavior," I reply. "I get it. I think."

We've both begun striding toward the back of the house when I hear a sound somewhere ahead—the low, murmuring thrum of human voices.

Only they're not uttering words.

More like *moans*.

A door is open ahead of us, and I tiptoe over and peek inside to see the prince and Valira. She's propped up on a large, solid wood desk, her bare legs wrapped around Tallin's waist as he drives himself into her with a frenzy that makes me want to avert my eyes.

I can see only part of Valira's face over Tallin's shoulder. Her eyes are sealed shut, and she looks as though she's wincing in physical or emotional pain—or perhaps it's delight—with every violent thrust. Sounds of pleasure erupt from both of them, and my stomach flips over on itself, disgust working its way rapidly through me.

I leap backwards, almost colliding with Thorne. I don't dare take hold of him for fear that there are cameras in the corridor. Instead, I simply nod toward the back of the house and we make our way quickly to the vast kitchen and beyond, onto a small, pretty terrace of gray flagstone.

"We don't have long," Thorne says. "We can use the excuse

that we were searching for Tallin, but eventually, someone's going to notice our absence."

"I know," I sigh, then say, "Maude—are there surveillance systems out here?"

~There are sentinel hounds roaming the grounds not far from us. I can only assume they have the means to record what they see. I'm not sure whether they capture audio.

"Damn it." I draw my eyes up to Thorne's, so tempted to bury myself in his chest and plead with him to wrap his arms around me.

"I know," he replies. "Look—I'm going to—"

A sound from inside the house silences him.

"We should head back in," I say, fearful of what will happen if Tallin finds us both out here.

Thorne nods once and then, as I'm about to head back toward the kitchen doors, grabs my arm.

I stare down at his hand for a moment, savoring the intimacy of his touch and the desire that floods me—desire so powerful that I have to fight every instinct to kiss him here and now.

"I'm going to find a way to get to you, Shara. Tonight, I'll disable the palace's surveillance and come to your suite..."

"No!" I whisper. "If he finds you there, he'll kill us both, and I can't lose you." Glancing sideways toward the house, I lay my hand on Thorne's cheek, fighting back the throb of longing in my chest. "I just...need to convince Tallin I'm truly on his side. I need him to trust me enough to stop watching every move I make."

"The ass-hat is supposed to be engaged to you, yet he's inside, fucking another woman in full view of anyone who happens by. And you're worried about him trusting *you*?"

"I don't care what or *who* he does, as long as he stays away from me. I just need to find a time when his guard is down, and then I promise—I will call for you. But I can't...*we* can't risk our lives, no matter how badly we want one another. Thorne—if we can gather enough information—if we can incriminate enough Nobles, then maybe we'll find our way to freedom on our own terms. Maybe we won't have to sneak around in the shadows anymore."

He looks like he's about to say something. I can feel the conflict in him, the painful, churning turmoil. I feel how badly he wants to throw caution to the wind.

"If I were any weaker," he whispers, pulling me close, "I would tear that beautiful dress off you and fall to my knees before you. My tongue and lips would show you every pleasure imaginable. Fuck, I can still taste you, Shara. Your scent surrounds me like a constant torment and a delight, every second of every day. Just know I'm starved for you—and I will not be satisfied until I've got my mouth on you."

It's all I can do not to tear the dress off and offer myself to him, here and now. "It's a torment for me, too," I whisper. "You don't know how I..."

Spotting a sudden flurry of movement inside the house, I curse under my breath, pull myself away from him, then slip inside.

CHAPTER
SIXTEEN

I HURL myself into the kitchen just in time to see Tallin, his eyes wild, combing his hands through his mussed-up hair.

"Where the hell have you been?" he snarls.

I throw him my best innocent look and say, "Outside, hoping to find you. I was told you were getting a breath of fresh air. Or was it another sort of breath you were after?" I ask the question while glancing over Tallin's shoulder at Valira, who is standing stiffly a few feet behind him. Her eyes are blank and expressionless, her mouth pulled into a grimace.

As usual, I can't tell what she's thinking. But I'm assuming it's *not* how much she adores Tallin.

The prince narrows his eyes at Thorne, who's standing behind me, tense and ready to fight if the need should arise. But Tallin lets out a quick breath and half-whispers, "Don't leave the guests without telling me first. Don't roam other people's grounds. You need to maintain the appearance that you're here to socialize, not to go romping off with our Guard."

At that, I let out a quick, aggressive laugh.

I don't care who Tallin sleeps with. I'd be perfectly happy if he were having sex with half of Kravan—as long as that half doesn't include me or anyone I care about. But his hypocrisy is irritating as hell.

"We'll discuss this further at the palace," Tallin says. "For now, return to the library and make sure you've assessed all the guests. I want you to be certain you haven't missed a Tethered among them."

"I'm already certain," I tell him, doing my best to hide the lie.

"Well, look again."

I obey his command and return to the library, where the guests are engaged in a heated conversation about the Capitol's state of chaos. I can't help but listen to their ranting and raving about the lowly Normals who live there and how they've neglected their homes. But the truth is, all I want to think about is Thorne's touch, and all I want to know is how long I'll have to wait until I can feel him inside me again.

For another torturous hour, I engage in conversation with the guests, pretending I have some idea what they're talking about. They speak of militias in the Capitol and of rebels among the Normals.

Yet they still seem intent on blaming the Tethered for all the wrongs of the world.

Once or twice, I catch Ellion Graystone watching me intently, his stare burning into my flesh. There's something intimidating about him, and strange—like he's able to see beyond my skin to some place far deeper inside me, and I wonder for a moment if he, like me, is a Hunter. Which would make him more dangerous than his mother—and more at risk of the prince's wrath.

But something tells me his power isn't quite as straightforward as mine. There's a darkness in it. The look in his eye reminds me too much of Tallin—it's troubled, pained, seemingly hidden behind a cold, hard façade.

When Tallin finally declares that it's time to return to the palace, I am beyond relieved. My face hurts from my forced smile, and my head hurts from trying to engage with bigots who have no intention of keeping an open mind about anyone or anything.

As we begin to make our way toward the door, Lady Graystone reaches for my hand with her prosthetic. It's cold to the touch, its grip tightly wrapped around my fingers.

Too tight.

She pulls me close and whispers, "I know why you're here. Choose wisely tonight when you speak to the king."

With that, she releases me and turns to talk to the others, and I walk away, my legs trembling beneath me.

When the prince and I say our goodbyes at the front entrance of the Prefect's house, Tallin lingers a particularly long time with Lord Malloy as the other guests wander out.

"My father will want a tennis match soon," Tallin says loudly, clapping the other man on the shoulder. "I'll have my people set up a date."

"That would be wonderful," Lord Malloy replies with a bow of his head. "I would be honored to play him again."

When we're safely ensconced in the Flyer and Thorne is once again in the pilot's seat, I tell Tallin I'm grateful he was gracious to Lord Malloy. "He really does seem like a nice man," I say. "Particularly compared to some of the rest of them."

The prince lets out a snort, but says nothing.

Valira, it seems, is headed back to the palace in her own Flyer. I don't ask Tallin about it; the truth is, I don't particularly care why she insists on traveling separately.

All I know is that sitting a few feet from Thorne once again without being allowed to touch him feels like a cruelty.

He pilots the vehicle expertly and before long, we reach the shores of the Palatine Estates. I watch as properties unfold below in the encroaching darkness, one after the other, until I recognize the Verdan grounds in the distance.

As Thorne prepares for our descent toward the palace, Tallin reaches for me, yanks me close, and tries to kiss me.

"Highness!" I cry, trying in vain to escape his grip. But he's too strong and manages to land his lips on my own.

I refuse to open my mouth to his. Refuse to let him think for a second that he is anything other than repugnant to me. I let out a sound that draws Thorne's eyes, and the Flyer hurtles sideways before he regains control of it.

Laughing, Tallin pulls away and says, "Easy now, big boy. Don't forget what I have in my pocket."

I shove him away and push myself as far toward the window as I can get, wiping at my lips with the back of my hand. My eyes are filled with hot tears, and I feel the raging desire to scream at the injustice of our situation.

"I know perfectly well what you have, bastard," Thorne growls. "I've felt its consequences—but I don't care. Touch her again, and I'll take your head."

Tallin reaches inside his pocket with a chuckle, extracts the disc, and presses the orb at its center, expecting Thorne to cry out in agony.

Instead, Thorne shoots the Flyer downward and we barrel toward the trees below.

"What the fuck are you doing, man?" Tallin shouts.

Thorne's voice is hoarse with rage when he says, "You and I need to have a little talk, your *Highness*."

CHAPTER
SEVENTEEN

THE FLYER LANDS VIOLENTLY in a field of tall grass, but Thorne maintains just enough control to keep us from getting injured —though I'm fairly certain he would be perfectly delighted if Tallin were to sustain a massive head trauma.

Thorne leaps out of his seat and opens Tallin's door, grabs the prince by the front of his jacket, and drags him outside.

Scrambling out of the Flyer, I watch in horror as Tallin pulls the silver disc from his pocket, clearly intending to shock Thorne into submission.

When the prince presses his thumb into the sphere at its center again, Thorne winces, lifts his chin, and says, "You really don't know, do you?"

"Know what?" Tallin asks, desperately pressing the contraption again and again. I can hear in his tone that he's trying—and failing—to sound strong.

The truth is, he sounds like a weak little boy.

"Thorne," I caution. "Don't push him. Don't forget he's a Tethered. I've seen what he..."

I've seen what he's capable of.

"I'll let him go once I've said what I need to," Thorne

assures me, then turns back to the prince. "I'm a Gilded Elite," he tells him. "And one of my powers allows me to take control of toys like the one in your hand and turn them against their abusive owners."

Tallin's eyes go wide as he tries to figure out what Thorne means. But a moment later, he shrieks in pain and drops the disc to the ground.

"Your shocker," Thorne snarls, "doesn't work on me unless I let it. There is no electronic device you could use on me that I wouldn't eventually control. That includes locks, weapons, or surveillance. I have let you think you have some small modicum of power over me, your goddamned Highness, because I want to protect Shara from you."

"I don't believe you," Tallin says, his voice practically a whine.

Thorne smiles. "I don't give a shit whether you believe me or not." With that, he shoves Tallin back against the Flyer's side. The vehicle whirs to life as Thorne's eyes darken, swirling with colors only I can see.

"Any time I choose," he says, "I can take you out. It might be a light switch you're touching. Your electric razor. Anything. I could kill you as easily as I could crush an ant, you despicable little shit."

Tallin's lip quivers, but he shakes his head. "You wouldn't kill me," he says. "If you did, the Royal Guard would tear you to pieces."

"You're right. I wouldn't." Thorne gives him a final shove, then releases him from his grip. "Because we have a job to do, and killing you would put an end to it. But I'm telling you right now—if you touch Shara again, I *will* destroy you. I don't know what sort of twisted power is churning inside you, Prince—but I really don't care. This game ends now. The woman I love is not your plaything. Do you hear me?"

Tallin swallows, then nods. "Fine," he says. "But I can't let you two be together. You know I can't. My father would...well, let's just say it wouldn't go well for any of us."

Thorne shoots me a look, his expression softening slightly. I can feel his thoughts, his emotions. I feel his hunger inside me as though it were my own.

"I know," he says, his voice tight. "There would be talk, and you would be forced to break up with your so-called fiancée."

He straightens his uniform and runs a hand through his hair, then steps over to me and pulls me close.

"Are you all right?" he asks softly.

"I am now," I reply.

I forget everything in that moment. The danger we're in. The watchful, enraged eyes of the prince of Kravan.

All I know is the feeling that the ground has fallen away from beneath our feet, and Thorne and I are somewhere else—a world far from our own, where we're allowed to live and to love.

He kisses me, his tongue sweeping against mine, my body aching for more...more...*more*.

But Thorne pulls away as a set of bright lights flares on the distant road. "We have to head back."

When we've enclosed ourselves along with Tallin inside the Flyer once again, a vehicle speeds by us, its driver oblivious to the fact that they came dangerously close to witnessing the murder of a prince.

We land a few minutes later in the palace grounds. Thorne opens the doors for the prince and me, and we descend, entering the palace together.

"I'll take my leave now, your Highness," Thorne says from behind us. "I will see you both very soon, I hope."

"Yes," I reply, looking him in the eye. "I hope so, as well."

With that, he disappears down a corridor to make his way to his quarters. My heart sinks as I watch him go, knowing that once again we'll be sleeping in our own beds, so close to one another...yet a million miles apart.

"What is it with you?" I ask Tallin when Thorne has left us. "Why are you so fucking cruel?"

"Me?" Tallin laughs. "I'm the cruel one? That bastard was going to kill me."

"No, he wasn't. He was just warning you." I speak the words with confidence, but I'm not entirely sure I mean them. I could *feel* Thorne's rage. I absorbed it in my bones, my very blood.

Tallin fixes me with a hard stare and says, "Trust me, Shara. I know hatred—and Thorne wanted me dead. He still does. I should have him killed for it, but I am letting him live tonight for you. I want you to remember it when the time comes."

Inside the palace, the prince ushers me to my quarters, warning me that if Thorne and I so much as glance at each other, he will report our rule violation to the king.

I enter my suite alone, cursing Tallin and our entire realm for inflicting this torture on us. All I want—all I *ask*—is a few minutes alone with Thorne.

The few fleeting moments we've had together, knowing they're all we'll ever be allowed, feel like the beginnings of death by a thousand cuts.

"I have to see him," I murmur. "I have to find his quarters, and—"

~*Not just yet,* Maude warns. *Someone is coming.*

CHAPTER
EIGHTEEN

As USUAL, Maude is right.

A few seconds after her warning, a knock sounds at my suite's door.

"Who is it?" I ask, grateful that I haven't yet slipped into my pajamas.

"Your handsome fiancé," an irritable voice grumbles from the hallway.

Rolling my eyes, I tell Tallin to enter.

He seems to grow even more annoyed when he says, "The king—my beloved father—wants to see you."

"Now?" I ask, skeptical. "Isn't it a bit late for meetings?"

"Yes, now," he barks. "I wouldn't keep him waiting, if I were you."

The way he speaks of his father, the king sounds like a tyrant. But the truth is, King Tomas has shown himself to be far kinder and more patient than Tallin could ever be. He's no saint, but at least there's *some* humanity in him.

"Fine," I say, and follow the prince out of the suite and down the hall. He refuses to look at me, still sore from Thorne's threats, no doubt.

"Did Valira make it back to the palace all right?" I ask.

"Yes. She's waiting in my chamber—which is in the same wing as my father's quarters."

Instant nausea swirls inside me, but I wish it away and focus on the task at hand. I have no doubt as to why the king wishes to see me, and I'm not looking forward to it—but given that Tallin invited Lord Malloy to play tennis at the palace, I have high hopes that he'll remain safe.

When we enter the king's private suite, a small but audible gasp escapes my lips. I've never seen anything like this living space filled to the brim with what look like priceless artifacts—ancient swords and shields, leather-bound books in glass cases, jewels, armor. The ceilings are covered in ornate paintings depicting scenes of warring men and angelic women, and I wonder as my eyes are drawn to them whether the painted events were real, or imagined by some artist or other.

"Ah, Lady Ingram," King Tomas's voice booms, and I pull my eyes down to see him slipping out of a vast bedroom with Lady Verdan by his side.

The sight of her turns my blood cold, but I swallow, manage a smile and a gentle bow of my head, and say, "Good evening, your Grace."

"My son has told me you identified Lord Malloy as a Tethered."

~*Getting right to the point, I see,* Maude whispers in my mind.

Her voice startles me.

"I..." I swallow as my eyes move from the king to Lady Verdan and back again.

"She did," Tallin says. "She identified him instantly and did not hesitate to inform me of his...status. She didn't let us down as I thought she would, and for that, I am grateful to her."

I twist to look at him, stunned that he appears to be singing my praises, albeit in a backhanded manner.

"He's a Velor," I explain to the king. "But when I studied him, I determined he's not dangerous. He only uses the power for pleasure."

"There are many Tethered who use their powers for pleasure," Lady Verdan retorts, raising a hand in the air, a sparking orb of flame appearing above her palm. "It doesn't mean they aren't a threat."

"I really don't think..." I say, but Tallin raises a hand to silence me.

"I've invited Lord Malloy to join you for a tennis match, Father," he says. "Perhaps you could have a look at him and gauge his threat level."

The king nods, a smile on his lips. "That sounds like an excellent idea. Shara—that is, *Lady Ingram*, you have my thanks. You have proven your worth already, though I fear I'll be asking a good deal more of you in the coming days."

"Of course, your Grace," I say, my stomach churning again. I'm not looking forward to any of it. It was hard enough to turn in a man who seems as innocent as a squirrel collecting nuts. There could be other Tethered among the Nobility who prove useful allies to Thorne and me. Tethered who, like us, want to see the system flipped upside down.

The last thing I want is to turn them in.

But if the king is willing to assess them in a reasonable manner—if he really is going to engage in a simple, friendly tennis match with Lord Malloy—then maybe there's nothing to fear, after all.

"And Thorne?" the king asks. "How was he this evening?"

I gawk at him, unsure as to whether the question is directed at me or at Tallin.

The prince, too, hesitates, glancing quickly at me before saying, "He did his duty and guarded me well, your Grace."

"I don't believe that for a moment," Lady Verdan chuckles,

the chill in her voice sending frost into my veins. "His only interest lies in bedding Shara, just as it always has. Perhaps I should have left him as a plaything for Devorah, after all."

I shoot her a look of pure, silent rage.

~*Careful now,* Maude cautions.

"My eldest daughter was so fond of him," Lady Verdan says. "Or, at least, aroused by him."

"I believe you mean step-daughter," I growl.

You vile bitch.

"Mother," Tallin says, his jaw tight. "Perhaps it would be best if you didn't speak of the Tethered as though they're objects in our possession."

My jaw almost hits the floor. Why the hell is Tallin, of all people, defending our kind? Is it because of Valira? Is he somehow protecting what little honor she's afforded as one of us?

Lady Verdan looks taken aback for a moment, then lets out a laugh. "You do realize that's just what they are, my son," she says. "We own them. We *paid* for them—or have you forgotten that important fact?"

Under his breath, Tallin hisses, "*We* are Tethered too, Mother. How would you feel if someone spoke of us in this way?"

Lady Verdan's hands curl into fists, and slowly, she raises an arm in the air, spreading her fingers to reveal another fireball rotating like a menacing shadow below her palm.

"Never, ever say those words out loud again, my son," she hisses. "Do you hear me?" Her eyes dart around the room. "There are listeners everywhere. Spies. Some of the few people who know the truth about you and me are in this very chamber—and if we allow that information to escape, we're as good as finished, you and I."

My mind veers to thoughts of Thorne—of our dream of a future together.

They'll never let us leave here alive. Not knowing what we know.

"There is to be another ball," the king announces, breaking through the sharp-edged hostility permeating the room's every inch. "In a week's time."

"Where?" Lady Verdan asks, clapping her hands together with delight, the fireball vanishing into thin air.

"At Lord and Lady Perrin's estate," King Tomas replies, pulling his eyes to mine. "I suspect it will be an excellent opportunity for our gifted houseguest to size up more of Kravan's Tethered traitors. Every last Noble in the realm is invited, naturally. I'll be disappointed, Shara, if you don't turn in at least a dozen of them after the evening is through."

"Yes, your Grace," I reply, forcing a half smile onto my lips despite the renewed nausea stirring up a storm inside me.

"Don't look so dejected," the king laughs. "What you're doing, Hunter, is for the greater good. Your father may be a cruel and vicious creature, but you? You are protecting the realm."

At the mention of my father, I balk. "You say my father is cruel. What exactly do you mean by that? Did he hurt someone? I keep hearing he's dangerous, but I have yet to see proof...your Grace."

The king and Lady Verdan exchange a quiet, knowing look, then King Tomas adds, "Let's just say he isn't as...compliant...as you are. He is an enemy of this realm, Shara. It gives me no pleasure to tell you such a thing, but it's the truth. Count it as a blessing that you never knew him. He has an agenda of his own, and if ever I find him, I promise you, it will not end well for him."

"I see," I reply, my heart swelling with pride for the man I've never known. Any enemy of the Nobility's is a friend of mine.

"You think he's still alive, then?" I ask.

"I'm quite certain of it, yes." He holds up his hand when he sees that I'm about to ask another question and adds, "Don't ask me where he is. The truth is, I don't know. I only know he's not in the employ of any of Kravan's Noble families—which means that technically, he is a fugitive. Your father is probably the most wanted man in all of Kravan." With a doleful shake of his head, he adds, "It's only a matter of days before I send my men out to find the monster at long last."

"Monster," I reply through gritted teeth.

~*Don't say it,* Maude warns.

"Yes, I'm sure you're right," I add with a sigh. "Now, if that's everything, your Grace..."

As I turn to leave, King Tomas snaps, "No. It's not all."

I pivot back to him, suddenly apprehensive. The man who seemed so kindly until a few minutes ago now looks almost fierce, his body rigid as if he's ready to pounce.

"Are you certain Lord Malloy was the only Tethered at the Prefect's dinner party? Absolutely certain?"

I struggle not to show the lie in my eyes when I reply. "Yes, I'm certain. I had a chance to study every guest thoroughly. Everyone else was a Normal. There's no doubt of it in my mind."

The king stares me down for a few more seconds before his expression softens and he says, "Then I thank you, Shara. That will be all."

As I leave the room, I breathe a long sigh of relief.

~*What is it, Shara? You seem worried,* Maude says as I pad along the corridor.

Does the king know something about the Graystones? Is he trying to entrap me—to catch me in a lie?

~*He's a difficult man to read. I'm not sure about Lady Graystone and her son. As to whether he's trying to entrap you—all I can say is, who the hell knows? It's anyone's guess.*

I roll my eyes when I think, *That's very helpful. Thank you, Maude.*

~I do what I can to make your life a constant misery.

Yes, you do. And you're so good at it.

CHAPTER
NINETEEN

WEARY, I head up to my distant wing of the palace, realizing only when I'm in my bedroom that it's now well past midnight, and I'm exhausted.

When I've showered and changed into a pair of crisp cotton pajamas, I throw myself onto the bed, falling asleep almost the moment my head hits the pillow.

I don't know how many hours have passed when a high-pitched cry jars me awake. I tell myself at first that it must have been part of a dream. I've never seen a soul in this entire section of the palace, other than Tallin, Valira, and a few servants who presumably spend the night in distant wings.

When it comes again—a blood-chilling cry of terror—I leap out of bed and run to the door, yanking it open. I sprint in the direction the sound came from, unsure what my plan is. I may be a Gilded Elite, but I've always been useless in the fighting ring.

Still, if someone's in trouble I need to sound the alarm, at the very least. I'll wake the whole palace if I need to.

I run until I reach the hallway that leads to Tallin's and the king's quarters as well as a number of other chambers where high-level Guards sleep.

When I spot two silhouetted figures in the dim light, I freeze in place.

One is a tall, broad-shouldered man, and the other is slumped on the floor, whimpering in pain.

It takes me only a moment to realize the man is Tallin.

The slumped figure...is Valira.

I leap toward them, my mind too addled to consider the danger I'm putting myself in. If I've caught Tallin in the midst of some act of violence, there's no telling what he'll do to punish me for it.

When I stop a few feet away, I see that Valira is dressed in a cotton robe that was once pure white. Its entire front is now stained deep crimson, the fabric torn with violent slash marks that look like they were inflicted by a blade.

Tallin is dressed in the same suit he was wearing earlier, its collar undone. He, too, is streaked with blood. When he turns to me, he looks distraught.

It's an expression I never would have thought possible—not for him.

As I pull my eyes back to Valira, a sickening memory comes to me of the vision I saw the night of the Prince's Ball, when I first touched Tallin.

His victims.

"Did you do this to her?" I hiss, crouching down next to Valira as the prince backs away, sweeping what appears to be a shaking hand through his hair. Is he nervous because I caught him in the act? Or is it that he regrets what he's done?

No. No way. Tallin isn't capable of remorse.

Valira's breathing is shallow, and she's barely conscious. The wounds in her chest are deep, parallel gashes, as if an enormous set of claws has raked itself across her flesh.

With my fingers splayed, I hold a hand a few inches from her torso, close my eyes, and ask my healing power to work its way through her body. I don't care if Tallin punishes me for it. I may not be overly fond of Valira, but she doesn't deserve to die for his sick, twisted pleasure.

Her wounds seal up, and her breathing slows instantly. I turn to Tallin again and growl, "Did you do this to her? Answer me!"

"Of course not!" he half-shouts. "What sort of monster do you think I am?"

I want to laugh and ask how much time he has.

But as I look him in the eye, confusion twists its way through my mind. His irises swim with color, a mix of shades melting into one another behind tears unwilling to fall.

Once again, I see the suffering of past victims. I see so much pain and fear...

But I can also see something else.

He genuinely cares about her.

"You told me she was waiting for you in your chamber," I tell him. "You were going to spend the night together."

"She was waiting for me when I left to collect you. But when I returned after our little rendezvous with my father, she was gone."

"Really?" My tone is skeptical. "Did you look for her?"

"Of course I did. I couldn't find her, so I went back to my quarters and waited. I ran out when I heard her screaming— but by the time I got here, the attacker had disappeared."

I don't believe him for a second. Why is Valira even here, in this hallway that leads to Tallin's quarters, if not because she was trying to escape his clutches?

"If you didn't attack her," I say, struggling to control my voice, "then who did?"

Tallin shakes his head. "Another Tethered, probably," he

says, avoiding my gaze. "A Guard—someone with anger issues. God knows, there are enough of those around here."

I scowl at him when I reply, "Maybe Valira can tell us herself."

I take her hand in mine. It's cold and trembling with shock, but she manages to open her eyes and look at me. There's pain in her features, but I'm not sure it's physical.

This is something far worse.

"Valira," I murmur. "Who did this to you?"

Her head lists to the side, then she manages a weak shake. "I didn't...see..." she breathes. "I don't know. I was heading to Tallin's quarters when..." Again, she shakes her head. "I can't say who it was."

I glance up at the prince, who's still avoiding my eyes.

Is she protecting him? If so, she's a fool.

If he did this to her in a fit of rage, he might succeed in killing her next time.

"Was it the prince?" I ask.

She shakes her head, her eyes moving weakly to Tallin's face. "No. Not the prince. Never."

"You should question your Guards," I tell Tallin, rising to my feet, anger stiffening my spine. "Though I suspect you know *exactly* what happened here."

"I didn't do it," he snarls again. "It's like she said. I would never..."

His voice is on the verge of breaking, as if it truly pains him to think of Valira being hurt.

For a moment, the prince seems almost human. Still, I tell myself not to let my guard down. This could be nothing more than an impressive act on his part.

"Get her into her bed," I tell him. "Bring her water and anything else she wants—unless you'd rather I ask a servant to do it."

Tallin shakes his head. "No. I'll look after her. Is it...all right if I lift her?"

"I don't need lifting," Valira replies, pushing herself to her feet. She manages to stagger toward the staircase, and Tallin takes hold of her, making sure she doesn't fall.

"Lady Ingram," he says over his shoulder.

"Yes?" I reply when I remind myself that's my "official" name.

"Please, don't tell anyone what happened here."

"I won't. But only for Valira's sake."

CHAPTER
TWENTY

WHEN TALLIN and Valira have disappeared, I turn to head back to my quarters but think better of it. I'm wide awake and freaked out, and I need to get some fresh air into my lungs. I want to stand under the stars and feel grateful that I'm alive— and it doesn't hurt that for once, I know there's no risk of Tallin following me and dragging me back inside.

I make my way down to one of the palace's kitchens and out onto a broad terrace, where I press myself against the stone railing, my breath quickened by the shock of seeing Valira so close to death.

She may be vulnerable, but she's quick. She's powerful in her way.

It's hard to imagine someone managing to get close enough to a Netic to slash them with a blade.

Unless she was intimately involved with the perpetrator...

I shake my head, telling myself not to jump to conclusions. She said Tallin didn't do it, and no good will come of it if I insist on accusing the prince again in his own home.

Clouds meander through the sky, half-obscuring the moon, and I lift my chin to marvel at the beautiful sight. Such a distant thing, the moon—oblivious to the trials of the small humans in our world.

For so many years, I didn't know what it was to see the sky. I had no real concept of a cloud except as a few abstract words or images I had come across in the few books I had access to. And now, seeing the clouds morph and change as the wind steers their fates, I tell myself never to take their loveliness for granted.

I wonder, staring up at the vast, open space above, how much there is to our world that I haven't even begun to imagine.

I've flown over much of Kravan by now. I've seen a few of its islands.

But Kravan can't be all there is. Surely there is far more than this one, small realm. I've read fictional accounts of people in distant lands—stories told by men and women whose lives sounded almost real.

I just wonder if they're still out there somewhere.

Are Tethered trapped inside Towers in each of those realms —or is there somewhere our kind is allowed to live in peace?

I shut my eyes and think of Thorne, wondering whether he and I will ever be able to stand under the stars together hand in hand, and revel in a sense of peace. Fate has always dictated that he and I are to be denied happiness, and Tallin has done everything in his power to keep that fate securely in place. But just now, it seems so arbitrary and so cruel that two people as insignificant to this universe as we are should be denied any small chance at joy.

"I wish you were here with me," I murmur. "I wish I could touch you, even just once, without being punished for it."

"May your wish be granted, my Lady," a deep voice says from behind me.

I spin around, convinced that I imagined the sound. But

sure enough, Thorne is standing a few feet from me in his Guard uniform, a bittersweet smile on his lips.

I'm torn between throwing myself into his arms or backing away and begging him to return to his quarters before he's seen by another Guard.

"If he finds us together out here..." I whisper, wincing. "He'll kill you."

Thorne holds out his fist then opens it, palm up, to reveal Mercutio's shining eyes staring up at me.

"This little mouse has informed me the prince is locked inside Valira's quarters, and it seems he plans to stay there for the night. The king is sound asleep. And I've disabled all cameras in this area of the grounds to loop their video feeds. As far as anyone knows, there's no one standing on this terrace right now. You and I are nothing but ghosts."

I smile to think he has so easily manipulated the palace's systems. But the smile quickly fades as I remember the risk we're taking.

"What's wrong?" Thorne asks softly. "You look worried."

He lays Mercutio down, and the mouse goes tearing off toward the inside of the palace.

"Someone attacked Valira," I tell him despite my promise to the prince. "They sliced her up badly, but I managed to heal her. I don't know if Tallin did it, but I wouldn't be surprised. He looked pretty guilty, and we both know he has serious anger issues."

"I wouldn't put anything past that asshole," Thorne replies, stepping closer to me. "I'm sure what happened earlier didn't help his mood. But if Valira is okay now, that's all that matters. I have to admit, I have no interest in discussing the prince just now."

As he edges toward me, I have to fight an instinct to back away from him—both for his protection and mine.

137

"Shara," he says when he's inches away, his head tilted slightly as if he's assessing me. His voice is silk when he says, "If you don't want me here, I can easily go back to my room."

"No!" I almost yell. I force myself to relax and then let out a quiet, pained laugh. "I want you here more than anything. I want you by my side every day and night." With those words, I feel everything inside me giving way. "I've been so worried, Thorne. About you—about us. I want you so much it's killing me. It's just...I'm afraid. After seeing what happened to Valira, and knowing what Tallin is capable of..."

The too-vibrant memory once again assaults my mind of the scenes that I saw when I first discovered the prince's powers. The victims were brutalized, terrified—tortured.

"It won't happen to us," Thorne says. "I won't let it."

With that promise, he takes hold of my waist and pulls me to him, his lips crashing into mine. When his tongue seeks out my own and his arms sweep around my body, my mind loses any and all control.

Thorne's desire mingles with my own, twisting and braiding into one entity as my every nerve awakens to take in the pleasure of his touch.

"Come with me," he whispers, pulling back and taking me by the hand. "I have a quiet place in mind—one where we can be alone for a little while."

He leads me to the far end of the terrace, and we don't bother to look back and make sure we're alone when we spring down a set of stairs into an entrance of the palace's vast hedge maze.

I've seen it from my window, and know how enormous it is —and how easy it would be to lose ourselves inside it for several hours.

Thorne guides me around at least a dozen turns before we

come to a small clearing with two curved stone benches positioned around a circular patio of paving stones at its center.

"We don't have much time," he says, his voice feral as he turns to me, cupping my face in his hands. "I know it as well as you do. But if I'm denied the pleasure of tasting you for one more minute, I'm going to lose my mind."

When he's led me onto the paving stones, his fingers fumble with the buttons on my pajama top, and he pulls it open, pushing it away from my shoulders.

"I've missed this sight," he moans, his eyes taking in my breasts, my stomach, my hips. "More than you can possibly know."

"Oh, I think I have some idea."

Our mouths collide again, and the kiss is violent with craving. My head swims with arousal, need winding its way through my body as if I've been injected with the most addictive drug in the world.

"I hope you can forgive me," Thorne says, pulling back. "There's something I've been craving for days, and I can't hold back any longer."

He falls to his knees before me, his hands slipping down my waist, and lets out the most gorgeous sigh I've ever heard. The cool night air strokes its way over my skin as he takes a nipple greedily between his lips.

"You're perfect," he moans, his hands cupping my breasts, his lips and tongue teasing me without mercy. "How the hell am I supposed to resist you every day when I know this body is so close at hand?"

"If it were up to me, you would never have to resist," I say in a strained voice, desire clenching at my insides.

As the power flows between us, I feel his pain, his frustration—but also the pure euphoria of finding our way to one another at last. I can sense the rush of blood through his body, the ache of desire assaulting him now. That same brutal desire is making me want to tear his uniform from his body, throw him to the ground, and take him inside me.

"Soon, beautiful," he says softly, reading my mind as he kisses his way down my belly. "Soon."

His fingers grip the seam of my pajama bottoms. He pulls them down slowly, his lips following their path, and I moan, bliss and anticipation intermingling deep inside me.

Mine, I think. *You're mine, now and always—no matter what happens.*

And I am yours.

When Thorne has pulled the bottoms down to my hips, he slips his hand inside them and groans as his fingers meet the slickness between my legs. He lifts himself to his feet, his eyes locking on mine. He watches me, intent on my face, as he takes in my pleasure.

"This..." he whispers, pinching the bundle of nerves gently then stroking a fingertip over it, "is what I crave when I think of being with you. My tongue on you, sending you slowly over the edge. My lips, sucking on you until you explode. I want nothing more in this world than your pleasure."

"I want yours, too," I insist, but he shakes his head.

"*This* is my pleasure. Everything you feel. Every twitch, every pulse of every nerve. I take it all for my own—and it is fucking beautiful."

He pulls the bottoms down until they're at my ankles, then, when I've stepped out of them, pushes my legs apart. I fall back onto one of the cold stone benches and Thorne gets on his knees again and buries his face between my thighs.

Ecstasy simmers its way through my core, my hips lifting almost against my will to meet the slow strokes of his tongue. He pushes one, then two fingers inside me, his moans of bliss vibrating against my flesh.

Fuck, that feels so good. My mind spins with sensation—his and mine, melded into an intoxicating, uncontrollable whirlwind. My blood pulses violently inside me, my powers stirring with the strength of our bond.

Thorne takes my clit between his lips, sucking gently as his fingers drive into me—teasing me with the promise of what is to come.

"I need you inside me," I say, desperate. "My body is aching for you. I can't stand waiting another second."

He looks up at me and shakes his head, the tip of his tongue flicking me in stubborn refusal to give me what I demand.

"I want you to come for me first," he breathes. "I insist on it."

"Oh," I laugh, pushing my hips forward so I'm balanced right on the edge of the bench. "You insist, do you?"

He slips his fingers out of me and strokes me as he pushes himself upward, taking the peak of one nipple gently between his teeth, then the other. He toys with me, flicking his tongue over the stone-hard tip and sending me into a series of shudders of pleasure.

"I do insist," he says again, moving back down and thrusting his fingers deep inside me. "I have lived and breathed in wait for this moment, right here. All I could think about in the cold of that cell was getting my mouth on you again. Whatever pain I was in, all I wanted was to taste you—to feel you writhe for me. Don't deny me this, or I'll fall into madness."

"I wouldn't want that," I say softly, throwing my head back and closing my eyes. "So I suppose I have no choice but to give in."

As his tongue works me in destructive, tormenting circles, I feel his voice in my mind. *Don't worry, Shara,* he growls. *I'll claim you as my own every chance I get. I need to feel you tight and wet around me—I need to show you how hard you make me every time I think of this beautiful body of yours.*

"You're showing me right now," I reply in a ragged whisper. *I'm going to...*

The words disappear as my back arches. The explosion rolls over me in a massive wave, power churning through my body, my hips bucking, his mouth still devouring me with each pulse, each throb of climax that assaults me.

Thorne doesn't let up until I'm spent, slouching back on the bench, a moan sliding down my throat.

"I love you," he says, his lips on my inner thigh. "I love you."

A smile twists its way over my mouth.

"Show me how much," I command.

"Show you?" he laughs, rising to his feet. "And here I thought I just did."

But he knows exactly what I'm asking for.

He undoes his pants and drops them, grasping his swollen length in one hand.

I slip down to the ground and take him in both hands, his velvet flesh delicious under my touch.

I want him inside me—now. But first, I want to tease him a little.

My lips close around the engorged head of his cock, my tongue working its way over him. He moans, raking his fingers through my hair.

"I'm not sure this is the best way to show you how much I love you," he breathes, and I smile around him, my hands stroking his shaft in slow motion.

"Then allow me to help," I tell him, taking him by the hand and guiding him onto the nearby grass. I lay him down on his back and step over him, one foot on either side of his hips.

"If there was ever a sexier sight on this earth, I can't imagine what it was," he says.

I bend my knees, reaching for his length and guide myself until he's pushing at my opening. My eyes lock on his face, taking in the strain in his features as he tries to resist thrusting himself deep inside me.

Slowly, I ease down until I've taken him in, inch by inch. With each movement comes a moan from his lips, I lift myself again so that he's almost free of me, then slip back down. Faster each time.

Thorne lets out a cry, and my hand goes to his mouth, a laugh rising up from deep inside me.

He takes hold of me, spinning us both around so that my back is to the ground, and presses himself up, his arms to either side of my head.

"You want me to show you how I love you," he says, pulling himself free so that the head of his cock is teasing my opening again.

I nod. "Show me."

He sheaths himself so deep inside me that my every nerve catches fire. It's all I can do not to shout his name, but I somehow maintain my composure, staring into his eyes as he does it again...and again.

"If we live to be a hundred, I will never get enough of you, Shara," he says, driving himself faster and faster into me, tearing open his uniform to reveal a slick, muscular torso. I reach for him, my body tingling with the intensity of our connection.

He leans down and kisses me, our tongues finding one another as I rock my hips upwards to meet his thrusts. "I love you," I whisper into his chest, watching him drive into me. "I love you, Thorne..."

He takes my lower lip between his teeth, sucking it in, and drives himself one last time, so deep inside me as he falls over the edge of a precipice, unleashing an explosion of searing heat into us both.

I wrap my arms and legs around him, pulling him closer, deeper still, as his body pulses, then shudders with the intensity of our mutual pleasure.

I moan against his neck, fire filling me, fueling me—nurturing me—and then, I let out a long, deep breath.

"How was that even better than the first time?" I whisper when the frenzy has subsided, wiping the hair from my damp forehead.

"Something tells me you and I would—*could*—only ever get better and better, beautiful. Someday, we'll have hours together...hours in our own bed, to do with as we wish."

"Don't make promises you can't keep," I tell him, reaching up and cupping his cheek in my hand.

"Oh, I promise," he says. "If it's the only good thing I ever do, I will find a way to free us both."

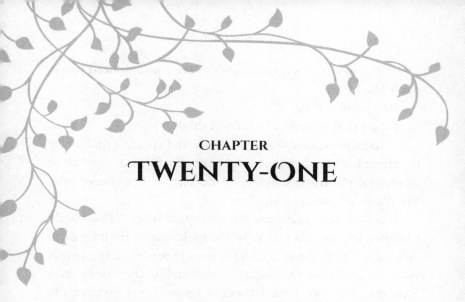

CHAPTER
TWENTY-ONE

THORNE and I lie on the grass next to the benches, his fingers stroking their way through my long hair as we stare up at the flawless sky.

"What was your impression of Lady Graystone?" I ask. "Other than the fact that you think she might be important to our future, I mean."

"I didn't exactly get to speak to her, so I can't say anything specific. She looked kind, I suppose—though looks can be deceiving." He chuckles. "She didn't seem to like Tallin too much."

I raise myself up onto one elbow and look at him. "Why do you say that?"

"I saw them exchange a couple of hostile looks." Thorne smirks. "It's possible I just imagined it."

"Or maybe Tallin knows something about her..." I muse.

"More likely she knows something about him. We both know he's vile."

"To put it nicely, yeah," I sigh. "Did you notice Lady Graystone's prosthetic hand?"

"I did, yes. It was quite a work of art. I also noticed it was her *left* hand."

He's right. It was.

I want to slap myself. "You don't think..."

"That she escaped from the Tower and couldn't find a way to extract her Maude unit, so had her entire forearm amputated to conceal the truth about her?" he says with a cheeky grin. "That's exactly what I think."

I lie back once again and let out a quiet laugh. "That would explain a lot, wouldn't it? Why she spoke out so confidently in defense of the Tethered who have been imprisoned. She knows what we've all been through." I contemplate the theory for a moment, then say, "But I thought no one ever escaped the Tower."

"There have been a few escapes," Thorne says. "They're just not acknowledged because the last thing the Prefecture wants is for Tethered to think there's a way out other than death. Maybe Lady Graystone is one of the few who have gotten away over the years. She must have found someone sympathetic to Tethered to take her arm without killing her."

Thorne sits up, his bare chest and the tense, ridged muscles of his abdomen prominent under the starlight. I twist my head to admire him, marveling at his perfection and cursing the world for denying me a life with him.

"One day, you and I will follow in her footsteps," he says softly, staring down into my eyes, his fingers stroking my cheek. "Not as Nobles, but as free people. I promise you that, Shara. We will be free."

"I want to believe that, but—" I begin, but before I can let out the pessimistic thought, he leaps on top of me, taking my wrists in his hands and pressing my arms gently into the cool grass.

"No buts," he says, pushing himself down, his lips brushing

over my collarbone then up my neck. "One day, we will live together with no tormentors, and every morning, afternoon, and evening, I will get to do this to you."

He lets go of my arms and slips down my body, his lips caressing their way along my torso until my hips roll under him, my thighs parting to welcome his mouth.

It's then that I see a stream of bright light flailing into the air some distance away, beyond the greenery that surrounds the clearing...then another, moving far too quickly through the hedge maze.

"Thorne!" I whisper, and he leaps up, yanking his uniform on. I follow suit, pulling my pajamas on and quickly buttoning them.

Thorne takes my hand, and we spring toward the maze's closest exit, deftly avoiding the lights and the Guards who carry them. A surge of power passes between us, and one by one, the lights go out and a chorus of curses rises up behind us.

I let out a laugh when we race across the terrace and throw ourselves inside the now dark palace.

"This is your doing, isn't it?" I ask. "The lights, I mean."

"*Possibly*," Thorne says, pulling me sideways into a thick curtain and wrapping it around us both. He kisses me with an intensity that courses through my veins like liquid fire, and I know he's thinking what I'm thinking.

We don't know if or when we'll ever be together again.

TWENTY-TWO

MAYBE I'M A FOOL, but for the first time since we were imprisoned in the Verdan House, a surge of hope has made its way through me. I feel alive again and free, despite the fact that I am trapped between the palace walls.

Some quiet voice deep inside me—deeper, even, than Maude's voice—is telling me we will find a way to heal this world.

A few minutes after I've crept back to my suite, a soft knock sounds at the door.

I leap to my feet and dash over, hoping that somehow, Thorne has found his way undetected to my quarters. But when I open the door, it's Valira who stands before me, looking as tall and strong as she ever has.

"May I come in?" she asks, her voice tense.

"Yes, of course. But what are you doing here? You should be resting, Valira."

"I don't need to," she says as she slips inside. "You were impressive, healing me like that. I feel better than ever."

When I've closed the door behind her, I offer up a confused smile and say, "I'm glad."

"I just wanted to thank you for what you did—and tell you that I will help you."

"Help me?" I ask, feigning confusion. "Help me to do what?"

She lowers her chin and smirks. "I'm not an idiot," she says. "I know perfectly well that you were with Thorne a little while ago. Going forward, maybe I can help facilitate your time together. And..." She looks down at her wrists, where she's once again wearing a set of silver cuffs similar to the ones I've seen Thorne wear. "Look..." she adds under her breath. "I know this isn't sustainable. You and Thorne—you're not safe for long here. The moment they think you've outlived your usefulness will be your last."

"Do you really think we don't know that?" I half-whisper.

"You've known it since before you came to the palace," she replies. "I know you're intelligent, as is Thorne. But for all your combined strength and intellect, you and he will not be able to escape this place. Not without some kind of miracle."

For a moment, I suck in my lower lip and stare at her, wondering if this is some kind of entrapment. Is she trying to get me to confess that escape is exactly what I have planned?

"There are rumors of an old tunnel system," she says when she sees I'm not going to ask. "Not the system you took to get into the palace, but one that leads under the water, all the way to the Capitol. They say the Nobles used those tunnels when they escaped in the days of the Rebellion. No one knows where they are these days. But if you can find out where the entrance is..."

I nod, understanding her meaning but unwilling to confirm my intention to escape.

"Valira—is Tallin the one who attacked you?" I ask. "Is that why you're helping me?"

Valira nods toward the couch and says, "Could we sit down?"

"Of course."

We slip over and seat ourselves at opposite ends of the couch. Valira frowns slightly when she says, "Before you ask—I know what Tallin is. I also know you've never liked me, and I don't blame you for it. I've been nothing but hostile toward you."

"Yeah. Why is that, again?"

She chuckles. "I assumed you were a traitor. I thought you were here to rise up above the rank of Tethered and crush our kind. But I'm beginning to suspect your motives are quite different."

"I want to expose Tallin and Lady Verdan," I tell her, knowing the risk I'm taking. "I want the truth to come out so that all of Kravan can know it's being ruled by liars. Monsters, even. That's why I agreed to come here, posing as a Noble. Well, that and getting Thorne and me released from Lady Verdan's less-than-welcoming accommodations."

"Most of Kravan knows there are monsters running things," Valira says woefully. "What good do you think it will do to expose Tallin, other than to add fuel to the fire that's already raging? You could start a civil war."

"A civil war may be what we need. The Capitol is already in ruins. It's not like it can get worse."

"Trust me—it can," Valira sighs. "Look—I've been to the Capitol. I've walked those streets, and they're no place for decent people, Normal or Tethered. There are things you don't know, Shara. You see the realm through the eyes of someone who holds out hope that things can change and improve. I see it through the eyes of someone who knows this realm is hanging on by a thin, gossamer thread that may snap at any moment."

"Then I need to figure out how to help Kravan. Let's start with you telling me who attacked you."

She looks away, her jaw tensing. "It wasn't Tallin, all right?

Believe it or not, the prince actually loves me. Probably too much."

When I stare at her in disbelief, she adds, "I've told you he's complicated. Tallin is...broken, quite literally."

"I can't disagree with you there," I say. "But tell me what you mean."

"You know what it is to be tethered to someone—to be connected to them, body and soul. I see it between you and Thorne. I can feel it in the air when you two are close. A powerful bond that grows stronger every time you two are near one another. I'm not sure you're aware of just how extraordinary a thing it is, to be able to find your tethered mate."

"I know it's rare. I know we're fortunate...even in our misfortune."

She nods. "Archyr and I are tethered," she says softly.

My eyes widen with surprise. "But..." I begin, but I'm not sure how to complete the thought.

She speaks the words I'm thinking. "How can I sleep with Tallin when I'm tethered to another man?" With a shake of her head, she says, "I do it for the realm. I do it for Archyr and all of us. I told you—it's for everyone's good."

"Tell me how," I say.

"There is something called a broken tether." Her voice is strained like it's difficult to get the words out. "Tallin found his mate a few years back—a Guard called Eva. He loved her with all the intensity that anyone feels when they find their tethered mate. But something happened to her. She was killed, and Tallin was shattered. He ranted and raved—and tore the palace apart. His powers, which had intensified, only grew stronger. There are rumors that he killed Guards during those days and ordinary human servants, but I don't believe any of it."

"You said his power grew. He must have been incredibly strong, and we've all seen his temper."

Valira combs a hand through her dark hair. "That's where you're wrong. I mean, he has a temper, of course. I don't know if I've ever met a person as tormented by rage as Tallin. But it's not what you think. His power...it's like a weakness, Shara." She pulls her eyes to mine, and I see then that they're filled with tears. "He feels what others feel. You know what I mean by that —I'm sure you've felt it with Thorne."

I nod. "I feel his emotions sometimes. His pain. His joy. Yes, I know."

"When Tallin's tether was broken—when Eva died—he lost the capacity to feel the joy of others. All he feels is pain, all day, all night, every day. He told me once that he feels the pain of every person he's ever met, driving at his mind like a drill. He still feels Eva's agony—the fear and suffering in the moments when she died."

"That's...horrible," I say.

I will never forgive Tallin for his cruelty. I'll never think kindly of him.

But I've felt Thorne's pain before, and I know its stark intensity. I know the brutality of it—and I cannot imagine feeling it times a thousand every minute of my life.

"It's where I come in...despite my attachment to Archyr," Valira says. "I love him with everything inside me. I know it hurts him, what I do with Tallin. But the only relief Tallin receives from his torment comes from me. My power allows me to extract some of that pain temporarily—to give him a little respite and to keep his mind from snapping entirely. When we have sex, he and I, it allows him to absorb something pleasurable, though it never lasts long. Still, in the meantime, it keeps him from losing control."

"What does that mean? What exactly happens when Tallin loses control?"

Valira inhales a long breath. "Chaos," she says. "It would be the end of his father's reign. The end of all of us."

"So, that's why you're classified as a Violet—why he protects you," I say pensively. "You're the only one who can keep him on an even keel. But does he really have to have sex with you? Can't you just take away his pain without...?" I shudder at the unspoken words.

She shakes her head, letting out a bitter laugh. "If only it were that simple. Sometimes, I think Tallin has convinced himself that he and I are meant to be...he thinks that's the reason he feels so much pleasure when we make love. He thinks it's *my* bliss that he's feeling, but he doesn't understand that I'm literally extracting pain from him, like drawing blood. And he fails to realize I can't heal him fully. No one can."

She lets out a sigh, then continues.

"He commits cruel acts sometimes as a means to temper his moods—almost like he's now addicted to hurting people. What he did to you at the ball—yes, I know." She flicks her eyes briefly to mine. "When he assaulted you, he felt your fear and your loathing. He thrives on it, because fear and loathing are something different from physical pain and torment. He assaulted you to feel powerful."

"That's no excuse," I tell her. "Look—I'm sorry for what he's going through, but what he did to me—it was horrible."

"I know," she says with a nod. "I'm not making excuses. I'm only offering an explanation. He isn't the powerful man everyone thinks he is."

"Do you love him?" I ask.

"No. But I don't hate him, either. The truth is, I pity him. He is a broken man who will never know what it is to be loved as I am. As you are. He will never again know a tether that isn't shattered—which means he will never mend."

"You tell me all this, but you say he's not the one who attacked you tonight."

"He wasn't."

"Who did it, then?"

She narrows her eyes at me, shaking her head. "I can't tell you that. I won't. Please, don't ask again."

"Does Tallin know who it was?"

"Yes, he does."

"Is he going to punish the attacker?"

At that, Valira stares down at her fingers, which are braiding themselves together. "In his way," she says. "He will."

"So, you're telling me it won't happen again?"

"I don't know. It may." She rises to her feet and paces, chewing on her thumbnail for a moment before saying, "You did a kind thing for me, despite my coldness to you. I would have died. I owe you for it. So I'm going to tell you that the Histories are kept in a vault in Lord and Lady Perrin's house— the one where the ball is being held in a week's time. It won't be easy to access it, though. They say it's impenetrable."

"Thorne could open any lock—" I begin, but Valira puts a hand up to stop me.

"I've heard it doesn't have traditional locks. Don't ask what that means, because I don't know. But look, Shara—I'm not convinced it's a good idea to try and find the Histories. I don't know what's in that vault, but there's a reason most of Kravan wants it kept hidden from view. The truth would be dangerous for everyone."

"Then why not burn the texts? Why keep them at all?"

"I don't know. All I can guess is that there's information in them that could wreak havoc on these lands. Information that would harm Nobles as well as others. Lies would be exposed—

far greater ones than the fact that Tallin and Lady Verdan are both Tethered. If you learn the truth, you may not like it, whatever it may be."

"But it could free us all," I say. "If I could get that truth to the people of the Capitol."

"You're assuming the truth paints our kind in a good light," Valira points out.

"Of course I am. The Nobles are lying about the Rebellion, I'm sure of it."

With a shake of her head, she says, "I pray that you're right. But you should know, Shara…there are Tethered like your father out in the world who are dangerous—far more so than any Noble. The Hunter is not the benevolent mischief-maker you may think he is."

"My father?" I leap to my feet, stepping toward her. "What do you know about him?"

Valira grimaces up at me and shakes her head. "Not as much as some do. I only know there are some who call him the Shadow. If you want information, you should talk to Evangeline."

"Wait—the Domestic in the Prefect's house?"

"Yes."

It feels like weeks now since I first laid eyes on her. After all that's occurred since, I'd forgotten she even existed.

"What does she have to do with my father?"

Valira rises to her feet and looks me in the eye. "I want to help you, Shara. But on this, you're on your own. Speak to Evangeline. She'll tell you what you want to know."

"There's no way I can get myself back to that house," I protest. "It would be impossible to come up with an excuse to visit."

"Nothing is impossible," Valira says. "You have a job to do, remember. Tallin will let you go wherever you like, so long as it involves the potential to uncover more traitors." She turns and steps over to the door, then pivots to face me. "Thank you again for healing me tonight. Archyr thanks you, too. But I need to get back to Tallin."

"Valira—" I want to plead with her to think about what she's saying. But with a shake of her head, she holds up a hand.

"You don't understand how I could care about such a man," she says. "Maybe I don't care, not really. But if I stop giving him what he needs, he'll kill Archyr—and that would kill me. Whatever you may have concluded about Tallin, he's not the one-dimensional sadist you think he is. He's complex. He's tortured. And his life, like ours, has him locked inside a prison. Its walls may be prettier than the Tower's, but trust me—it's just as ugly when you take a close look at it."

Without another word, she leaves, closing the door behind her.

CHAPTER
TWENTY-THREE

THE FOLLOWING MORNING, I find Tallin and the king sitting in stony silence on the terrace just outside the dining room.

I seat myself and pour a cup of coffee, eyeing each of them as I try to piece together what they could possibly have been talking about before I came out.

"Shara," King Tomas says with a smile. "I understand you used your healing power last night on one of our Guards."

Swallowing a swig, I nod and force my eyes onto his. Knowing all I know—and *don't* know—after last night, I'm not sure this is a conversation I want to have.

In the king's eyes is a shadow of what appears to be genuine concern.

Tallin, on the other hand, looks both guilty and defeated. In spite of everything Valira told me last night, I still find it hard to believe he didn't have some hand in her injuries, and his expression does little to assuage my suspicions.

"Do you know what happened to Valira?" King Tomas asks me.

"No, your Grace," I say. "Only that someone cut her deeply several times, with a weapon...or, possibly, a set of steel claws."

"I see. And how did you happen upon her so late at night?"

I have no idea whether to tell him she was with Tallin. For all I know, the king still isn't aware of their occasional trysts.

I decide to take a chance and tell the truth—partially, at least. "Prince Tallin had already come upon her in the hallway, and he was in the process of helping her. I could see she was in pain, so I healed her. She didn't tell us what happened, and it seems the prince saw nothing."

"Did you not ask who attacked her?"

I scrutinize King Tomas, wondering if he's testing me again. Did he hear our conversation last night, somehow? Did he have surveillance in place to monitor us—or did he listen in via Valira's Maude unit, perhaps?

"I did ask," I say after swallowing down my nerves. "I wished to know if she needed protection from her assailant. But she was adamant that she didn't see who it was that attacked her."

The king seals his lips then smiles with a surprising warmth, the skin at the corners of his eyes crinkling. "I see. Thank you for your help, Shara. I suppose I was hoping to get to the bottom of this. If we have a rogue Guard in the palace—one who's going around attacking young women—well, I would want to know about such a thing. Wouldn't you?"

"I would, yes. If I find out, your Grace, I promise I will tell you immediately."

"I know you will," he replies. "You've been a wonderful asset and addition to the palace, Shara dear. I want you to know how much I appreciate you."

"Thank you, your Grace."

Across the table, Tallin glowers at his father, but I do my best to ignore him.

"Tell me something," the king adds, "does Valira have any

close friends among the Royal Guard that you know of? Anyone she might spend time with?"

I glance sideways at Tallin, convinced that he's trying to give me a quick shake of his head. "No, your Grace," I say. "Not that I know of."

I refuse to put a target on Archyr's back, and I have no doubt Tallin is just as intent on protecting him. Besides, I can't imagine Archyr hurting Valira, however envious he may be of her strange relationship with the prince.

No more words are spoken for several minutes, and it's the king who finally breaks the silence, rising to his feet and grunting, "I need to begin my day. Perhaps I'll see you both at dinner."

He storms off without a word to his son.

I'm tempted to ask Tallin when the king started despising him. When I first saw them at the Prince's Ball, they seemed close and jovial—yet everything I've seen in the palace since tells me otherwise. Is this a new phenomenon—or were they simply hiding it with so many guests around?

"Did you get some sleep?" Tallin asks, his voice brittle as a shard of glass.

"A little," I reply. "You?"

"Eventually." He pulls his eyes to mine and adds, "Thank you for what you did for Valira."

It seems entirely counter to Tallin's nature ever to thank anyone for anything, so I choose to accept it with as much grace as I can muster.

"I did it for her—not for you," I say coldly. "I want you to know that."

"I'm well aware."

I hesitate a beat before adding, "When I first met Valira, I wasn't sure I liked her. But I'll admit she's growing on me."

Tallin takes a sip of his coffee before replying. "She keeps her cards close to the vest, but I'm sure you've figured out by now that she is inherently good. Which means I don't deserve her, and I know it perfectly well. If I were a kind and decent man, I would offer her the world. I would provide quarters for her to share with...*him*. But I can't bring myself to let her go—I can't bear to release her from my grip. No one in this palace deserves her—not even Archyr."

"Archyr?" I ask, pretending not to know what he means.

He glances at me sideways, his chin down, shoulders hunched as though his insides were troubling him. "I know they care deeply for one another. I'm not as stupid as you might think."

"Then why—" I begin to ask, but I stop myself to gather my thoughts. "Why do you..."

"Demand her attentions?" He lets out a derisive snicker. There's a grittiness to his voice that sounds like genuine pain. "There are no excuses, Shara. There is nothing I can say, except that Valira keeps me human. Just barely, I'll admit. But human, all the same. As I said, I don't deserve her. I'm draining the life from her, and I know it."

"So, why not send her to the Capitol to start a new life? If you know what you're doing to her, why not set her and Archyr free? Maybe you could find another way to...*mend*."

"Because I'm selfish!" he snaps. "I'm afraid of what I'll become if I lose her. But I fear for her, too. The Capitol is no place for decent people. I know what that city has become, and I wouldn't wish it on my worst enemy."

"What, exactly, has it become?" I ask, recalling what little I saw of the Capitol after leaving the Tower. Burnt-out husks of former homes. Destroyed roads, fallen trees, and shattered roadways.

"A war zone," Tallin declares. "A calculated disaster area, orchestrated by those who don't want the Normals to rise up against them. It is chaos, ruled from the shadows by cruel minds."

Choosing my next words carefully, I nod. "Speaking of cruel minds," I say, doing my best to segue into the question I've been afraid to ask, "There's something I'd like to do today, with your permission."

"Don't tell me you're going to request that Thorne share your quarters with you. I may be feeling particularly vulnerable this morning, but I will never grant that wish."

"I'm not foolish enough to ask for that, your Highness."

Tallin lets out a chuckle, then says, "What, then? Chocolates? Flowers?"

"I..." I swallow, gathering the strength I need to finish the sentence. "I want to go back to the Prefect's house. I'd like to speak to his wife, Susan."

And their servant Evangeline.

Shock widens the prince's eyes, and he stares at me, incredulous. "You're serious? A few days ago, you were terrified by the idea of being seen by the Prefect, afraid he would recognize you. Besides which, his wife is horrible."

"All the same, I'd like to speak to her."

"Why?"

I've been waiting for this question. I've thought of little else, in fact, since Valira told me the servant Evangeline had information about my father.

"When I spoke to Lady Weston," I reply, "I got the impression she knew some things...about other Nobles. She's a gossip, which makes it easy to prod her mind. I'd like to see if I can extract some information. Maybe she could inadvertently steer me in the direction of a few more Tethered traitors."

Tallin contemplates this for a few seconds, then raises his brows and shrugs. "I suppose I could invite the Prefect to tea this afternoon, to get him out of his house. I can make up some bullshit excuse to do with the Tower. Renovations or something. That will give you an opportunity to visit in private with his wife." With a sneer, he adds, "But if you think this is some clever ploy to get some alone time with Thorne, think again. I'm not sending him to pilot you. You two would end up fucking in the Flyer like a couple of drunken teenagers."

"Is that something teenagers do?" I ask with an attempt at light laughter. "I wouldn't know. I never saw a Flyer or a drop of alcohol until I left the Tower—and I haven't exactly had a ton of opportunities to make out in vehicles since."

"It's something Normals used to do," he replies wistfully. "So they tell me, anyhow."

"Maybe you'd be willing to let Valira pilot the Flyer. You trust her, don't you?"

"I do. But—do you really think she's up to it? You're the one who healed her."

"She's fine," I assure him, though I'm not entirely certain I'm right. "But I have no doubt she'll tell you if she'd rather not."

"I'll go speak to her now." Tallin pushes himself away from the table and rises to his feet. "I'll have my people summon the Prefect for a two p.m. meeting. I'll see to it that you have at least an hour or two to speak to his irritating wife."

"That should be plenty," I tell him. "Thank you."

"You will report any findings to me, of course."

With a smile, I say, "That's the whole point."

With that, Tallin leaves me on the terrace. I sip my coffee, looking out over the exquisite grounds and wondering what I will learn this afternoon about my father, the man they call the Shadow.

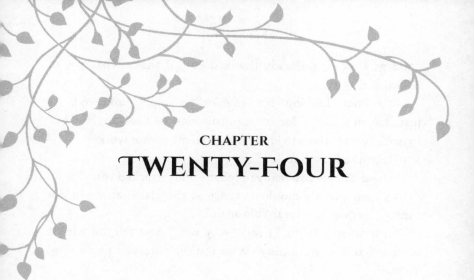

CHAPTER
TWENTY-FOUR

AT 1:30 P.M., after I've received word that Tallin has made the necessary arrangements, I head out the palace's main entrance, where a silver Flyer awaits.

Valira greets me with her usual formality, nodding once before gesturing to the vehicle and saying, "Get in."

I look over my shoulder at the two members of the Royal Guard who are watching us, wondering if they're surprised by her tone. If they are, they sure as hell aren't showing it.

I suppose Valira addresses everyone in that way—except for Tallin and his father, that is.

I climb into the backseat and buckle myself in, staring out the window in hopes of seeing Thorne on the grounds somewhere. When there's no sign of him, I pull my attention back to Valira.

"How are you feeling?" I ask.

"Fine," she replies, her tone curt and clipped.

"Your wounds are all healed?"

She eyes me in the mirror as the Flyer lifts off and soars toward the high wall surrounding the grounds. "Yes," she says.

"And as I recall, I already thanked you, if that's what you're fishing for."

"I'm not looking for thanks," I reply, annoyed. "I just...haven't had a lot of opportunities to heal anyone but myself. I was curious to know how well my power worked."

"It worked just fine."

"Good. So, are you ready to tell me who attacked you?"

I watch Valira's shoulders tense as she glares at me in the mirror. "Seriously, Shara? This again?"

"If it wasn't Tallin," I say, "why won't you tell me who it was? What are you hiding? Who the fuck are you protecting, Valira?"

She looks temporarily frazzled, then shakes her head. "No one. And you should stop asking foolish questions, unless you want to die."

I let out a laugh. When I asked for Valira to accompany me today, I was not expecting this level of hostility. "Is that a threat?"

"Not from me," she says. "But you know where my loyalties lie, *Lady Ingram.*"

"With a lying fraud of a prince," I say. "One who's proven himself violent. So you can't blame me for questioning your judgment."

She brakes abruptly and navigates the Flyer downward, landing a little aggressively on a bare stretch of gravel road. With the press of a button, loud music begins to blast out through a set of speakers in the passenger doors.

"Watch yourself," Valira hisses, twisting in her seat. "Do you have a death wish or something? Are you forgetting we are probably being monitored? We're in a vehicle that belongs to the Royals. They have ears everywhere, Shara."

"The Royals want to know who hurt you as much as I do."

Valira snorts. "You're wrong about that."

The truth is, my fear of the Royals has diminished over time —which probably makes me a fool.

Still, King Tomas has been nothing but kind to me since I entered the palace. Tallin has proven surprisingly restrained, despite his foolishness in the Flyer last night. And something about seeing him looking so helpless when Valira was wounded —so pained, so unable to do anything but whimper—made me realize he's more fragile than I ever knew.

Maybe one day, I can use that fragility to my advantage.

As I sit in silence, Maude vibrates a reminder under my skin, almost like she's laughing at me.

~Valira is right, you know. I've detected multiple listening devices in this vehicle. You're probably safe, however. I suspect it's Tallin who planted them here, and he will most likely not punish you for discussing what unfolded last night. Still, I suspect he's not keen on being called a fraud.

You think? I reply silently with a roll of my eyes. *You know, you could have warned me about the listening devices.*

~If you like, I can go back to nagging you regularly. The truth is, I sort of miss it. Now, apologize to the young lady or I'm afraid she'll rip your face off and wear it like a hat.

"I'm sorry, Valira," I blurt out. "I didn't mean to offend you. I suppose I was just hoping..."

"You were hoping we were friends now, or something equally ridiculous," she retorts. "I can't be friends with you, Shara. I won't. So get that notion out of your head. You and I... we're not the same. We never will be. You have a chance at a normal life—and maybe you'll find it one day. But I won't. Not now, not ever. So please—just let me live my twisted existence."

I don't know what's happened in Valira's life to turn her into this person—this damaged human who thrives on Tallin's attention and covers for those who have injured her to within an inch of her life. I can't imagine what level of self-loathing a person has to engage in to get to that point.

But it's none of my damned business. If she wants to be a miserable human being, that's her prerogative.

She turns the music off and lifts the Flyer off the ground once again, aiming for the Prefect's lands miles away.

I don't say another word. All I want to think about now is getting some answers about my father. What sort of man is he? Where is he now? And how does a Domestic in the Prefect's house know him?

Valira lands us on the grounds after what feels like a long flight. "I'll be waiting here when you're done."

"I'll be back in an hour," I tell her as I open the door to step out. "If I don't return, come find my corpse."

"It will be my pleasure."

THIRTY SECONDS or so after I ring the bell, the door opens inward to reveal Evangeline, the Domestic I encountered briefly the previous evening.

This time, I study her more closely. The lines of her face, the curve of her lips, her chin. I know I never met her before the dinner, yet she looks oddly familiar.

I shake my head, telling myself I'm only imagining it.

"Lady Ingram," she says, her voice quivering slightly. "I... heard you were coming to see Lady Weston. She's in the garden enjoying a cup of tea. I'll bring you right through."

"Give me a moment," I say, glancing around.

Maude, I ask silently, *any surveillance here in the foyer?*

~A small camera in the far corner. No audio, only video. It's old, and not working terribly well. I suspect the Prefect's most reliable security system is his collection of murder-hounds.

166

You mean the mechanical watchdogs?

~Yes—those.

Let's hope we don't meet any of them today, then.

"Evangeline," I say out loud, "the truth is, I'm here to see you."

"Really?" She looks over her shoulder, clasping her hands together. It's only now that I see they're shaking.

"Really."

"Quickly, come into the salon, please," she instructs, guiding me toward an open doorway.

When we're inside the room, she closes the door behind us and says, "There's no surveillance here. Lady Weston considers this room her private sanctuary. But you and I don't have much time before she realizes something is amiss."

As she speaks, she studies my face intently, just as she did the last time I was here.

"I was told you might be able to give me some information about a man they call the Hunter," I say quietly. "Do you know him? Do you have any idea where he might be?"

"Oh, I know him well. May I ask why you want to find him?"

I seal my lips shut and shake my head. "I can't tell you that," I say. "It's a...personal matter."

"A personal matter," she replies with a chuckle. "Yes, I see." She turns to a window at the far end of the room and peers out, then says, "Do you know what my power is?"

"Why would I know that?" I ask, a blatant lie in my voice.

She lets out a disquieting laugh, and pivots back to me. "Because of who you really are. I know as well as you do that your name is not Lady Johanna Ingram."

CHAPTER
TWENTY-FIVE

"I don't know what you're talking about." The lie claws at my throat. "Everyone knows I'm Lady Johanna Ingram, from Pembroke Isle."

How can this Domestic possibly know the truth about me?

Surely Valira didn't tell her. As frosty as she is, she doesn't exactly strike me as the sort of woman who goes around disclosing classified information at the drop of a hat—not even to someone close to her. I've never met a more tightly sealed book than Valira.

"You're *not* Lady Ingram," Evangeline says. "It's all right—I haven't told my Proprietor, and I never will. You have my word on that."

"You don't need to tell your Proprietor," I retort, glancing at her left arm. "Don't you have an implant? Don't they monitor you?"

A shake of her head. "Most Proprietors don't monitor Domestics who have been in their service for more than a year. The Prefect and his wife watched me like a hawk when I first started working for them. They deemed me non-threatening, not to mention useless. The fact is, Maude units are implanted in the Tower to determine our natures early on and train us against...certain emotions. Out here in the real world, it's assumed we're already well-versed in acting as loyal servants to the Nobility."

"It doesn't matter," I say, forcing a falsely haughty tone into my voice. Clearly, I made a mistake in coming here. I have some choice words for Valira when I get back to the Flyer. "You seem to have me confused with someone else. Now, if you'll excuse me—"

I take a step toward the door, but Evangeline moves quickly, positioning herself in front of me. "There are things most people forget during the course of their lives," she says. "Early memories. Pain. Faces, even. It's true that I shouldn't have known your face—I hadn't seen it in so long, after all."

I pull back, wondering if I should make a run for it. She's not making any sense. In fact, right now, she sounds completely unhinged.

The truth is, her power is as mysterious to me as Tallin's was. As I look into her eyes, all I can see is a series of what look like dream fragments. Cloudy visions of a white room, where I hear people shouting but can't make out any faces.

Perhaps I'm seeing her memories—but we all have those. Don't we?

"It's all right," she says, stepping over to a small wooden table under the window and picking up a sharp letter opener. "I know your nature—your goodness. Tell me something," she says, pushing its tip into her palm. "Would you heal me if I were hurt?"

"Heal you? I...couldn't...I'm not a..."

But before I can spew any more lies, she pulls the blade along her skin, leaving a red streak in its path. The cut is deep—deeper than any letter opener should be able to slice—and I leap over and take her by the wrist, panicking.

If I heal her, she'll know the truth. But if I don't...

"Are you insane?" I hiss. "You'll bleed all over the carpet."

Already, the blood is trickling down her hand toward her wrist and threatening to spill to the off-white, pristine carpet beneath our feet.

"Heal me, Shara," she says, her blue eyes locked on my own.

My heart rate accelerates, my palms instantly clammy with panic. "My name is Lady Ingram," I insist again, my voice breaking.

Evangeline shakes her head. "Don't bother. I know where you were born. Not because I'm a Hunter like your father, but because of who I am to you. I've seen my own face in your mind —from the very first time you opened your eyes to the moments just before they took you from me."

I stare at her swirling irises, and I see it then—I see a woman whose heart has been broken more than once.

A woman whose child was taken from her.

A woman who, like me, can *heal*.

She presses her palms together and inhales deeply, looking me in the eye. When she holds her hands up again, the wound is gone.

Intaking a breath, I whisper, "You're..."

I can't bring myself to say the words. They're too huge, too momentous.

My mother.

"Do they know?" I ask in a whisper. "The prince—the Prefect—anyone else? Do they know we're related?"

She shakes her head. "Not as far as I can tell," she says. "I can't imagine the prince would have let you come here today if he suspected as much."

"But *you* knew," I tell her. "The first time we saw each other, there was something in your expression, like you recognized me."

"It hit me like a hurricane threatening to blow me over," she says. "The revelation was so powerful I thought it might destroy me. I'm so sorry I couldn't tell you then. It's only—you looked like a Noble, dressed like that. You can understand my confusion...my hesitation. Saying such a thing could have gotten you killed—and probably me, as well."

"I understand. But...how did you know I was your daughter?"

"Truthfully, I'm not sure. I just did. I once received a letter in the post—one from an unidentified sender. With it was a photo of you when you were twelve years old, inside the Tower. Your face hasn't changed that much since. And I suppose some long-lost maternal instinct told me who you were."

"Have you figured out who sent it? The Warden, or..."

She shakes her head. "The Warden doesn't contact mothers after we've given birth in the Tower. All ties are supposed to be severed. I have my suspicions, but I can't know for certain."

Emotions collide and explode inside me. I have never had a mother. I've told Maude more than once that she's as close as I've ever come.

I don't know how to be a daughter.

And it's clear, looking at Evangeline now, that she's as baffled as I am. The Tethered are kept from emotion all our lives. We don't know how to feel properly, and when we do, it comes in frenzied bursts so violent that they nearly kill us.

"And my father," I say, reminding myself that by now, Lady Weston must be wondering why we haven't shown up outside.

"Your father," Evangeline says softly, warily eyeing the door. "Well, I haven't spoken to him in a long time. We were together in secret several times over the years when I was in my early twenties. When I was taken to the Tower to give birth to you, he watched and waited for me, then found me afterward, at great risk to himself. He looked after me in the months that followed

—helped me to cope with the sense of loss I was feeling. When I fell pregnant a second time, it came as a shock to us both, as you can imagine."

"Wait..." I say, but I'm interrupted by the sound of sharp footsteps hitting the stone floor at the far end of the hallway. "A second time?" I whisper. "Are you telling me I have a sibling?"

She nods, casting her eyes warily to the door. "A younger sister. But she wasn't born in the Tower," she breathes. "There's so much I want to tell you, Shara—so much you need to know."

Evangeline moves to open the door, but I grab her arm.

"Where is she?" I hiss. "Where is my sister?"

~*Shara,* Maude warns silently as the percussive footsteps approach. *The lady of the house is coming. And Evangeline is not supposed to touch anyone—not even kin.*

"I've heard your father is in the Capitol," Evangeline whispers. "That's all I know. They say he's changed since I knew him —that he's grown dangerous and unpredictable. Be wary if you go looking for him."

I step away, releasing her from my grip just in time to hear, "Ah, *there* you are, Lady Ingram!" as the door flies open. "What are you two doing in here?"

"I'm so sorry, Lady Weston," I reply with a smile. "I asked your Domestic to bring me to this lovely room. I saw its window from the outside and thought it looked charming. She was simply showing me some of the architectural details."

As Lady Weston glides into the room, my mother bows her head, clearly terrified of her Proprietor. She gives me one last, apologetic look over her shoulder before disappearing from view.

I know in my shredded heart that it's the last I'll see of her for a long time, and all I want in this moment is to steal her away.

I came here with one question, and now I have a million of them.

MY MIND RACES a mile a minute as Lady Weston and I head out to the back garden for tea.

When we seat ourselves, I'm a quivering, useless mess, barely able to string a sentence together. All I want is to find Evangeline again and ask her more questions about my father and the sister I didn't know I had until a few minutes ago.

When Lady Weston asks why I wanted to meet with her, I lie...poorly.

"I just...needed an escape from the palace, to be honest," I tell her. "I love the royal grounds. They're absolutely exquisite. But there are so many people milling about all the time, and your property—it's so lovely and relaxing. I thought since the Prefect was headed to visit the prince today, it would be a perfect time for me to come and see you again."

Lady Weston looks surprised, but seems to accept my words at face value.

I can't say I blame her for her shock. I wasn't exactly polite to her the last time we met. As I recall, I came perilously close to punching her.

"Well, I'm so pleased," she replies. "Tell me—will you be attending the ball next weekend? I must admit, I haven't yet picked out a dress."

"I will—but I haven't chosen one, either. I'm looking forward to it. I'm curious to meet Lord Perrin."

"You may not meet him at all. He's quite reclusive." Lady Weston grins, and I can't quite read what's going on behind her eyes. "A strange sort, very mysterious. I'm quite shocked he wants to hold a ball at all, though he does have the perfect house for it. It's absolutely enormous." She leans forward and half-whispers, "They say the Histories are kept in the vault inside his home."

With a laugh, I ask, "Does everyone know that? Because you're not the first person to mention it. It kind of seems like it's not much of a secret."

"I shouldn't have said anything," she says with a laugh. "The Prefect would kill me. But it doesn't matter who knows, anyhow—the Histories are absolutely impossible to access. No one can get into that vault—even though they say many have tried."

I fidget with my tea cup. "I suppose the reason the texts are entrusted to Lord Perrin is because he's so secretive?"

She shakes her head. "As I understand it, he's never seen them. But honestly, I've never understood why *anyone* keeps records of the pre-Rebellion times. No good can—or will ever—come of it. Those who know the truth are long dead, and that's for the best. The texts could destroy our lands if they came to light—at the very least, they would ruin things for the Nobles."

She gives me a knowing look, and my curiosity surges to new, dangerous levels.

"I always thought the Tethered waged war on the Normals and drove the Nobles from the Capitol," I say, forcing my voice into a conspiratorial tone. "Is there something I don't know?"

"That's what everyone in power wants us to believe, isn't it?" Susan replies. "But I don't suppose you and I will ever know the whole truth, will we?"

She glances around as if looking for watchers before she adds, "Look—I've heard rumors. Things that should never be uttered—not even by the most powerful of men. But when you live with the Prefect, you tend to overhear things, you know?"

"Oh?" I ask, offering up a complicit smile. "What sorts of things?"

"Let's just say the king isn't as powerful as we tend to believe—and his position is precarious, at best." She looks like she's about to spill several hundred pounds of contraband information when she shakes her head, sits back in her chair and her smile fades. "We shouldn't talk like this. No one should. It's all speculation, anyhow. If I told you what I've heard, I would be punished for it, whether I'm the Prefect's wife or not. But let's just say, there's a reason the Quiet War continues to rage between Nobles. There are some who want to usurp the throne because they feel King Tomas is too weak to face the deluge that may one day hit if the Capitol's Normals ever learn the truth about the past."

I pull my chin down, averting my eyes when I ask, "And what truth is that?"

When Lady Weston doesn't reply, I glance at her, only to see her studying me intently. "You ask a lot of questions, Lady Johanna Ingram," she says, and I'm convinced there's veiled accusation in her tone. "I'm surprised you haven't learned by now that it's a bad idea."

Forcing a quiet laugh, I say, "You're right—I tend to be too inquisitive. I'm sorry if I've offended you."

"Not at all. I'm only looking out for you." She breathes out a long sigh before adding, "Seeking information about the pre-Rebellion era is punishable by death, or worse. There's no need for you or me to look for that information, as intriguing as it may be. It's best we just learn to coexist in an imperfect world."

I stare at her for a moment too long before saying, "I understand."

Damn it. I thought we were onto something there.

~You shouldn't trust her, anyhow, Maude whispers to my mind. *Don't count on Nobles to give you the truth—ever. They're not on your side. They look out only for themselves.*

But she knows something—and I really think she wanted to share it with me.

~The only absolute truth is locked inside a vault, and you have no access to it, Shara. No one does. Perhaps it's time to let it go.

There has to be a way in, Maude. Otherwise, what's the point in storing the Histories there?

~Shara—I'm warning you to stop.

Fuck that.

"Lady Weston," I say abruptly, leaping to my feet. "I've taken up enough of your time. Thank you so much for letting me sit in your beautiful garden with you, but I really should get back to the palace."

"Are you certain you don't want to stay for dinner? The Prefect will be home soon."

The thought of seeing him again sends a shudder of unease through me. "I'm sure. Thank you, though. I'll see you at the ball next week?"

With a nod of confirmation, she escorts me around the house to the waiting Flyer and we say our goodbyes.

When I'm sealed inside the vehicle, Valira asks, "Was your visit a success?"

It's a friendlier question than I expected from her, but then, I can tell without asking that she's not talking about Lady Weston.

She wants to know if I managed to speak to Evangeline.

"It was...interesting," I say.

"Yes," she replies as she sets the engines whirring to life. "I thought it might be."

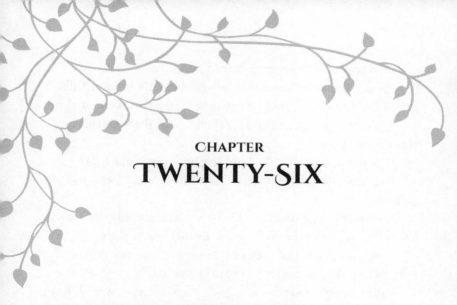

CHAPTER

TWENTY-SIX

ALL I CAN THINK about on the way home is Thorne.

I *need* to tell him what I've learned—to share the enormity of the truth that has been weighing me down since the moment my mother revealed her identity.

"Valira," I say when we've been traveling for a little while.

"Yes?" Her tone is reserved, but not so icy-cold as it has so often been.

"I want to speak to Thorne. Do you have any idea how I can see him?"

At first, she doesn't reply, and for a cynical minute, I wonder if she's enjoying my discomfort.

But when she turns the music on once again, blasting it so loudly through the speakers that I'm tempted to slam my palms over my ears, I understand her hesitation.

"Tomorrow evening," she says over her shoulder as I lean forward, getting as close as I can. "There's a cocktail party at Lord and Lady Nelson's place. Word has it that Thorne will pilot the Flyer again."

"Then I have a favor to ask of you."

"You want me to keep the prince occupied."

I nod. "You seem to be the only person able to hold Tallin's attention. Maybe you could work your magic and...soothe him."

She seems to tighten, and I feel instantly like I've said something terribly wrong.

"I'm sorry," I tell her. "I shouldn't have put it like that."

"It's all right—it's my lot in life. I'll do what I can to help you."

I'm beginning to wonder if her tone has altered because she knows what just occurred between Evangeline and me.

"Did you know the Prefect's Domestic was my mother?" I ask. "Is that why you wanted me to go see her?"

Valira nods. "Even if she hadn't told me, I would have known. I could feel the emotion inside her—pain, mixed with joy. So few of us get to meet our parents, and when Evangeline saw you—well, it seemed like you two should have at least one chance to meet properly."

I'm not sure what to say, so I simply reply, "Thank you."

Part of me wants to pour my heart out and tell her I don't know how to feel—that it was one of the most overwhelming moments of my life, and I have her to thank for it.

"Do you know anything about your own parents?" I ask.

"I was told once that my father is a Normal...and that it's my mother who is a Tethered. That's all I know, and I expect it's all I'll ever know. Like I said, most of us never get the chance you had today."

"I didn't feel a bond with Evangeline, in case it makes you feel any better. I mean, I *liked* her—she seemed genuinely kind. But maybe the bond between parent and child is severed in the Tower the moment they steal us away. Maybe we miss them less than we think, because we've evolved not to need them."

Valira goes silent for a minute, and I wonder if she's planning on telling me I still talk too much.

Instead, she turns down the music.

"Fuck it," she says, her voice shaky. "I don't care who hears this. Some days, I wish for my mother so badly it hurts. I don't know her, of course, but I...I wish I had someone in my life who loved me unconditionally. Someone who could talk me down from the ledge where I stand so often. Even if I've never known her, I wish more than anything that I could weep in her arms."

I never expected such words from Valira, and now I'm not sure what to say in response. "You must know how much Archyr cares about you. I'm sure he loves you unconditionally."

She snickers and wipes at her eye with the back of her fingers. "He must, to put up with everything that goes on between Tallin and me." With a sigh, she adds, "I know he loves me. I also know I don't deserve him."

I begin to protest, but Valira shakes her head. "It's all right. You of all people don't need to protect me, Shara. Like Archyr, you're kinder to me than I deserve. I suppose I push you both away because I feel pain in each of you, and I can't take any more pain. Not on top of what Tallin inflicts on me."

"I understand," I lean back in my seat. "But I'm sure Archyr thinks you deserve him."

"He does," she replies softly. "And I love him for it. In an ideal world, he and I could be together. You and Thorne could be together, too. But *this* world is fucked up, and you and I both know it."

She's not wrong. Denying us this one, simple thing—being with the person we love most—is a monstrous act.

I will never forgive the Nobility for the abuse we endure at their hands.

"Could I ask you a question?" I murmur.

Valira turns her head to throw me a look. "All you *do* is ask questions," she replies with a fake sneer.

"Fine. I'll turn it into a statement, then." I clear my throat.

"You don't seem to hate Tallin. I suppose I'm still confused by that."

"No, I don't hate him, because I *know* him," she snaps, then inhales a quick breath as if to silence herself. "Look, I know he seems like a monster to you. I get it. Maybe he is. But trust me when I say I've seen a side to him that most people don't know about. A lot of Proprietors would have terminated me ages ago. I'm not the most useful Tethered, and I'm certainly not the most pleasant to be around. But Tallin defends my right to stay in the palace and in the world. He keeps me alive. He's also the reason Archyr never has to risk his life in the Championship. The prince looks out for us—and I can promise you, he's looking out for you and Thorne too, in his own twisted way."

"He nearly *killed* Thorne," I retort. "He's threatened me multiple times since I arrived at the palace. Not to mention that he let us both rot in the Verdan dungeon far longer than we should have."

"I never said he was kind," Valira says. "Only that he isn't as bad as people think."

Part of me wants to argue with her, but there's no point. She'll never see Tallin through my eyes, and I'll never understand how she tolerates being used for his own pleasure.

In spite of everything, I like Valira. Enough, at least, to want to shake her and plead with her never to be with Tallin again.

The only problem is, I *need* her to be with him. I need her to take him aside tomorrow night and keep him occupied long enough for me to talk to Thorne.

I'm desperate to tell him what I learned today about both my parents...and the sister I never knew existed.

"I'll keep Tallin distracted tomorrow evening," Valira says, reading my mind. "And maybe one day, you'll understand why I'm willing to give him so much of myself. But you need to do something in return."

My chest tightens, but I nod. "I'll do whatever you ask of me."

"Find a way to free our people," she says. "Once and for all."

CHAPTER
TWENTY-SEVEN

I DON'T LEAVE my quarters this evening—not even for dinner. I'm too excited by what I discovered today and terrified I'll divulge too much if I should run into the wrong person.

All I want is for time to pass quickly so I can find my way to Thorne again.

I'm about to change into my pajamas when, around nine p.m., a knock sounds at the suite's door.

"Come in," I call out, my heart sinking. There's little doubt in my mind of who it is—and I'm in no mood to tolerate his presence.

I wait, my breath imprisoned in my chest, as the door flies open and Tallin wanders in.

"I've come to see what progress you made this afternoon," he says, throwing himself onto the couch a foot or so from where I'm sitting. "Did Lady Weston offer up any dirt?"

"Dirt?" I echo before my distracted brain kicks in.

"Yes. Gossip. News. Juice. Tea. Whatever the cool kids are calling it these days."

Shit.

I'd totally forgotten the alleged reason I went to the Prefect's in the first place.

"I...no," I reply. "No dirt. Lady Weston wasn't exactly forthcoming, and I'm sure she would have begun to grow suspicious if I'd asked too many questions."

Tallin cocks his head to the side, examining me for a moment before saying, "Pity. Well, there's always tomorrow evening."

"Tomorrow evening?" I ask, feigning ignorance. I'm not sure whether Valira was officially allowed to tell me about the cocktail party. "Is there something happening then?"

"Did I forget to tell you? Ah, well, it must have slipped my mind." The prince pulls at a loose thread on the couch cushion. "We're to head over to Lord and Lady Nelson's for a little cocktail party in their garden. By the way, I asked for a little black dress to be added to your wardrobe earlier today. Something appropriate for the occasion. It should be waiting in your closet as we speak."

"Thank you," I reply, already dreading the garment. If Tallin chose it, it's probably too short, too low-cut, and too tight, all at once.

I study him for a moment, contemplating everything Valira told me about him. Tallin has always seemed entirely one-dimensional. He's an asshole—an arrogant, cruel prick who loves making my life unpleasant, and as an added bonus, takes delight in watching other Tethered murder one another.

It's hard to believe someone who's suffered the pain Valira described would wish it on others—yet Tallin seems to do exactly that.

"May I ask you something, Highness?"

He pulls his eyes to mine, narrowing them when he says, "Of course, my lovely fiancée. Go right ahead."

It takes more than a little effort to lighten my voice when I ask, "What, exactly, is your power?"

For a moment, he freezes, his jaw clenching tight as if he's about to hurl a barrage of curses at me. But he gains control over whatever rage was threatening to overtake him, smiles, and pulls his eyes to the fireplace.

"I thought you saw my power when you touched me at the Prince's Ball," he says. "Did you not?"

With a shake of my head, I reply, "I saw people who were either in pain or dead. I saw horrible wounds—and I assumed you had inflicted them." The honesty in my words is a risk, I know—but then, I want him to be honest with me, too. "But I didn't see how they were wounded."

"Ah." He rises to his feet, steps over to the fireplace, and leans against its surround. He lowers his chin, eyes darkening when he adds, "You don't want to know, Shara. Trust me. No one should wish that knowledge upon themselves."

Without expanding on the thought, he pulls away and strides over to the door. "Be ready at six tomorrow evening. And keep your mind sharp. I need you to hunt down more Tethered —You know, for the good of this lovely realm of ours and all that."

The door shuts a moment later, and as usual, I'm left with more questions than answers.

Tallin's reaction to my question wasn't at all what I had expected. I had braced myself for unbridled rage, or boasting about his plethora of kills...or something.

Instead, he was evasive.

If I didn't know him, I'd even say he seemed *ashamed*.

IN THE MORNING, the maid who tends to my room announces that the king wishes for me to join him for breakfast.

"Do you know why?" I ask as she parts the curtains to let the sunlight in. I'm grateful to see that Mercutio has already taken off for his morning patrol of the palace. I can only imagine that the sight of a small mouse on the windowsill would make the maid shriek in horror.

"No idea, my Lady," she says, lowering her voice to add, "but I should warn you—I've heard he's in a bit of a mood."

Great. Just what I need—a cranky monarch.

When I've dressed and trekked through the enormous building to hunt down the king on the dining room's terrace, I'm relieved to see he's sitting alone.

"No prince?" I ask, taking a seat opposite him as the breeze catches wisps of my long hair.

"The prince is sleeping in this morning," King Tomas tells me with a frown. "With his...*friend.*"

Without thinking, I reply, "You know about their...?"

I stop myself, but too late.

"Their vile relationship?" he asks with a snort of derision. "Yes. I know. I'm deeply sorry for the insult he's inflicting on you by behaving this way, Shara. Honestly, it's pathetic how he runs to that woman every time he feels the slightest bit out of sorts. He's such a sensitive boy—so vulnerable. And they say *women* are the members of the weaker sex."

I ignore his casual misogyny. "With respect, Prince Tallin usually strikes me as the least vulnerable person I've ever met."

"You don't know him," the king says, casting his gaze to the distance and staring in the direction of the Capitol. "He's..." He lets out a wry laugh. "Well, let's just say my son is a disappointment. If he weren't heir to the throne, perhaps I'd concern myself less with his pathetic nature. But I don't suppose anyone wants a weak-willed man like Tallin taking the reins of this realm—and I can't say I blame them."

I have no idea how I'm supposed to reply to such an appraisal. Nor do I begin to understand why the king would choose to confide these less than savory feelings to me, of all people.

After a momentary silence, he pulls his eyes to mine. "How are you feeling, Shara? Are you settling in well? I realize your first couple of days have been a whirlwind."

"I'm...fine," I say with the warmest smile I can manage. Then, after a mere moment's contemplation, I add, "Though I'll admit, I wish I could speak to Thorne now and then."

The king raises an eyebrow. "I know how it feels, you know—not to be able to be with someone you love." He nods toward the Verdan property to the west. "Kravan's rules are cruel to more than just Tethered servants. To this day, Daphne and I can't marry. There's too much risk involved, you see...so I am forced to seek comfort in other ways—as is she."

Other ways?

I shudder to think what he could mean by that. Am I to understand King Tomas has other lovers?

As far as I know, Lady Verdan never invited male guests into the house while I was there.

I could be wrong.

"You will see your Thorne tonight," he assures me. "Perhaps you two can find a little time on your own at the cocktail party —after you've assessed the guests, of course."

My eyes go wide with surprise. "Wouldn't that be an insult to the prince? I mean, speaking to Thorne might...irritate him a little."

"The prince spent last night fucking the brains out of a member of the Guard," the king grunts. "I wouldn't worry too much about insulting him. Just be careful. Tallin doesn't take kindly to disrespect, as I'm sure you've figured out by now."

"I'm aware," I say. "Your Grace, I need to ask...is there a particular reason you wanted me to have breakfast with you this morning?"

King Tomas nods. "I simply wanted to learn of your progress. For instance, are there any more Tethered Nobles on your radar—or is it only Lord Malloy thus far?"

I swallow, steeling myself for yet another lie. "I'm afraid I've only detected Lord Malloy's power. I'll keep an eye out tonight, naturally, and report to you if I find any more."

"Good, good. I'm quite sure you'll spot a few at the cocktail party. Just remember—whatever your heart may tell you, they're not your friends. They're cowards who have been concealing themselves behind a façade of wealth for an age— infiltrators into the Nobility. They're nothing more than opportunistic liars."

I want to point out the obvious—that Tallin, too, is a liar who hides his true identity behind a mountain of riches.

To say nothing of Lady Verdan.

But the silent warning Maude issues reminds me that there's no way I should take such a risk, particularly as there's no possible benefit to me.

"Here's the thing, Shara," King Tomas says softly, leaning in close, a twinkle in his eye. "It may seem like all is well in the land of Kravan—but the truth is, too many Nobles thirst for power these days. The more of it they have, the more they want. They demand more Tethered servants. More money. More *every*thing. The only thing keeping the order is me. It's why the law states clearly that there can only be two Tethered in most Noble homes. It would be too dangerous if I were to allow entire military forces to build up in the houses of my enemies. Do you see what I'm saying?"

I do—though I have no idea why he's telling me all of this.

"Of course, I understand."

"Good." He lays his hand on top of mine for a moment, issuing a sad smile. "If I had my way, Kravan would be quiet, peaceful, and filled with benevolent people. But it's undeniable that an incorrigible part of human nature is to be ambitious. It's our reason for living, really. It's also one reason we Normals feel the need to train all ambition out of the Tethered—why we don't want your kind itching for power. You're strong in body, but weak in mind. It's why you tend to make such excellent servants."

Thank you for speaking about Tethered as though we're a bunch of lobotomized pack mules, I think.

~Watch it, donkey, Maude warns. *You're making a face, and the king isn't stupid.*

Obediently, I nod, offering up a faint smile. "Yes, your Grace."

"Lady Verdan and I will be attending the Perrins' ball next week," the king says, pulling back and gazing toward the Verdan grounds again. "Daphne will be pleased to see you again."

"Will she, now?" My snide tone is conspicuous, but I don't particularly care. There's no point in pretending Daphne Verdan likes me even a little.

The king chuckles. "Believe it or not, she respects you, my dear. She acknowledges your usefulness, just as I do. She also appreciates your efforts, though she would never admit as much. Daphne's reserve doesn't allow her to be effusive in her praise."

"Will her step-daughters be at the ball?" I ask, ignoring his obvious lies.

"They may—but I wouldn't worry, if I were you. They've been warned to keep quiet about the goings-on with the prince.

All they know is that there's something secret and important happening inside the palace."

I want to laugh. The idea that Devorah could see me on the prince's arm and keep her mouth shut is ridiculous. I'd be shocked if she didn't jump up and down, shrieking to every member of the Nobility that there was an intruder among them.

The sound of a door opening distracts me, and I look over to see a servant striding out to the terrace. She stops next to the king and leans down to whisper something in his ear.

"Ah," King Tomas says, laying his cloth napkin on the table and rising to his feet. "I'm afraid I have to leave you, Lady Ingram. I have a pressing appointment I don't wish to miss."

When the king has made his way inside, I rise to my feet and stroll over to the terrace's railing to look out onto the Royal grounds.

In the distance, by the entrance to the vast hedge maze, I spot a tall, broad-shouldered man in a Royal Guard uniform. He's facing me, and when our eyes meet, he offers up a quiet nod, lifting one hand ever so slightly in greeting.

Thorne.

What I wouldn't give to leap over the railing and sprint over to him. But even as I contemplate it, he turns away and steps into the hedge maze, disappearing from view.

"I'd stay put if I were you, Lady Ingram, however appealing the scenery may be at this moment."

The voice is familiar and deep, but I can't entirely place it until I turn to see that Archyr is standing in the doorway, his arms crossed and a grin on his lips.

"Thorne would like to come to you as badly as you want to go to him," Archyr says, striding over to the table, his eyes locked on the distant hedge maze. "Trust me."

"I know," I sigh. "I just wish..."

"We all wish for many things." He takes a seat, snatching an apple from the fruit bowl that's currently acting as a centerpiece.

"What are you doing here, anyway?" I ask, stepping over to join him at the table. "I didn't know Guards could just wander into the king's private dining room."

"We can't, normally. But the king asked me to look in on you when he jogged by me just now. For some reason, he thinks you need babysitting."

"I'm fine."

"I know you are. I'm the one who wanted company, so I told him I'd come see you."

"Oh." We exchange a look, and I know exactly what he's thinking. After all, the king *did* mention that Tallin spent the night with Valira. I have no doubt Archyr is aware of it, too. "Does it bother you?" I ask.

He grinds his jaw and lowers his chin, his expression darkening. "Of course it does. I fucking hate when they spend the night together. But it's not like I can do anything about it. He needs her like most of us need air."

"Isn't there some other woman—some other Tethered—who could take her place?"

"No!" Archyr retorts, his voice jagged. He takes an almost vengeful bite of the apple, then, slouching back in his chair, says, "Sorry. Not your fault. But no, there is no other Tethered who can give the prince what he needs. I suppose the positive side is that Valira is so important to Tallin that he'll do anything to keep her alive. And, by extension, me. He keeps me alive to keep her happy—and in return, the prince gets his medication in the form of sex with the woman I love." He lets out a snicker. "Ridiculous, isn't it? He keeps me from certain death, but what's the point in living if I can't be with her?"

The last sentence feels like a knife threatening to pierce my heart. There's something so desperate, so sad—almost *weak*—about it. Yet I understand it fully.

Every moment that I spend so close to Thorne but so far from him—far from his voice, his touch, his lips on mine, feels like a vicious form of torture.

"We're not like Normals, you and I," Archyr says. "Not in any way, shape, or form. Our emotions run as deep as marrow, and it kills us slowly when we're torn from the person we're connected to. Keeping two bonded mates apart is a cruelty that most Normals can't even begin to fathom. Tallin is a Tethered. He should know better, yet he acts like Valira is his. Deep down, he knows it's not true."

"She's *yours*," I say, but Archyr shakes his head.

"She belongs to no one. None of us does. That's what's so beautiful about love, and so painful. We *choose* to surrender our hearts and bodies to one another. Because we feel it so deeply

191

that it's just...right. I would lay down my life for Valira a thousand times, because I love her—and if I can only have a few fleeting moments with her until the end of my days, I will have to be satisfied with that. She gives me something she could never give Tallin. Above all else, I know what it is to be loved by her and how fragile that love is."

I glance around, realizing all of a sudden that we're engaged in a conversation we probably shouldn't be having.

"Don't worry," Archyr says. "No one is listening to us. The king is paranoid that if he's recorded, it'll be used against him—so he doesn't allow devices in his private chambers. Plus..." he adds, holding up his arm to reveal a wrist piece like I've recently seen Valira wearing. "A Blocker," he says. "Handy things, these."

"I thought devices like those were illegal—but it seems they're all the rage around here."

"Oh, they're illegal," Archyr laughs. "Then again, so is a Tethered prince fucking a member of the Royal Guard. The laws of Kravan don't exactly apply between the palace's walls, in case you hadn't noticed."

"Except when it comes to keeping us from the people we love," I retort bitterly, my eyes locking once again on the hedge maze's entrance. I wonder if Thorne is cursing our fate as much as I am right now. "I would give anything for a different world," I say softly, wishing he would reappear. "One where we all had an equal chance at happiness."

"They say there are many realms in this world. Realms where Tethered flourish—where we're not only accepted, but free to love, to rule, to be ourselves." Archyr combs a hand through his reddish hair and, snickering, says, "Can you imagine that? I mean, how unlucky were we to have been born in the Tower instead of in one of those far-off lands? Yet we live in Kravan, where a few men and women claim ownership of us simply because they believe it to be their right. What would happen if they were brought to their knees, I wonder? What if they learned we aren't as submissive as they think?"

"I don't know," I reply, leaning toward him and whispering, "but I intend to find out."

He raises an eyebrow, frowning. "Many have tried over the years, you know. They say that in the Capitol, there's an entire movement—a whole army of Tethered, just waiting to wage war."

"So why don't they?"

Archyr chuckles. "You've *seen* the Capitol—right?"

"Yeah, from a distance. It's a mess."

"It's a mess by design. It's a mess because it gets bombed by drones on a regular basis. The more havoc the bombs wreak, the harder it is for anyone to live a productive life. Every single person in the Capitol spends the bulk of their energy rebuilding, over and over again. It's futile. It's appalling." He glances over his shoulder toward the dining room and adds, "But I will say, the king knows exactly what he's doing."

"You really think it's King Tomas who's orchestrating the chaos? He doesn't really seem..."

I'm about to say he doesn't seem like the sort of man who would do something like that. He's been kind to me, and understanding. Then again, he welcomes the Crimson Championship to his home each year and watches Tethered tear each other apart.

The truth is, I have no idea what sort of man he really is.

Archyr scoffs. "It's no secret. Everyone knows it's his doing. It's pretty smart, actually. If you want to make your enemies weak, distract them with their own desperate need for survival. If they're struggling to put food on the table, they won't notice there's a monster lurking in the shadows, waiting to devour them."

At that image, I shudder.

"I hope you get to see Thorne tonight," Archyr says, changing the subject abruptly. "Valira told me yesterday that she plans to keep Prince Not-So-Charming occupied while you have a moment to yourselves."

I'm about to respond with an apology when he holds up a hand and shakes his head. "It's all right. It hurts like hell to know she's with him when I want her so badly, but I'm not being eaten away by jealousy, believe it or not. If her sacrifice can help you and Thorne spend some time together, I'm all for it. At least she's surrendering pieces of her soul for a good cause. Besides, she owes you for saving her life."

"She told you about that?"

Archyr nods. "And before you ask, I don't know who attacked her—but there's no question in my mind that she's protecting someone."

"Three guesses as to which someone that might be," I reply with a roll of my eyes.

"I wouldn't dare accuse the bastard. I'm just grateful she's okay. And I'm glad she can help you and Thorne out."

"It's just that I've had so little time with him. We need a chance to talk. To...well..."

"I think the word you're hunting for is *fuck*," Archyr snickers.

"I was going to say 'to plan,' actually," I reply with a half-smile.

"There's nothing to stop you from planning while fucking," he shrugs. "I suspect it's a lot more fun that way."

"You're irredeemable."

"You love it."

A laugh explodes from my throat. "I hate to admit it, but I knew the first moment I met you that I'd like you, even though you *were* a total dick."

"Why, thank you. I'll take that as the highest compliment."

"You should."

We both go silent for a minute, then I say, "Archyr—you really don't want to say who you think attacked Valira the other night?"

A look of quiet rage passes over his face, then he shakes his head. "I have a theory, but it's nothing I have any power to act on. Still, if ever I'm proven right, I can't be held accountable for my actions. I'll kill the bastard myself, I swear."

I'll kill the bastard.

It sure as hell sounds to me like he's talking about Tallin.

I push myself to my feet, looking out toward the gardens one last time. "I think I'm going to go rest for a little. Something tells me it's going to be a long one."

"That's what she said."

"Behave yourself, Guard," I groan, then turn to head inside. But before I've taken a step, I add, "I really hope you and Valira get your happy ending one day."

"Thank you, Shara," he replies. "So do I."

CHAPTER
TWENTY-NINE

INSTEAD OF HEADING to my quarters, I decide to go for a stroll in the palace gardens.

The likelihood of finding Thorne in the hedge maze is close to zero. Chances are that the only reason he stepped into the maze's depths earlier was to convey a silent message to me—a reminder of what transpired between us under the stars the other night.

Still, I can't help but feel hopeful with each step I take. The thought of finding him alone, if only for a few minutes, makes my heart race. The palpable memory of his lips crashing against mine, his powerful hands taking hold of my waist...It's enough to propel me effortlessly forward.

I'm sorely tempted to start sprinting when I see two familiar figures emerging from the maze—neither of whom is Thorne.

To my shock, one of them is Lady Graystone, and the other is King Tomas.

My heart is still racing, but now it's for another reason entirely.

"What's she doing here?" I murmur. "And with *him*, of all people?"

~*Visiting, I imagine,* Maude replies. *She's a Noble, after all.*

"But it's so risky. What if he figures out what she is?"

~*Shara, if the king hasn't figured it out by now, he's not going to. Besides, his body language tells me he's quite at ease with her. I'd guess their relationship is quite an...intimate one.*

She's right. The king looks completely relaxed.

Too relaxed.

His hand is on Lady Graystone's back, a broad smile on his lips, and as I watch them move out of the maze, he leans in and kisses her on the cheek.

Lady Graystone lets out a laugh that sounds like wind chimes. She says goodbye, then strides directly over to me, giving the king a final wave of her golden hand as he makes his way toward the palace's doors.

I guess I'm not going on a Thorne-hunt after all.

"Lady Ingram," Lady Graystone says as she nears me. "How lovely to see you."

"And you," I say, glancing around to see if anyone is watching us. "Do—do you and the king meet often?"

I realize as I ask the question that it almost sounds like an accusation, but I let it lie.

"Not as often as I'd like," she says, taking me by the arm. "Lady Verdan isn't exactly fond of me, as you can probably imagine. Come—let's go for a wander in the maze, shall we?"

It's an offer I can't possibly refuse.

The best-case scenario is that we run into Thorne. The worst-case is that I get to spend some time deciphering the enigma that is this woman.

"Will you be at the cocktail party this evening?" she asks. "Doing your usual reconnaissance work?"

I debate internally for a moment before asking, "How exactly do you know about that?"

"I know many things. Let's just say I'm well connected. But don't worry—your secret is safe with me."

I let out a nervous laugh. My secret seems to pale in comparison to her own. I, at least, am under the king's protection. "I've barely done any reconnaissance," I tell her. "And what I have done wasn't exactly thorough, was it?"

"I'm not sure what you're getting at, my dear."

I stop walking and turn to face her, staring into her swirling eyes. "Aren't you worried that the king will figure out what you are? His sole mission in life right now is to find Tethered hiding among the Nobility."

With a shrug of her shoulders, she says, "Not really, no. Still, I appreciate you keeping our secret—Ellion's and mine. I know what you've risked for me, and I won't soon forget it. Your loyalty to your own kind is admirable."

As we begin walking again, I reply, "I didn't want anything to happen to you. It didn't seem fair. Besides, I was tasked with finding one Tethered at the dinner party, not three."

"Well, then. I suppose we all lucked out that evening."

Yes, I think. *I just hope Lord Malloy sees it that way.*

"Tell me," Lady Graystone adds, "What happens when all of this is over? When your mission is accomplished, and the king no longer has any use for you?"

"I suppose I'll go back to being a servant for some Noble or other." I utter the words confidently, though I know full well that such a simple fate is unlikely at best.

"Oh, come on, Lady Ingram," she laughs, squeezing my arm as we come to a bend in the maze. "It's me you're talking to. I know what you are—you don't need to sugarcoat the truth."

"The truth is, I don't know what will happen to me. The

king has been kind to me, so I suppose I'm hoping he'll show mercy."

"Oh, I suspect he will. He's fond of you, and by extension, your handsome lover."

At that, my cheeks heat.

"As long as Thorne remains safe, I'll be happy," I say.

"Ah, but wouldn't you prefer if you could continue to pose as a Noble? Wouldn't it be better if you and Thorne could simply exist in our world, alongside people like Ellion and me?"

Our world.

She speaks the words effortlessly, as if she's so assimilated into the society of Nobles that it doesn't even occur to her that she belongs here as little as I do.

"The prince would always be suspicious of us," I protest. "And to be honest, I'd rather *change* the world so that everyone —wealthy, poor, Tethered, Normal—could live on equal footing."

Lady Graystone lets out another laugh, and I'm beginning to wonder if her jovial nature is all for show. "You're so lovely, aren't you? Oh, to be young and idealistic again. The world, in your eyes, has so much potential. You know, I envy you, Lady Ingram. I really do. I was once like you. I thought I could run away and start a new life—one in which I was respected and treated like a human. A life free from threat."

"You did," I tell her. "Isn't that what this is? The life of a Noble who gets invited to the palace for afternoon walks with the king himself? It sounds to me like running away paid off for you."

I curate my words carefully. I'm not even remotely convinced that what Lady Graystone and the king did in the maze was just a walk.

In fact, I'm starting to think there's a reason Tallin seems to dislike her intensely.

"Since we're telling the truth, I may as well confess that running away nearly cost me my life." She holds up her prosthetic hand. "When I lost this arm, I nearly bled out. Yet it was the only way to free myself. My enemies would have tracked me —and killed me. It was a kindly surgeon in the Capitol who removed it."

"You told me you lost it in a crash," I reply.

"Ah, but that was in front of Nobles. I know perfectly well that you've figured out the truth of it—that I lost my arm to free myself. And believe me when I tell you I had to summon a good deal of cash in exchange for the privilege of parting with my limb. But in the end, it was worth every conjured penny."

"How long were you in the Capitol?"

"A few months. It was a difficult, brutal experience."

"Because you were being hunted?"

She glances sideways, a smile ticking up her lips, and says, "In a manner of speaking, yes. There were some who wanted to destroy me for what I was—and you would be amazed at how cruel people can be. But I managed to evade the worst of them. I met a Noble couple who were there on business, and they agreed to take me in, to adopt me as their own daughter. I was young, you see. Still in my teens—and I was pregnant by then, with Ellion."

My eyes widen with shock.

"Oh, don't look so stunned," Lady Graystone says. "It's not like you haven't had sex, is it?"

"I suppose not," I confess. "But fortunately, I haven't gotten pregnant. There are fertility suppressors in our implants. Did your pregnancy happen after—"

I gesture to her arm.

"After it was removed?" she asks. "Yes, now that I think of it. Still, fertility suppressors fail on occasion, like everything else in this world."

I'm tempted to ask who Ellion's father is, but it's none of my business. I can only assume he was some young man in the Capitol—someone giving comfort to an escaped Tethered.

"They don't talk about the suppressors much," I say softly. Perhaps in Lady Graystone's time, they didn't talk about them at all. "They don't like to encourage Tethered to think about sex or pregnancy, except to treat both like the worst sorts of felonies."

"For the record," Lady Graystone says with a smile, "My pregnancy was the furthest thing from a felony. Ellion is an absolute blessing, and I'm very fortunate."

"Oh—I didn't mean to say you weren't. I just meant that if I were in this situation and pregnant, well—it wouldn't be good."

"No, I suppose not. It would cause quite the stir if Prince Tallin's lovely fiancée showed up to social functions with a baby bump."

I have no desire whatsoever to continue discussing this particular topic, so I veer off course and say, "Tell me something—when you were in the Capitol, did you ever hear of a man called the Hunter, or...the *Shadow*?"

Lady Graystone stops in her tracks, her spine stiffening.

"I'm sorry," I stammer. "Did I say something wrong?"

"I know of the Shadow," she replies, a chill in her voice. "He is a cruel man. One of the worst I've ever encountered."

My heart sinks. "You've met him?"

She nods. "They say he's the most powerful Tethered in the Capitol, and I believe it. There was a time when he used his power for good—to protect others of our kind. But now, it's said that he's gathering an army to his side to take on anyone who doesn't believe in his cause. His people kill with impunity. Violent bodyguards surround him at all times. He lords over the Capitol like a wolf, watching, waiting, and assessing. Anyone who's deemed a threat dies. It doesn't matter whether they're Tethered or Normal."

"You said he's gathering an army. What does he intend to do with it?"

Lady Graystone looks deep into my eyes when she says, "He intends to sow chaos, my dear. Some say his followers are the ones who wreak havoc on the Capitol, setting fires and destroying lives. He forces ruin on the population, then demands they pay him in return for protection. He's essentially a mob boss, using powerful, amoral Tethered rebels to do his dirty work for him."

I'm tempted to point out that her words are in direct contradiction with Archyr's, but I think better of it. Given that she seems close with the king, it would be foolish to point out he's allegedly behind the Capitol bombings.

"If you find yourself tempted to learn more about the Shadow, Lady Ingram, or rather, *Shara*...Don't. Whoever he is to you, he's not worth it."

There was a moment earlier when I was on the verge of telling her the Shadow is my father. That my mother lives the life of a Domestic, serving in the Prefect's house.

But now, I don't know *what* to say.

"Do you think there's an actual chance the Shadow and his people will rise up against the Nobility?" I finally ask.

Her voice is cold now. "There's a chance. But if they do, they will die. The king has the best Crimson Elites in the land serving him, and they are beyond loyal. The best of the best are sent to the palace—and the second best end up serving powerful Noble families. The only Tethered in the Capitol are the ones who slipped through the cracks or managed to fly under the radar. They're untrained, unmanageable, and an absolute mess."

"You've seen them, then?"

"I've seen their handiwork," she says with a wince. "Let's just say there's a reason I didn't choose to raise Ellion in that city. It's an ugly, brutal place—and if you want to know why, look no further than those who live there. I may not support locking our kind up for years, but sometimes, I admit, I think it's a wise and cautious move."

She's contradicting what she said at the Prefect's dinner, when she insisted that it was wrong to incarcerate our kind—to deprive us of love, of life.

Was she simply lying that night?

Is she lying *now?*

I've heard so many conflicting reports about the Capitol that I don't know what to think anymore.

Still, Lady Graystone is the first person I've met who has actually lived there, and she has no reason to lie to me. Her word must mean *something.*

"Lady Ingram," she says, squeezing my arm once again and turning me back toward the maze's exit. "I'm afraid I must head home to prepare for the cocktail party. But I have one little piece of advice to impart to you before I say goodbye."

"Oh? What's that?" I ask, my mind more muddled than ever.

She turns to me, takes my face in her hands, and smiles. "Do yourself a favor, and stop asking questions. Don't go digging so deep that you end up in hell."

AT FIVE O'CLOCK, I slip into the little black dress Tallin selected for me. It's sleeveless, fitted, stretchy, and cut just above the knee. With it is a pair of shoes with heels so high that I feel like a giant when I slip them on.

I don't hate the outfit by any means, but when I study myself in the mirror, knowing the prince chose it for me, my first instinct is to gag.

It's clear by now that Tallin is trying to present me to Kravan's society as nothing more than his dress-up doll. A pretty, mindless creature who has nothing to offer the world but her body, which he insists on putting on full display.

I suppose I should be grateful that he doesn't expect me to actually befriend Nobles or engage in witty conversation with them. All he's ever asked of me—other than pretending I actually get aroused in his company—is to look them in the eye and determine whether or not they're frauds.

While Maude helps me apply my makeup, I remind myself with a jolt of excitement that there's a possibility that I'll see Thorne in an hour or so.

Think of him, I tell myself. *Not the prince.*

"Maude, do you have a guest list for this cocktail party?" I ask while she takes control of my hands, twisting my hair into an elegant style that she insists is "in vogue" at the moment.

~I don't, but I can probably access one, she tells me. *Is there a particular guest you'd like to know about?*

"Yes. Ellion Graystone. Will he be there?"

She goes silent for a few seconds, then says, *~Apparently, he will be in attendance.*

"Good."

I still don't know exactly what it is that Thorne saw in his mind's eye that led him to believe the Graystones will be important to us. But there's something about them that I want—no, *need*—to figure out, especially after my strange conversation with Ellion's mother today.

I can't help but like Lady Graystone. She's warm, inviting, and friendly—for the most part. But after this morning, I find her more puzzling than ever.

She seemed genuinely bitter when she spoke of the Capitol —particularly where my father is concerned. She's far more comfortable in the presence of Nobles than rebels.

Then again, it's hard to blame her for that.

Being thrust from life in the Tower into the middle of a warring city would be difficult, to say the least.

Perhaps she was telling the truth. Maybe my father, the man they call the Shadow, really *is* cruel and vicious.

Maybe I'll be better off if I never meet him.

The trouble is, he's the only one who knows anything about my sister.

SHORTLY BEFORE SIX, after slipping the platinum bands onto my wrists and tucking Mercutio into a beaded ivory clutch, I navigate the palace's multitude of labyrinthine hallways until I reach the main entrance, where a Flyer awaits.

Thorne is standing in uniform just outside the vehicle, and he nods a surreptitious greeting when our eyes meet.

"Are you doing okay?" I ask, striding quickly toward him, stopping a mere few inches away.

"Better now than I have been in some time," he says with a hint of a smile, his hand brushing against my own. Unspoken words pass between us, the sensation of his touch enough to make me want to risk any punishment Tallin might throw our way.

I can't fucking stand being apart from you, he tells me, his voice as clear in my mind as if he spoke the words out loud.

And I can't stand spending every waking hour wishing for you.

I'm about to step even closer, my desire to kiss him overwhelming, when I hear a man clearing his throat.

I don't need to turn around to know Tallin is standing a few feet away, watching us like a vulture assessing the carrion he's about to tear to shreds.

When I pivot toward him, I see that Valira is by his side dressed in her uniform, her expression blank.

"I'm so very sorry," Tallin says loudly, eyeing Thorne and then me. "Have we interrupted a beautiful moment of intimacy?"

"No intimacy, your Highness," I hasten to reply as Thorne tenses. "I was just asking how our Guard is doing."

Tallin lets out a snort, then begins moving toward the Flyer. He stumbles, listing to one side as Valira grabs his arm, stabilizing him.

Thorne and I exchange another furtive look. There's no doubt we're thinking the same thing:

The prince is shit-faced.

Tallin's words are slurred, but more than that, he looks like he's about to double over and release any half-digested food in his belly.

"Valira will sit in the back with me," he announces with some effort. "Lady Ingram, I'm afraid you'll have to shit—I mean *sit*—in the front."

I stare at him, stunned. Is this an act of benevolence or self-ishness? Is Tallin so horny that he insists on manhandling Valira—or has she somehow convinced him to let Thorne and me sit together for the duration of the ride?

Either way, I can't deny my gratitude.

Without a word, I slip into the passenger's seat while Thorne ensures Tallin and Valira are sealed into the back. When we're all inside, Thorne sets the engine purring and makes quick work of the Flyer's takeoff.

"Don't get any foolish ideas," Tallin warns, leaning forward. "I don't want you two licking one another's tonsils while we're airborne."

"Of course not, your Highness," Thorne says. His hostility is subtle enough that Tallin doesn't seem to notice it—but I can feel the pulsing desire stewing inside him to throw the prince out the window.

We haven't flown more than five minutes when I hear movement in the back seat. I glance over my shoulder to see that Tallin is pulling Valira's uniform open, his lips slipping over her neck.

She throws me a "Don't watch" warning look before taking him gently by the arm. I turn back to face the windshield and hear her say, "Soon, Highness—we'll find a quiet corner of the Nelson residence tonight—I promise."

"Fine," Tallin sighs, pulling away from her, and once again, I'm filled with gratitude for Valira's sacrifice. *She's planning to come through on her promise to distract the bastard while I spend time with Thorne.*

"Did you know, Shara," Tallin says, his voice lilting like off-kilter music, "that Lord Nelson despises me?"

"Surely not," I reply, glancing sideways at Thorne, whose narrowed eyes are fixed on the distant horizon.

"Oh, yes," Tallin laughs. "He wants me dead. He's tried to get the Prefect to assign him Tethered servants with violent powers, just for evenings like this one when he might have a chance to end me. But my father—*dear old Dad*—has seen to it that Nelson only receives useless Greens or other Harmless Tethered. Then again, perhaps I should let one of his Greens kill me. Maybe I *deserve* to die."

"Highness," Valira says gently. "Come on, now. You know you don't mean that."

"I've done terrible things, my darling," he laments, and I genuinely can't tell whether he's being ironic or sincere. "You know I have."

"Maybe you need some strong coffee," I tell Tallin, twisting around in my seat again. "Something to perk up your mood."

"Coffee won't fix me. There is a war raging, Shara. Haven't you seen the signs?"

Sure I have. It's why he's forcing me to hunt down Tethered, isn't it?

"Not really," I lie through my teeth. "You and your father must be doing a good job of keeping it in check."

Tallin laughs. "My father. Yes, what a peacekeeper *he* is."

"Highness," Valira says again, and this time, Tallin shuts his mouth and leans on her shoulder, closing his eyes.

I take advantage of the moment to turn to face forward and ease my hand slowly toward Thorne's. When my fingers land on his skin, I feel it—the energy, the power that twists and braids between us like a binding flame when our bodies touch. It's almost too much to bear, but when I move to draw my hand away, he takes it protectively in his, engulfing it so completely that I gasp with the pleasure of it.

I crave you.

At first, I'm convinced he said the words out loud, but when I look over, his lips are sealed, his eyes intent on the land unfurling below.

I crave you, too, I reply silently, hoping the words reach him.

It seems they do, because the tiniest flicker of a grin pulls his lips upward.

When we hear Tallin stirring in the back seat again, Thorne releases my hand. I pull it into my lap and force myself to stare out the window.

Thorne's voice resonates through my mind one more time. *If I don't get to be with you again soon, I might just have to kill the drunk bastard in the back seat. They can imprison me for the rest of my days, but if I get to spend one night with you first...it will be worth it.*

THIRTY-ONE

FROM THE AIR, Lord and Lady Nelson's house looks even larger than the Prefect's substantial residence.

I don't know anything about our hosts other than what Tallin has said, but I can't help but snicker to think we're about to cross the threshold into the home of a man who despises the prince—possibly as much as I do.

As we circle around for a landing, I study the properties to the west and east of the Nelsons'. Each is equally impressive, forbidding, and surrounded on all sides by the typical high walls that separate members of the Nobility from one another.

When I spot an outbuilding on the periphery of the Nelson grounds, a hint of hope blooms in my chest. I glance at Thorne, wondering if he, too, has seen it, and the curl of his lips tells me he's thinking what I'm thinking.

We'll sneak over there after dark.

Then again, given Tallin's current state, we may not have to wait too long. The prince is still leaning against Valira, mumbling nonsensical words to himself. He's in no state to sit up, let alone attend a social function.

I could heal him out of his stupor, I suppose.

But I won't.

"You all right?" I ask when he opens his eyes and peers hazily at me.

"Fine," he replies, though nothing in the contortion of his mouth fills me with confidence that he's speaking the truth.

"Highness, are you sure you don't want to return to the palace?" Valira asks, cupping his cheek with her hand.

There's something so intimate in that gesture, so kind and sympathetic, that I find myself puzzled and admiring at once. As much as I know Valira loves Archyr, there is a soft spot in her heart for the cruel, vile prince that I will never understand.

"No!" Tallin snaps, sitting bolt upright, his eyes seeming to focus suddenly. He slaps himself across the face with a violence that startles me, and I turn back in my seat to face forward, avoiding any and all contact.

As unhinged as Tallin can be, I've never seen him as erratic as this. I can only hope he doesn't wreak havoc on the party.

When Thorne has landed the Flyer and we've made our way inside the Nelson residence, a cold, eerie feeling settles under my skin.

For all its impressive attributes, the house is dark on the inside and a little dreary, with beige walls and artwork to match. The Nelsons, it seems, aren't keen on showing off their wealth as the Royals do. The place looks like it was thrown together by an incredibly dull person with no appreciation of beautiful things.

Our hostess strides toward us when a housemaid has guided our small group into the foyer. There's a tight smile on Lady Nelson's lips, but when her eyes land on Tallin, it straightens into a grimace.

"Your Highness," she says. "How lovely to see you."

"And you, Lady Nelson," he replies with a bow of his head.

Somehow, he's managing to sound relatively normal. Maybe the slap across his face was all he needed.

If only he'd asked me to administer it, I would have been more than happy to oblige.

He gestures to me when he adds, "This is Lady Ingram, my fiancée."

With those words, my mind jolts to life. I'd almost forgotten I was still wearing the diamond ring on my left hand, and that I came here to play a role.

"The other guests are out in the garden," Lady Nelson says, nodding to me without offering up an actual greeting. I'm beginning to see why Tallin doesn't feel welcome here. "We'll stay out there until dusk when the insects come out, then make our way into the Great Room."

"Thank you," Tallin replies, staggering toward the back of the mansion as though he knows exactly where he's going. I follow him, with Thorne and Valira behind me.

When we step into the back garden, I see that forty or so guests have already gathered under a broad white tent, dressed in elegant, expensive-looking outfits suitable for such an occasion. Most of the women are wearing knee-length dresses like mine, drinks in their well-manicured hands. As with the impractical black leather pumps Tallin provided for me, their high-heeled shoes sink into the soft grass.

I find myself envying the men, who are more sensibly dressed in trousers and button-down shirts of linen or cotton.

A few Guards from various homes linger here and there, watching over their Proprietors as though expecting a brawl to break out.

"A few warring Houses are represented here," Tallin murmurs, pulling close to me as if he's read my expression. "Men and women who would happily see my father dethroned, and me dead. They don't trust me any more than I trust them—

bunch of jackals. The only way we can win this war is to elimi-
nate the most dangerous of our enemies. So get to work, Lady
Ingram."

When a middle-aged man strolls over to say hello, Tallin
pulls away from me and shakes his hand, smiling from ear to
ear as if he hasn't just confessed that he despises everyone here.

He introduces me to the man, whom he simply calls
"Prescott." After a minute of surface-level conversation, I
excuse myself, telling the prince I want to take a look at the
grounds. He nods his assent, glancing over at Thorne and
signaling that he's to stay put.

"Damn it," I mutter. Not that I expected to be able to sneak
off with him just yet—but I would have liked to keep him close
by, at least.

~A suggestion for you, Maude says. *Perhaps you should wander
through the house rather than the grounds. There will be plenty of
time for that later.*

Why do I get the impression you're up to something? I ask her
silently.

~Because I am. Just don't ask what it is.

I hate when she plays coy with me. But if I know one thing
about Maude, it's that there's always a reason for her behavior.
As much as she pisses me off on occasion, she has never yet led
me astray.

Then again, there's a first time for everything.

I'm already on edge as I make my way back into the house,
some sort of sweet pink beverage in hand.

*This isn't where the Histories are kept. So what, exactly, are we
doing?* I ask Maude as I peer down the beige hallway.

~Trust me—there's something even more interesting here.

You're going to keep me in suspense until we find it, aren't you?

~But of course.

I make my way down the long hallway, passing an enormous chamber to the right that must be the Great Room. Servants are already in the process of preparing for the point later in the evening when the guests flood inside. Long tables are laid with champagne flutes and cocktail glasses, as well as hors d'oeuvres and plates, napkins, and décor.

The servants ignore me for the most part, though one or two glance up and study me for a few seconds before realizing they're being rude and pulling their eyes away. They're curious about the prince's future wife—their future queen—as ridiculous as the thought of it is.

I want to shout, "I will never marry that bastard! Stop looking at me!" but it would take several more alcoholic drinks before I could muster the courage to even consider it.

~*Maybe later,* Maude says, reading my desire.

I wasn't actually *going to do it, Maude.*

~*That's what everyone says before they lose their inhibitions.*

Come on, now. When have you ever known me to lose control?

~*Do you really want a list? All right. When you sprayed yourself with Lady Verdan's perfume. When you read her diary, against my advice. Then at the ball, when you screamed Ilias's name. Afterwards, when you leapt into bed with—*

Okay. Enough. You've made your point.

When I've nearly explored the entirety of the house's main floor, I'm about to curse Maude for steering me inside when a voice hisses my name.

My *real* name.

"Shara?"

I spin around to see a young woman in a Guard's uniform, a violet crest on the left side of her chest.

"Oh, my God," I breathe when my eyes land on those of my oldest friend. *"Nev!"*

CHAPTER
THIRTY-TWO

I HAVEN'T SEEN Nev since our last day in the Tower.

The day I was flown to the Verdan home for the first time, and my life changed in unfathomable ways.

I open my mouth to warn my old friend not to call me by my real name. But it seems Nev's Maude unit is one step ahead of me, because she winces in obvious pain then lets out a sharp curse.

"Noted, Maude," she says. "Jeez, you don't have to be such a cruel mistress, you know."

She looks into my eyes, offers up a little bow, and says, "Lady Ingram, is it? Welcome to the Nelson home."

"I...thank you," I reply. *Maude—can you do something about her A.I.?*

~Done. I've temporarily scrambled her unit. You have a few minutes before it comes back online.

I grab Nev by the wrist, pulling her into the room she just came out of, which appears to be a large office. After I've closed the door behind me, I turn to face her.

"What the fuck are you doing here, dressed like one of them?" she whisper-hisses. "I feel like someone spiked my drink with hallucinogens—except I haven't even *had* a damned drink."

"Where do I start?" I say, my heart racing with the shock that hasn't yet abated. "I have so much to tell you, Nev. About my Proprietor, Lady Verdan...Thorne...I don't even know where to start."

"Wait—" Nev sputters. "Did you say Thorne? As in *the* Thorne? Sir Hottiecakes, king of fuckable men? The one dude in the world that I would switch sides for?"

My brows meet when I chastise, "Nev."

"Sorry—but I totally would."

"He's my..." I'm about to explain to her that Thorne and I are in love when a more pressing concern drives its way to the forefront of my mind. "It doesn't matter. Look—what do you know about the Crimson Championship?"

Her shoulder shrugs upward. "I know it's a competition every year at the palace. I've heard it's cut-throat, literally. I guess it turns out Ore trained us to be psychotic killers for a reason."

You don't know the half of it, I think.

"Did you..." My eyes move to the floor, courage deserting me. I clear my throat, then manage, "Have you heard about Ilias?"

"I have an acquaintance who works at the palace. Someone I've run into on my errands. I asked about Ilias a while back— I'd heard he'd made Royal Guard, if that's what you mean."

"He did," I tell her, my heart sinking. I can see in her eyes that she doesn't know what happened the night of the Prince's Ball. "Nev," I say, taking her by the hand. "He's dead."

"Dead..." She steps backwards, pushing herself away from me. Tears well in her eyes when she says, "No—he *can't* be."

I reach for her again, knowing I'm taking a risk spending so much time with her, let alone touching her.

"He was killed in the Crimson Championship. I was there. I saw everything. He was always loyal to the Nobility, and he paid for it with his life."

"Oh, God. Poor Ilias. That was his dream," she says, then swallows and collects herself, shaking her head as if dislodging the horror of it. "Members of the Royal Guard die all the time. I guess I shouldn't be surprised. It's just..."

She's trying to appear stoic, but I know Nev. This is only temporary—a mask she's putting on to cover up the conflagration of emotion that's searing her insides.

Later, when she's alone, she'll allow herself to process the loss of our oldest friend.

"Ilias's dream is a nightmare for many, it turns out," I tell her. "The Royal Guard are treated like fighting dogs—and a lot of Crimson Elites from other Noble houses end up dying in the Championship, too."

"Meanwhile, you're wearing the garb of a Noble," she reminds me. "You hardly look like you're living a nightmare. You still haven't told me what the hell is going on."

She speaks the words without malice, but I can feel the anger simmering inside her, as if I've betrayed everything I used to be.

"I'll tell you," I say. "But you may not believe it."

I spend the next few minutes explaining everything that's happened. Finding Lady Verdan's diary, thinking it belonged to Devorah. My love-hate-love relationship with Thorne. My deal with the prince and the king to keep me free of the dungeon so long as I cooperate.

And, last of all, I tell her about my powers.

"A Gilded Elite," Nev breathes when I reveal the truth. "Who knew you were one of the most powerful of all of us? We all watched you get your ass handed to you a hundred times, at least."

K. A. RILEY

"All thanks to Maude," I chuckle. "Not that I was ever much of a fighter. Still, she helped create the illusion that I'm totally useless, so I guess I owe her my thanks."

"Who the hell programmed her?" Nev asks. "Maude units aren't supposed to betray the Prefecture like that."

"I...have my suspicions," I say, not wanting to tell her everything I've learned about my parents. "But I'm not convinced it matters anymore. Once the prince is done using me, I'm sure he plans to kill me and Thorne. Unless..."

Something occurs to me then, and apparently Nev can tell, because she shakes her head and says, "Oh, shit. What's going on in that terrible mind of yours?"

I take her by the hand and squeeze. "We need your help. I have to get into the vault at the Perrin home during the ball next Friday. Do you know the place?"

"I've been there once, with my Proprietors when they were there for an overnight and needed extra security. But I'm not exactly invited, Shara—I mean, Lady Ingram."

"It doesn't matter. You can port there, right?"

Nev considers this. "I don't usually use my powers for anything more than getting to the shops," she says. "But I suppose I could meet you at the back of the property, if we arrange a time. I should point out that this is a horrible idea, and we'll probably all end up dead."

"Trust me—we're dead if we don't do this."

"Um, no," Nev chuckles. "According to my calculations, *you're* dead. I'll be just fine, living here in my sad beige wonderland, minding my own damned business."

"Please," I say. "For all the Tethered in Kravan—just do this one thing."

"Of course I'll do it, you doofus."

I clap my hands together—probably too loudly—and say, "Good. Let's say we'll meet at the servants' entrance at ten

218

p.m. By then, half the guests should be drunk out of their skulls."

"What's this about, anyhow?" Nev asks. "Why the hell would you want to get into some vault? Seriously, if we get caught..."

"I need to see the Histories," I interrupt.

"The Histories? Wait—do you mean..."

I nod. "The account of Kravan before the Rebellion. I need to know what this realm was like back then. The Nobility is going to great lengths to hide the truth—and I believe that truth will be the key to freeing the Tethered."

"Holy shit," Nev says, shaking her head. "But I can't possibly help you with that. It would be insane, Shar. Even if we managed to get into the vault, laying our eyes on the Histories is a crime punishable by death."

"I know," I tell her as a sound outside the room draws my eyes briefly to the door. "But if I can record the information, I can bring it to the Capitol, to the rebels there. I can use it to unite them and inspire another uprising."

"There won't be any uprising," Nev hisses, her eyes darting to the door. She can hear the same thing I do—hard footsteps moving quickly toward us. "Look—forget it. Just find a way to escape. Get yourself somewhere safe and far from here, and live a happy life. I've heard there are other realms out there, Shar— lands where things aren't so bad as here. There must be a way to—"

Before she can finish, the door flies open. Nev and I move quickly apart, looks of terror in our eyes.

But it's not Tallin or one of Lord Nelson's servants who's come.

It's Thorne.

I stare at him, my pulse racing.

"The prince has noticed your absence, Lady Ingram," he

says, his tone frosty until he lays eyes on Nev and recognizes her.

He steps into the room, closing the door behind him. "I'm so sorry—but I have to take her from you."

"It's okay," Nev says, fixing her eyes on me. She takes my hands in hers and adds, "Look—I'll come next Friday. I promise. But I can't promise I can get us inside the..." She peers at Thorne, then whispers, "*Vault.*"

"If you're willing to try, it's all I can ask."

"Of course I'll try. But for the record, you two are insane. You know that, right?"

"I'm not sure there's a sane person in all of Kravan," Thorne says. "Now, Shara needs to come with me, or there will be hell to pay."

I throw my arms around Nev, hugging her for the first time since we were small.

A moment later, I follow Thorne out into the hall.

"In a couple of hours, we can be together for a little," he says under his breath as I accompany him. "Valira told me she has plans for the prince."

I nod. "Once she's taken him away, I'll slip out to the back of the property. You and I need to talk about our plans for the night of the ball."

"Talking is fine," he agrees with a sly smile. "But I need to do more than just speak to you, Shara. I'm going to lose my mind if I can't..."

He stops short when Tallin appears, striding toward us.

"Where the hell have you two been?" he snarls, murder in his eyes.

"I was just...exploring the house," I reply. "Thorne came to get me, to bring me to you."

Tallin looks as if he's about to accuse me of lying when his expression softens, as if he's just done the calculus and realized Thorne was by his side until a couple of minutes ago.

"Fine," he says. "But Lady Ingram, you have some mingling to do and some Nobles to assess."

"Yes, your Highness," I say, bowing my head slightly when a servant wanders by.

As Tallin snatches me by the arm to drag me back outside, I shoot Thorne one final look over my shoulder.

Soon, I mouth silently. And with that, Maude buzzes a gentle warning in my arm.

~Be careful, she says. *Something tells me there's trouble brewing.*

CHAPTER
THIRTY-THREE

THE FIRST PERSON I spot when I've separated myself from Tallin is Lady Graystone, who's standing with her son, Ellion, and a couple I haven't met.

From several feet away, their conversation appears to be jovial and friendly enough, but when the two leave Ellion and Lady Graystone behind, they look pleased to be rid of them.

I watch as Ellion excuses himself and slips away from his mother to head toward a table at the far end of the massive white tent, where hors d'oeuvres and drinks are laid out.

Before I approach, I peer around to see that Tallin is currently occupied with another couple, Valira lurking close behind him. Thorne has positioned himself by the house's back entrance, and I can tell instantly that, like me, he's wishing we were anywhere but here.

When I'm sure it's safe to do so, I head over to Ellion, slipping up next to him to reach for a small cheese tart.

"Nice evening, isn't it?" I say.

"Nice enough," he replies coldly.

He begins to step away from me, but I stop him with a few quick words. "It must be difficult for you."

"What must?" he asks with a huff. When he turns to me, his irises swirl with color, and for the first time, I feel close to seeing his power—and I'm beginning to understand why it was so hard to decipher in the past.

If I'm assessing him correctly, he sees people's minds, their thoughts. Possibly even their emotions.

Yet, for some reason, he can't see *mine*...and I suspect it irks him.

It's probably why he dislikes me so intensely.

~Yes, Maude says. *Keep telling yourself that's why.*

Shut it.

"What I'm saying is that it must be hard to be here. Hiding in plain sight," I tell Ellion with a sigh, stepping closer to him. "Just as I am."

"Ah." He glances over my shoulder at another Noble as she grabs a plate of hors d'oeuvres, then heads back to her companion. "My mother told me you're a Hunter," Ellion says softly, the last word sliding from his lips with a dose of disdain. "Working for the Royals while you pose as Tallin's fiancée. Lucky you."

"Don't worry. I'm not going to tell them about you or your mother."

"Why not?"

"Two reasons. One, I haven't detected violence in you."

"And two?" he asks.

"I'd prefer to keep two to myself. Besides, if your power is as impressive as I suspect, shouldn't you be able to read my thoughts?"

"Even if I wanted to, I couldn't. A Hunter keeps their guard up—or so the old saying goes."

"I didn't realize there was an old saying about Hunters," I chuckle. "But if you read minds, aren't you a Hunter, too? Can't you tell who's a Tethered, and who's a Normal?"

"It doesn't work quite like that," he sneers, his eyes down-cast as if he'd prefer to avoid the question entirely.

"I see. Well...I'm intrigued by your skill, as well as the fact that your mother is a Conjurer."

"Yes," Ellion says with more enthusiasm. "Almost anything you can conceive of. Jewelry. Money. Food, water. She can call it all up with her mind."

"So, you two must be incredibly wealthy."

Ellion issues me a crooked smile in spite of himself. "We do all right."

I nod toward Lady Graystone, who's been accosted by a small group of women. "Her arm," I say, my eyes fixed on her prosthetic. "She lost it because she couldn't remove her implant herself, I assume?"

Ellion frowns. "Something like that."

"Do you know how she escaped the Tower?"

For a moment, he looks surprised by the question.

"I...don't know. We don't talk about those days. All I know is that she found her way to freedom and has lived the life of a Noble ever since."

"As have you," I observe. "And your father...?"

It's a bold question. But I can see that Ellion has had a few drinks, and this may be my best chance to extract information from him and figure out why it is that Thorne thinks he and his mother are potentially useful allies.

"My father is...absent," Ellion says. "Not that I mind. My mother and I enjoy our life of relative solitude. We have the good fortune of having been left in peace—at least, for the most part."

"I don't mean to disturb your peace," I say under my breath. "But maybe you could help me—in return for my keeping your secret."

"Why do I get the feeling I'm not going to like this?"

I shrug. "No idea. But I'd like to play a little game."

Ellion grinds his jaw for a moment. "To be honest, Lady Ingram, I'm not fond of games—except those where I get to set the rules. But if you're willing to keep your mouth shut to protect my mother and me, I suppose I'll go along with whatever game you have in mind."

"Good." I smile and turn to face the crowd of milling guests. "Tell me, then. Do you know if any of these Nobles are particularly hostile to the prince or the king?"

Ellion narrows his deep-set eyes at me. "This feels like a trap."

"Not a trap. I'm simply asking for your help. You may as well put those powers of yours to good use. If you can see into people's minds, maybe you can tell me what some of the guests think about the Royals."

"Fine." He looks around, his eyes moving from guest to guest.

"Lord and Lady Chaplin over there—they despise the king. They want him unseated, and a new king named—someone outside the line of succession."

I look over to the couple he's speaking of. I hadn't noticed them before now, but even from this distance, I spy the color swimming in Lady Chaplin's eyes—and then, deep in my mind like a distant memory, I see a Tethered Guard dead on the ground, his skin scorched a gruesome reddish-brown.

"A Conflag," I say, identifying her as a fire-starter—a power similar to Lady Verdan's.

"Really?" Ellion says, the slightest hint of admiration in his tone. "You can tell that from here?"

I nod. "Unfortunately for them, yes."

"And you're going to report them?"

"I haven't decided yet. But if I don't report someone today, the king will grow suspicious. Tell me—do you like the Chaplins? Are they decent people?"

"No. They're awful. Worse than the Royals, by far."

Those words surprise me. It's clear by now that neither Ellion nor his mother likes Tallin—though I wonder if it has anything to do with the fact that Lady Graystone seems to be carrying on a quiet, illicit relationship with the king.

God help her if Lady Verdan ever learns of it.

"Anyone else?" I ask. "Anyone you think is bad news for you or your mother, for instance?"

"Everyone at this fucking party is bad news for us," he sneers. "If any of them knew what we were, we'd both be dead."

Still, he names off a list of six or seven Nobles, most of whom turn out to be Normals. I make a mental note of the two Tethered among them.

As Ellion is about to leave, I say, "I've heard you and your mother might have a connection with the rebels."

It's a lie—sort of. Thorne only said he thought the Graystones would be useful to us—nothing specifically about rebels.

But if there's a chance they could help us get to the Capitol, I fully intend to take advantage of it.

"Where did you hear that?" Ellion asks, his voice taking on a nervous edge.

"Doesn't matter. Is it true?"

"There's a Tethered who moves between the palace and the Capitol undetected—a Stealther. My mother speaks to him on occasion to learn what's been going on."

Interesting, I think. *Maybe that's the real reason Lady Graystone was at the palace this morning.*

"And?" I ask. "What *is* going on?"

"Nothing you need to hear about." Ellion begins to walk away without another word, but I grab his arm.

"I could end you with a word to the prince," I say under my breath. "You know that."

With his eyes darkening, he turns to me. "What do you want to know? That the rebellion is in shambles? That the city's constant bombings mean half the rebels are dead and the others are blaming one another? That the Normals are hunting Tethered in the streets? Is that what you want to hear? Because *that's* what's happening, Lady Ingram."

I stare into his eyes, trying desperately to read him, to determine whether he's telling the truth. If only I could speak to Thorne, to ask him to look into the future again and tell me what it is that he sees.

Why are the Graystones important? What does he know that he's not telling me?

I swallow, afraid to summon the words lingering on the edge of my mind. "Is the man they call the Shadow still in the Capitol? Do you know if he's still alive?"

"I...don't know. But if you're smart, you won't mention him out loud again. That man is a curse—and the most dangerous Tethered Kravan has ever known...That is, until you came along."

"I'm not as dangerous as you think."

"No?" he asks. "You showed a good deal of interest in the Histories at the dinner party the other night. I'd say that makes you dangerous."

"I don't really care about any of that," I tell him a little too emphatically.

"Right. I'm sure you have no desire to learn the truth about Kravan's past—just as no one else does." His voice drips with sarcasm.

"What's that supposed to mean?"

"Come on. Surely you're not this dense," he hisses, then leans in closer and whispers, "The real reason Nobles have been

227

breaking into one another's houses for years is to try and gain knowledge—any snippet of the Histories they can get their hands on. There's a theory going around that the truth would dissolve the king's power and turn the entire system on its head —so you can understand why people *want* that knowledge. It's also the *real* reason the Histories aren't kept in the palace, where the king could easily destroy them."

"What do you think is in those texts, Ellion?"

He looks around, then lowers his chin and says, "Lies, I've heard. Plain and simple. Kravan will suffer a blow if they're ever uncovered. So I'm telling you now—don't do something stupid, Shara. If the king loses his throne, every Noble—Tethered or Normal—will be at risk. Don't you see? If another Rebellion occurs, *we* will be the first targets."

"If war breaks out, we could join the rebels," I tell him. "Fight on the right side of history. With your power and your mother's, you could both be incredible assets for the side striving for equality."

An expression comes over his face that I can't quite read. *"Equality,"* he says. "Why is everyone so hung up on that concept? We're not equal, and you know it as well as I do. Some people deserve to serve. Others deserve to lead."

"You think King Tomas deserves to lead?"

With a strange smile, Ellion shakes his head. "No, I don't. But I think there are far worse men and women for the job. So, until a better ruler comes along, I will happily continue to hide in plain sight along with my mother, while his throne remains secure. But when the next ruler comes—if it's who I think it will be—the tide will turn. Kravan will see a renewal of its glory days."

I try in vain to read his face. Surely he can't be talking about Tallin. "And the Tethered?"

"Any Tethered worth their salt will know it is better to serve willingly than to die."

With that, he leaves me standing on my own.

Ellion Graystone is confusing as hell.

Part of me feels sympathy for him. His entire life has been spent looking over his shoulder, warily assessing the rest of the world for threats.

But wariness aside, there's something about him and his mother that feels...*off*. Then again, perhaps it's just that they've both concealed the truth for so long that neither of them has ever learned to trust other people.

I can't say I blame them.

CHAPTER
THIRTY-FOUR

I'VE BEGUN QUIETLY SEARCHING the grounds for Thorne when I see Tallin lurching toward me on unsteady legs.

He's even more intoxicated now than he was in the Flyer, and I watch him with disgust as he nearly falls to the ground a few feet away.

"*You're* shupposed to be hobnobbing with Nobles," he scolds, wagging a finger in my face when he's managed to straighten up. "Not shquatting in a corner by yourshelf. Your...*self.*"

With that, he turns back to the crowd and leans an elbow on my shoulder, still swaying from side to side.

"I'm studying the guests from a distance," I tell him, doing my best to support him without actually laying a hand on him. "By the way, I've got some information for you—a few new Tethered to add to the list."

"Oh? Do tell."

"Later," I say, batting my hand through the air to ward off the stench of alcohol.

I notice in that moment that the sun is hanging low over the horizon. It will be dark soon—which means the party will move inside, and I'll have a chance to conceal myself in the guest house with Thorne. That is, if I can get rid of the foul prince. "Where's Valira? I thought she was going to stick close to you."

"Around here somewhere," he half sings, waving a hand in the air as if he's conducting an orchestra. "I suppose I ought to go find her." He glances down at me with a ridiculous, foolish grin on his lips. "Will you be all right on your own, sweet little thing?"

"Don't call me that," I snarl under my breath.

"Oh—I'm sorry. Would you prefer that I called you *my dearest love*?"

I roll my eyes at him. "Just go. Find your lady friend, with my blessing. Then maybe it would be a good idea if you found a place to lie down."

"You're probably right." To my delight, Tallin does as I tell him, tripping over his feet as he shuffles toward the house's back entrance.

He passes Lady Graystone on his way and for a moment, the two stop and have a word. I can't hear them, but I can see from their body language the conversation is less than friendly.

At one point, Tallin reaches for her shoulder, gripping it hard, and Lady Graystone shoves him away with what sound like a few choice words.

When they've finished their brief conversation, Lady Graystone, to my surprise, strides over to me.

"Hello, Lady Ingram," she says. "How are you this evening?"

"I'm fine, thank you," I reply, unsettled by a quiet menace in her tone. "And you?"

"Very well," she says, holding up a hand as I've seen Lady Verdan do before. A small item appears at the center of her palm —a ring identical to the one I'm wearing. She picks it up and hands it to me, but it fades away a moment later. "Your prince, on the other hand, is three sheets to the wind."

"I apologize for his state," I offer. "In my defense, he was like that when he got into the Flyer."

"Not surprising. He and Lord Nelson aren't exactly close. They've had a few altercations in their time." She nods toward our host, who's busy chatting with a couple of middle-aged Noble lords. "Lord Nelson is what you might call a shit-stirrer. Then again, so is the prince."

"What do you mean, exactly?" I ask, even though I know perfectly well what a pain in the ass Tallin is.

Lady Graystone moves closer, nodding toward Lord Nelson. "Rumor has it that he has sent Crimson Elites to various Nobles' homes to ransack them, looking for anything he can use to incriminate them and elevate his own rank in society in the process. He's gone after some who are close to the prince—and though Tallin can't prove anything, it's safe to say there are a few trust issues where Nelson is concerned."

"I still don't understand why we're here, then," I muse. "Why would Tallin agree to attend this party in the first place? He's not the type to do things that make him miserable, if he can avoid it."

"Because you have a job to do, naturally." Lady Graystone peers out at the guests, who have started making their way inside. "And I suspect Tallin is desperate to please his father. So, tell me—how goes the hunt?"

"I'd rather it weren't going at all," I tell her. "I'm pretty well ready to let the wealthy eat their own, and I want no part of it. But I have no choice."

"No, I suppose you don't. I would do the same in your place, naturally. But you know—you *have* been offered a wonderful life. You're engaged to a prince, for God's sake. Maybe you should consider embracing that, instead of conspiring to let the Nobility implode."

I gawk at her, so stunned that I nearly laugh. "You can't be serious. I would never in a million years consider marrying...that."

It's not the first time she's suggested I simply try to become a part of the despicable Nobility and forsake everything I care about, and the very suggestion is grotesque.

"Well, then, perhaps you should think about marrying someone Tallin sees as competition. My son, for instance."

I'm not about to entertain the prospect, but still, I ask, "You think the Prince sees Ellion as competition?"

"I'm sure you've noticed by now that the prince is intimidated by everyone and everything—and my son in particular terrifies him. But they stay out of one another's way, for the most part. Tallin has enough sense to do that, at least."

"Do you think Tallin knows Ellion can read minds?" I half whisper.

Lady Graystone's eyes widen with surprise. "It seems your skills aren't as honed as I'd thought, Hunter. My son does far more than read minds."

I don't know what she means by that, but the menace in her voice sets the hair on the back of my neck on edge.

"What exactly is his power, then?" I muster, though I don't particularly crave a reply.

"Let's just say it's one that instills fear in the hearts of many —even if they don't yet know it. One of these days, you'll see it in action, and trust me—it's quite remarkable."

Inadvertently, I pull away from her. As much as I've found myself enjoying Lady Graystone's company, something about her demeanor tonight seems as menacing as anything Tallin has ever thrown my way—and that's saying a lot.

"I should probably mingle a little," I tell her, mustering a pathetic attempt at a smile. "I'll see you soon, I hope."

"Yes, yes," she replies with a wave of her golden hand. "You should go out there and enjoy yourself, while you still can.

Why don't you see if you can find that handsome Guard of yours?"

"I will," I nod, my eyes scanning the crowd, desperate to spot Thorne again. "I'll do that."

As I stride away from Lady Graystone, all I can think about are the four ominous words that fell from her lips like shards of ice.

While you still can.

I SLIP into the main house to find Valira making her way toward the central staircase.

"The prince is tired," she tells me, her voice taking on a quiet formality as if she's worried we'll be overheard. "He's in one of the second floor bedrooms, and I'm going to see to it that he gets some rest for an hour or so."

The look she issues me then is filled with quiet meaning, and I nod gratefully, thanking her for her service as a couple of guests approach. "I don't suppose you've..."

"Seen Thorne?" Valira asks with the vaguest hint of a smile as the Noble couple passes us. "Yes. I believe he's patrolling the garden—ensuring that there are no entry points where infiltration of the grounds is a possibility. With the prince here, it's best to be cautious, as I'm sure you can imagine." With that, she winks. "Last I saw Thorne, he was at the far end of the grounds —near a small guest house. Perhaps you should seek him out there."

My heart thuds against my ribcage, and I come dangerously close to letting out a triumphant cry. "Yes, of course. Thank you. I'll see if I can find him."

I turn to head back down the hall toward the garden. At that same moment, Lord Nelson's booming voice summons guests into the Great Room for more drinking and merriment.

I squeeze my way through the cresting wave of a crowd until I'm standing outside under the stars, which have begun to reveal themselves one by one against the onyx veil high above our realm.

I've never come close to getting over the beauty of the sky, whether it be daytime or nighttime, rain or shine. But tonight, with the cool breeze stroking my skin and the anticipation of seeing Thorne, the exquisite expanse seems more lovely than ever before.

In the encroaching darkness, I can barely make out the few stragglers still working their way toward the house. I'm about to start my rapid trek toward the far end of the property when a quiet, familiar voice says, "Back right corner—just follow the path. The guest house is small but cozy. I've made sure there's a fire in the hearth and clean sheets on the bed."

With my cheeks burning, I spin around to see Nev smiling at me. "Thank you," I reply, wanting desperately to hug her again, but fearful that we'll be seen. *You don't know what you've done for me—for us.*

"It's no problem," she replies with a wink. "Anything for you, Lady Ingram. I'll see you next weekend?"

"Next weekend," I echo. "I'm looking forward to it."

"I just hope you know what the hell you're doing." She vanishes instantly, porting herself back inside, and I let out a little laugh before I make a beeline for the guest house.

By the time I've found the small outbuilding and spotted Thorne through the window, silhouetted against a sea of warm light, my heart has begun racing wildly in my chest.

Trembling with anticipation, I slip inside, closing the door behind me.

It's almost impossible to resist leaping on Thorne the second my eyes land on him, standing by the fireplace. His jacket is off, the sleeves of his white shirt rolled up to his elbows to display his powerful forearms.

We gawk at each other for a few seconds, like we're encountering one another for the first time and unsure of the rules of conduct. When our eyes meet, I feel my powers churn inside me, amplified by our bond—our insatiable, unrelenting attraction. My senses are heightened, my desire endless—and every bit of pain, anxiety, and fear I've suffered over the last few days melts away as Thorne's strength feeds my mind and body.

For a moment, I close my eyes and delve deep, my mind linking so tightly with his that I feel his need as acutely as my own. When I look at him again, the color seems to deepen in his flesh. His eyes, which are often serious and angry these days, soften, his lips twitching playfully.

"You are so fucking beautiful." His voice is a low, intoxicating growl. "Do you have any idea how much I want you right now?"

I shake my head, summoning him. "Show me."

He moves like a shot, leaping over and pressing me back against the solid door. Then his hand is in my hair, pulling it loose so that it cascades down beyond my shoulders. His fingers trail down my neck, an inhalation catching in his throat when he reaches the strap on my black dress, pulling it off my shoulder and letting it fall lower still until he realizes I'm not wearing a bra.

"You're lucky I didn't know there was only one thin piece of fabric keeping me from you," he moans, the backs of his fingers slipping down my breast until they reach the peak of my nipple. I tighten, a sigh pushing its way out from between my lips.

"You're wearing too many clothes, yourself," I breathe, reaching out to undo his shirt. He tears it off and drops it to the ground, his powerful abdomen flexing with the movements. His torso narrows toward the waistband of his pants and I let out an audible breath as I take in the gap between the fabric and his flesh, hunger gnawing at me.

It's cold in this little guest house—this perfect, isolated haven—in spite of the flames licking at one another inside the fireplace. But the chill only serves to invigorate us both.

I need him inside me.

I want to say the words...yet I'm desperate for this moment to go on forever. I want to watch him slip onto his knees—which he does at my silent bidding, his tongue teasing my nipple as he pulls the other strap down, yanking my dress to my waist.

A hand slips up the inside of my thigh, and Thorne rises to his feet again, looking into my eyes as he finds the seam of my panties and pulls them gently aside, sliding a finger over my slickness.

In the same moment, I reach for him, cupping his length through his uniform, and he lets out a long, low moan of delight.

"If I didn't know how much you wanted me before, I have some idea now," I purr as he leans down and brushes his lips over my neck, curling his fingers possessively inside me.

"I'm glad it's so obvious," he chuckles, his tongue slipping over my skin as fire stirs and flares in the depths of my veins.

I part my legs, inviting him to give me more of himself.

He strokes me slowly, slipping down so his mouth can tease its way over my breasts, his mind focused solely on my pleasure. Our sensations meld and become one, and I feel his bliss as I slide a hand inside the front of his trousers and take him in hand to match his strokes, his shaft steel-hard against my palm.

"I need you," I tell him. "I need to feel every inch of you inside me, Thorne. Now."

"Soon," he promises, yanking my dress down and off along with my panties, so all that's left are the high-heeled shoes I'm only now growing accustomed to.

"Now!" I insist, laughing.

Falling to his knees, he says, "As much as I would love to oblige, Lady Ingram, I have other business to attend to."

Thorne cups the backs of my thighs in his strong hands, spreading them still farther apart, then lifts my leg over his shoulder. His mouth is on me now, his tongue delving deep in defiance of my command.

If anyone were to push the door open, our temporary bliss would come to a shattering end—as, no doubt, would our lives. But all I can think of as I stand perched on one leg, Thorne's lips and tongue sending me into a state of oblivion and beyond, is how utterly perfect this moment is.

My back arches against the door, my face raised to the ceiling, eyes closed, as I revel in his skill, his pure, unabashed lust—his desire to once again send me over the edge into an abyss of ecstasy.

He flicks the end of his tongue over me in quick, agonizing strokes, his fingers delving deep inside me, stretching me wide as my body throbs against him in anticipation of his beautiful cock.

"I can't stand this," I moan. "I want you—I'm serious. You need to fuck me."

"I will fuck you," he says. "Once you come for me, Shara. I need to feel it. I need you to surrender to me—and then, I'll give you exactly what you want. I promise—I will take you hard."

Oh, God. The thought of it—of him driving into me with the fervor I'm craving so cruelly—it's almost more than I can take.

Another flick of his tongue, and another, and then I tense, my fingers coiling tightly in his hair.

"Good girl," he groans against me. "You're so close, aren't you?"

But I can feel how much he wants to keep me there on the brink. He wants me to linger in that place where I stand on the precipice's rim, my body on the very verge of explosion.

His lips take in my clit and he sucks gently, his tongue tormenting me with a feather-light touch. It's almost *too* good—a sensation so fleetingly delectable that I never want to allow myself the devastation of falling over the edge.

"That's it," Thorne moans against me, the words vibrating me toward the inevitable. "Come for me, and then I'll give you what you want most in the world."

I'm about to beg him to let me fall to my knees, to take him in my mouth and do the same for him that he's doing for me, when a wave of scalding heat passes through my body, every nerve throbbing and exploding with pleasure. I cry out without a care in the world for who may overhear me.

"Oh, good girl," he breathes, teasing my clit with the tip of his nose as the last pulses leave my body. "You're so fucking good."

I'm about to plead with him when he rises to his feet and, in one swift series of motions, slips his pants down, lifts me, and—parting my legs wide—thrusts himself deep inside me.

He kisses me deeply, the taste of sex on his lips and tongue, my legs hooking around his waist as he pulls out then thrusts again, tearing me apart in the most delicious of ways.

My core coils with delight, his pleasure flooding my mind, braiding with my own so that I can no longer distinguish my ecstasy from his.

"You're the most beautiful woman I've ever seen," Thorne moans, pinning my wrists over my head with one hand as he drives into me without mercy. "All I have to do to get hard is think about you—picture your eyes, your lips. The *taste* of you."

I tighten around him, never wanting to release him from my grip.

But he's too strong for me. He pulls out and lifts me, one arm under my legs, to carry me over to a solid-looking table, where he sets me down. Reading his wishes, I twist around and bend over, spreading my arms and legs wide in submission.

He teases me, the head of his swollen cock slipping over my clit, then takes hold of my waist with both hands. He eases inside me slowly at first, then all at once, drawing a cry from the depths of my chest.

"Do you want more?" he whispers, leaning in close.

"Yes," I tell him.

He pulls out again. "Say it," he commands. "Tell me what you want from me."

"All of you," I breathe. "Every inch."

"Who am I to deny you?" he asks, then drives into me hard and fast until every nerve in my body is on fire. I cry out again and again with each thrust, acutely aware of how fully he feels the pleasure he's gifting me—the absolute, unrelenting wholeness of *us*.

"Come for me, Thorne," I rasp, my voice coarse with need. "Come inside me. I need to feel it. I want you to surrender, just like I did."

"Are you sure?" he whispers, teasing. He knows exactly what I want.

"I'm sure."

He straightens, his hands grasping my hips, sheathing himself deep. The power between us intensifies with each movement, each thrust igniting the inferno that is our unbreakable bond. I feel his strength, his mind, his every nerve ending —and I know how deeply he feels mine, too.

He pulls out suddenly, turning me around and lifting me onto the table. His lips are on mine as I rock my hips against his, taking every inch of him as though this, right here, will be the end of us...and of all things.

I feel myself slipping once again toward the perfect, endless abyss of pleasure that overtook me just a little while ago, and only hope he feels it as keenly.

"Come with me," he groans against my mouth. "Can you feel how close I am?"

"I feel *everything*."

He bites my bottom lip, taking it between his teeth, and an instant later, our mouths crash together alongside the wave that takes us both at once, a shuddering, devastating explosion washing over us.

When he falls against me, his breath heaving, I wrap every bit of myself around his body, refusing to let him go for anything in the world.

I have spent too much time apart from him. Too much time desiring him, searching for him, *wishing* for him.

And in this perfect *now*, he's mine—and the entire world belongs to us.

CHAPTER
THIRTY-SIX

WHEN I FINALLY RELEASE HIM from my grip, Thorne takes me by the hand and leads me to a small bedroom off the guest house's main area.

We slip into the bed together, and I lie on my back. He slides over me, a hand cupping my neck possessively, his lips against my own.

"Thorne," I say softly when he pulls back to look into my eyes.

The last thing I want to do right now is dive into an intense conversation, but I need to tell him what's happened—the momentous revelation that collided with me while he and I were separated.

"What is it?"

It feels surreal to reply, "I met my mother."

"Wait—*what*?" he breathes, rolling onto his side to prop himself up on his hand. "How? Where?"

I turn my face to his. "At the Prefect's, believe it or not."

He looks confused beyond words, so I fill him in on Valira's encouragement to head back to the Prefect's home and meet with Evangeline. I tell him about my younger sister who allegedly exists in the world somewhere, and fill him in on what my mother said about my father.

"I know the Hunter—or the Shadow, or whatever we're supposed to call him—is powerful. I know he scares people. But I feel *drawn* to him, Thorne. I want desperately to find him the second we can leave this place. In the meantime, the king and Tallin still expect me to report Tethered Nobles to them. I don't want to do it. But if I lie and tell them I haven't spotted any, they'll suspect something is up."

"So don't lie. Choose wisely instead."

"What does that mean?"

Thorne lets out a long breath. "Look—there are good and bad Tethered. If you discover there are Nobles in this realm who are vicious bastards *and* have powers, maybe telling the king about them is the best possible move."

"But what if—"

I can't help thinking about my conversation with Ellion about the Chaplins. If they're as awful as he thinks, there's no way the king will simply let them go on living their lives.

At least, I don't think there is.

"You're worried the king will have them killed," Thorne says softly. "But Lord Malloy is still alive, isn't he? Maybe what you're doing is nothing more than simple surveillance. Thanks to you, the Royal Guard can keep an eye on anyone who seems like a potential threat. It doesn't mean they'll be murdered—only that they'll be monitored."

"But they may be killed," I reply. "They could die because of me." I let out a sigh, and I know without asking that Thorne can feel the oppressive weight bearing down on my shoulders.

"Shara," he says, his voice gentle. "If they die, it will be because the king and his son are monsters. Not because of you. You are good and kind. I love you for that, and so many other reasons. And one day, you and I will find a way to free our people—all because you made this sacrifice. If I had the means, I would take you by the hand right now and we would get away, you and I. Together. We'd run until there was nowhere left to run...and only then would we stop. I can't stand seeing you in pain. I can't stand feeling your sorrow. But always know that I'm with you. I give you my strength—my heart. Every bit of me is yours."

With tears in my eyes, I roll onto my side and, slipping my fingers through his thick, dark hair, I pull myself to him, kissing him deeply enough to forget for a moment where we are, and what we're up against.

"I love you," I tell him, pressing my forehead to his. "You know that, don't you?"

"As surely as I know my own mind," he whispers. "I've never been more confident of anything in my life. For all my misfortune, I am the luckiest man in the world—because I have you."

He holds me for a time as the tears stream down my face. I'm sure it's streaking the makeup Maude so carefully helped me apply, but I don't care about anything right now, except the injustice in our world.

"We need to get you out of here," Thorne says, stroking my skin with his fingertips. "We have to make our move, and soon. You and I need to be free of the palace and of the Palatine Hills. We have to get ourselves to the Capitol, or eventually, it won't be the Tethered posing as Nobles we need to worry about. It'll be..."

He doesn't need to say the words for me to understand his meaning.

It'll be us.

"As soon as I've seen the Histories, we'll find a way," I promise. "Next Friday, with Nev's help, we'll get what we need, and we'll leave the Palatine Estates for good."

"Shara..." Thorne twists a finger through a long strand of my hair. "What if the Histories aren't enough to inspire an uprising?"

I pull away just enough to look into his eyes. "What do you mean? Why wouldn't they be?"

"Because from what I've heard from the other members of the Royal Guard, the Capitol is in a state of chaos, and it gets worse every day. Worse than you and I know, even. They say each day is a fight for basic survival. People are angry—feral, even. Families are constantly being torn apart at the seams over political disagreements, even as they starve. I don't know what you'll find in the secret texts, but it would take more than a little scandal to unify our people. The only thing the Capitol's citizens really want is a chance at a normal life—it's the same desire the rest of us feel. They're probably exhausted—and in no state to fight a war."

"Then let's hope the Histories inspire them," I say. "With Mercutio's help—and my Maude—maybe I can record what I see. I don't even need to *steal* the Histories from the vaults; I just need to know what's in them—and be able to prove it."

"What do you think you'll learn? What could possibly cause such a seismic shift that the Capitol will rise up?"

From anyone else, the question might sound snide. But from Thorne, I know it to be protective.

He only wants to save me from the pain of realizing how cruelly unfair the world really is.

"Have you seen something?" I ask. "Something that tells you we'll fail?"

He goes silent for a moment. "I've seen things," he confesses. "All I can say is that my visions of the future are... inconclusive. Look—I'm not afraid to try, but I am afraid of seeing you hurt or disappointed by the outcome if things go awry."

"I can't say I wouldn't be disappointed," I confess. "As for hurt—don't forget, I'm a Healer."

"I'm not talking about that kind of hurt," he chuckles bitterly. "Then again, you know that already."

I cup his cheek in my hand, staring into his swirling eyes when I say, "Thorne, I think I'm *meant* to see those texts, and I'm meant to tell the world about them. I wish I could explain better than that, but I can't."

"I just hope you're right—if only for your sake."

Taking hold of my waist, Thorne flips me onto my back and slips over me again, his arms bracing by the sides of my head, supporting his sculpted, beautiful torso above my own.

"Now," he says, pressing himself between my legs and inspiring a long moan to rise from the base of my throat, "I believe we have time for one more before we have to make our way back."

"What if someone comes looking for us?" I ask, nervously eyeing the door. "What if..."

Thorne flings a hand out, and I hear a mechanism whirring. A lock—an electronic one—has just ensured that no one will come bursting in. With another flick of his hand, a set of opaque blinds descend over the windows, blocking out any inquisitive eyes from looking in.

"Impressive," I laugh.

"Oh, that's not all I can do," he says, pushing himself inside me an inch at a time so that my breath catches in my chest.

The guest house's lights flicker, then glow with intense brightness—then go out. All that remains are the embers in the fireplace casting an orange glow on the floor just outside the bedroom.

"You were serious when you told Tallin you could electrocute him," I say with a chuckle.

"Dead serious," he replies.

He pushes himself a little deeper inside me, and the lights flare back to life. Another moan rises in my chest.

"Why did you let him think he could hurt you?" I ask. "When he first used the shocker on you?"

"Because," Thorne says, kissing my neck, "when you convince your would-be oppressor they hold the power, their guard lowers...and it becomes easier to snatch that power back. I wanted Tallin to think he was stronger than I am. It's far easier to vanquish an arrogant man than a cautious one."

He sheathes himself deep, and I cry out.

"But let's never utter his name again," he whispers, "at least not while we're in this position, beautiful thing. The bastard prince has no idea what it is to feel love like I feel for you—and maybe *that* will prove his downfall."

With a nod of assent, I close my eyes, devouring the sensation of our two bodies becoming one, our emotions and our every pleasure melding until I don't know where Thorne's mind ends and mine begins.

No, I think. *Tallin has no idea what this feels like.*

No one who understands this kind of love could possibly be so cruel.

WHEN THE TIME comes for us to go our separate ways, I pull my dress back on, fighting the desire to march into the group of assembled guests and announce that I am no longer willing to play by their rules.

Thorne and I have been robbed of our lives, but before we came along, countless other Tethered were robbed of their own.

I don't want to return to the palace only to report our kind to King Tomas. Hell, I don't want to return to the palace at all.

I want to steal a Flyer and soar over the water until the

vehicle loses power, or we find another realm—one where we would be welcomed with open arms.

"Do you think we'll ever be allowed to be together?" I murmur, fighting back fresh tears as Thorne wraps his arms around me from behind, resting his chin on my crown.

"Allowed?" he asks, and I can feel him shaking his head. "No. But when has that ever stopped us?"

I turn and kiss him deeply, absorbing the taste and scent of him, the feel of his chest under my palms.

And then, I check my makeup in a small mirror by the door, leave him alone, and hike back toward the Nelson house, my heart breaking just a little more with each step.

THIRTY-SEVEN

By some miracle of fate, I manage to slip back inside the Nelson house unnoticed and make my way to the Great Room where most of the other guests are gathered.

The space is enormous, with stone arches supporting its high ceiling. A cacophony of booming, drunken Noble voices bounces off the walls to create a constant roar, and the general vibe of hostility sets me instantly on edge.

I move through the room, studying Noble after Noble, assessing, searching for people I can report to the king with a clean conscience.

It doesn't take long before I've noted the identities of several Tethered, each sadistic in their way. When I don't know their names, I glide over to whatever Guard is closest and ask, memorizing any information they impart.

Thorne assured me before I left the guest house that he would wait several minutes then follow along behind me, and I'm relieved when I see him enter the vast chamber after a little while. He positions himself by the Great Room's main doors, a satisfied grin on his lips.

I smile too, both with the vivid recollection of what just

occurred between us, and the knowledge that Valira has kept her promise and prevented Tallin from catching on.

I only wish we could do this every day.

I move around the room, scanning the crowd for any Tethered I might have missed. Here and there, someone stops me in my tracks, wanting to make small talk, but I always manage to find an excuse to leave their side after a minute or two.

Eventually, I slip out of the room, my hand brushing Thorne's gently as I pass him.

"Are you all right, Lady Ingram?" he asks in that smooth, delicious voice of his.

"Just looking for the prince," I tell him.

"I believe he's on the second floor. Third bedroom on the left."

"Thank you...Thorne," I say, and it's a struggle to resist throwing myself at him then and there, in front of an audience of Nobles who are just waiting to witness a scandal.

I find Valira standing in a doorway on the second level, chewing on her nails as she watches Tallin writhing on the bed on the other side of the room. He's coated in perspiration, his eyelids fluttering.

"What's happened?" I ask, panicked as I rush to his side— not so much out of concern for him as fear for Valira's safety.

"I gave him a little something," she confesses. "I'd hoped it would help him sleep, but..."

There's a distinct glint in her eye—something mischievous, even playful.

She drugged the prince?

~Looks like it, Maude replies.

"I'm sure he'll be fine," I say, but just in case, I lay a hand on Tallin's chest and summon my healing power.

The last thing I want is for Valira to get into trouble after what she did for Thorne and me tonight.

Tallin's heart is racing wildly, but my touch calms it until his chest begins to rise and fall steadily, his fluttering eyelids settling.

"I want to thank you," I tell Valira. "I owe you."

"I was only repaying a debt I already owed you," she says. "Now, we're even."

With a quick flick of my hand, I issue the last of my healing to Tallin, whose eyes snap open. He shoots up, an expression on his face that tells me he's not entirely sure where he is.

"We're at the cocktail party," I say. "Remember?"

When his gaze lands on Valira, he reaches for her. She glides over and takes his hand, and he pulls her close. She combs her fingers through his hair and holds him as he presses his face to her stomach.

Their relationship remains a baffling mystery to me, and one day, I'd like to understand it. But not today.

"I have no desire to stay here," Tallin grunts. "But my father will be displeased if we return to the palace with only one or two Tethered to report."

He pulls his eyes up to mine, questioning.

"I've identified five Tethered," I tell him. "Each of them poses a potential threat."

"Five!" he repeats, pulling free of Valira as if my words have given him the strength he needs. "Are you sure?"

"Completely," I say. "I'll give their names to your father."

The truth is, I encountered seven. But two of them were Harmless, married to Normals, and I can't bring myself to turn them in. The others violently beat or killed at least a few of their Tethered servants.

Maybe I've become a coldhearted monster, but I no longer have qualms about sentencing cruel people to cruel fates.

"Good," Tallin says, closing his eyes. "Thank you, Shara. In that case, I think it's time to head home."

One more week, I think as we fly back. *One week, and we can finally find our way out of this hell. Thorne and I can be together. We can secure a place to stay in the Capitol—maybe even find a way to live as two people in love—two people who want nothing more than to be free and happy.*

The Capitol may be a shit-show, but something tells me Thorne and I could turn even the most uninhabitable house into a paradise of our own making...if we only had a chance.

I glance over at him, a smile on my lips.

My body and mind feel rejuvenated by our bond—and right now, it feels like there's nothing in the world that could bring us down.

We only need to survive.

One.

More.

Week.

CHAPTER
THIRTY-EIGHT

IN THE MORNING, I make my way to the king's dining chamber for breakfast, only to find him waiting for me along with Lady Verdan.

When I walk in, the two of them look tense, almost as if they've been arguing, or worse. I stop in my tracks, wondering whether I should leave and return later.

"Lady Ingram!" the king bellows, his voice so aggressive that it bounces off the walls. "Come, sit down with us."

I do as he asks, my eyes locked on Lady Verdan, who doesn't look at me. Not that I mind—the last thing I want is to share a moment with my former Proprietor. But something about her seems coiled more tightly than usual, like she's a mouse trap about to snap.

There was a time when the look on her face would have intimidated me. But last night strengthened me down to the marrow of my bones, and I will not allow her to make me feel small—not now.

Not ever.

"So," King Tomas says, ignoring her and focusing solely on

me as he hands me a cup of coffee. "How did last evening go? I hear our beloved son was somewhat intoxicated."

"It was fine," I tell him, ignoring the last sentence. No way am I going to confirm in front of Daphne Verdan that her son made a spectacle of himself. "Very pleasant, actually."

I take a swig of coffee, mentally preparing myself for further questions.

"I've heard you and Ellion Graystone have hit it off," the king observes, his eyebrows raised, his tone jovial.

I nearly choke. Where the hell did he hear that? Surely Valira wouldn't have told him—she wasn't even around when Ellion and I were talking.

Was she?

"Oh?" I say with a swallow.

"Yes. It seems you two have become fast friends."

Lady Verdan flinches like the king's words have pricked at her flesh.

"Well..." I begin, eyeing her for a moment before pulling my attention back to the king. "He seems...nice."

"Nice?" Lady Verdan spits, unable to keep her ire in check. "That little prick wouldn't know *nice* if it hit him in the face with a crowbar."

"Now, darling," King Tomas says, laying his hand on top of hers. "There's no need to be cruel."

She stares daggers at the king, and I find myself wishing I could go back in time ten minutes and warn myself against entering the dining room.

I don't know what the hell is going on between these two, but I want no part of it.

"You know what a snake he is—not to mention his vile mother," Lady Verdan hisses. "Despicable, both of them."

I bury my face in my coffee cup to hide my smirk. The truth

is, I'd like to release a full-on belly laugh at the irony of Daphne Verdan referring to any other human as despicable.

I've never met anyone more odious than her.

~Perhaps not, Maude tells me. *But maybe you should work harder at masking your disgust. You're making that face again.*

I pull my mouth into a neutral position, then lay my cup down and sit back, watching the bickering couple as the tension in the room thickens.

If I didn't know better, I'd say Lady Verdan *fears* the Graystones. But why would she? If anything, it should be the other way around. They're the ones hiding their true natures. They're in danger of discovery, while she has the protection of the king and all his Guards.

Maude, do you have any clue what's going on here? I ask silently.

~None, she admits. *But if I were to assess Lady Verdan's body language, I would say she's jealous.*

You think she knows the king spends time with Lady Graystone?

~I have little doubt.

In that case, I'm surprised Daphne has allowed Lady Graystone to survive this long.

"What were your findings last night?" King Tomas asks, redirecting his attention toward me.

"Findings?" My spine tightens as I pull my eyes back to him. "You mean..."

He lets out an aggravated huff. "Did you uncover any more Tethered?"

"Oh." For a moment, I was worried he suspected the Graystones. "A few."

I proceed to rattle off the list of names I collected last night.

At the mention of the Chaplins, Lady Verdan's head snaps around and she locks her eyes on mine. I can't quite tell whether she's surprised or horrified.

"Really?" she says. "Interesting. Yet I always knew there was something malevolent in them."

"Lady Chaplin is a Conflag, somewhat like you," I tell her with no attempt to mask my disgust for those with her set of skills. "She's violent—and if I had to guess, I'd say she's killed a few of her Crimson Elites in the hopes of being assigned stronger ones. I've seen some of her handiwork in my mind's eye."

"Well done," King Tomas says, clapping his hands together. "You really are impressive, Hunter. I'll be sorry to lose you when the time comes."

Lady Verdan shoots him a look of warning, and any feeling of newfound confidence leaves me instantly.

Is that what they were discussing when I walked in? When to rid themselves of me—of Thorne? Do they already have a date chosen?

"I simply mean when the day comes for you to leave the palace," the king assures me, seeing the look on my face. "Most likely, you will be placed in a new home, not far from here. I'll make sure you're well looked after, of course."

"And Thorne?" I ask. "What about him?"

"Well," King Tomas laughs. "Naturally, I can't have you two placed together—it wouldn't be fair to either of you. But trust me, he'll receive the best possible treatment. Who knows? I may even keep him here to serve as a high-level Royal Guard."

I smile, though there is no doubt in my heart that he's lying through his teeth.

"Now, my dear, are you looking forward to the ball next Friday?"

"I am," I tell him, and there's no lie in those words—though I would never divulge *why* I'm excited. "Very much."

"Good. I'm sure you haven't forgotten that last time there was a ball, you made quite an impression on Kravan's Nobles.

Perhaps you could approach this one with a little more...reserve."

I force out a laugh, then say, "Things have changed since then. No one needs to worry that there will be an encore performance. For one thing, I'm assuming there will be no Crimson Championship at this ball."

"No indeed," the king says. "No Championship. Consider this gathering a respite from all I've asked you to do over the last days."

I try but fail to decipher his meaning. "You still want me to hunt for Tethered, though—don't you?"

"Of course. Seek them out and report back to me. But you've done such a wonderful job already that I think it's time you sat back and enjoyed yourself, if only for a little."

The words on their own seem kind and gentle enough, but there's something ominously final in them...as if the ball will put an end to any enjoyment I'm ever to be allowed.

Still, I tell myself to shake it off. It's not as if I can *avoid* attending the ball—and not as if I want to. It will be the most important night of my life, and if all goes well, it could change the course of Kravan's history.

CHAPTER
THIRTY-NINE

I RETURN TO MY QUARTERS, where I change into a yellow cotton dress with thin straps tied into bows and a knee-length, full skirt.

I don't know how or when, but I intend to find my way to Thorne today. After the king's tacit warning, all I want is to look into his eyes and feel my strength renewed.

My first destination is the hedge maze. I'm already striding across the palace's vast lawn toward its nearest entrance when I hear, "Good morning, Lady Ingram. How are you today?"

I turn to see Archyr standing next to a sapling, watching me intently.

"I'm all right," I say, stepping toward him. "And you?"

"Not bad at all," he beams.

"The grin on your face makes me think you might be a little better than not bad," I tell him. "Let me guess...the prince is taking a little while to recover from the cocktail party."

Archyr winks at me, nodding. "It seems he drank a little too much, poor man. He's been in bed ever since. And so have I...if you know what I'm saying."

"I take it you haven't been *alone* in that bed," I laugh, temporarily forgetting my worries.

"Hell, no," he says, stretching his arms overhead as though recovering from a long workout. "Where would be the fun in that?"

"Well, I'm happy for you. Genuinely. May the prince spend many more days puking his guts out."

"Cheers to that," Archyr chuckles.

A moment later, his smile fades as he pulls his attention to something behind me, and I turn to see what he's looking at.

Valira is making her way rapidly across the lawn toward us —and she doesn't look happy.

At first, I'm convinced she's about to tear into me for talking to Archyr. But when she stops, her breath coming in short bursts, she says, "Lord Malloy is dead."

"Lord Malloy?" I ask. "The man from the Prefect's dinner party?"

"The same." From the look in her eyes, she's more concerned about me than about him.

"How did—" I begin, but I'm not sure I want to finish the question.

"Heart attack is the official cause of death," Valira says. "He was playing tennis with the king, and when he went to shower, he collapsed. It happened here, in the palace."

I intake a breath, reluctant to admit how relieved I am that it was natural causes that killed him.

"He was healthy," Archyr says. "I've met him a few times. He was only forty-six."

"It happens, I suppose," Valira replies. "But yes—it was a shock. The king has already offered to cover the costs of a funeral service."

"Was anyone with him when it happened?" I ask. "The king, or anyone else?"

"I don't know yet. And the surveillance systems were being rebooted, so there's no record of anyone entering the shower room after the match. It's possible Lord Malloy just played too hard—though I can't imagine why anyone would actively try to beat the king."

"Let's hope that's all it was," Archyr mutters. "Because it all sounds pretty damned sketchy, if you ask me."

"Be careful," Valira cautions him. "You don't want anyone thinking you've been leveling accusations at the Royals."

He grimaces and says, "Hey, I said nothing accusatory. It does seem a little fishy, though, given that Lady Ingram here reported Lord Malloy just a few days ago."

"You know about that?" I raise an eyebrow.

"Pillow talk." He shrugs, and Valira looks at me with a sheepish lowering of her chin.

"I tell him things," she says. "Everything, truth be told. It's the only way we stay sane. We trust each other completely, so there's no such thing as a secret between us."

"I understand, believe me," I reply. There's nothing in the world I would keep from Thorne.

I want to think Lord Malloy's death was nothing more than an unfortunate twist of fate—the same sort that has inflicted itself millions of times over the history of humanity.

But a quiet, queasy feeling in my gut warns me it may not be so simple.

"I should head inside," I finally say, suddenly feeling like a third wheel. "Could you do me a favor?"

Valira nods silently.

"If you see Thorne, ask him to find me. I need to talk to him."

Archyr's lips tick upward. "Going to engage in a little secret bumping of uglies, are you?"

"Archyr," Valira says with a roll of her eyes.

"Sorry," he replies with the flash of a white smile. "I meant to say *illicit fucking*."

"Like I said, I want to talk," I lie through my teeth.

"I bet you do. With your mouth on his—"

"Stop it, you two," Valira interrupts, nodding toward me. "Lady Ingram—I'll let Thorne know he's to find you as soon as possible. I'm sure he'll be eager to...discuss security measures for the upcoming...ball."

I can't help chuckling at what somehow sounds like another sexual euphemism. "Thank you."

As I head back toward the palace, I think about Lord Malloy and wonder whether he'd still be alive if I hadn't reported him.

~It's not your fault, Maude tells me when my gut clenches with worry.

No? Whose fault is it, then?

~If he was murdered, it was clearly the murderer's fault. If he died of natural causes, then we can blame Mother Nature—not that such a being actually exists.

If he was murdered, I say, *I blame myself. I gave the king a motive. Tallin gave him an opportunity by inviting Lord Malloy to the palace.*

~No matter. Until the moment comes when you kill a person, you are no murderer, Shara. That may change one day soon, however.

What does that mean, Maude? What are you trying to tell me?

~Only that you need to prepare yourself for some difficult days ahead. But I promise you—I will be right here by your side...whatever may come.

HOPING to distract myself from thoughts of Lord Malloy, I head back inside to roam the palace's halls, aimless in my trajectory.

When I reach a broad hallway on the second level, I notice a figure striding toward me from a stairway at the far end. In the moment when our eyes meet, I spot a dark shape scurrying off, and I know without question that Mercutio had a hand in telling Thorne to seek me out.

My little shadow.

"Lady Ingram," Thorne says with a bow of his head and a telling smirk. "Valira sent me to find you, and a certain rodent told me where you could be found. Are you in need of anything on this fine day?"

"A tranquilizer," I tell him with a laugh as he turns to accompany me on my stroll. "I'm freaking out."

He speaks low when he replies, "About the ball?"

I nod. "I feel like something momentous is going to happen." I glance sideways. "Have you..."

"Have I seen what will happen that night?" he asks, the muscles in his jaw twitching.

"I take it that's a yes."

He looks around, then, taking me by the hand, pulls me into a room on the right side of the hallway. I look around and realize we're surrounded by glass cases, each of which appears to contain one or more maps.

Thorne seals the door, locking it, and then begins to pace the length of the chamber.

"I've seen a little," he says as I lean back against the door, my hands clasped nervously behind my back. "I'm not sure what to make of it."

"That doesn't sound good."

"It's not good—but it's not bad, either," he says, stopping and turning my way, his hazel eyes reflecting the map room's dim light. "Nothing is clear. I've seen darkness and shadow. I've heard a voice—one I don't recognize. Everything in my mind is jumbled and abstract, like it's swimming with pieces to a puzzle, but I don't know how to put it together."

"Do you know if Nev and I will manage to get into the vault?"

He shakes his head. "I'm not sure," he says. "All I know is you'll..."

"I'll what?" I ask as he moves closer to me.

Gently, he takes hold of my arms, pulling my hands from behind me, and pins them above my head.

With his other hand, he undoes one of the straps of my dress, then the other, and pulls the soft fabric down to my waist.

"You didn't answer my question," I tell him as his eyes lock on the sight before him.

Letting out a long sigh, he cups my breast in his hand, stroking the pad of his thumb over my nipple, and a reluctant moan rumbles up my throat.

"You'll be fine," he concludes, leaning down to kiss my neck.

My head cranes to the side to accept the caress of his lips. "Everything will be okay."

"Will it?" I ask in a whisper. "Will we manage to get out of here, Thorne?"

He reaches down and pulls up the skirt of my dress, yanking my panties aside. Releasing my hands, he undoes his pants and lets them drop to the ground. Taking hold of my waist, he lifts me effortlessly.

I wrap my legs around him as he presses the swollen head of his cock to my opening.

"I can't say," he whispers, thrusting deep inside me and cupping a hand over my mouth as I cry out. "I can only hope— and so can you. I want to be with you, Shara. Forever. I never want to be separated again, and I will fight with everything in me to make sure it never happens."

I look into his eyes, searching for a lie. But all I see is his love —his sincerity.

If he sees an unpleasant future for us, he's hiding it well.

"I don't want to be separated, either," I tell him. "I hate the thought of it."

He draws himself out again, then buries himself deep, his mouth colliding with mine, my tongue lashing at his own.

Tears stream down my cheeks as I suppress a cry of ecstasy. I hold onto him, like letting go will mean losing him forever. In my mind's eye, a vision of an uncertain future forms—darkness, confusion. *Fear.*

The shadow he spoke of.

This is *his* power, borrowed temporarily from his mind. I'm witnessing what *he* witnessed...and it makes no sense.

If he's seeing it at the same time, he doesn't let on. Instead, he presses me into the door, driving into me like the world is about to end. I cling to him, desperate, needful, terrified of some distant, horrible fate neither of us can see.

"Lie down," I command.

Without a word, he draws himself out of me and obeys, lying on his back, his length held tight in his fist.

Slipping over him, I spend my rage on him, my frustration, my fear...my love. I set our pace, drawing myself slowly upward, tormenting him with the sensation—the slow withdrawal—before I take him inside me again and again.

He pushes his hand between us, stroking me with his thumb as I writhe above him, forcing me toward the cliff's edge with each small, perfect motion.

"You know just how to touch me," I say. "Does it feel as good for you as it does for me?"

"Better," he tells me. "Because I live for this."

When I finally fall over the edge, he comes with me, heat rolling over us in one exquisite wave...

Until, all of a sudden, my mind flashes with a horrifying vision.

I see Thorne on his knees, hunched over in a desolate place I don't recognize. He's surrounded by men in gray masks, weapons in their hands. All around him lies ruin—broken walls, shattered windows, and shards of metal, twisted and bent.

As I stare at this future version of him in my mind's eye, I can feel a surge of fear infiltrating his heart—not for *his* safety... but for mine.

"What is it?" he asks when a gasp emerges from my chest.

"I—I don't know. I don't understand what I'm seeing—except that...you're in danger and far away."

"That's impossible." He lets out a low chuckle. "I'll never let you out of my sight," he promises, pushing a strand of hair behind my ear. "Not after the ball. We're going to escape this place together, Shara. We're going to be free, you and I."

266

I nod, trying desperately to convince myself he's right. "I know. It was just a dream, or something. But..."

"You saw one of my visions," he whispers. "It's got you worried."

"It looked like you were in the Capitol. There were men in masks, and it seemed like you..."

Like you were their prisoner.

"Yes," he says. "I've seen it, too. But Shara, not all my visions come to pass. I've had a few that involved Tallin and a gray cat, and I assure you—there's no cat in the palace. The king is allergic and forbids them, for one thing. Like you said, sometimes these visions are nothing more than dreams invented by my overactive subconscious. Don't worry."

Gently, I rise to my feet, pull the dress up, and tie my straps as he yanks his trousers upward and stands.

"If we get our hands on the secret texts," I whisper, "I can only hope they tell us how to get to the Capitol. We won't be safe here once the king decides we're useless to him."

"I know," Thorne says, nodding toward the glass cases that house the room's display of maps. "Maybe one of these will tell us how to get where we want to go once we've made our way out of this place—not that I've ever been taught to read maps."

"Me neither."

Maps were forbidden to those who grew up in the Tower. We weren't taught about Kravan's various islands or its topography, and all we could do without windows was speculate about the Capitol. Nobody in our cohort even knew that Kravan was made up of a series of islands.

Encased in glass are several maps painted on parchment and pinned to a wooden board. They are mostly wordless—just drawings of distant lands. One depicts a pure white territory, designed to look as though it's a frozen wasteland. Another shows a long, jagged-looking green island, surrounded on all sides by mountain peaks.

On another map, I notice a triangle with an arrow pointing upward and a square with a downward arrow. Another map has the opposite—a square with an upward arrow.

"I think these symbols have to do with populations," Thorne says. "Tethered versus Normal, maybe?"

"What makes you say that?"

"I saw a notebook one time in the Tower, when I was a teenager. My Warden had a list of the Tethered he oversaw, and another list of the Normals who worked on our level. The Tethered were..."

"Triangles," I say. "Right?"

He nods.

"Unfortunately, that information doesn't help us figure out a way out of here."

"No," Thorne agrees. "But the maps tell us there are other realms out there—and some of them seem to be vast. It seems the Royals are aware of them...but I suspect no one else is."

"Then why have these maps sitting here on display? Anyone could have walked in here."

"I don't think that door was supposed to be open," Thorne tells me, thrusting his thumb toward the hallway. "Maybe a servant left it that way by accident. Or maybe someone was trying to help us."

"Help us? Who would want to do that?"

Thorne shrugs. "Your guess is as good as mine. But something has been racing around in my mind for days, Shara—a question that's never been answered."

"Everything in our lives is a question," I say with a sigh.

"True—but..." He steps over and pulls me close, kissing me tenderly. "Have you ever given any more thought to who reprogrammed your Maude unit when we were in the Verdan house?"

"Of course I've thought about it," I reply. "But I don't have any theories. For a minute there, I wondered whether it could have been my mother—but she was as surprised to discover me as I was to discover her, so I don't think so."

"What about your father?"

"My...father?" I pull back to study his face and determine whether he's serious. "Really?"

"They say the Shadow is resourceful and stealthy, like a cat burglar. I've heard there are Tethered who make their way to and from the Capitol on occasion."

With a nod, I reply, "Apparently Lady Graystone speaks to a Stealther sometimes. I suppose it's possible they know my father—but the Graystones aren't fans of his, so I can't quite imagine it."

"Still—if your father is as clever as he sounds, maybe he finds his way into the palace occasionally."

I press my hands to Thorne's chest, kiss his chin, and say, "You think my father left the door to this room open so I could get laid in here? Really?"

"Not likely," Thorne chuckles. "But I think it's possible he—or someone else—did it to open your eyes to how large the world is beyond Kravan. Didn't you say you have a sister out there somewhere?"

At that, my expression shifts. "I assumed she was in the Capitol, hiding out with my father. You don't think..."

I turn and glance at the maps.

"She could be out there somewhere," I say. "Which means I would never find her."

"We don't know that. All I know is that it was too easy to find you today—too easy to sneak in here after days when we've been kept apart. It's almost like someone is guiding us to each other—like they're feeding us information. The question is why."

"Maybe someone is trying to show us lands where equality exists," I reply. "Trying to give us hope."

"Or take hope away," Thorne murmurs, pressing a kiss to my forehead. He pulls me close, holding me against his chest. I breathe into the percussive throb of his heart, wishing I could stay like this forever.

"You told me once you suspect the Graystones are a key to all this," I murmur. "Do you think there's a chance they're the ones helping us?"

"I suppose it's possible." But his voice is strained, as if he knows something I don't.

"What is it?" I ask, forcing myself to pull away.

"Since that vision I had—the one where I saw them—I haven't seen the Graystones in my mind's eye. It's like they're hiding from me—but I don't know why."

"Well...maybe we'll find out at the ball."

Thorne's face turns grim when he says, "That's what I'm afraid of."

OVER THE NEXT SEVERAL DAYS, my life falls into a surprisingly pleasant routine, and the worries that have nagged at me since I first came to the palace begin to fall away.

In the mornings, I eat breakfast with the king, Tallin, or both. Neither seems particularly interested in making conversation with one another or me, which suits me just fine.

The king dotes on me, inquiring daily as to my health, my happiness, and my general comfort, while Tallin does little more than grunt reluctant greetings my way.

I wander the palace grounds each morning, then nap.

Thorne and I agreed before leaving the map room that we would meet each night at the stroke of midnight in our secret spot inside the hedge maze.

Every time we meet, I expect to have an army of Crimsons descend upon us...but they never do.

It's almost as though they've been ordered to stay away—but we tell ourselves that's far too much to hope for.

We make love each night like it's the last time we'll ever see one another, our powers and feelings growing with each encounter. My desire for him increases with each meeting, and each time we part, it feels like torture.

I know without asking that we both fear what will happen after the ball.

Every Noble in Kravan will be attending, and if I do my job well, my time at the palace will come to an abrupt end. By then, I'll have given King Tomas every bit of information I can possibly gather.

Though I allow myself to hope and dream that the Histories will provide us with what we need to escape our fates, a sense of dread creeps its way into my chest every time I think about the future.

What if we can't access the vault? What if there are no texts in the Perrin home?

Worse still, what if the texts paint the Tethered in a negative light?

Every question breeds more questions—and every answer leads me back to the same place:

We need to escape the palace as soon as we possibly can.

ON THE LAST night before the ball, as Thorne and I lie in an exhausted tangle on the grass, I finally summon the courage to ask the question that's been weighing on me for days now.

"What exactly did you see that convinced you the Graystones have a part to play in Kravan's future?"

Thorne stiffens, pulling me closer, then says, "Do you really want to know?"

I nod and murmur, "Yes."

I feel Thorne's body tighten next to mine. "I saw Tallin lying bloody on the ground. Ellion and Lady Graystone were standing over his body."

CHAPTER
FORTY-ONE

WHEN LATE AFTERNOON hits on the day of Lord and Lady Perrin's ball, I find myself trembling with anticipation...though I'm not entirely sure I should be.

I'm about to take the greatest risk of my life. I intend to break into a vault that's apparently impossible to find, let alone open. I'm willingly seeking out texts that are forbidden to every citizen of Kravan, including the king himself.

It seems that at some point in the last few weeks, I've lost my mind.

In my suite's closet, I find an assortment of new gowns, each more beautiful than the last. One of them—a stunning silk dress with a skirt so full you could hide a small army under it— is deep crimson, and far too similar to the gown I wore to the Prince's Ball.

I lay a few other options out on my bed, mulling them over. After trying each of them on, I settle on a gown the same deep blue as the sky's depths on a clear, cold day. Its bodice is fitted, its banded straps are off-the-shoulder, and it's absolutely perfect.

It even has pockets, though I don't suppose I'll make use of them...except, perhaps, as a temporary home for Mercutio.

I'm grateful to discover a pair of long white satin gloves on my nightstand, which I intend to wear instead of my silver wrist bands in order to conceal the telltale markings of a Tethered on my left arm.

When Maude has assisted me in applying my makeup and styling my long brown hair into loose waves, I slip into the dress. As beautiful as it is, perhaps my favorite thing about it is the fact that it's not flashy or conspicuous—and tonight, of all nights, I need to remain understated. If anyone notices me heading off to find Nev at ten p.m.—if anyone should follow me —it would not go well for either of us.

I don't know what I'm likely to discover in the vault. So many people have offered up conflicting theories that I've had to clear my mind of all of them and simply hope for the best possible outcome.

When seven o'clock rolls around and I've finally scarfed down a little of the dinner that was sent to my room an hour ago, I grab Mercutio from the windowsill, tucking him into my clutch, and head down to the palace's main entrance, where I find Tallin dressed in a set of black tails.

The prince takes me by the hand, his voice almost charming when he says, "Ah, Lady Ingram. How lovely you look."

"Thank you," I tell him, glancing sideways at Thorne, who's standing next to the Flyer and watching me with a look of famished admiration.

For all the prince's finery, I'll take Thorne in his black dress uniform any day.

Many times over, if I were allowed.

Forcing my eyes from his face and glancing around, I ask, "Where is the king? I thought he was coming tonight."

Please tell me he's not. It would make life so much simpler.

"He took a separate Flyer, piloted by Valira, to pick up Lady Verdan and her daughters."

"Her daughters are coming?" I say, and my eyes meet Thorne's as my heart rate accelerates to precarious levels.

"Don't worry," Tallin says softly. "My mother has assured me Devorah and Pippa will never speak a word about you to anyone, on pain of death."

I can't help snickering. We all know Tallin's mother is a psychopath who's not at all opposed to killing members of her own family. Something tells me her threat against the young women is a hundred percent sincere—whether they realize it or not.

"I'll take your word for it," I say, striding past the prince to climb into the Flyer. Tallin scrambles in next to me, but to my surprise, he doesn't reach for me or make lewd comments. Instead, he leans against his door and stares out the window.

Thorne climbs silently into the pilot's seat, and within a minute, we're airborne.

SOME TIME LATER, we reach the Perrin estate only to see a large group of Nobles making their way inside the main house. The sprawling estate stretches over an enormous plot of land, complete with a pond, pool, tennis courts, and several outbuildings. It's almost as lavish as the palace itself, and I scan the property from the air, trying to figure out where the servants' entrance is.

~Southwest corner, Maude's voice says. *Next to the basketball court.*

How do you know?

~I've tracked down the blueprints for the house.

What about the vault?

It takes her a moment to reply.

~It's next to Lord and Lady Perrin's library—but it looks like there's no access from the hallway.

Oh—so there's a hidden door or something?

~The vault has no door whatsoever.

What?

~According to the most recent plans for the house, the vault is fully enclosed and encased in several inches of steel. There is one small access panel on one of its walls, but that's it. I believe it was built before the house itself.

Wait—you're telling me the Perrin house was built around *it?*

~That's exactly what I'm saying. The vault, it seems, was constructed toward the end of the Rebellion, generations ago. I suspect the texts have been hidden inside it ever since. There is no door. No lock. Nothing at all. Apparently, no one was ever meant to open it.

This is why I need Nev.

Maude, a Porter can bring someone with them when they use their powers, right? Nev could transport someone past a wall, no matter how thick?

Again, the A.I. seems to ponder that for a moment, then says, *~Yes, provided they're touching you. But there are certain risks involved.*

Like what?

~If Nev doesn't port to the correct location—let's say she accidentally ends up mere inches from the steel wall while holding onto you —you could end up inside *that wall.*

That sounds bad.

~I suspect it's not pleasant.

When Thorne has landed, we climb out of the vehicle and head into the Perrin home, my arm in Tallin's.

For once, I don't recoil at his touch.

Maybe it's the excitement of the evening—the thrill of

knowing how close Thorne and I are to escaping this life and starting over elsewhere.

Or maybe it's just knowing that tonight, I have the chance to learn a truth that's been hidden ever since the Rebellion.

All I know is that ten o'clock can't come soon enough.

FORTY-TWO

THE INSTANT we walk into the house, I see why the Perrin estate was deemed a perfect location for a ball.

The enormous foyer, with its extraordinary crystal chandelier, is large enough to hold a hundred guests. Just beyond it lies a vast ballroom. Twelve more chandeliers hang from its high ceilings by silver chains, illuminating the gleaming marble floors, fluted columns, and elegant wall sconces scattered around the space.

I'm overwhelmed by the sheer number of guests who have already begun dancing to bombastic music performed by what looks like a full-sized orchestra at the far end of the room.

"Impressive," I say as we saunter in.

"Isn't it?" Tallin replies. "But remember, my dear—this isn't a night to let your guard down. You still have a job to do."

He doesn't need to remind me that I'm here to hunt Tethered.

But I have no intention of doing so.

All I care about tonight is what will occur at ten o'clock, and until then, nothing else matters.

Tallin introduces me to a few Noble couples as we tour the

room, and each time we finish making small talk with them—
while Thorne stalks along behind us—the prince turns my way,
an inquisitive look on his face.

"No," I tell him each time. "They're not Tethered."

A few of them are, of course. A Healer, like me. A Netic, like
Valira. I spot a few with dull talents like the ability to calculate
complex mathematical equations quickly, or, in one case,
impressive swimming skills. But I have yet to see one Tethered
at the ball that I would deem a threat.

After a while, I spot Lady Graystone and Ellion making
conversation on the far side of the room with the king and Lady
Verdan.

That seems like a terrible idea, I tell Maude silently.

~Perhaps the Graystones like to live dangerously.

"I'm going to go over and chat with them," Tallin tells me.

"I think I'll stay here, if that's all right."

The prince looks me up and down, then says, "Fine. Don't
go far."

I assure him I won't and watch him go, grateful that he
didn't insist I accompany him. I observe his interaction with his
parents for a moment, then slip over to get myself a glass of
punch at a nearby table.

Thorne watches me intently, careful not to get too close. I
turn toward him while I sip my drink—just as a young woman
with a shock of blond hair walks over and lays her hand on
his arm.

I nearly spit my punch all over the floor.

Oh, shit.

It's Devorah, the older of Lady Verdan's two stepdaughters.
When she touches Thorne, he tightens, his lips pulling into
something approaching a sneer.

She doesn't seem to take the hint, because she eases closer
to him, whispering something in his ear, then turns my way. He

gestures toward me and to my surprise, Devorah steps over and nods her head in greeting.

I mirror her movement, watching the king and Lady Verdan out of the corner of my eye. I'm relieved when I see they're too occupied with Tallin and the Graystones to notice us.

"Shara," Devorah whispers.

"*Lady Ingram*," I correct, a warning in my tone.

"Of course. Lady Ingram."

Her voice isn't the hard bite I'm used to from her, but softer, more lilting—almost reverent.

"Don't worry," she says. "I won't give away your true identity."

"So why, exactly, are you talking to me?" I hiss. This feels dangerous and stupid, to put it mildly. If Lady Verdan sees us together, I can't imagine she'll react well.

Devorah takes hold of my wrist and leads me toward the nearest door and out. A moment later, we find ourselves standing in a narrow hallway just outside the ballroom, ensconced in shadow. "Look," she says, "I've discovered some things since you, um...*left*."

"Left?" I snicker. "Your stepmother threw us in the family dungeon."

"I didn't know there were cells in our basement. I don't go down there. I didn't know a *lot* of things. I'm sure it's for you to believe, but it's true. Like—I didn't know for a long time what my stepmother really is."

My eyebrows arch in surprise. "Are you saying you know now? Did she tell you?"

Devorah shakes her head. "Hell, no. She would never. I saw it for myself." She shifts on her feet, then adds, "Our last Tethered before Thorne—Timothy was his name—disappeared one day a few years back. Daphne told me she'd let him go, but one day when I was out in the garden, I saw a ring that he used to wear. A small silver thing. I knew it because it had a dragon's face on it, and I've always liked dragons."

Get on with it, I think.

"It was poking out from a pile of earth," she whispers.

"Maybe there's an innocent explanation. He could have dropped it when he was working out there."

She shakes her head.

I have no idea why I'm defending Lady Verdan to her, anyway. The woman is a sociopath. She killed her own husband —Devorah's and Pippa's father. She killed her parents, by her own admission. Who the hell knows how many other people she's murdered over the years?

"I saw more than just the ring," Devorah murmurs. "When I got close and looked in the garden...he was...*there.* Under the ground. I dug at the earth a little with my foot. I nearly passed out when I saw a hand—it was burnt and horrifying. At first, I thought maybe a member of the Royal Guard had killed him or something. But I had seen her—Daphne—my stepmother, I mean. I'd seen her summon flame and lightning when she thought she was alone. I know she's a Tethered, like you and Thorne."

I look into her eyes, trying to determine whether that's the extent of her knowledge.

Is she aware the prince of Kravan is her half-brother?

Does she know her stepmother killed her father, Milo Verdan?

~There's no way Lady Verdan would allow Devorah to live to tell about it if she knew, Maude assures me.

You're probably right.

"Watch your back, Shara," Devorah whispers. "This isn't going to end well for you—this charade you're putting on. I don't know why you're doing this—posing as a Noble. And I realize I haven't always been nice to you..."

"You've *never* been nice to me, Devorah."

"Fair enough. Okay, fine, I've been a bitch. But I never wanted you dead. I just didn't like how Thorne looked at you. But none of that matters now. I'm worried about what's going to happen."

"Why do you say that? What have you heard?"

She looks around to make sure we're not being watched, then takes me by the arm and pulls me toward the shadowy depths of a nearby alcove.

"The other night, I was downstairs in the salon. I heard my stepmother let someone into the house—a woman. They argued for a few minutes in the foyer. I heard your name come up, and Thorne's. I heard the word 'terminate' more than once. You know what that means, right?"

My heart sinks to new depths.

I've known this reality would hit eventually—that the day would come when the king realized I was no longer useful.

I just didn't expect to hear about it from Devorah, of all people.

"Yeah. I know what it means when Nobles terminate Tethered. Do you know who the other woman was?"

Devorah shakes her head. "Someone important, I think. Another Noble—but I don't know her. It sounded like they think you're a threat—you and Thorne, both."

"You think your stepmother's got something planned for us?"

"I *know* she does. Look, I don't like you, Sha—I mean, Lady Ingram. At all. I haven't exactly made a secret of it. But I've always had a soft spot for Thorne—and I'm scared he's going to end up like Timothy."

"He won't," I assure her. "Thorne is powerful. I've seen him take down an entire cohort of Tethered."

Devorah looks skeptical to the point of amusement. "I'm

not sure even Thorne would be able to take on someone who can summon fire. And I *know* you couldn't. Whatever magical powers you may have, you're not some warrior princess."

She's right.

I have no great strength. My powers have nothing to do with violence or battle. I'm a weakling, by anyone's standards. The greatest power I wield is my ability to hunt Tethered—and that is quickly losing its value, thanks to the service I've already rendered the king.

"It's not magic," I lament.

"Then how the hell are you going to survive? If my mother's talking termination, it's serious."

"I have no idea. But I'll think of something. Thorne and I have made it this far without getting ourselves killed. All we need..."

Is a little time.

"Look, we're prepared for whatever may come," I say at last, though the words feel hollow and pointless. "But to be honest, I'm not sure the king would hurt me."

King Tomas has always been kind to me—even treating me like a daughter. At least, as I imagine a daughter should be treated. He's consoled me when I felt down, reassured me, and invited me to be a part of the family. And for the last several days, he's turned a blind eye when Thorne and I met for nightly trysts—despite the fact that I know perfectly well that the king normally sends out nightly patrols to check on the grounds.

As cruel as Lady Verdan is, I don't see Tomas standing idly by while she burns one or both of us to death.

Devorah levels me with a look that reminds me a little too much of a gargoyle—her shoulders hunched, her eyes filled with judgment.

"I hope you're right," she mutters. "For Thorne's sake. Just watch out—and keep an eye on the prince. That guy gives me the creeps."

"Thank you. I will."

I guess that means she doesn't know Tallin's her half-brother.

~Astute observation, Maude replies, snide as always.

Before Devorah has a chance to walk away, I call her name softly.

"Yes?"

"Did your stepmother hire—I mean *purchase*—a new Domestic yet?"

"Not yet," she says. "We have a new Guard, but he's some old guy who's, like, thirty. He seems all right, though."

"You might want to suggest to Lady Verdan that she look into acquiring a Domestic called Evangeline. She's working for the Prefect, but they're thinking of getting rid of her. Just...don't tell Lady Verdan I was the one who recommended her."

Devorah crinkles her nose. "Evangeline? She's not some hot nineteen-year-old, is she? I have enough competition from Pippa for hot guys."

"No—a lot older than nineteen," I laugh. "She's nice. I think you'd like her. Plus, I'd feel better if I knew you were looking out for her."

I'm not convinced that working for Daphne Verdan is any safer for my mother than working for Lady Weston and the Prefect. But at least she might have a chance to survive a few more months if she makes the move.

Devorah looks at me like I've lit my head on fire, then offers up a strangely warm smile and nods. "Okay—thank you, Shara." Whispering, she leans in close and says, "Lady Ingram, I mean."

She turns away just in time to see Lady Graystone leaving the ballroom and heading toward the house's main doors.

"Holy shit," Devorah says.

"What is it?"

"That woman—she's the one who was arguing with my mother about you and Thorne. I remember her prosthetic hand."

With that, she leaves me to my wretched solitude, a thousand new questions stirring inside my mind.

CHAPTER
FORTY-THREE

"WHAT DID DEVORAH WANT?" Thorne asks when I've found my way back to his side.

"Let's just say she's been looking out for us—and she's a slightly better person than I took her for. We need to be careful tonight, Thorne."

"Just a few more hours." He utters the words out of the corner of his mouth, hands clasped behind his back as he watches the guests mingle and dance. "Then we'll have some answers, and we can figure out how to get the hell out from under the Royals' noses."

A feeling of foreboding settles over me, a grim cloud hovering above my mind. "What if we don't find what we're hoping for?"

"Hey—no need for pessimism. You're starting to sound like me." Thorne smirks. "Besides, what exactly *are* we hoping for? The likelihood of finding some magical formula for bringing peace to Kravan or bringing down the king is basically zero. If we're really lucky, the texts will tell us how to get to the Capitol without getting ourselves killed. I'd say that's a lofty enough goal."

Just as he finishes speaking, Lord Nelson walks by, and I nod toward him, watching him leave before whispering, "There's got to be something in the vault that's important. I don't know how or why, but I'm sure of it. There's a reason it's been hidden all this time."

"I just hope you're right. But for the record, I have a bad feeling about all of this."

~So do I, Maude says.

"Shut your nonexistent mouth," I mutter.

Thorne, who knows exactly who I'm talking to, chuckles.

"I'm going to patrol for a little," he says. "I'll figure out how to reach the servants' entrance from inside the house so we don't have to go scrambling for it at the last second."

Before Maude has a chance to point out that she knows exactly where it is, I whisper, "Yes, Maude—we know. Just let him confirm your theory."

I spend over an hour moving around the ballroom and making small talk with this and that Noble, some of whom I've met before. A few sadistic Tethered stand out, and I take note of them, calling on Maude to give me their names. But the truth is, I have absolutely no intention of reporting them.

If all goes well tonight and Thorne and I manage to make our escape, there will no longer be any need to impart the names of traitors.

AFTER A TIME, I spot Ellion Graystone across the room. He's standing on his own as usual, intently watching a middle-aged man in a set of gray tails dancing with a much younger woman.

Ellion's eyes are narrowed as he observes the couple, and I pull my focus to them, wondering what's got him so fascinated.

It's only when I watch the man attempt to kiss the young

woman—which results in her slapping him hard and storming off—that I look back at Ellion, who's now laughing.

The man who just got slapped, meanwhile, looks temporarily confused, as if he has no idea what just transpired. After a few seconds, though, his confusion turns to horror. He runs after the woman, calling out in desperate apology.

"Holy shit," I say under my breath. "I was so wrong."

"Wrong?"

Thorne has just stepped up to my left, and his eyes, too, have landed on the apologetic Noble.

"I thought Ellion's power was mind-reading," I tell him, "but his mother said it was more than that. I didn't understand what she meant—couldn't figure him out. But now, I think I see."

"See what?"

I turn to Thorne, panicked. "I think he took control of that man—the one on the dance floor. I think Ellion *made* him kiss that young woman."

"Made him? You mean to say he's a Bender?"

"Is that what it's called?" I ask. "I've never encountered one."

Thorne nods. "They're a special—and horrible—breed of Tethered. When I was in the Tower, we had one in our cohort who took control of our Combat Trainer. The trainer ended up in the infirmary and the Bender disappeared. The theory was that he'd taken control of every Guard and Warden until he'd managed to escape the Tower and hide out in the Capitol. Their kind is so dangerous, they're not even labeled Crimson or Gilded—they're given their own classification."

As I watch, Ellion turns our way and fixes his eyes on me, and I'm convinced I see him wink.

He knows I know.

"I wonder if we could ever persuade him to manipulate Tallin or the king," I whisper.

Thorne shakes his head. "He wouldn't do it—not if he has any sense of self-preservation."

I draw my gaze away from Ellion with a shudder, grateful that he seems unable to penetrate my mind.

"If you ever feel him digging around in your head, you'll let me know—won't you?" I ask, desperation in my eyes when they meet Thorne's.

"I will. But don't worry—I suspect Ellion is too smart to try that sort of shit with me."

With a smile, I tell him I'm going to keep wandering until the time comes to meet up with Nev. "I don't want anyone to get suspicious that we're plotting—not when we're this close."

Thorne nods and heads off on another patrol, and I turn just in time to spot Tallin in the midst of a lively discussion with Lord Twain. Valira is standing close by, keeping an eye on him.

I've just started making my way toward them when I hear the king's voice calling me over.

"Lady Ingram! Come!"

I glance over to see him standing with Lady Verdan and Lady Graystone—a strange, uncomfortable sight, particularly given what Devorah told me earlier.

I step over, bowing my head. "Your Grace," I say.

"How are you enjoying the evening's festivities?" the king asks over the roar of a lively waltz.

"Very much," I lie. "And you?"

King Tomas smiles first at Lady Verdan, then Graystone, and says, "I can't possibly complain with such lovely companions by my side, can I? Tell me, has this evening been a...success?"

"Yes, your Grace. Definitely a success."

Another lie.

"Good, good. Excellent. Well, you should go about your

business. Go back to my ridiculous son and make a man of him, would you?"

Whatever he means by that, the imagery my mind conjures is enough to make me gag.

"Yes, your Grace," I reply, my eyes veering to a large clock on the opposite wall.

A jolt of adrenaline forces a gasp from my throat.

9:45.

It's nearly time to head to the servants' entrance.

With a reverent curtsy, I leave the king and his two companions and head off in search of Thorne. It's only a minute or two before I discover him in a hallway leading toward a servant's kitchen in another wing of the house.

"I'll lead you to the meeting place," he says. "But first—"

He takes me by the hand and pulls me close, looking up and down the hall to make sure no one is watching. "Are you sure you want to do this? There's a ton of risk involved, Shara, and I'm talking about more than the mere danger of trying to port into an unknown room."

"I know," I say. "And yes, I want to do this. If I can only have one chance at freedom and a life with you, Thorne, I'm going to take it."

His eyes brim with affection. "Well, I can't exactly argue with that, can I?"

I glance both ways, then kiss him. It's quick and fleeting, but filled with so much meaning and love that my chest warms with all the courage I could possibly need.

I lock my eyes on his and whisper, "Let's go risk our lives."

NEV IS ALREADY WAITING OUTSIDE, the cool night air making her shiver despite her Guard's uniform.

"I'm so happy you came," I tell her. "I'm surprised—but grateful—that the Nelsons didn't bring you as their bodyguard. Every Noble here seems to have one."

"My Proprietors hire outside people for that job," Nev moans. "They don't like me leaving the house—which means I only have a few minutes to do this, so we'd better get cracking."

I reach into my clutch to make sure Mercutio is with me. Under the touch of my finger, I feel him stirring slightly, and I tell him to be patient. "Only a few minutes, now."

Thorne accompanies us back inside, watchful as he guides us, with Maude's help, through the back servants' corridors until we reach the Perrins' library.

To my relief, its door is unlocked, and we push our way in to find the room empty, other than the thousands of contraband books lining a multitude of floor-to-ceiling shelves.

"Who the hell *are* these people?" Nev asks under her breath. "Nobody is allowed to own this many novels—I mean, other than the king."

"I suspect Lord and Lady Perrin get special privileges for being the keepers of the Histories, or something," I tell her. "They need to be kept happy in this house, for obvious reasons. If they move or decide to demolish the estate..."

"It would be bad, I guess," Nev admits.

When we're inside, Maude guides us toward the far wall, which, like the others, is concealed by shelves.

~*The vault is six feet ahead of us,* she says out loud so that Nev can hear her. *It's nine feet by nine feet.*

"Can you work with that?" I ask Nev.

"I think so. I'll port us both ten feet in—that should give us room for error."

~*Error, in this case, could result in death,* Maude chimes in, audible once again.

"Thanks, Maude," Nev says. "Super-helpful advice there."

"The king may note our absence," Thorne reminds us. "You'd better get in there."

"You?" My eyes go wide. "You're not coming in with us?"

"He can't," Nev says. "I've tried porting two people along with me, but it doesn't work. Even one is a risk—two would be insane."

"It's okay." Thorne kisses me gently on the forehead. "Maude and Mercutio will record anything you see. I'll meet you back by the servants' entrance." He takes me by the hand then kisses me one last time. "Don't die, okay?"

"You never let me do anything," I mock-pout.

"As if I could ever *stop* you."

"You two are nauseating," Nev moans. "And I really do have to get home, so can we please get a move on?"

"Fine," I say with a laugh. "We'll be as quick as we can. Promise."

With a nod, Thorne backs away. I can feel his nervous energy from where I stand—fear for our safety mingling with excitement about what Nev and I are about to see.

"You good?" Nev asks, and I nod.

I take hold of her hand and squeeze it tight, my pulse racing.

"Then here we go," she says, and the world drops violently out from under my feet, only to jar itself right back into place a moment later.

I peer around, not daring to step forward or backward. At first, all I can see is a thick veil of darkness. I'm still holding tight to Nev, who seems as disoriented as I am.

Of course it's dark, I think. *Why would there be a light in a room that's been cut off from the world for decades?*

There's a sudden flicker of light, and an old-fashioned lantern illuminates, its flame springing to life.

"How...?" I breathe, wondering if there's some sort of motion detector at work.

And then, I see it.

"Shara..." Nev says, clinging tightly to my hand. "Who the hell is *that*?"

SITTING at a table in the room's center is a person, small and frail. The figure is hunched over the lantern, a set of pale, colorless eyes focused on the flickering flame.

When the voice comes, it's brittle—the rasp of an elderly woman. "Never did I think a Hunter would enter the vault. And yet, it makes perfect sense."

I spin around, eyeing the walls, searching for a door. Shelves. Books. *Anything* to tell me I'm not dreaming.

"Who *are* you?" I can hear the apprehension in Nev's voice. "Where are the texts?"

"To answer the first question, I am known by a select few as the Storian," the woman says, turning her head our way. "To answer the second question, there are no texts, dear girl."

"The...Storian...?" I ask, my voice quaking. I shouldn't fear this woman, as fragile as she is. But there is an aura of immense power in this strange room.

It's as though she holds the key to my future, even if I don't yet understand how that's possible.

I try and force myself to look into her eyes—to determine

what her power could be—but all I see in them is creamy whiteness. No swirl of color. Nothing at all.

"Yes, Hunter," she says. "I *am* a Tethered, like you, and I have lived in this room since the end of the Rise."

"The Rise," I echo, looking at Nev to see whether she has any idea what that means.

"You call it the Rebellion," the Storian says. "But *that* is far from the truth. My job—my only occupation in this world—is to hold onto the past."

"I don't understand. What, exactly, is your power? You've been here longer than any person has ever lived. How are you..."

"Alive?" She locks her eyes on mine as though she can see everything inside me. With a jagged finger poking at her temple, she says, "I hold history in my mind's eye. All that Kravan once was—and all that led to its downfall."

"But...how do you survive?" Nev says, looking around. "How do you eat, sleep...everything else a person does?"

The Storian lets out a quick, cackling laugh, then says, "I don't live. Not in the way you think. I have no need of sleep, of food. My mind keeps me occupied while I am awake."

"But you're so...*old*."

The statement would normally seem incredibly rude, but something tells me the woman won't take it personally.

"I'm kept alive by what I know," the Storian says. "And only when I pass my knowledge to the next Storian—or Kravan is freed—will I be allowed to leave this place. That is the law."

I don't have time to ask her where this so-called law came from, so I simply say, "Can you tell us about Kravan's history? What led to the Rebellion—I mean, the Rise?"

"I cannot tell you," she says, and with that, my heart sinks.

"What do you mean, *cannot tell*?" Nev half-shouts, her hands raking through her hair. "After all this, we're supposed to leave here with nothing?"

"That's not what I said."

Slowly, the Storian rises to her feet and steps over to me, her face in shadow. She looks up into my eyes and says, "You are not a mere Hunter, Shara. It is the wrong name for your particular gift. Here, let me show you."

I can feel Nev growing impatient by my side as she shifts from foot to foot, clearly wanting to get on with it—whatever *it* is.

With a long, pointed fingernail, the Storian slices into her own palm—just as my mother did with the letter opener in the Prefect's home. A trickle of blood slips from the wound, black in the darkness, and the Storian takes hold of my hand, clenching it with a surprisingly powerful grip.

At first, I think she's asking me to heal her. But with her touch, my mind explodes.

I feel myself falling to my knees, overwhelmed by a thousand emotions all at once.

Pain. Joy. Fear. Jubilance.

Defeat.

Somewhere in the far distance, I hear Nev and Maude calling to me, concern wracking their voices. But I can't answer.

My head is reeling with a churning sea of information. I see everything at once—every inch of the Capitol in the days when it was a beautiful, prosperous city, and no Tower shot up at its center.

I see Tethered and Normals living together in their pretty homes, surrounded by gardens and friendly neighbors. Ships arrive in a southern harbor that no longer exists. Vehicles move along the Capitol's streets. There are schools, and my heart aches to see so many happy children running around in green parks with their parents by their sides.

The Capitol was so different then from what I've witnessed in my few brief glimpses. It wasn't an island situated at

Kravan's center, surrounded on all sides by the broad channels I've seen from the air. Instead, Kravan was one land, connected, with roads running through it—all the way from the Capitol to the Palatine Estates.

There was a leader—a woman called President Brant, elected by the people. Her government met inside an underground chamber at the Capitol's center known only as the Citadel. For a time, she was respected, even loved.

From the Citadel ran long tunnels, leading to every corner of Kravan. These were the passageways Valira once told me about—the routes the Nobles used to escape when the Rebellion began. I can see them in my mind, like a series of veins channeling blood from one part of the realm to another.

Only, in those days, it wasn't *called* a realm.

There was no king. No queen. No Nobles—and no indentured servants. Kravan's citizens lived in a land of equality, and the only power granted to individuals came from the population itself.

I see in an instant how it came to pass—how the Rise began. A wealthy businessman named Quinton hired a small army of mercenaries and commanded them to storm the Citadel. They killed the president and every member of her government. Civilians were forced against their will to build the Tower, and those who didn't support Quinton were herded inside and locked in the cells that would one day be known as Whiterooms.

Quinton named himself king and claimed the palace as his own after having its residents murdered. He cut the realm off from every other land. Ships were outlawed, except for a precious few allowed to bring in goods from distant locations.

In my mind I see fighting and chaos in the Capitol. Bloodshed, anger, and blame are all propagated by lies about the "violent" Tethered. Posters announce in capital letters that our kind has destroyed Kravan—that the Tethered are the reason the shipments ceased and the population began to starve.

I watch in horror as a full-blown war breaks out, with armed men now known as the "Royal Guard" killing civilians on both sides of the battle.

And then, I watch as the streets fall silent. Bodies litter the Capitol—Tethered and Normal alike. A massacre has decimated Kravan's former population.

An entire new generation of Normal and Tethered is born inside the Tower, and every child is raised to believe Kravan has always been ruled by a king...and that the Tethered have always been the enemies of Normals.

Every Tethered is raised to believe their sole purpose in life is to serve the Nobility. The Rules of Kravan are drafted, and Tethered are killed when they dare break them.

Over time, the land that was once beautiful and whole is ruined, with deep channels carved into its surface to separate its regions—to keep rich from poor and to isolate the informed from the ignorant, the powerful from the weak.

Anyone with knowledge of the past is killed.

Books are burned.

Newspapers are outlawed.

One by one, the new generation of imprisoned Normals is released to live in the Capitol once again. Some are deemed worthy of Nobility by Kravan's so-called "king" and are invited to live on what are now the outer islands, in the sprawling estates once occupied by Tethered and Normal alike. Walls are built between the properties, grim reminders of the hostilities that once nearly brought down the realm.

The elderly man who once declared himself king—one of the few who knows the truth about the past—declares that no Tethered shall ever again be born outside of the Tower. There will be no evidence of a past in which Kravan's population was free.

The words "prison" and "election" are banned from the realm's vocabulary.

Thousands more visions cross my mind simultaneously—lives lived, deaths, births, conflict, bombings of the Capitol by rebel militias.

And then, just for a moment, my mind stops and focuses when a man appears—tall, with brown hair and piercing blue eyes. He stands at the center of a desolate street, dressed in black, and calls out to his followers.

Without understanding why, I know this man is my father, the one some call the Shadow.

The visions begin moving at a mile a second again, mere flashes coming at me far too quickly to register. Yet every flash enters my consciousness like an entire lifetime I've lived, felt, witnessed. The sensation is overwhelming.

It's also a horror.

Not only am I witnessing the birth of entire generations, but their deaths as well, and all of it is colliding with my consciousness at once.

When it finally ends, I crumple to the floor, heaving with exhaustion.

The Storian stands over me, the wound in her hand now healed.

"What the hell was that?" Nev shouts. "What have you done to her?"

"I have given her the truth," the Storian says. "All of it.

"Shara?" Nev asks, crouching down and taking me by the shoulders. "Are you all right?"

"We have to go back!" I cry. "They'll be searching for us! It's been hours..."

"It's only been a few seconds," Nev protests, concern filling her voice. "It's all right."

I'm shaking when I look up at the Storian.

"What's happened to me?" Hot tears streak down my cheeks. "What have I become?"

"Nothing, except what you always were," she says. "It's your power, Hunter, that allowed you to gather those memories, just as I did so long ago. You absorbed my gifts for a time. You can absorb those of other Tethered as well."

I shake my head. "No—I should only have been able to *see* your powers. What just happened...it was something else."

"A Hunter can take on the powers of anyone whose blood she touches," she says softly, her voice almost musical. "Only temporarily—for a few minutes, at the most. But a few minutes were more than enough for you to take on all of the memories I have held onto for so long. They live inside you now, and one day soon, you will reveal them to the realm of Kravan. You will show our people the truth—once you come to understand which parts need exposing."

"I don't want the memories," I say miserably. I sound like a child. I feel like one, too—desperate to be held, to be soothed. Desperate for the mother I barely know.

I don't want this burden. I don't want this trauma. I don't want the pain of rifling through what's now living in my mind —to uncover the horrors that need exposing to the world.

"The truth is the only path to freedom," the Storian says, nodding toward Nev. "You have allies. You have friends. They will help you. But I warn you—this night will be brutal and cruel, Shara. What happened here is only the beginning."

Ice infiltrates my veins. "What does that mean?"

"It means you will be tested. Every part of your life has led to the hours to come—everything. But you must find your strength if you are to turn the tide."

"I don't understand," I whimper.

"I know," the Storian says, her voice filled with kindness. "But go. Take what I've given you. A storm is coming, and only you can put an end to its fury. Tell no one what you've seen— not until the time is right."

"But what about you?" I ask, gesturing to the thick walls. "How can you live like this?"

"I have lived like this for many years, and I will live this way until you have done what you need to, and Kravan is freed. Perhaps after all, it's my fate to be the last Storian this land ever knows."

It's almost like she's something other than *alive*—like she simply...*is*. Like she's an animated creation who comes alive only when others are present, but remains dormant the rest of her days. I can't imagine she's seen another person since she was first encased in this horrific, dark vault.

"Maybe you could come with us..." I glance at the walls, willing them to vanish.

The Storian shakes her head. "The walls aren't what's holding me here. Now, go. And good luck to you."

Nev takes hold of my hand, and within moments we're standing in a small bedroom in another wing of the Perrin home.

"No," I gasp when I realize what we've done. "She'll die, Nev. We have to go back..."

"She's ancient," Nev says, her voice straining as if she knows my pain. "We can't help her, Shar. But...I need to get back to the Nelson property before the other servants realize I'm gone. You should go find Thorne."

I throw my arms around her and squeeze tightly. "I don't know what's going to happen," I say, my mind still swimming with memories that don't belong to me. "Never tell anyone what happened in there, Nev."

"I won't. Trust me. No one would believe me, anyhow."

"That's probably true." I pull back and wipe at my eyes. "Look—when this is all over, we'll find each other, okay?"

Nev nods, and I'm pretty sure I see uncharacteristic tears in her eyes, too. "We will. I promise."

I say one last goodbye, then leave the room and make my way rapidly down the hall toward the back stairway. I race down the stairs, nearly twisting an ankle in my desperation to reach the back entrance.

Whether or not I'm allowed, I need to tell Thorne what I've absorbed—though it would take a decade or more to describe it all.

At the very least, I need to tell him about a tunnel I saw, tucked among thousands upon thousands of visions—one that leads from the crypt in the palace's lowest level all the way to the Capitol.

If Thorne and I can find that entrance, we can escape...

Tonight.

CHAPTER
FORTY-FIVE

When I arrive at the servants' entrance, Thorne is nowhere to be seen.

At first, panic threatens to send me into the throes of a cardiac incident—but then, I remind myself of what Nev said about how it only took a matter of seconds for me to receive all the Storian's memories.

Maybe Thorne went another way. Maybe he ran into Tallin, or Valira, or someone who held him up for a few minutes.

I'm still mulling over the abundance of *maybes* when a low voice speaks.

"Shara."

I twist around, my heart racing with the shock of hearing my real name uttered in this place.

The prince is standing before me, with Valira by his side—and neither of them looks pleased.

"Lady Ingram, you mean." I speak the words sternly, but something in Tallin's eyes tells me that for once, he didn't mean any offense.

"You're looking for Thorne," Tallin says. "But you're not going to find him. I'm sorry."

Two men wearing Royal Guard insignias step around him, lunging at me. One of the men takes me hard by the arm, and when I try to jerk myself away, his grip only tightens.

Shit.

"What's going on here?" I ask in my best *I'm a Noble, and I deserve to be treated with respect* tone.

"Thorne was found in the Perrins' library a few minutes ago. Strangely, three people were seen entering that library—but only he came out. You can see how that was suspicious to the house's owners. I've also come to discover that the Histories were stored in a vault next door to that very library."

"I don't know what you're talking about," I say, fully aware of how ridiculous the lie is.

"Look, Shara," the prince says with a huff of exasperation. "I would have happily ignored your little transgression. My father, on the other hand, will not, and he's ordered that you be brought to the palace immediately. I don't suppose you're going to tell me where your Guard friend is."

Given that he already knows where Thorne is, he can only mean Nev—but there's no way I'm willing to utter her name.

"Like I said, I don't know what you're talking about."

"Fine," Tallin retorts, nodding to the Guards. "You know what to do."

The man who's clenching my arm in his fist drags me around the back of the house toward the gravel drive and beyond, until we reach the Flyer that brought us to the Perrin residence. Tallin and Valira follow along behind.

"Valira," I say over my shoulder as I stumble toward the vehicle. "What's happened to Thorne?"

"He's..." she begins to say, but stops herself.

"It's fine, my darling," the prince tells her, making no effort to conceal his fondness for her. "Go ahead. Tell her."

"The king had him carted off," she says. "I don't know

where he's gone, but it's not the palace. I watched his Flyer take off. It was...headed south."

"South," I stammer.

Toward the Capitol.

But why? What reason could the king possibly have for sending him there? If King Tomas is angry with us, shouldn't he bring us back to the palace for whatever punishment he intends to inflict?

"I'm sorry, Shara," Valira says. "I didn't want this for him—for you. I tried to—"

But Tallin grabs her hand and whispers something to her, and she stops talking.

All five of us—Tallin, the two Guards, Valira and I—pile into the Flyer together, with me in the back between the two enormous men. Valira pilots the Flyer, and Tallin sits next to her, a hand possessively clutching her thigh.

When we get to the palace, the larger of the Guards takes hold of me again—he's a behemoth and powerful—and drags me out of the vehicle. Without giving me a chance to catch my breath, he forces me inside and down several hallways until we reach a stairway that leads downward.

"See to it that she's locked away in one of the cells," Tallin calls out. "My father will get to her soon enough."

Maude, I think as the Guards drag me down the stairs and along a narrow, dark corridor. *Does the king know what I saw?*

~The king likely suspects, she replies. *I imagine he'll want to keep your mouth shut.*

By that, I assume you mean he'll want me dead.

~That is, unfortunately, exactly what I mean.

Isn't there some way you can help me out of here? Give me super-strength, or...

~I can only work with the muscles you have, Shara. And unfortunately, you have noodle arms and the legs of a praying mantis.

Not helpful, Maude.

~Sorry.

One of the Guards opens a thick wooden cell door, shoving it inward, and the other tosses me inside like a sack of flour. I land hard on my side, wrenching my wrist.

Yet again, I find myself in a damp, cold cell. Except this time, I don't even have the comfort of knowing Thorne is nearby.

When the Guards have left me alone to rot, I push myself to my feet, shivering as I slip over to the door. I'm still wearing the blue gown, which does little to offer warmth. The shoes I've worn all evening are on the brink of falling apart, their heels damaged and barely hanging on.

I kick them off and tear off the white gloves, tossing them to the ground, then rip Tallin's engagement ring from my finger and drop it to the floor.

There is no longer any need to carry on this ridiculous act.

A small, barred window in the door is the only source of light, and what little light there is in the corridor diminishes when the Guards leave.

Where are you? I murmur, my mind reaching for Thorne.

At first, there's no response.

Then...

Pain.

My head feels as though someone is taking a battering ram to it repeatedly, trying to break their way into my skull.

"What are they doing to him?" I cry.

~I wish I knew, Maude tells me. *I can only feel the pain you're feeling—not the exact cause of it. It feels like he's being forced to separate from you. Like...someone is trying to break your tether.*

Another surge of pain hits, and I scream this time, falling to my knees, then crumpling to the floor.

If this is what Tallin felt when his tether with Eva was severed, I understand now why he's so broken. The agony of it is total—devastating. Every nerve is excruciating. Every inch of me cries out for relief.

When the surge finally passes, I search for Thorne with my mind.

Our tether won't break. Not while we're both alive.

He's still out there.

Only a faint shadow of him—but he's still with me.

I have to find him. This has to stop.

The creaking of a door meets my ears, and a beam of light pours into the cell.

One kind of agony has just ended, but another is about to begin.

CHAPTER
FORTY-SIX

KING TOMAS' voice echoes off the cell's walls, a torturous, arrogant sound that makes my skin crawl. "Ah, my dear. How sad it is to meet under these circumstances."

"What do you want?" I snarl, pain stabbing at my insides.

Thorne is still out there somewhere—and with each moment that he's torn away from me, the agony grows.

"To start, I'd like you to give me the names of every Noble Tethered you saw at the ball this evening."

"No."

"Shara!"

My name shoots from his mouth like a projectile aimed squarely at my mind. It is a name that carries no power, no weight. The name of a Tethered, disposable and unwanted.

Once, my kind had surnames. We had histories.

It was a so-called "king" like Tomas who robbed us of them.

"No," I say again. "I will not give you any names." I don't conclude the statement with "your Grace."

The truth is, I'd sooner call him *You piece of shit.*

"What the hell do you mean, no?" King Tomas spits. "I'm not offering you a choice."

"And I'm not offering *you* one," I retort. "Where is Thorne?"

The king steps toward me, looking like he's ready to strike me across the face. At the last moment, he growls, "He's on his way to the Capitol."

At least he's telling me the truth, I guess.

"Why?"

"That is no concern of yours—but if you must know, I have sent him to find your father, the man known as the Shadow."

My heart turns to ice with those words.

I *want* to find my father. I'd like to see for myself whether or not he's the monster everyone claims. But...

My mind flashes with the sickening vision I had when Thorne and I were in the map room. I saw him on his knees, surrounded by men in gray masks...and he was in danger.

Who were those men?

"If you want the names of the Tethered I identified tonight —some of whom want you dead, your *Grace*—then you will bring Thorne back here. Until then, I refuse to say anything."

The king lets out a hearty, diabolical laugh. "Do you really think the Tethered are what I care about most? Do you think I've *ever* lost sleep over a few traitors in our midst?" He crouches next to me and takes my chin roughly in hand, pulling my eyes to his. "Tell me what you saw in the vault."

Fear infiltrates his eyes, mingling with quiet, terrifying rage.

My brows meet, my voice filling with venom when I reply, "I saw the truth. About you—about this realm. All of it."

The king studies me for a moment, then shoves my face aside like my flesh has burned him.

"I see. And just what were you intending to do with that so-called *truth*?"

I clam up. There's no way I'm telling him a damned thing. Not until Thorne is by my side again.

"No matter," the king says. "I have plans for you—something that will, perhaps, jar you out of this unfortunate reluctance to cooperate." With a click of his tongue, he adds, "I thought you and I were friends, my dear. I thought we had an understanding."

"I thought you were a half-decent human, but it turns out we've both been wrong about a lot of things, doesn't it?"

He whips his head around. "Guard!"

A Royal Guardsman appears in the doorway. "Yes, your Grace?"

"Bring in her friend. They'll stew here for a little before we take Shara to the arena."

As the king storms out of the cell, my blood runs cold.

I haven't returned to the arena since the night of the Prince's Ball. The night when Ilias was killed and when my life was turned on its head.

In fact, I've avoided it like the plague, circumventing it each time I wandered the palace.

I'm about to ask Maude why the king would want to bring me there when Valira comes stumbling into the cell. As I rise to my feet, the Guard who shoved her glares at me then turns to leave, sealing the door behind him.

Around Valira's neck is a large metal collar that looks as if it's digging into her flesh. Her eyes are cold and lifeless, and I know without asking that the collar is preventing her from using her powers.

"What's happening?" My voice is raw with panic. "Why did they put you in here?" It's only then that I notice that one of her eyes is swelling up, and her cheek is red where it looks like someone struck her. I leap over and take her by the shoulder, examining her. "Did Tallin do this to you?"

As I ask the question, I slip my hand up to her cheek, healing her almost instantly.

My powers have grown stronger in the last week, thanks to

my bond with Thorne. *Too bad I lack the strength to break through these damned walls.*

"It wasn't the prince," she replies. "Tallin has never injured me."

"Who, then?" My voice is hard-edged. I've lost the patience to deal with Valira's avoidance of the truth. "Who keeps attacking you? Is it a Guard?"

She narrows her eyes at me, then lets out a quiet laugh. "You've really lived a lovely life between these walls, haven't you? Just completely oblivious to what goes on daily in this fucking place."

Backing away, I cross my arms over my chest. All I want is to get out of here—to get to Thorne. I'm in no mood to entertain Valira's insinuations that my life is some kind of paradise on earth.

"King Tomas has had you wrapped around his finger," she says when I refuse to reply. "He's not the sweet man you seem to think."

"I've never thought he was sweet," I retort. "No one who hosts the Crimson Championship could be kind—besides which, he just had me locked up in this cell, in case you hadn't noticed."

"You're in here without any wounds, though. Before the beloved king had *me* thrown in here, he did me the honor of beating me."

My jaw drops open.

"Tomas—the king—he hit you?"

Valira raises her hands to waist height and shakes them in jest. "Surprise," she mutters. "It's hardly the first time."

Rage seeps through my pores, and I want to cry out, but Maude warns me against it. "Why the fuck would the king want to hurt you? What's wrong with him? Does he hate you or something?"

"He doesn't care about me enough to hate me. He did it to punish Tallin."

"How?" I shake my head involuntarily. "I need you to explain this to me, Valira. Once and for all."

With a heavy sigh, she steps over to the wall and slides down until she's sitting on the floor, knees bent up to her chin, her arms wrapped around her calves.

"Tallin's power first showed itself when he was very young. Fifteen." She looks me in the eye. "I wasn't here then, but some of the Guards were. They say there was an incident where the prince was in his chamber and something happened to make him angry. They say Tallin had found a little gray cat and wanted to keep it as a pet. The king ordered it killed."

"A *cat*," I breathe, recalling Thorne telling me about a vision he'd had about Tallin. *But his visions are of the future, not the past...*

Aren't they?

~Perhaps Thorne is more skilled than he knows, Maude says.

"When Tallin found out, he exploded," Valira continues. "Literally. Fire burst from him, shooting in every direction. The room and everything in it was utterly destroyed."

With a jolt of horror, I recall a girl in the Tower named Cher who caused an explosion in her Whiteroom—at least, that was what we all assumed. I remember cleaning up afterwards and seeing the streak of black soot left in her wake.

We never saw her after that incident, and to this day, I have no idea whether she lived or died. If she and Tallin share a power, then I can only imagine how terrifying the prince must be when he truly loses his temper.

Valira brushes her hair from her eyes and looks away. "The king was delighted when Tallin's power revealed itself."

"What the hell? Why?"

"Because he realized his son was a weapon—the greatest in

his entire arsenal. If Tallin could do that at fifteen, imagine what he would do when his powers were fully formed. That was how King Tomas saw it, at least."

"Tallin really is his mother's son, isn't he?" I mutter. "Except his mother seems to have a little control over her power."

"She may well, but the prince has no control. Like I said, it's more like an explosion—in the same way you or I might shout when we get angry, he's a human bomb. Most people think someone with his so-called gift would die, but it doesn't hurt him. He's what they call a *Volatile*—someone whose emotions bring out their powers. Each time the explosion comes, it gets stronger and stronger."

"Which is why the king wants to manipulate it," I muse.

"Tallin told me once that at first, he loved the power," Valira says. "When he was sixteen, he would set off controlled blasts in various bunkers underground—ones the king had built just for him at the far end of the grounds. The explosions were so powerful that the palace's construction team had to rebuild some of the structures multiple times. It all seemed to be going according to plan until Tallin fell in love with Eva."

"The Guard—his tethered mate, you mean."

Valira nods. "He was eighteen when he fell for her. She was kind and strong. A Velor."

I know what a fucking Velor is, Tallin spat at me when I told him about Lord Malloy's power. No wonder he was so angry when he said the words.

"The king knew they loved one another. But he hated that the moment Tallin fell for her, the prince changed. He lost interest in growing angry—in using his rage for destruction. He refused to train in the bunkers. He knew that his bond with Eva was making him stronger, and he knew his next explosion would be highly destructive. In those days, Tallin was relatively calm, or so they tell me. He wasn't afflicted by the pain that's now a constant torment."

"You told me Eva died," I'm almost reluctant to hear anything more. "How did it happen?"

"The king, being a Normal, wanted his Tethered son to become as powerful as he possibly could. Tomas has always been convinced that solitude makes a man stronger than love... and he wanted to put an end to Tallin's bond with Eva. I'm not sure whether Tomas knew about broken tethers and how destructive and brutal they can be. I don't know if he realized what he was doing to his son when..."

She cuts herself off, as if the thought of it is too much to bear.

"What did he do?" I ask.

Valira lets out a quiet, bitter laugh. "King Tomas knew the best way to anger Tallin was for Eva to get hurt, and so he made sure it happened. He sent a Guard to her chamber one night, just before Tallin was to arrive. The Guard forced himself on her, and when Tallin showed up, he caught the man on top of her."

Nausea surges up in my chest, but I remain silent, waiting for the rest of the grim tale.

"Tallin lost his mind. His rage consumed him—and as much as he tried, he couldn't contain it." Valira's voice trails off, and she wipes the back of her hand over her eyes. "Eva died. And it was Tallin's power—enhanced, ironically enough, by their love—that killed her. *He* killed her, and to this day, it torments him like a living nightmare. All day, every day, he feels the agony he inflicted on her as he broke their tether. He hears her screams. He..."

I step over and crouch down, my hands on Valira's knees, as a series of sobs breaks her.

"You take his pain away," I say softly. "You're the only one who can."

For the first time, I understand what she's sacrificed for the rest of us. What she's given of herself and stolen from Archyr, just to protect Tallin and the residents of this palace from his rage.

She is a literal human shield, the only thing standing between Tallin and chaos.

My eyes well with hot tears as I crouch down and take hold of Valira, pulling her close.

"I'm so sorry," I whisper. "This should never have happened to you—or to him."

She shakes her head. "Tallin is a bastard, and there's no denying it. He's cruel. But his father is so much worse. His mother, too, is terrible. She approved all of it."

"Why am I not surprised?" I snarl, pulling back and rising to my feet. "Look—we need to get out of here. There's a way to get to the Capitol, Valira, and I know where its entrance is. I want you to come with me."

"Even if we could get out of this cell, I'm not leaving Archyr. I'm not leaving Tallin, either. The next time his power shows itself, he could take half of Kravan with him. I can't risk that."

"Maybe we should let him destroy this particular half," I reply with an attempt at a smirk. "Maybe it's time to burn this place to the ground."

"Doesn't matter," she scowls. "Like I said, I can't leave Archyr. I love him. I will die for him if I must."

A wretched thought strikes me then.

"Do you know why they're planning to bring me to the arena?" I ask. "Do you think they're going to make me fight?"

"I don't know. The king's motivations usually aren't kind, so it's entirely possible that you'll be shoved in there with some Guard or other."

"Thorne told me he had a vision," I muse, "of Lady Gray-stone and Ellion, standing over Tallin's body. He seemed to think it would come to pass. Maybe..."

"Maybe he did have that vision," Valira retorts. "But if I were you, I wouldn't count on those two Graystone assholes to help you. I've heard they have an agenda of their own. There are rumors that Ellion—"

Before she can finish speaking, the cell door flies open, and a Guard steps in.

"I'm to bring you to the arena, Lady Ingram. The king says if you're so eager for the truth, it's time you learned it."

CHAPTER
FORTY-SEVEN

THE GUARD LEADS me out of the cell and down the corridor, his shoulders so broad that they threaten to collide with the walls to either side.

"Do you know *why* the king has summoned me?" I ask as jovially as I can. "Why couldn't he give me the truth in the cell?"

"Not a clue," the man grunts.

As we move, I take hold of the long blue skirt of my dress, only realizing when I've got it clenched in my fingers that somewhere during the course of the evening, I lost track of my clutch.

The clutch Mercutio was in.

Maude, I ask silently, desperately. *Do you know what happened to him?*

~I'm not entirely sure. I'm sorry, Shara. It's possible he's still at the Perrin estate.

If he's there, he'll never make it back to the palace. Their estate is miles away, on one of the neighboring islands, and there's an immense channel between us.

As terrified as I am and as desperate to see Thorne again,

the thought of losing Mercutio wrenches at my heart in an entirely new way.

~He'll be all right, Maude assures me. *I've never encountered a more resourceful mouse.*

How many mice have you encountered?

~Not many.

"Do you know who else will be coming to the arena?" I ask the Guard. There's no longer any effort in my voice to conceal my misery.

"Why the hell would I know that?" he growls. "All I know is the prince was asked to attend."

My devastation is instantly replaced with fear.

Oh, God. Maude—you don't think the king is going to force me to fight Tallin, do you? The king might try to make him use his powers on me, or...

~Do you want an honest answer, or a kind one?

Honest.

~I don't see you leaving that arena alive.

What's the kind answer?

~It'll probably be a quick death.

WHEN WE STEP into the arena a few minutes later, the meager contents of my stomach turn instantly into spikes jabbing at my insides.

Tallin is standing, his shoulders hunched, at the far end of the fighting ring. The king is next to him, with Lady Verdan on the other side.

Other than that...we're alone.

The Guard shoves me to the arena floor then turns to head back to the hallway.

I stare at Tallin, whose face is pale and beaded with sweat—his body frail-looking, almost pathetic.

For the first time, I feel genuine, painful sympathy for him.

Unfortunately, sympathy won't save my ass—and it won't make up for all the cruelty the prince has thrown my way over the weeks.

There's no denying that Tallin has led a complicated life, with cruel parents. But at least he *has* parents. At least he had the opportunity to grow up somewhere other than a cold, sterile cell. He was never forbidden to love, to feel. He was never tortured by an internal voice that was programmed to keep him in check and punish him when he dared to care for someone. He wasn't forced to fight his friends weekly, or told every day of his life that he was an inferior, horrible being.

So, my sympathy, it turns out, is short-lived.

The king is dressed in an elegant, dark gray suit, his hair slicked back. The kindness I've noted so often in his eyes is gone, and all I see now are the eyes of a snake—a cruel man who revels in torturing his son and beating women.

I despise him.

"You're wondering how we managed to get a man as powerful as your Thorne to leave the Palatine Estates and head to the Capitol," he says, examining his cuticles briefly, a smile on his lips. "Aren't you?"

"I know you didn't hurt him badly," I retort. "So he must have agreed to go because you threatened to hurt *me*."

Pulling his chin up to stare into my eyes, King Tomas says, "Not exactly." He turns to the entrance closest to him, nodding once. "There are other ways to persuade even the strongest Tethered to do your bidding. I happen to have one such way at my disposal."

I have no idea what he's talking about, and I'm telling

myself I don't particularly care when, with a gesture of the king's hand, two figures appear from the shadows.

Lady Verdan's head swivels quickly around, a look of pure, searing hatred in her eyes as Ellion Graystone and his mother step into the arena.

What.

The.

Fuck?

"Shara," the king says. "I believe you know Lady Graystone and Ellion."

"I've had the pleasure," I say, narrowing my eyes at both of them. Are they here to help me? To take me away from this god-awful place?

"Ellion has informed me he lacks the ability to control you," Tomas says. "I believe he admires that about you. However, he had little trouble with your lover."

"Thorne..." I say, staring into Ellion's eyes. "What did you do to him?"

Ellion laughs. "You know perfectly well that I took control of him and forced him into a Flyer. He's now walking the streets of the Capitol." He clicks his tongue. "It's not a safe place for the Royal Guard, let me tell you. If my instincts are correct, he'll be dead by tomorrow's end."

A shudder rips its way through me.

He's still alive. He's all right. I can feel him, if only faintly.

I can still get to him.

"Why would you..." I stammer, my eyes shifting from the king to Ellion, and back again. "Why did you do this?"

A malicious grin spreads across Ellion's lips. "Because I was asked to. I will give your Thorne credit—he fought hard. Resisting me nearly killed him, in fact." He locks his deep-set eyes on mine when he adds, "It seems he cares for you deeply, Shara. That's unfortunate for you both."

Bile pushes its way up my throat, but I refuse to be sick in front of him or to show any other form of weakness. Instead, I force myself to straighten and, wiping my brow, fix Ellion with a glare.

"I hope you know," he continues, "it gives me no pleasure to hurt you. You—who protected my mother and me, despite knowing the king might have had your head for it. He has a history of killing Tethered, you know. He has a particular love of taking young women's lives. Perhaps you've seen some of his victims in your mind's eye."

"The king isn't a Tethered," I spit. "Of course I don't see his cruel acts in my mind. But I know he's beaten Valira more than once."

"Oh, but not just Valira." Ellion pulls his eyes to Tallin then. The prince is barely standing now, his head swinging lazily from side to side as if he's about to lose consciousness. "Isn't that right, Highness? Why don't you show Shara again, so that she may understand what she's seen in the depths of your soul?"

Tallin pulls his glazed eyes to mine. After a moment, they swirl with color, and once again, I see the violence I witnessed the first time we met—the man and two women I saw the night of the Prince's Ball...and then another victim, lying crumpled on the floor of one of the palace's hallways. At first, she's blurry, as if Tallin can't quite bring himself to confront the memory.

But after a few seconds, she comes into focus. She's dressed in a white robe with a series of angry, red slash marks across her chest.

Valira.

"Tallin didn't hurt her." I pull my eyes to the king. "It was you. *You* attacked her—to try and inspire your son's wrath."

One of the prince's feet lifts off the ground, then the other, and he staggers toward us like a marionette on tangled strings. He slouches in front of me, his eyes dim.

"Tell her," Ellion commands.

"No," Tallin replies, swatting at the other man like he's an irritating gnat.

"Tell her what he does to you."

"Stop it!" I cry, taking hold of Tallin's arm to steady him. "I know what the king does and why. I *know* what a cruel bastard he is."

"Tsk," King Tomas says with a laugh. "I'm the only one in this room who's *normal.*"

"You're a fucking psychopath," I snarl. "Torturing people so your son absorbs their pain—knowing what it will do to him."

"If he had any real strength in him, he would *harness* the pain," Tomas says. "He would let it fuel his rage and the weapon he was meant to be. But he's weak...unlike his brother."

"Brother?" I sputter.

Lady Graystone glances over at Lady Verdan, nods her head, and says, "My dearest sister. How nice to see you twice in one night."

FORTY-EIGHT

SISTER?

My mind is threatening to implode with every piece of new knowledge that's penetrated it tonight. The Histories. Everything Valira told me about Tallin's power and his father's abuse.

But this—*this*—is insane.

"Didn't you know, Shara?" Lady Graystone asks. "Did Daphne never tell you she had a sibling?"

I'm about to shout an emphatic *no* when Maude reminds me I'm wrong.

~Lady Verdan told you she had a sister. It was some time ago, granted—and a lot has happened since.

A vivid memory comes to me then, as clear as Lady Graystone's eyes on her handsome yet devious face. When I was in the Verdan house—before she locked me in the dungeon—Daphne did say something about a sibling.

"My sister and I are both Tethered—you'd like her. A real spitfire, that one. She and I aren't close, but we admire one another grudgingly for what we've done to survive this long in a world that hates our kind."

Why didn't anyone ever tell me? I ask Maude. *Why keep it a secret?*

~I have a bad feeling we're about to find out.

"If she's Lady Verdan's sister," I say softly, "then Ellion and Tallin..."

"Are cousins," Lady Graystone says. "Only, in their case, they're half-brothers, as well. Our family tree is, admittedly, a little skewed."

This has to be a depraved, ridiculous nightmare, because it makes no sense.

"But...the only way they could possibly be half-brothers is if..." My eyes move to King Tomas, who nods, a cruel grin on his lips.

"Like many of Kravan's residents, you weren't aware that I have two heirs," the king says.

Holy shit.

It's no wonder Lady Verdan has such disdain for Lady Graystone and Ellion. I'm beginning to think they're even worse than she is.

"You lied to me," I snarl at Lady Graystone. "About everything. But...why? Why not just tell me who you were?"

A smile creeps over her lips. "For one thing, it's not a commonly known fact that I am Lady Verdan's sister. There are rumors, naturally—and a select few who know Ellion is second in line to the throne. But none of that has anything to do with the reason I chose to befriend you from the start, Shara dear."

"Then why?" My throat is parched, my voice a rasp.

"I asked that you be sent to dinner at the Prefect's," she says, "to determine whether you would protect Ellion and me if given the chance. I wanted to know where your loyalties lie, and I will admit, you didn't disappoint. I've had my eye on you for some time—ever since I learned the Hunter's daughter was in the Tower, years ago. Do you know—" she adds, holding up her golden hand, "it was actually your father who took my arm?"

"My father?" I repeat, the wind knocked out of me. "Why the hell would he...?"

I watch her eyes as she stares me down with a look of superiority that's sickeningly familiar. *How did I not see it before? She's so similar to Lady Verdan—the shape of her mouth, her eyes.*

The main difference, though, is that Lady Verdan is honest about her awfulness.

Lady Graystone, on the other hand, lured me in from our first moment together. I liked her. I felt sorry for her, and at times, I even cheered silently for her and Ellion.

"I knew the second you saw my hand..." She waves her prosthetic mockingly at me, "that you would feel empathy for me. *Poor Lady Graystone had to sacrifice her arm because the world is so cruel to our kind. But she escaped! She made it in the outside world, posing as a Noble.*" She lets out a wild laugh. "What better rags-to-riches story?"

"You were never in the Tower," I breathe. "No. Of course you weren't. Not if your parents were Nobles."

"I've never stepped foot in that godforsaken place. I was, however, in the Capitol—that part was true. After I learned of my pregnancy, I fled. My sister, as you know well, has a temper on her—and I didn't imagine she would love hearing that Tomas was my lover, as well as hers." She lets out a snicker and shoots her sibling a sidelong look. "The Capitol was relatively kind to me, too—until I encountered your bastard of a father. If you want to know what happened to my arm, look no further than his cruel band of assholes."

I gawk at her, completely baffled.

"Why would he...?"

"Slice off my arm?" She shrugs. "Isn't it obvious? He didn't —but he knew I was a Noble hiding among the masses in his beloved city of ruin." She eyes her son then and adds, "The man who became known as the Shadow also knew I was pregnant— and somehow, he knew who the father was—which made my child incredibly valuable to him and his followers. Imagine—an army of rebels raising the king's second heir as their own? The scandal it would cause! It was all strategy to that prick. I was nothing more than an asset, and my son was a weapon."

"You still haven't explained how you lost your arm," I point out, narrowing my eyes in irritation.

"Your dear daddy didn't want to lose me—I was worth my weight in gold. So in order to track me, he had his minions place an implant in my arm. He does that, you know, Shara—your father is as much a tyrant as any Normal who imprisons Tethered. And trust me when I say his implants are far worse than those the Tower inflicts. *You* got an A.I. unit—but I got daily torture. If I strayed more than a few feet from the perimeter where he was holding me captive, I spent the next several days in bed, recovering from the pain."

"I'm so sorry to hear that," I say with a sneer. "But it's not like he locked you up for nineteen years and never allowed you to know your parents, is it?" I step toward her, my brows meeting. "Oh, that's right. *Your* parents are dead—because your sister *killed* them."

Lady Graystone and Lady Verdan exchange a look, and I can feel the dark cloud of hatred swirling between them.

A cruel laugh rises up in Lady Graystone's throat. "Shara has some balls on her, doesn't she? She'll make an excellent queen, after all is said and done."

I freeze in place. What the hell does she mean, *queen*?

Maude? Do they actually think I'm going to marry Tallin?

~I don't know, Maude replies. *I'm not sure I want to know.*

"This bitch won't be marrying my son," Lady Verdan spits, answering the question. "I'd sooner die than allow it."

"*Allow* it?" Lady Graystone cackles. "Oh, you're in no position to allow anything, Daphne, my darling sister."

Lady Verdan shoots a look toward the king, her lips forming a tight line. "Is that a threat, Lyana?"

Lyana. So, Lady Graystone has a name.

Not that I give a shit.

"You've had your shot, Daphne," she tells her sister. "I gave you the chance years ago to have your son raised in the palace while mine lived in the shadows, cowering like a wretch inside our home. Yours has proven a worm, while mine has grown powerful."

"Tallin is no worm. He's..." Lady Verdan glances at her son. His face is pale, his hair soaked with sweat. He's clearly terrified —but of what, I'm not entirely sure. "He feels too deeply. That's all."

"His emotions are exactly what we need," King Tomas says. "Bring in his lover and her tethered mate," he commands to the Guard standing by the door. "It's time."

"What are you doing, Father?" Tallin asks, his voice teetering on the brink of failure. He forces himself to straighten, the fog temporarily leaving his eyes.

"I'm simply taking away your drug," the king replies. "Your crutch. It's time to let your power shine, my Son."

"No! You can't! Please, Father...Don't do this."

Tears streak his cheeks as he stumbles toward the king, who holds out his hands to steady him.

"Valira is not worthy of a prince—and a prince should not be fucking a Tethered."

"*I am* a Tethered," Tallin exclaims, raising his chin to stare his father down.

"You are a weakling. Your power drains you of strength, when it should have the opposite effect. You, my son, are a grave disappointment. I've been patient with you, but it's time you learned to be a man."

"A man!" Tallin cries. "You did this to me, Father! You inflicted this pain on me when you...when you..."

He falls to his knees, breaking down in a series of gut-wrenching sobs.

I back up slowly toward the wall. The power swirling and twisting through the air is palpable and terrifying.

I don't know what's about to happen—but whatever it is, it will be catastrophic.

"It's time," King Tomas says, rubbing his hands together. "Enough with exposing all the family secrets. It's time to put an end to those who know too much—don't you think?"

He's going to have us all killed.

~Yes, Maude says. *It's looking that way.*

CHAPTER
FORTY-NINE

W̲H̲E̲N̲ V̲A̲L̲I̲R̲A̲ A̲N̲D̲ A̲R̲C̲H̲Y̲R̲ A̲P̲P̲E̲A̲R̲, framed in one of the arena's entryways, Tallin lets out a wail of rage.

I don't blame him for it. I want to scream, too, as my eyes lock on each of them in turn.

Archyr is standing tall, his eyes fixed on the woman he loves. Their hands are clasped together as if they know exactly what fate is about to befall them.

The collar is no longer locked around Valira's neck, which must mean she's expected to use her powers.

To what end, I can only imagine.

This moment marks the first time they've ever been allowed to hold hands in front of an audience. The first time they've let it be known that they are bound together.

It is a brutal irony that they're revealing their love to the very people who want them dead.

"Valira," King Tomas calls out. "You have long provided an important service to my son. I *would* thank you for it..." He glances over at Tallin, who has pressed himself against the arena's wall as if he wishes to disappear into it. "But I'm afraid you've only fed into his weakness. It's high time he learned to live without your particular sort of...care."

Tallin shakes his head desperately. "No, Father," he says mournfully, turning to face the woman who has long shielded his mind from chaos. "You can't do this. Please, Valira—I need you. *Please.*"

Lady Verdan sneers with disgust as her eyes slip over the woman who has relieved her son's pain so many times over the months.

"You never needed her, Tallin," she says, her voice inhumanly cold. "You tell yourself you do, but only because she gratifies you sexually."

"No, Mother!" he protests. "It's nothing to do with..."

"Of course it is!" she snaps. "You will see, my Son. You have no need of some Violet whore. You'll be better off without her."

"No..."

Never have I seen Tallin look so destroyed—so weak and vulnerable.

Never before have I cared for him as much as I do in this moment as I watch his soul breaking into fragments, irreparable and agonizing.

"It's been a while," the king announces, ignoring his son's torment, "since we've had the pleasure of witnessing a battle between the palace walls. I thought it might amuse Shara here to see what will be in store for her and Thorne if ever he manages to return from the Capitol."

"He's really going to make them fight?" I whisper.

~It looks that way, Maude replies. *The good news? It sounds like the king intends to keep you alive.*

"I'm not sure that's good news at this point."

"Father!" Tallin shouts, taking a step toward the king. His rage is palpable and terrifying, but I can see him fighting it back —struggling to keep his emotions in check for the protection of those he cares about. He knows better than anyone that if he unleashes his wrath, every person in this palace could lose their lives. "You can't do this."

"Can't I?" King Tomas asks.

"Your Grace," I shout. "Valira has protected your palace—your people. Your family. Why would you punish her for it?"

The king twists my way, ire in his eyes. "Don't pretend you're unaware that I've inflicted punishments on her in the past, Shara dear. Perhaps it isn't obvious yet that I quite *enjoy* hurting Tethered servants—and Valira is particularly deserving, given that she has disgraced this house on many occasions. As my lovely Daphne said, she's nothing more than a whore."

"What the hell is wrong with all of you?" I spit. "You know what happened when Tallin's tether was broken. Why would you inflict that sort of pain on someone else? Why hurt Valira and Archyr like this?"

"Because they know far too much—as do you," the king replies calmly. "Tonight marks a turning of the tide, if you will. It's time to put an end to the Quiet War—and to show the rebels in the Capitol what it is to be afraid. It's time my eldest son came out of his shell and revealed to the world what true power is."

I roll the words over in my mind, knowing the king can only mean one thing.

He intends to weaponize Tallin—and there's only one way to do so.

"Now," Tomas calls out. "Valira. Archyr. It's time." With that, he leans back against the wall and grins as a Guard wheels a large rack holding ten or more weapons—everything from daggers to swords to spears.

But Valira and Archyr don't step to the ring's center. Instead, they simply remain in place, their hands locked together.

"I will not fight," Archyr announces. The color swims in his eyes, his power strengthening with his proximity to Valira. "Unless, your Grace, you care to take me on."

I knew the moment I first met Archyr that he was a *Brutal*—a Tethered with enormous physical strength. If he chose to, he could snap the king like a twig.

Kill the fucker, I want to growl. *End him, Archyr.*

But he won't. He's an honorable man.

He's no murderer.

The king lets out a howl of laughter. "You *will* fight your lady love," he says. "And the fight will continue until one or both of you are dead."

"No." This time, it's Valira who speaks. "I won't hurt him. He won't hurt me. You can imprison us, or kill us yourself. But you cannot ask two tethered mates to kill one another. You have your laws, your Grace—and we have ours. We will not break them willingly."

"Your laws mean nothing to me," Tomas snarls, then issues a quick nod to Ellion. Lady Graystone's silent son steps forward, flicking a hand through the air as if swatting at an insect.

Archyr seems to turn to stone for a second, his limbs locking in place. From between gritted teeth, he lets out a roar of anger, fighting the strength of Ellion's power.

But the king's second son is strong. He quickly takes over Archyr's mind, dragging him away from Valira as though his feet are made of lead. She holds onto his hand with every ounce of strength she possesses, but Archyr yanks himself away, stumbling several feet until he reaches the weapons rack. He grabs hold of a dagger, taking it in hand and grasping it like his life depends on it.

Turning to face Valira, he freezes again, shaking his head slightly. I hear the words, "No, no, no..." repeated faintly as he struggles against the might of Ellion's mind.

King Tomas applauds gleefully. "That's the stuff!" he shouts. "Now, the woman."

Ellion holds Archyr in place as his attention shifts to Valira, forcing her to lift one foot, then the other, and hurtle herself toward the arena's center.

When she's a few feet from Archyr, her arm shoots out as though she's a marionette who's being controlled via a long set of overhead strings.

A long, jagged spear lifts from the weapons rack and flies at Archyr, who manages to hurl himself out of the way just in time to avoid being impaled.

Archyr forces himself upright, and Valira cries out in ire and frustration.

Ellion lets out a laugh, forcing the Netic to hurl another of the rack's blades, and another, until finally, she manages to strike Archyr, the cruel blade of a dagger lodging itself deep in his shoulder.

He falls to his knees, grabbing hold of the weapon's hilt. I watch him tremble in shock as he draws it from his flesh, every bit of his strength doing battle with the Bender.

Desperate, I leap toward Archyr, but the king stops me in my tracks.

"Heal him, and Lady Verdan will kill them both!" he shouts. "It will hurt—trust me."

My eyes flick to my former Proprietor, whose grin oozes with smug delight.

As I watch in horror, Valira fights her trembling arm, forcing it back down to her side.

She knows what's happening, I murmur. *She knows she's killing him.*

"That's the thing," the king calls out as if he heard what I just said. "The beauty of mind-control, you see, is that the person being controlled *knows* it. They're aware of their actions, however reprehensible they might be. They simply can't fight their own body. Isn't it wonderful?"

With a small flick of Ellion's fingers, Archyr rises to his feet and hurls the bloody dagger at Valira, who manages to dodge it, throwing herself into the arena's dirt floor. In retaliation, Archyr lunges at her, grabbing her by the throat and squeezing so tight that her face turns instantly red.

With desperate gasps erupting from her chest, Valira thrusts a hand in the air, and again, an object hurtles toward Archyr. This time, it's a light fixture that she's pulled loose from the arena's wall. It crashes against his head, leaving behind a wound on the side of his face as he plummets to the ground.

A stream of blood is trickling down his cheek now, and it's all I can do not to leap forward and use my power to heal him.

"You two cannot win this fight!" King Tomas calls out, triumphant. "There will be no victor here!"

Valira rises to her feet, a hand at her throat—hoarse breaths struggling their way out of her chest. She stares down at Archyr, her eyes shining with tears that refuse to fall.

"Kill me!" Archyr shouts. "Valira—you have to!"

"No," she rasps. "I won't. Not for anything in this world."

She looks over at Tallin, who's sinking slowly to the floor, his face in his hands. He can't—won't—watch the last thread of his sanity snap for his parents' amusement.

His father is torturing him with this spectacle. Devastating him deliberately, just to force so-called *strength* into him. And I despise the king for it.

Archyr and Valira circle one another slowly, but at first, they don't strike out at each other. Instead, they move like two prowling cats taking stock of one another's attributes.

"This is growing dull," the king calls out. "Let's end it."

Ellion slips a little closer to the arena's center, holding up a hand to take control again.

But Archyr shakes his head.

"No," he says. "Give us a minute. Let us end it on our own terms."

"Fine," Ellion replies, holding his hands up in mock surrender. "*One* minute. Then I end this."

Archyr nods, then sets his sights on Valira once again.

"I love you," he says as they continue to move in a slow circle, one foot crossing over the other on the arena's dirt floor. "You know that. I have always loved you, since the day we met."

"I love you, too."

Archyr is circling around toward the king now, never taking his eyes off Valira. "Whatever happens," he tells her, "I want you to live a good life."

With tears streaming down her face, she shakes her head. "I don't want any kind of life. Not without you. Arch..."

But he's not listening anymore.

In one rapid motion, he spins around and lunges toward the ground, grabbing the dagger that struck him in the shoulder. He hurls himself at Ellion, the blade raised high, ready to meet its mark.

But Ellion is too quick.

With a simple gesture of his fingers, he sends Archyr flailing, the blade tight in his hand, his spine twisting until his entire body has turned to face Valira once again.

Oh, God, I say under my breath.

Archyr trips toward Valira, the blade still high in the air.

I expect her to do something. To defend herself, to fling another projectile at him.

But instead, she simply...waits.

Archyr cries out as the knife comes down almost far enough to plunge into Valira's chest. At the last second, he manages to fight Ellion's control, twisting himself around again.

But a moment later, he's behind Valira, an arm wrapped around her, the blade at her throat.

My pulse is vicious and aggressive in my veins, my heart beating its way up my throat. I want to run to Ellion, to throw him to the ground and put an end to this madness, once and for all...

But I can't.

He may not be able to control me, but he's far stronger than I am—and he has Lady Verdan and Lady Graystone on his side.

"Do it," Valira says, the blade pressing into her skin hard enough to draw blood. "Archyr—finish this, and maybe they'll let you go. It's me the king wants killed, and you know it."

"No," he growls against the force of Ellion's might. "I won't..."

"Archyr!" Valira screams as he pulls the weapon away. With one final burst of strength, he draws the blade across his own neck.

Blood streams down his throat, and he falls to his side on the arena floor, Valira crumpling into a pile next to him.

She reaches for him, then looks up, her vacant eyes meeting mine, her mouth dropping open.

I spring toward her, shouting, "I can heal him!"

The truth is, though, I suspect it's already too late.

Valira shakes her head, a hand slipping down to cup his pale cheek, tears landing on his blood-soaked skin.

"It's too much," she murmurs. "Too much."

"Valira." I reach for her, but she pulls back and looks me in the eye.

"I'm so sorry," she says, reaching for the blade that's lying next to Archyr.

"No—" I breathe when she clenches it in her hand, her eyes landing on Tallin.

The blade pierces her chest, and she falls to the ground next to her tethered mate.

The cry that erupts from the prince's chest is the most brutal, horrifying sound I've ever heard, and my heart breaks for him.

A second later, my heart *stops*.

CHAPTER
FIFTY

THE NIGHTMARE UNFOLDING before me is both surreal and horrifying.

Valira and Archyr lie dead at the center of the arena.

Nausea churns inside me as I watch Tallin rise to his full height, his skin pulsing with angry orange veins. The swirling irises of a Tethered have been replaced with the searing glow of fire and flame.

Even from a distance, I can feel the power in him, the rage—the undeniable potential for devastation.

"You have both tortured me so many times," he snarls, his eyes moving from his father to his mother and back again. "You've forced me to absorb their pain so that I would submit to your will. But don't you see? You've turned me into a beast. You have ripped my soul away and torn a hole in my heart that will never mend. Do you understand that? Do you even *care*?"

His voice is shrill and menacing, and his mother—a woman I didn't know was capable of fear—takes a step back, terror festering in her eyes.

For a moment, I'm certain Tallin is going to attack her. His chest is heaving, his face beading with sweat. I can feel it as I watch him—power, pestilent and awful, flowing through the air in a toxic mist.

"*There* it is," King Tomas says, stepping forward and clapping his hands together. On his face is an expression that's half jubilant, half fearful. "*There's* the strength you'd lost, my son. Come, now, you must save it for a time when we need it. We'll have the Guards clean this place up, and we'll lock Shara away until she agrees to be your wife. Imagine the power you two would possess if you combined your strength—the power your children would have. Together, you could take down every enemy of the realm. You could—"

"Silence!" Tallin cries, taking a long step toward the king and his companions, fingers spreading and arms outstretched. Flames spin and coil around his flesh, manic waves of rage fueled by grief.

Lady Graystone smirks, more amused than fearful, while her son stands by her side, his eyes intent and cruel.

"You," Tallin snarls, staring the Graystones down, his chin lowering. "Fucking *cowards*, both of you. I should end you." He raises his arms, chains of fire cycling around them like fast-moving asps.

"Ellion," Lady Graystone says, her smile fading. "Take his mind. *Now*."

"I—" her son replies, and I can see the strain in him as he struggles to focus. "I'm trying."

"I *told* you," Tallin snarls. "My parents created a goddamned monster." He pulls an arm back as if he's about to lash out at them—to unleash devastation.

Fear seizes at my chest when I envision the mayhem that now feels inevitable.

"Tallin, don't do this!" I shout. "You'll kill everyone in the palace."

"Do you think I care?" he asks, his skin crackling with gruesome orange veins. "Do you really think anyone in this place deserves to live, after what you've seen tonight?"

"I...I don't know. But this isn't the way." I swallow hard, seeking my courage, then say, "Let Kravan decide. Let the people take back what they once lost, and let this land heal. Tallin, you have the power to change this realm for the better. It wasn't always run by a tyrant. I know it can flourish once again if we help it."

He stares into my eyes, and for a moment, I'm convinced he's contemplating it.

But then a sound rumbles in his chest, crescendoing until a full-on laugh barrels up his throat.

"There is nothing in this realm worth salvaging," he spits. "My dear father has seen to it."

With that, he turns to face his parents again.

"Now, what should I do with you two?"

The king's back is pressed hard against the arena's wall. He's too far from the exit to flee, but if he did try and escape, I have no doubt Tallin would unleash the full strength of his powers.

"Daphne," the king growls. "Get your son in check. Control the bastard."

"*My* son," Lady Verdan snarls. "Oh—you mean the one whose power you have long tried to harness so that you could turn him into a living bomb? The one you consider a grave disappointment because he's not cruel enough for your liking?"

"Call. Him. *Off.*"

Lady Verdan laughs, her eyes locked on Tallin. "No. I don't think I will, Tomas."

The prince takes a step toward the king, his searing hands curling into horrifying fists.

"Don't do this, Highness," I plead. "Think of Valira—"

He twists toward me, flames swirling around his face and

neck. "Do *not* say her name!" he cries, his gaze moving to her lifeless body. "Never say it again."

I nod, holding out a submissive hand and taking a step closer. "I'm sorry. But..."

I pull my eyes to the king and Lady Verdan, hatred in my heart for both of them. "I want them to pay for everything they've done. But not like this. Tallin, think about what you're doing."

"I've thought about it a million times," he retorts, nodding toward Valira. "She has always kept me from acting on my rage. But she's gone now. And if you're smart, Shara, you'll leave, too. Go—find your Thorne. You don't want to see this. You don't deserve to be part of this toxic, dysfunctional shit-show."

He lifts his hands toward his parents, the horrific sound of crackling embers filling the air.

But just as he's about to unleash his wrath, Tallin jerks his head around unnaturally then doubles over in agony.

That's when I see Ellion Graystone moving slowly toward him, his chin low, eyes focused. He's close to taking control of the prince's mind—and I can only imagine what will happen if he succeeds.

"Stop it!" I cry, fear ripping its way through me. But Ellion keeps moving toward his half-brother while Tallin cries out in pain, crashing hard to the ground.

Lady Graystone laughs again. "It would be a damned shame if Tallin and the king were to die here and now, wouldn't it? A damned shame if *my* son were to find his way to the throne."

With that, a memory jabs at my mind of something Ellion said to me at the cocktail party when we were discussing King Tomas.

When the next ruler comes—if it's who I think it will be—the tide will turn. Kravan will see a renewal of its glory days.

Something tells me he wasn't talking about the days of President Brant.

He was talking about the days of the Rise—the event that is now referred to as the Rebellion. The days when Tethered were first imprisoned, and civilians were murdered in the streets.

Ellion knows, somehow, what happened during those dark days.

So many times, I've wished for Tallin's death and for Lady Verdan's. I've wanted to bring the Royal family to its lying, hypocritical knees.

But now, all I want—aside from Thorne—is to see these devious assholes live to witness an *actual* Rebellion. I want them to feel the wrath of Kravan's people, those who have been lied to for so many years.

I need to get to the Capitol. I need to make it happen.

I hold the Storian's memories—the greatest weapon the people of Kravan have.

Desperately, my eyes move to the blades scattered here and there along the arena's floor.

If only I could get to them, I think. *If only my aim were true.*

~Shara, Maude whispers into my mind. *Remember what the Storian said about your power. You are more than a mere Hunter.*

She's right.

I am.

"I'm sorry, my friend," I say, reaching down to swipe a finger over the blood staining Valira's chest.

The shock of her Netic power collides with my mind, and I reach my arms out, drawing the weapons into the air and aiming them at Ellion and his mother. They hover there, trembling as if in anticipation of their fates.

"Hey!" I shout as Tallin lies on the ground, struggling against Ellion's mental hold.

Ellion turns my way, rage creasing his brow, but says nothing.

"You were right, you know," I tell him, my hands at shoulder height, the weapons moving with me as I take one step, then another, gaining control over the temporary power. "We aren't all equal. Some of us deserve to lead...and others deserve to die."

I hurl my hands forward, and the weapons fly.

Lady Graystone ducks, almost avoiding injury—but one lone dagger tears into her arm, drawing a sharp cry from her lips.

Ellion isn't so fortunate. He screams when a blade lodges itself in his thigh, breaking his focus.

Scrambling to his feet, Tallin turns his head my way, and for an instant, his eyes go clear, the flame extinguishing.

"Run!" he breathes before the fire rekindles in his irises.

Without another thought, I obey his command.

CHAPTER
FIFTY-ONE

I DON'T KNOW if it's adrenaline, Maude's control, or Valira's strength that's fueling me, but I fly through the palace's hallways like a gust of wind.

Guards watch me tear by them, stunned into silence at the sight of a woman in a torn, filthy blue gown, her feet bare, a cascade of tears staining her cheeks.

I want to tell them to run, to hide—but in all likelihood, they would throw me back into my cell.

"Maude," I call out. "Can you get me to the crypt?"

Somewhere behind me, screams and desperate cries ring out. The floor trembles beneath my feet as if the earth itself is shattering.

Is Tallin killing his father? His mother? The Graystones?

Has Ellion taken control of him again?

None of it matters.

All I care about is finding the tunnel, getting to the Capitol, and finding my way to Thorne before it's too late.

A barreling explosion shakes the palace's foundations. A flash of light bounces off the walls, but I don't turn to witness the destruction unfolding behind me.

With my filthy skirts gathered in my fists, I run from death.

Maude assumes full control of my body, and every muscle, every tendon pushes itself to its limit until I'm tearing down a set of marble stairs to reach a large, wooden door with a keypad embedded in the wall to one side.

~The code is five-one-four-zero, Maude tells me, and I input it with a shaking hand. The door flies open, and I leap through just as another explosion meets my ears. Somewhere in the distance, I hear what sounds like an immense slab of stone crashing to the ground.

I glance around, knowing without a doubt that I'm inside the crypt I saw in my mind's eye when I absorbed the Storian's memories. *The door to the tunnel is close.*

"I know where to go," I cry, and Maude tells me she, too, knows. She propels me forward until I reach a large stone casket situated in the far corner of the vast, dark, underground chamber.

The tomb of the first king of Kravan—the bastard who set the Rebellion in motion and declared himself monarch.

On top of the casket is a life-sized carving of that very king, and for a moment, I stare at it, baffled. The figure is bearded, and clenched in his hands is a long sword.

"What do I do, Maude?" I ask, my voice tremulous as another explosion sends debris falling from the ceiling.

~There has to be a mechanism to open the tunnel, she says. *Try finding a button—a lever. Anything.*

I pull at the sword's hilt, then the king's carved stone beard, but nothing happens.

Finally, I circle the tomb and spot a few words carved around the perimeter of the stone casket.

Here lies King Quinton, who saved Kravan from Tyranny.

"That's some impressive next-level bullshit," I sneer.

~Focus, Shara.

I examine the letters. After the word "King" is a small flower —what looks like a rose—carved into the stone.

I press it, and to my surprise, it disappears, receding into the surface. The sound of grinding stone meets my ears, and the casket begins to slide across the floor, revealing a dark stairway leading downward.

"Light, please," I say, and instantly, my left arm illuminates with the faint green reminder that I was once deemed a Harmless Tethered.

I'm about to take my first step into the stairwell when a small, dark shape scurries up and climbs onto my left foot.

"Mercutio!" I cry, reaching down to take the mouse in my hand. "How..."

~He must have stowed away on the king's Flyer. Clever little thing.

When another blast sounds and the crypt shakes from the violence of it, I tuck the mouse into my pocket and run down the stairs, holding my left arm out in front of me to provide enough light so that I don't kill myself in the process.

The moment my foot hits the ground at the base of the stairs, the grinding of stone begins again. The tomb slides back into place, trapping me underground and isolating me from my horrific enemies.

I don't know what happened back there. I don't know whether Tallin is alive or dead.

I don't even know if Kravan still has a king.

All I know, staring into the abyss, is that I will be walking for a long, long time.

EPILOGUE

HEARTBREAK ISN'T what people think it is.

It's not the shattering of a brittle organ into tiny fragments, like a vase exploding against marble.

Instead, it's the rapid spread of a cruel, invasive emotion. It's a cresting wave of sorrow that wends its way through your chest until you feel like you can no longer breathe, let alone stand.

It is the loss of a part of yourself that you will never get back, regardless of what fate may befall you.

I am a Healer. But a broken heart is something I'm powerless to fix.

If Prince Tallin is still alive, he's beyond my reach. His rage —the very rage Valira fought so hard to quell—is his power, and it has consumed him.

I can only hope my despair doesn't do the same to me.

I've walked for hours now, staggering along on bare, bloody feet. The cold stone beneath my soles is a mercy, at least, and the tunnel is damp and quiet. For once, I'm not surrounded by people who despise my kind.

All I have to keep me company are Maude and a dormant mouse. Every now and then, I reach my mind out in search of Thorne, but each time I do, I'm met with silence.

"You're out there," I say softly. "You have to be."

But it's only when his voice comes to me after six hours in the tunnel that I'm certain of it.

A mere gust of wind, swift and fleeting.

Shara...

I collapse against the rounded wall, sobbing. Every emotion that has built up inside me over the last few days—every fear, every bit of sorrow, of hope, of bliss—is releasing itself now with the knowledge that Thorne is alive.

I can see him, as I saw him once in a vision. He's on his knees, his chin low. Men in gray masks surround him inside a large structure of dark stone, its ceiling high and vaulted. Instantly, I know it's the Citadel—one of the few intact buildings left in the Capitol, concealed as it is deep underground.

I can feel Thorne's mind—his love. How desperate he is to get back to me.

But I can also feel his hope waning.

He doesn't know I'm coming...he can't feel **me**.

Something has happened.

I cry out for him, but no response comes.

Our tether is intact...but just barely.

My chest heaves, my pulse quickening, and I push myself away from the wall to begin walking once again.

"I am Shara," I say, wiping my hand across my eyes. "Healer, Hunter, and Keeper of the Histories. I will bring the truth to Kravan's people. And if I have to fight my way through a million of our enemies to get to you, Thorne...then *that's what I'll do.*"

BROKEN

*The End of Book Two of the **Thrall Series***

The series continues with *Queen,*
coming in September 2024.

COMING SOON

The Thrall series continues with Queen,
coming in September 2024!

ALSO BY K. A. RILEY

DYSTOPIAN BOOKS

THE AMNESTY GAMES

THE RESISTANCE TRILOGY

THE EMERGENTS TRILOGY

THE TRANSCENDENT TRILOGY

| TRAVELERS | TRANSFIGURED | TERMINUS |

ACADEMY OF THE APOCALYPSE

EMERGENTS ACADEMY | CULT OF THE DEVOTED | ARMY OF THE UNSETTLED

THE RAVENMASTER CHRONICLES

ARISE | BANISHED | CRUSADE

THE CURE CHRONICLES

THE CURE | AWAKEN | ASCEND | FALLEN | REIGN

VIRAL HIGH TRILOGY

APOCALYPCHIX | LOCKDOWN | FINAL EXAM

RISE OF THE INCITERS | INTO AN UNHOLY LAND | NO MAN'S LAND

Fantasy Books

A KINGDOM SCARRED | A CROWN BROKEN | OF FLAME AND FURY

SEEKER'S SERIES

Seeker's World |Seeker's Quest | Seeker's Fate | Seeker's Promise |Seeker's Hunt | Seeker's Prophecy (Coming soon!)